THE TOWER TREASURE

Joe toppled over the railing into space!

Hardy Boys Mystery Stories

THE TOWER

TREASURE

BY

FRANKLIN W. DIXON

NEW YORK
GROSSET & DUNLAP
A NATIONAL GENERAL COMPANY
Publishers

In this new story, based on the original of the same title, Mr. Dixon has incorporated the most up-to-date methods used by police and private detectives.

CONTENTS

Contents

CHAPTER I

The Speed Demon

FRANK and Joe Hardy clutched the grips of their motorcycles and stared in horror at the oncoming car. It was careening from side to side on the narrow road.

"He'll hit us! We'd better climb this hillside—and fast!" Frank exclaimed, as the boys brought their motorcycles to a screeching halt and leaped off.

"On the double!" Joe cried out as they started up the steep embankment.

To their amazement, the reckless driver suddenly pulled his car hard to the right and turned into a side road on two wheels. The boys expected the car to turn over, but it held the dusty ground and sped off out of sight.

"Wow!" said Joe. "Let's get away from here before the crazy guy comes back. That's a dead-end road, you know."

The boys scrambled back onto their motorcycles and gunned them a bit to get past the intersecting road in a hurry. They rode in silence for a while, gazing at the scene ahead.

On their right an embankment of tumbled rocks and boulders sloped steeply to the water below. From the opposite side rose a jagged cliff. The little-traveled road was winding, and just wide enough for two cars to pass.

"Boy, I'd hate to fall off the edge of this road," Frank remarked. "It's a hundred-foot drop."

"That's right," Joe agreed. "We'd sure be smashed to bits before we ever got to the bottom." Then he smiled. "Watch your step, Frank, or Dad's papers won't get delivered."

Frank reached into his jacket pocket to be sure several important legal papers which he was to deliver for Mr. Hardy were still there. Relieved to find them, Frank chuckled and said, "After the help we gave Dad on his latest case, he ought to set up the firm of Hardy and Sons."

"Why not?" Joe replied with a broad grin. "Isn't he one of the most famous private detectives in the country? And aren't we bright too?" Then, becoming serious, he added, "I wish we could solve a mystery on our own, though."

Frank and Joe, students at Bayport High, were combining business with pleasure this Saturday morning by doing the errand for their father.

Even though one boy was dark and the other

fair, there was a marked resemblance between the two brothers. Eighteen-year-old Frank was tall and dark. Joe, a year younger, was blond with blue eyes. They were the only children of Fenton and Laura Hardy. The family lived in Bayport, a small but thriving city of fifty thousand inhabitants, located on Barmet Bay, three miles inland from the Atlantic Ocean.

The two motorcycles whipped along the narrow road that skirted the bay and led to Willowville, the brothers' destination. The boys took the next curve neatly and started up a long, steep slope. Here the road was a mere ribbon and badly in need of repair.

"Once we get to the top of the hill it won't be so rough," Frank remarked, as they jounced over the uneven surface. "Better road from there into Willowville."

Just then, above the sharp put-put of their own motors, the two boys heard the roar of a car approaching from their rear at great speed. They took a moment to glance back.

"Looks like that same guy we saw before!" Joe burst out. "Good night!"

At once the Hardys stopped and pulled as close to the edge as they dared. Frank and Joe hopped off and stood poised to leap out of danger again if necessary.

The car hurtled toward them like a shot. Just when it seemed as if it could not miss them, the driver swung the wheel about viciously and the sedan sped past.

"Whew! That was close!" Frank gasped.

The car had been traveling at such high speed that the boys had been unable to get the license number or a glimpse of the driver's features. But they had noted that he was hatless and had a shock of red hair.

"If I ever meet him again," Joe muttered, "I'll —I'll—" The boy was too excited to finish the threat.

Frank relaxed. "He must be practicing for some kind of race," he remarked, as the dark-blue sedan disappeared from sight around the curve ahead.

The boys resumed their journey. By the time

they rounded the curve, and could see Willowville in a valley along the bay beneath them, there was no trace of the rash motorist.

"He's probably halfway across the state by this time," Joe remarked.

"Unless he's in jail or over a cliff," Frank added.

The boys reached Willowville and Frank delivered the legal papers to a lawyer while Joe guarded the motorcycles. When his brother returned, Joe suggested, "How about taking the other road back to Bayport? I don't crave going over that bumpy stretch again."

"Suits me. We can stop off at Chet's."

Chet Morton, who was a school chum of the Hardy boys, lived on a farm about a mile out of Bayport. The pride of Chet's life was a bright yellow jalopy which he had named Queen. He worked on it daily to "soup up" the engine.

Frank and Joe retraced their trip for a few miles, then turned onto a country road which led to the main highway on which the Morton farm was situated. As they neared Chet's home, Frank suddenly brought his motorcycle to a stop and peered down into a clump of bushes in a deep ditch at the side of the road.

"Joe! That crazy driver or somebody else had a crack-up!"

Among the tall bushes was an overturned blue sedan. The car was a total wreck, and lay wheels upward, a mass of tangled junk.

"We'd better see if there's anyone underneath," Joe cried out.

The boys made their way down the culvert, their hearts pounding. What would they find?

A close look into the sedan and in the immediate vicinity proved that there was no victim around.

"Maybe this happened some time ago," said Joe, "and—"

Frank stepped forward and laid his hand on the exposed engine. "Joe, it's still warm," he said. "The accident occurred a short while ago. Now

I'm sure this is the red-haired driver's car."

"But what about him?" Joe asked. "Is he alive? Did somebody rescue him, or what happened?"

Frank shrugged. "One thing I *can* tell you. Either he or somebody else removed the license plates to avoid identification."

The brothers were completely puzzled by the whole affair. Since their assistance was not needed at the spot, they climbed out of the culvert and back onto their motorcycles. Before long they were in sight of the Mortons' home, a rambling old farmhouse with an apple orchard at the rear. When they drove up the lane they saw Chet at the barnyard gate.

"Hi, fella!" Joe called.

Chet hurried down the lane to meet them. He was a plump boy who loved to eat and was rarely without an apple or a pocket of cookies. His round, freckled face usually wore a smile. But today the Hardys sensed something was wrong. As they brought their motorcycles to a stop, they noticed that their chum's cheery expression was missing.

"What's the matter?" Frank asked.

"I'm in trouble," Chet replied. "You're just in time to help me. Did you meet a fellow driving the Queen?"

Frank and Joe looked at each other blankly.

"Your car? No, we haven't seen it," said Joe. "What's happened?"

"It's been stolen!"

"Stolen!"

"Yes. I just came out to the garage to get the Queen and she was gone," Chet answered mournfully.

"Wasn't the car locked?"

"That's the strange part of it. She was locked, although the garage door was open. I can't see how anyone got away with it."

"A professional job," Frank commented. "Auto thieves always carry scores of keys with them. Chet, have you any idea when this happened?"

"Not more than fifteen minutes ago, because that's when I came home with the car."

"We're wasting time!" Joe cried out. "Let's chase that thief!"

"But I don't know which way he went," Chet protested.

"We didn't meet him, so he must have gone in the other direction," Frank reasoned.

"Climb on behind me, Chet," Joe urged. "The Queen can't go as fast as our motorcycles. We'll catch her in no time!"

"And there was only a little gas in my car, anyway," Chet said excitedly as he swung himself onto Joe's motorcycle. "Maybe it has stalled by this time."

In a few moments the boys were tearing down the road in pursuit of the automobile thief!

CHAPTER II

The Holdup

CHET MORTON's jalopy was such a brilliant yellow that the boys were confident it would not be difficult to pick up the trail of the auto thief.

"The Queen's pretty well known around Bayport," Frank remarked. "We should meet someone who saw it."

"Seems strange to me," said Joe, "that a thief would take a car like that. Auto thieves usually take cars of a standard make and color. They're easier to get rid of."

"It's possible," Frank suggested, "that the thief didn't steal the car to sell it. Maybe, for some reason, he was making a fast getaway and he'll abandon it."

"Look!" Chet exclaimed, pointing to a truck garden where several men were hoeing cabbage plants. "Maybe they saw the Queen."

"I'll ask them," Frank offered, and brought his motorcycle to a stop.

He scrambled over the fence and jumped across the rows of small plants until he reached the first farm hand.

"Did you see a yellow jalopy go by here within the past hour?" Frank asked him.

The lanky old farmer leaned on his hoe and put a hand to one ear. "Eh?" he shouted.

"Did you see a fellow pass along here in a bright yellow car?" Frank repeated in a louder tone.

The farmer called to his companions. As they ambled over, the old man removed a plug of tobacco from the pocket of his overalls and took a hearty chew.

"Lad here wants to know if we saw a jalopy come by," he said slowly.

The other three farm hands, all rather elderly men, did not answer at once. Instead, they laid down their hoes and the plug of tobacco was duly passed around the group.

Frank grit his teeth. "Please hurry up and answer. The car was stolen. We're trying to find the thief!"

"That so?" said one of the men. "A hot rod, eh?"

"Yes. A bright yellow one," Frank replied.

Another of the workers removed his hat and mopped his brow. "Seems to me," he drawled, "I did see a car come by here a while ago."

"A yellow car?"

"No—'twarn't yeller, come to think of it. I guess,

anyhow, it was a delivery truck, if I remember rightly."

Frank strove to conceal his impatience. "Please, did any of you—?"

"Was it a brand-new car, real shiny?" asked the fourth member of the group.

"No, it was an old car, but it was painted bright yellow," Frank explained.

"My nephew had one of them things," the farmer remarked. "Never thought they was safe, myself."

"I don't agree with you," still another man spoke up. "All boys like cars and you might as well let 'em have one they can work on themselves."

"You're all wrong!" the deaf man interrupted. "Let the boys work on the farm truck. That way they won't get into mischief!" He gave a cackling sort of laugh. "Well, son, I guess we ain't been much help to you. Hope you find the critter that stole your hot rod."

"Thanks," said Frank, and joined the other boys. "No luck. Let's go!"

As they approached Bayport, the trio saw a girl walking along the road ahead of them. When the cyclists drew nearer, Frank's face lighted up, for he had recognized Callie Shaw, who was in his class at Bayport High. Frank often dated Callie and liked her better than any girl he knew.

The boys brought their motorcycles to a stop

beside pretty, brown-eyed Callie. Under one arm she was carrying a slightly battered package. She looked vexed.

"Hi, Callie! What's the matter?" Frank asked. "You look as if your last friend had gone off in a moon rocket."

Callie gave a mischievous smile. "How could I think that with you three friends showing up? Or are you about to take off?" Then her smile faded and she held out the damaged package. "Look at that!" she exclaimed. "It's your fault, Chet Morton!"

The stout boy gulped. "M-my fault? How do you figure that?"

"Well, dear old Mrs. Wills down the road is ill, so I baked her a cake."

"Lucky Mrs. Wills," Joe broke in. "Callie, I'm feeling terribly ill."

Callie ignored him. "That man in the car came along here so fast that I jumped to the side of the road and dropped my package. I'm afraid my cake is ruined!"

"What man?" Joe asked.

"The one Chet lent his car to."

"Callie, that's the man we're looking for!" Frank exclaimed. "Chet didn't lend him the car. He stole it!"

"Oh!" said Callie, shocked. "Chet, that's a shame."

"Was he heading for Bayport?" Joe asked.

"Yes, and at the speed he was making the poor Queen travel, you'll never catch him."

Chet groaned. "I just remembered that the gas gauge wasn't working. I guess the car had more gas in it than I thought. No telling where that guy may take my Queen."

"We'd better go to police headquarters," Frank suggested. "Callie, will you describe this man?"

"All I saw," she answered, "was a blur, but the man did have red hair."

"Red hair!" Frank fairly shouted. "Joe, do you think he could be the same man we saw? The one who wrecked his own car?"

Joe wagged his head. "Miracles do happen. Maybe he wasn't hurt very much and walked to Chet's house."

"And helped himself to my car!" Chet added.

Frank snapped his fingers. "Say! Maybe the wrecked car *didn't* belong to that fellow—"

"You mean he'd stolen it, too!" Joe interrupted.

"Yes—which would make him even more desperate to get away."

"Whatever are you boys talking about?" Callie asked.

"I'll phone you tonight and tell you," Frank promised. "Got to dash now."

The boys waved good-by to Callie and hurried into town. They went at once to Chief Ezra Collig, head of the Bayport police force. He was a tall, husky man, well known to Fenton Hardy and his two sons. The chief had often turned to the private detective for help in solving particularly difficult cases.

When the boys went into his office they found the police chief talking with three excited men. One of these was Ike Harrity, the old ticket seller at the city ferryboat office. Another was Policeman Con Riley. The third was Oscar Smuff, a short, stout man. He was invariably seen wearing a checkered suit and a soft felt hat. He called himself a private detective and was working hard to earn a place on the Bayport police force.

"Smuff's playing up to Collig again," Joe whispered, chuckling, as the boys waited for the chief to speak to them.

Ike Harrity was frankly frightened. He was a timid man, who had perched on a high stool behind the ticket window at the ferryboat office day in and day out for a good many years.

"I was just countin' up the mornin's receipts," he was saying in a high-pitched, excited voice, "when in comes this fellow and sticks a revolver in front of my nose."

"Just a minute," interrupted Chief Collig, turning to the newcomers. "What can I do for you boys?"

"I came to report a theft," Chet spoke up. "My hot rod has been stolen."

"Why, it was one of those crazy hot rods this

fellow drove!" Ike Harrity cried out. "A yellow one!"

"Ha!" exclaimed Oscar Smuff. "A clue!" He immediately pulled a pencil and notebook from his pocket.

"My Queen!" shouted Chet.

Chief Collig rapped on his desk for quiet and asked, "What's a queen got to do with all this?"

Chet explained, then the chief related Harrity's story for him.

"A man drove up to the ferryboat office and tried to hold up Mr. Harrity. But a passenger came into the office and the fellow ran away."

As the officer paused, Frank gave Chief Collig a brief account of the wrecked blue sedan near the Morton farm.

"I'll send some men out there right now." The chief pressed a buzzer and quickly relayed his orders.

"It certainly looks," Joe commented, "as if the man who stole Chet's car and the fellow who tried to hold up the ferryboat office are the same person!"

"Did you notice the color of the man's hair?" Frank asked Mr. Harrity.

Smuff interrupted. "What's that got to do with it?"

"It may have a great deal to do with it," Frank replied. "What was the color of his hair, Mr. Harrity?"

"Dark brown and short cropped."

Frank and Joe looked at each other, perplexed. "You're sure it wasn't red?" Joe asked.

Chief Collig sat forward in his chair. "What are you driving at, boys? Have you some information about this man?"

"We were told," said Joe, "that the guy who stole Chet's car had red hair. A friend of ours saw him."

"Then he must have turned the jalopy over to someone else," Chief Collig concluded.

At this moment a short, nervous little man was ushered into the room. He was the passenger who had gone into the ferryboat office at the time of the attempted holdup. Chief Collig had sent for him.

The newcomer introduced himself as Henry J. Brown of New York. He told of entering the office and seeing a man run away from the ticket window with a revolver in his hand.

"What color was his hair?" Frank asked eagerly. "Did you notice?"

"I can't say I did," the man replied. "My eyes were focused on that gun. Say, wait a minute! He had red hair. You couldn't miss it! I noticed it after he jumped into the car."

Oscar Smuff looked bewildered. "You say he had red hair." The detective turned to Mr. Harrity. "And you say he had dark hair. Somethin' wrong somewhere!" He shook his head in puzzlement.

The others were puzzled too. Frank asked Mr. Brown to tell once more just when he had noticed the red hair.

"After the fellow leaned down in the car and popped his head up again," the New Yorker replied.

Frank and Joe exchanged glances. Was it possible the red hair was a wig and the thief had put it on just before Mr. Brown had noticed him? The boys kept still—they didn't want any interference from Smuff in tracking down this clue.

Harrity and Brown began to argue over the color of the thief's hair. Finally Chief Collig had to rap once more for order. "I'll send out an alarm for both this holdup man and for Chet's car. I guess that's all that can be done now."

Undaunted by their failure to catch the thief, the Hardy boys left police headquarters with Chet Morton. They were determined to pursue the case.

"We'll talk with Dad tonight, Chet," Frank promised. "Maybe he'll give us some leads."

"I sure hope so, fellows," their friend replied as they climbed onto the motorcycles.

The same thought was running through Frank's and Joe's minds: maybe this mystery would turn out to be their first case!

CHAPTER III

The Threat

"You're getting to be pretty good on that motorcycle, Frank," Joe said as the boys rode into the Hardy garage. "I'm not even scared to ride alongside you any more!"

"*You're* not scared!" Frank pretended to take Joe seriously. "What about me—riding with a daredevil like you?"

"Well," Joe countered, "let's just admit that we're both pretty good!"

"It sure was swell of Dad to let us have them," Joe continued.

"Yes," Frank agreed. "And if we're going to be detectives, we'll get a lot of use out of them."

The boys started toward the house, passing the old-fashioned barn on the property. Its first floor had been converted into a gymnasium which was used after school and on week ends by Frank and Joe and their friends.

The Hardy home, on the corner of High and Elm streets, was an old stone house set in a large, tree-shaded lawn. Right now, crocuses and miniature narcissi were sticking their heads through the light-green grass.

"Hello, Mother!" said Frank, as he pushed open the kitchen door.

Mrs. Hardy, a petite, pretty woman, looked up from the table on which she was stuffing a large roasting chicken and smiled.

Her sons kissed her affectionately and Joe asked, "Dad upstairs?"

"Yes, dear. He's in his study."

The study was Fenton Hardy's workshop. Adjoining it was a fine library which contained not only books but files of disguises, records of criminal cases, and translations of thousands of codes.

Walking into the study, Frank and Joe greeted their father. "We're reporting errand accomplished," Frank announced.

"Fine!" Mr. Hardy replied. Then he gave his sons a searching glance. "I'd say your trip netted you more than just my errand."

Frank and Joe had learned early in their boyhood that it was impossible to keep any secrets from their astute father. They assumed that this ability was one reason why he had been such a successful detective on the New York City police force before setting up a private practice in Bayport.

"We ran into some real excitement," Frank said, and told his father the whole story of Chet's missing jalopy, the wrecked car which they suspected had been a stolen one also, and the attempted holdup at the ferryboat office.

"Chet's counting on us to find his car," Joe added.

Frank grinned. "That is, unless the police find it first."

Mr. Hardy was silent for several seconds. Then he said, "Do you want a little advice? You know I never give it unless I'm asked for it." He chuckled.

"We'll need a lot of help," Joe answered.

Mr. Hardy said that to him the most interesting angle to the case was the fact that the suspect apparently used one or more wigs as a disguise. "He may have bought at least one of them in Bayport. I suggest that you boys make the rounds of all shops selling wigs and see what you can find out."

The boys glanced at the clock on their father's large desk, then Frank said, "We'll have time to do a little sleuthing before closing time. Let's go!"

The two boys made a dash for the door, then both stopped short. They did not have the slightest idea where they were going! Sheepishly Joe asked, "Dad, do you know which stores sell wigs?"

With a twinkle in his eyes, Mr. Hardy arose from the desk, walked into the library, and opened a file drawer labeled "W through Z." A moment later he pulled out a thick folder marked WIGS:

Manufacturers, distributors, and retail shops of the world.

"Why, Dad, I didn't know you had all this information—" Joe began.

His father merely smiled. He thumbed through the heavy sheaf of papers, and pulled one out.

"Bayport," he read. "Well, three of these places can be eliminated at once. They sell only women's hair pieces. Now let's see. Frank, get a paper and pencil. First there's Schwartz's Masquerade and Costume Shop. It's at 79 Renshaw Avenue. Then there's Flint's at Market and Pine, and one more: Ruben Brothers. That's on Main Street just this side of the railroad."

"Schwartz's is closest," Frank spoke up. "Let's try him first, Joe."

Hopefully the boys dashed out to their motorcycles and hurried downtown. As they entered Schwartz's shop, a short, plump, smiling man came toward them.

"Well, you just got under the wire, fellows," he said, looking up at a large old-fashioned clock on the wall. "I was going to close up promptly tonight because a big shipment came in today and I never have time except after business hours to unpack and list my merchandise."

"Our errand won't take long," said Frank. "We're sons of Fenton Hardy, the detective. We'd like to know whether or not you recently sold a red wig to a man."

Mr. Schwartz shook his head. "I haven't sold a red wig in months, or even rented one. Everybody seems to want blond or brown or black lately. But you understand, I don't usually sell wigs at all. I rent 'em."

"I understand," said Frank. "We're just trying to find out about a man who uses a red wig as a disguise. We thought he might have bought or rented it here and that you would know his name."

Mr. Schwartz leaned across the counter. "This man you speak of—he sounds like a character. It's just possible he may come in to get a wig from me. If he does, I'll be glad to let you know."

The boys thanked the shopkeeper and were about to leave when Mr. Schwartz called, "Hold on a minute!"

The Hardys hoped that the dealer had suddenly remembered something important. This was not the case, however. With a grin the man asked the boys if they would like to help him open some cartons which had arrived and to try on the costumes.

"Those folks at the factory don't always get the sizes marked right," he said. "Would you be able to stay a few minutes and help me? I'll be glad to pay you."

"Oh, we don't want any money," Joe spoke up. "To tell you the truth, I'd like to see your costumes."

Mr. Schwartz locked the front door of his shop,

then led the boys into a rear room. It was so filled
with costumes of all kinds and paraphernalia for
theatrical work, plus piles of cartons, that Frank
and Joe wondered how the man could ever find
anything.

"Here is today's shipment," Mr. Schwartz said,
pointing to six cartons standing not far from the
rear entrance to his shop.

Together he and the boys slit open the boxes
and one by one lifted out a king's robe, a queen's
tiara, and a Little Bopeep costume. Suddenly Mr.
Schwartz said:

"Here's a skeleton marked size thirty-eight.
Would one of you boys mind trying it on?"

Frank picked up the costume, unzipped the
back, and stepped into the skeleton outfit. It was
tremendous on him and the ribs sagged ludi-
crously.

"Guess a fat man modeled for this," he remarked, holding the garment out to its full width.

At that moment there was a loud rap on the
front door of the store. Mr. Schwartz made no
move to answer it. "I'm closed," he said, "Let him
rap."

Suddenly Frank had an idea. The thief who
used wigs might be the late customer, coming on
purpose at this hour to avoid meeting other people. Without a word to the others, he dashed
through the doorway into the store and toward
the front entrance.

He could vaguely see someone waiting to be admitted. But the stranger gave one look at the leaping, out-of-shape skeleton and disappeared in a flash. At the same moment Frank tripped and fell headlong.

Mr. Schwartz and Joe, hearing the crash, rushed out to see what had happened. Frank, hopelessly tangled in the skeleton attire, was helped to his feet. When he told the others why he had made his unsuccessful dash to the front door, they conceded he might have a point.

"But you sure scared him away in that outfit," Joe said, laughing. "He won't be back!"

The boys stayed for over half an hour helping Mr. Schwartz, then said good-by and went home.

"Monday we'll tackle those other two wig shops," said Frank.

The following morning the Hardy family attended church, then after dinner Frank and Joe told their parents they were going to ride out to see Chet Morton. "We've been invited to stay to supper," Frank added. "But we promise not to get home late."

The Hardys picked up Callie Shaw, who also had been invited. Gaily she perched on the seat behind Frank.

"Hold on, Callie," Joe teased. "Frank's a wild cyclist!"

The young people were greeted at the door of the Morton farmhouse by Chet's younger sister

Iola, dark-haired and pretty. Joe Hardy thought she was quite the nicest girl in Bayport High and dated her regularly.

As dusk came on, the five young people gathered in the Mortons' kitchen to prepare supper. Chet, who loved to eat, was in charge, and doled out various jobs to the others. When he finished, Joe remarked, "And what are you going to do, big boy?"

The stout youth grinned. "I'm the official taster."

A howl went up from the others. "No workee, no eatee," said Iola flatly.

Chet grinned. "Oh, well, if you insist, I'll make a little side dish for all of us. How about Welsh rabbit?"

"You're elected!" the others chorused, and Chet set to work.

The farmhouse kitchen was large and contained a group of windows in one corner. Here stood a large table, where the young people decided to eat. They had just sat down when the telephone rang. Chet got up and walked out in the hall to answer it. Within a minute he re-entered the kitchen, his eyes bulging.

"What's the matter?" Iola asked quickly.

"I— I've been th-threatened!" Chet replied.

"Threatened!" the others cried out. "How?"

Chet was so frightened he could hardly speak, but he managed to make the others understand that a man had just said on the telephone, "You'll never get your jalopy back. And if you don't lay off trying to find me or your car, you're going to get hurt!"

"Whew!" cried Joe. "This is getting serious!"

Callie and Iola had clutched their throats and were staring wild-eyed at Chet. Frank, about to speak, happened to glance out the window toward the barn. For an instant he thought his eyes were playing tricks on him. But no! They were not. A figure was sneaking from the barn and down the lane toward the highway.

"Fellows!" he cried suddenly. "Follow me!"

CHAPTER IV

Red Versus Yellow

By THE time the Hardy boys and Chet had raced from the Mortons' kitchen, the prowler was not in sight. Thinking he had run across one of the fields, the three pursuers scattered in various directions to search. Joe struck out straight ahead and pressed his ear to the ground to listen for receding footsteps. He could hear none. Presently the three boys met once more to discuss their failure to catch up to the man, and to question why he had been there.

"Do you think he was a thief?" Joe asked Chet. "What would he steal?"

"Search me," the stout boy replied. "Let's take a look."

"I believe he was carrying something, but I couldn't see what it was," Frank revealed.

The barn door had not been closed yet for the night and the boys walked in. Chet turned on the lights and the searchers gazed around.

"Look!" Frank cried suddenly.

He pointed to the floor below the telephone extension in the barn. There lay a man's gray wig.

"The intruder's!" Joe exclaimed.

"It sure looks so," Frank agreed. "And something must have scared him. In his hurry to get away he must have dropped this."

Frank picked up the wig and examined it carefully for a clue. "No identifying mark in it. Say, I have an idea," he burst out. "That man phoned you from here, Chet."

"You mean he's the one who threatened me?"

"Yes. If you know how, you can call your own telephone number from an extension."

"That's right."

Chet was wagging his head. "You mean that guy bothered to come all the way here to use this phone to threaten me? Why?"

Both Hardys said they felt the man had not come specifically for that reason. There was another more important one. "We must figure it out. Chet, you ought to be able to answer that better than anybody else. What is there, or was there, in this barn to interest such a person?"

The stout boy scratched his head and let his eyes wander around the building. "It wouldn't be any of the livestock," he said slowly. "And it couldn't be hay or feed." Suddenly Chet snapped his fingers. "Maybe I have the answer. Wait a minute, fellows."

On the floor lay a man's wig

He disappeared from the barn and made a bee-line for the garage. Chet hurried inside but was back in a few seconds.

"I have it!" he shouted. "That guy came here to get the spare tire for the jalopy."

"The one you had is gone?" Frank asked.

Chet nodded. He suggested that perhaps the man was not too far away. He might be on some side road changing the tire. "Let's find out," he urged.

Although the Hardys felt that it would be a use-less search, they agreed to go along. They got on their motorcycles, with Chet riding behind Joe. The boys went up one road and down another, covering the territory very thoroughly. They saw no parked car.

"Not even any evidence that a driver pulled off the road and stayed to change a tire," Frank re-marked. "No footprints, no tool marks, no treads."

"That guy must have had somebody around to pick him up," Chet concluded with a sigh.

"Cheer up, Chet," Frank said, as they walked back to the house. "That spare tire may turn out to be a clue in this case."

When the boys entered the kitchen again, they were met with anxious inquiries from Callie and Iola.

"What in the world were you doing—dashing

out of here without a word?" Callie asked in a shaking voice.

"Yes, what's going on? You had us frightened silly," Iola joined in. "First Chet gets a threatening phone call, and then suddenly all three of you run out of the house like madmen!"

"Calm down, girls," Frank said soothingly. "I saw a prowler, and we were looking for him, but all we found was this!" He tossed the gray wig onto a chair in the hall.

Suddenly there was a loud wail from Chet. "My Welsh rabbit! It's been standing so long it will be ruined!"

Iola began to giggle. "Oh, you men!" she said. "Do you suppose Callie and I would let all that good cheese go to waste? We kept that Welsh rabbit at just the right temperature and it isn't spoiled at all."

Chet looked relieved, as he and the others took their places at the table. Although there was a great deal of bantering during the meal, the conversation in the main revolved around Chet's missing jalopy and the thief who evidently wore hair disguises to suit his fancy.

Frank and Joe asked Chet if they might take along the gray wig and examine it more thoroughly. There might be some kind of mark on it to indicate either the maker or the owner. Chet readily agreed.

But when supper was over, Callie said to Frank with a teasing gleam in her eyes, "Why don't you hot-shot sleuths examine that wig now? I'd like to watch your super-duper methods."

"Just for that, I will," said Frank.

He went to get the wig from the hall chair, and then laid it on the kitchen table. From his pocket he took a small magnifying glass and carefully examined every inch of the lining of the wig.

"Nothing here," he said presently.

The hair was thoroughly examined and parted strand by strand to see if there were any identifying designations on the hair piece. Frank could discover nothing.

"I'm afraid this isn't going to help us much," he said in disgust. "But I'll show it to the different wig men in town."

As he finished speaking the telephone rang and Iola went to answer it. Chet turned white and looked nervous. Was the caller the man who had threatened him? And what did he want?

Presently Iola returned to the kitchen, a worried frown on her face. "It's a man for you, Chet. He wouldn't give his name."

Trembling visibly, Chet walked slowly to the telephone. The others followed and listened.

"Ye-yes, I'm Chet Morton. N-no, I haven't got my car back."

There was a long silence, as the person on the other end of the line spoke rapidly.

"B-but I haven't any money," Chet said finally. "I— Well, okay, I'll let you know."

Chet hung up and wobbled to a nearby chair. The others bombarded him with questions.

The stout boy took a deep breath, then said, "I can get my jalopy back. But the man wants a lot of money for the information as to where it is."

"Oh, I'm glad you're going to get your car back!" Callie exclaimed.

"But I haven't got any money," Chet groaned.

"Who's the man?" Frank demanded.

There was another long pause before Chet answered. Then, looking at the waiting group before him, he announced simply, "Smuff. Oscar Smuff!"

His listeners gasped in astonishment. This was the last thing they expected to hear. The detective was selling information as to where Chet would find his missing jalopy!

"Why, that cheap so-and-so!" Joe cried out angrily.

Chet explained that Smuff had said he was not in business for his health. He had to make a living and any information which he dug up as a detective should be properly paid for.

Frank shrugged. "I suppose Smuff has a point there. How much does he want for the information, Chet?"

"His fee is twenty-five dollars!"

"What!" the others cried out.

After a long consultation it was decided that

the young people would pool their resources. Whatever sum they could collect toward the twenty-five dollars would be offered to Oscar Smuff to lead them to Chet's car.

"But make it very plain," Frank admonished, "that if it's not your jalopy Smuff leads us to, you won't pay him one nickel."

Chet put in a call to Smuff's home. As expected, the detective grumbled at the offer of ten dollars but finally accepted it. He said he would pick up the boys in half an hour and take them to the spot.

About this time Mr. and Mrs. Morton returned home. Chet and Iola's father was a good-looking, jolly man with his son's same general build and coloring. He was in the real-estate business in Bayport and ran the farm as a hobby.

Mrs. Morton was an older edition of her daughter Iola and just as witty and lighthearted. But when she learned what had transpired and that her son had been threatened, she was worried.

"You boys must be very careful," Mrs. Morton advised. "From what I hear about Smuff, this red-haired thief could easily put one over on him. So watch your step!"

Chet promised that they would.

"Good luck!" Callie called out, as Smuff beeped his horn outside the door. "And don't be too late. I want to hear the news before I have to go home."

Frank, Joe, and Chet found Smuff entirely un-communicative about where they were going. He seemed to enjoy the role he was playing.

"I knew I'd be the one to break this case," he boasted.

Joe could not resist the temptation of asking Smuff if he was going to lead them to the thief as well as to the car. The detective flushed in em-barrassment and admitted that he did not have full details yet on this part of the mystery.

"But it won't be long before I capture that fel-low," he assured the boys. They managed to keep their faces straight and only hoped that they were not now on a wild-goose chase.

Twenty minutes later Smuff pulled into the town of Ducksworth and drove straight to a used-car lot. Stopping, he announced, "Well, here we are. Get ready to fork over that money, Chet."

Smuff nodded to the attendant in charge, then led the boys down a long aisle past row after row of cars to where several jalopies were lined up against a rear fence. Turning left, the detective finally paused before a bright red car.

"Here you are!" said Smuff grandly, extending his right hand toward Chet. "My money, please."

The stout boy as well as the Hardys stared at the jalopy. There was no question but that it was the same make and model as Chet's.

"The thief thought he could disguise it by painting it red," Smuff explained.

"Is that your guess?" Frank asked quietly.

Oscar Smuff frowned. "How else could you figure it?" he asked.

"Then there'll be yellow paint under the red," Frank went on. "Let's take a look to make sure."

It was evident that Smuff did not like this procedure. "So you doubt me, eh?" he asked in an unpleasant tone.

"Anybody can get fooled," Frank told him. "Well, Chet, let's operate on this car."

The detective stood by sullenly as Frank pulled out a penknife and began to scrape the red paint off part of the fender.

CHAPTER V

The Hunt Is Intensified

"HEY!" Oscar Smuff shouted. "You be careful with
that penknife! The man who owns this place
don't want you ruinin' his cars!"

Frank Hardy looked up at the detective. "I've
watched my father scrape off flecks of paint many
times. The way he does it, you wouldn't know
anybody had made a mark."

Smuff grunted. "But you're not your father.
Easy there!"

As cautiously as possible Frank picked off flecks
of the red paint in a spot where it would hardly
be noticeable. Taking a flashlight from his pocket,
he trained it on the spot.

Joe, leaning over his brother's shoulder, said,
"There was light-blue paint under this red, not
yellow."

"Right," Frank agreed, eying Smuff intently.

The detective reddened. "You fellows trying to

tell me this isn't Chet's jalopy?" he demanded. "Well, I'm telling you it is, and I'm right!"

"Oh, we haven't said you're wrong," Joe spoke up quickly. Secretly he was hoping that this was Chet's car, but reason told him it was not.

"We'll try another place," Frank said, straightening up, and walking around to a fender on the opposite side.

Here, too, the test indicated that the car had been painted light blue before the red coat had been put over it.

"Well, maybe the thief put blue on and then red," said Smuff stubbornly.

Frank grinned. "We'll go a little deeper. If the owner of this establishment objects, we'll pay for having the fenders painted."

But though Frank went down through several layers of paint, he could not find any sign of yellow.

All this time Chet had been walking round and round the car, looking intently at it inside and out. Even before Frank announced that he was sure this was not the missing jalopy, Chet was convinced of it himself.

"The Queen had a long, thin dent in the right rear fender," he said. "And that seat cushion by the door had a little split in it. I don't think the thief would have bothered to fix them up."

Chet showed his keen disappointment, but he was glad that the Hardys had come along to help him prove the truth. But Smuff was not giving up the money so easily.

"You haven't proved a thing," he said. "The man who runs this place admitted that maybe this is a stolen car. The fellow who sold it to him said he lived on a farm outside Bayport."

The Hardys and Chet were taken aback for a moment by this information. But in a moment Frank said, "Let's go talk to the owner. We'll find out more about the person who brought this car in."

The man who ran the used-car lot was very co-operative. He readily answered all questions the Hardys put to him. The bill of sale revealed that the former owner of the red jalopy was Melvin Schuster of Bayport.

"Why, we know him!" Frank spoke up. "He goes to Bayport High—at least, he did. He and his family moved far away. That's probably why he sold his car."

"But Mr. Smuff said you suspected the car was stolen," Joe put in.

The used-car lot owner smiled. "I'm afraid maybe Mr. Smuff put that idea in my head. I did say that the person seemed in an awful hurry to get rid of the car and sold it very cheap. Sometimes when that happens, we dealers are a little afraid to take the responsibility of buying a car, in case it is stolen property. But at the time Mr. Schuster came in, I thought everything was on the level and bought his jalopy."

Frank said that he was sure everything was all right, and after the dealer described Melvin Schuster, there was no question but that he was the owner.

Smuff was completely crestfallen. Without a word he started for his own car and the boys followed. The detective did not talk on the way back to the Morton farm, and the boys, feeling rather sorry for him, spoke of matters other than the car incident.

As the Hardys and Chet walked into the Morton home, the two girls rushed forward. "Did you find it?" Iola asked eagerly.

Chet sighed. "Another one of Smuff's bluffs," he said disgustedly. He handed back the money which his friends had given to help pay the detective.

Frank and Joe said good-by, went for their motorcycles, and took Callie home. Then they returned to their own house, showered, and went to bed.

As soon as school was over the next day, they took the gray wig and visited Schwartz's shop. The owner assured them that the hair piece had not come from his store.

"It's a very cheap one," the man said rather disdainfully.

Frank and Joe visited Flint's and Ruben Brothers' shops as well. Neither place had sold the gray wig. Furthermore, neither of them had had a customer in many weeks who had wanted a red wig, or who was in the habit of using wigs or toupees of various colors.

"Today's sleuthing was a complete washout," Joe reported that night to his father.

The famous detective smiled. "Don't be discouraged," he said. "I can tell you that one bit of success makes up for a hundred false trails."

As the boys were undressing for bed later, Frank reminded his brother that the following day was a school holiday. "That'll give us hours and hours to work on the case," he said enthusiastically.

"What do you suggest we do?" Joe asked.

Frank shrugged. Several ideas were brought up by the brothers, but one which Joe proposed was given preference. They would get hold of a large group of their friends. On the theory that the thief could not have driven a long distance away because of the police alarm, the boys would make an extensive search in the surrounding area for Chet's jalopy.

"We'll hunt in every possible hiding place," he stated.

Early the next morning Frank hurried to the telephone and put in one call after another to "the gang." These included, besides Chet Morton, Allen Hooper, nicknamed Biff because of his fondness for a distant relative who was a boxer named Biff; Jerry Gilroy, Phil Cohen, and Tony Prito. All were students at Bayport High and prominent in various sports.

The five boys were eager to co-operate. They agreed to assemble at the Hardy home at nine o'clock. In the meantime, Frank and Joe would lay out a plan of action.

As soon as breakfast was over the Hardys told their father what they had in mind and asked if he had any suggestions on how they might go about their search.

"Take a map," he said, "with our house as a radius and cut pie-shaped sections. I suggest that two boys work together."

By nine o'clock his sons had mapped out the search in detail. The first recruit to arrive was Tony Prito, a lively boy with a good sense of humor. He was followed in a moment by Phil Cohen, a quiet, intelligent boy.

"Put us to work," said Tony. "I brought one of my father's trucks that he isn't going to use to-day." Tony's father was in the contracting business. "I can cover a lot of miles in it."

Frank suggested that Tony and Phil work together. He showed them the map, with Bayport as the center of a great circle, cut into four equal sections.

"Suppose you take from nine o'clock to twelve on this dial we've marked. Mother has agreed to stay at home all day and act as clearing house for our reports. Call in every hour."

"Will do," Tony promised. "Come on, Phil. Let's get going!"

The two boys were just starting off when Biff and Jerry arrived at the Hardy home on motorcycles. Biff, blond and long-legged, had an ambling gait, with which he could cover a tremendous amount of territory in a short time. Jerry, an excellent fielder on Bayport High's baseball team, was of medium height, wiry, and strong.

Biff and Jerry were assigned to the section on the map designated six to nine o'clock. They were given further instructions on sleuthing, then started off on their quest.

"Where's Chet?" Mr. Hardy asked his sons. "Wasn't he going to help in the search?"

"He probably overslept. Chet's been known to do that," Frank said with a grin.

"He also might have taken time for a double breakfast," Joe suggested.

Mrs. Hardy, who had stepped to the front porch, called, "Here he comes now. Isn't that Mr. Morton's car?"

"Yes, it is," Frank replied.

Chet's father let him off in front of the Hardy home and the stout boy hurried to the porch. "Good morning, Mrs. Hardy. Good morning, Mr. Hardy. Hi, chums!" he said cheerily. "Sorry to be late. My dad had a lot of phoning to do before he left. I was afraid if I'd tried to walk here, I wouldn't have arrived until tomorrow."

At this point Mr. Hardy spoke up. "As I said before, I think you boys should work in twos. There are only three of you to take care of half the territory." The detective suddenly grinned boyishly. "How about me teaming up with one of you?"

Frank and Joe looked at their dad in delight. "You mean it?" Frank cried out. "I'll choose you as my partner right now."

"I have a further suggestion," the detective said. "It's not going to take you fellows more than three hours to cover the area you've laid out. And there's an additional section I think you might look into."

"What's that?" Joe inquired.

"Willow Grove. That's a park area, but there's also a lot of tangled woodland to one side of it. Good place to hide a stolen car."

Mr. Hardy suggested that the boys meet for a picnic lunch at Willow Grove and later do some sleuthing in the vicinity. "That is, provided you haven't found Chet's jalopy by that time."

Mrs. Hardy spoke up. "I'll fix a nice lunch for all of you," she offered.

"That sure would be swell," Chet said hastily. "You make grand picnic lunches, Mrs. Hardy."

Frank and Joe liked the plan, and it was decided that the boys would have the picnic whether or not they had found the jalopy by one o'clock. Mrs. Hardy said she would relay the news to the other boys when they phoned in.

Chet and Joe set off on the Hardy boys' motor-cycles, taking the twelve-to-three segment on the map. Then Mr. Hardy and Frank drove off for the three-to-six area.

Hour after hour went by, with the searchers constantly on the alert. Every garage, public and private, every little-used road, every patch of woods was thoroughly investigated. There was no sign of Chet's missing yellow jalopy. Finally at one o'clock Frank and his father returned to the Hardy home. A few moments later Joe and Chet returned and a huge picnic lunch was stowed aboard the two motorcycles.

When the three boys reached the picnic area they were required to park their motorcycles outside the fence. They unstrapped the lunch baskets and carried them down to the lake front. The other boys were already there.

"Too bad we can't go swimming," Tony remarked, "but this water's pretty cold."

Quickly they unpacked the food and assembled around one of the park picnic tables.

"Um! Yum! Chicken sandwiches!" Chet cried gleefully.

During the meal the boys exchanged reports on their morning's sleuthing. All had tried hard but failed to find any trace of the missing car.

"Our work hasn't ended," Frank reminded the others. "But I'm so stuffed I'm going to rest a while before I start out again."

All the other boys but Joe Hardy felt the same way and lay down on the grass for a nap. Joe, eager to find out whether or not the woods to their right held the secret of the missing car, plunged off alone through the underbrush.

He searched for twenty minutes without finding a clue to any automobile. He was on the point of returning and waiting for the other boys when he saw a small clearing ahead of him. It appeared to be part of an abandoned roadway.

Excitedly Joe pushed on through the dense undergrowth. It was in a low-lying part of the grove and the ground was wet. At one point it was quite muddy, and it was here that Joe saw something that aroused his curiosity.

"A tire! Then maybe an automobile has been in here," he muttered to himself, although there were no tire marks in the immediate vicinity. "No footprints, either. I guess someone tossed this tire here."

Remembering his father's admonitions on the value of developing one's powers of observation, Joe went closer and examined the tire.

"That tread," he thought excitedly, "looks familiar."

He gazed at it until he was sure, then dashed back to the other boys.

"I've found a clue!" he cried out. "Come on, everybody!"

CHAPTER VI

The Robbery

JOE HARDY quickly led the way into the swampy area as the other boys trooped along, everyone talking at once. When they reached the spot, Chet examined the tire and exclaimed:

"There's no mistake about it! This is one of the tires! When the thief put on the new one, he threw this away."

"Perhaps the Queen is still around," suggested Frank quickly. "The thief may have picked this road as a good place to hide your jalopy until he could make a getaway."

"It would be an ideal place," Chet agreed. "People coming to Willow Grove have to park at the gate, so nobody would come in here. But this old road comes in from the main highway. Let's take a look, fellows."

A scrutinizing search was begun along the abandoned road in the direction of the highway. A moment later Frank and Chet, in the lead, cried out simultaneously.

"Here's a bypath! And here are tire marks!" Frank exclaimed. To one side was a narrow roadway, almost overgrown with weeds and low bushes. It led from the abandoned road into the depths of the woods.

Without hesitation Frank and Chet plunged into it. Presently the roadway widened out, then wound about a heavy clump of trees. It came to an end in a wide clearing.

In the clearing stood Chet Morton's lost jalopy!

"My Queen!" he yelled in delight. "Her own license plates!"

His shout was heard by the rest of the boys, who came on a run. Chet's joy was boundless. He examined the car with minute care, while his chums crowded around. At last he straightened up with a smile of satisfaction.

"She hasn't been damaged a bit. All ready to run. The thief just hid the old bus in here and made a getaway. Come on, fellows, climb aboard. Free ride to the highway!"

Before leaving, the Hardys examined footprints left by the thief. "He wore sneakers," Frank observed.

Suddenly Chet swung open the door and looked on the floor. "You mean he wore *my* sneakers. They're gone."

"And carried his own shoes," Joe observed. "Very clever. Well, that washes out one clue. Can't trace the man by his shoe prints."

"Let's go!" Chet urged.

He jumped into the car and in a few seconds the engine roared. There was barely sufficient room in the clearing to permit him to turn the jalopy about. When he swung around and headed up the bypath, the boys gave a cheer and hastened to clamber aboard.

Lurching and swaying, the car reached the abandoned road and from there made the run to the main highway. The boys transferred to Tony's truck and the motorcycles, and formed a parade into Bayport, with Frank and Joe in the lead. It was their intention to ride up to police headquarters and announce their success to Chief Collig.

"And I hope Smuff will be around," Chet gloated.

As the grinning riders came down Main Street, however, they noticed that no one paid any attention to them, and there seemed to be an unusual air of mystery in the town. People were standing in little groups, gesticulating and talking earnestly.

Presently the Hardys saw Oscar Smuff striding along with a portentous frown. Joe called out to him. "What's going on, detective? You notice we found Chet's car."

"I've got something more important than stolen cars to worry— Hey, what's that?" Detective Smuff stared blankly, as the full import of the discovery filtered his consciousness.

The boys waited for Smuff's praise, but he did not give it. Instead, he said, "I got a big mystery to solve. The Tower Mansion has been robbed!"

"Good night!" the Hardys chorused.

Tower Mansion was one of the show places of Bayport. Few people in the city had ever been permitted to enter the place and the admiration which the palatial building excited was solely by reason of its exterior appearance. But the first thing a newcomer to Bayport usually asked was, "Who owns that house with the towers over on the hill?"

It was an immense, rambling stone structure overlooking the bay, and could be seen for miles, silhouetted against the sky line like an ancient feudal castle. The resemblance to a castle was heightened by the fact that from each of the far ends of the mansion arose a high tower.

One of these had been built when the mansion was erected by Major Applegate, an eccentric, retired old Army man who had made a fortune by lucky real-estate deals. Years ago there had been many parties and dances in the mansion.

But the Applegate family had become scattered until at last there remained in the old home only Hurd Applegate and his sister Adelia. They lived in the vast, lonely mansion at the present time.

Hurd Applegate was a man about sixty, tall, and stooped. His life seemed to be devoted now to the

collection of rare stamps. But a few years before he
had built a new tower on the mansion, a duplicate
of the original one.

His sister Adelia was a maiden lady of uncertain
years. Well-dressed women in Bayport were
amused by her clothes. She dressed in clashing
colors and unbecoming styles. Hurd and Adelia
Applegate were reputed to be enormously
wealthy, although they lived simply, kept only a
few servants, and never had visitors.

"Tell us about the theft," Joe begged Smuff.

But the detective waved his hand airily. "You'll
have to find out yourselves," he retorted as he hurried off.

Frank and Joe called good-by to their friends
and headed for home. As they arrived, the boys
saw Hurd Applegate just leaving the house. The
man tapped the steps with his cane as he came
down them. When he heard the boys' motorcycles
he gave them a piercing glance.

"Good day!" he growled in a grudging manner
and went on his way.

"He must have been asking Dad to take the
case," Frank said to his brother, as they pulled into
the garage.

The boys rushed into the house, eager to find
out more about the robbery. In the front hallway
they met their father.

"We heard the Tower Mansion has been
robbed," said Joe.

Mr. Hardy nodded. "Yes. Mr. Applegate was just here to tell me about it. He wants me to handle the case."

"How much was taken?"

Mr. Hardy smiled. "Well, I don't suppose it will do any harm to tell you. The safe in the Applegate library was opened. The loss will be about forty thousand dollars, all in securities and jewels."

"Whew!" exclaimed Frank. "What a haul! When did it happen?"

"Either last night or this morning. Mr. Applegate did not get up until after ten o'clock this morning and did not go into the library until nearly noon. It was then that he discovered the theft."

"How was the safe opened?"

"By using the combination. It was opened either by someone who knew the set of numbers or else by a very clever thief who could detect the noise of the tumblers. I'm going up to the house in a few minutes. Mr. Applegate is to call for me."

"I'd like to go along," Joe said eagerly.

"So would I," Frank declared.

Mr. Hardy looked at his sons and smiled. "Well, if you want to be detectives, I suppose it is about as good a chance as any to watch a crime investigation from the inside. If Mr. Applegate doesn't object, you may come with me."

A few minutes later a foreign-make, chauffeur-driven car drew up before the Hardy home. Mr.

Applegate was seated in the rear, his chin resting on his cane. The three Hardys went outside. When the detective mentioned the boys' request, the man merely grunted assent and moved over. Frank and Joe stepped in after their father. The car headed toward Tower Mansion.

"I don't really need a detective in this case!" Hurd Applegate snapped. "Don't need one at all. It's as clear as the nose on your face. I *know* who took the stuff. But I can't prove it."

"Whom do you suspect?" Fenton Hardy asked.

"Only one man in the world could have taken the jewels and securities. Robinson!"

"Robinson?"

"Yes. Henry Robinson—the caretaker. He's the man."

The Hardy boys looked at each other in consternation. Henry Robinson, the caretaker of the Tower Mansion, was the father of one of their closest chums! Perry Robinson, nicknamed "Slim," was the son of the accused man!

That his father should be blamed for the robbery seemed absurd to the Hardy boys. They had met Mr. Robinson upon several occasions and he had appeared to be a good-natured, easygoing man with high principles.

"I don't believe he's guilty," Frank whispered.

"Neither do I," returned his brother.

"What makes you suspect Robinson?" Mr. Hardy asked Hurd Applegate.

"He's the only person besides my sister and me who ever saw that safe opened and closed. He could have learned the combination if he'd kept his eyes and ears open, which I'm sure he did."

"Is that your only reason for suspecting him?"

"No. This morning he paid off a nine-hundred-dollar note at the bank. And I know for a fact he didn't have more than one hundred dollars to his name a few days ago. Now where did he raise nine hundred dollars so suddenly?"

"Perhaps he has a good explanation," Mr. Hardy suggested.

"Oh, he'll have an explanation all right!" sniffed Mr. Applegate. "But it will have to be a mighty good one to satisfy me."

The automobile was now speeding up the wide driveway that led to Tower Mansion and within a few minutes stopped at the front entrance. Mr. Hardy and the two boys accompanied the eccentric man into the house.

"Nothing has been disturbed in the library since the discovery of the theft," he said, leading the way there.

Mr. Hardy examined the open safe, then took a special magnifying glass from his pocket. With minute care he inspected the dial of the combination lock. Next he walked to each window and the door to examine them for fingerprints. He asked Mr. Applegate to hold his fingers up to a strong light and got a clear view of the whorls and lines on the inside of the tips. At last he shook his head.

"A smooth job," he observed. "The thief must have worn gloves. All the fingerprints in the room, Mr. Applegate, seem to be yours."

"No use looking for fingerprints or any other evidence!" Mr. Applegate barked impatiently. "It was Robinson, I tell you."

"Perhaps it would be a good idea for me to ask him a few questions," Mr. Hardy advised.

Mr. Applegate rang for one of the servants and instructed him to tell the caretaker to come to the library at once. Mr. Hardy glanced at the boys and suggested they wait in the hallway.

"It might prove less embarrassing to Mr. Robinson that way," he said in a low voice.

Frank and Joe readily withdrew. In the hall they met Mr. Robinson and his son Perry. The man was calm, but pale, and at the doorway he patted Slim on the shoulder.

"Don't worry," he said. "Everything will be all right." With that he entered the library.

Slim turned to his two friends. "It's got to be!" he cried out. "My dad is innocent!"

CHAPTER VII

The Arrest

FRANK and Joe were determined to help their chum prove his father's innocence. They shared his conviction that Mr. Robinson was not guilty.

"Of course he's innocent," Frank agreed. "He'll be able to clear himself all right, Slim."

"But things look pretty black right now," the boy said. He was white-faced and shaken. "Unless Mr. Hardy can catch the real thief, I'm afraid Dad will be blamed for the robbery."

"Everybody knows your father is honest," said Joe consolingly. "He has been a faithful employee—even Mr. Applegate will have to admit that."

"Which won't help him much if he can't clear himself of the charge. And Dad admits that he did know the combination of the safe, although of course he'd never use it."

"He knew it?" repeated Joe, surprised.

"Dad learned the combination accidentally. It was so simple one couldn't forget it. This was how it happened. One day when he was cleaning the library fireplace, he found a piece of paper with numbers on it. He studied them and decided they were the safe combination. Dad laid the paper on the desk. The window was open and he figured the breeze must have blown the paper to the floor."

"Does Mr. Applegate know that?"

"Not yet. But Dad is going to tell him now. He realizes it will look bad for him, but he's going to give Mr. Applegate the truth."

From the library came the hum of voices. The harsh tones of Hurd Applegate occasionally rose above the murmur of conversation and finally the boys heard Mr. Robinson's voice rise sharply.

"I *didn't* do it! I tell you I *didn't* take that money!"

"Then where did you get the nine hundred you paid on that note?" demanded Mr. Applegate.

Silence.

"Where did you get it?"

"I'm not at liberty to tell you or anyone else."

"Why not?"

"I got the money honestly—that's all I can say about it."

"Oh, ho!" exclaimed Mr. Applegate. "You got the money honestly, yet you can't tell me where it came from! A pretty story! If you got the money honestly you shouldn't be ashamed to tell where it came from."

"I'm not ashamed. I can only say again, I'm not at liberty to talk about it."

"Mighty funny thing that you should get nine hundred dollars so quickly. You were pretty hard up last week, weren't you? Had to ask for an advance on your month's wages."

"That is true."

"And then the day of this robbery you suddenly have nine hundred dollars that you can't explain."

Mr. Hardy's calm voice broke in. "Of course I don't like to pry into your private affairs, Mr. Robinson," he said, "but it would be best if you would clear up this matter of the money."

"I know it looks bad," replied the caretaker doggedly. "But I've made a promise I can't break."

"And you admit being familiar with the combination of the safe, too!" broke in Mr. Applegate. "I didn't know that before. Why didn't you tell me?"

"I didn't consider it important."

"And yet you come and tell me now!"

"I have nothing to conceal. If I had taken the securities and jewels I wouldn't be telling you that I knew the combination."

"Yes," agreed Mr. Hardy, "that's a point in your favor, Mr. Robinson."

"Is it?" asked Mr. Applegate. "Robinson's just clever enough to think up a trick like that. He'd figure that by appearing to be honest, I'd believe he is honest and couldn't have committed this robbery. Very clever. But not clever enough. There's plenty of evidence right this minute to convict him, and I'm not going to delay any further."

In a moment Mr. Applegate's voice continued, "Police station? Hello . . . Police station? . . . This is Applegate speaking—Applegate—Hurd Applegate. . . . Well, we've found our man in that robbery. . . . Yes, Robinson. . . . You thought so, eh?—So did I, but I wasn't sure. . . . He has practically convicted himself by his own story. . . . Yes, I want him arrested. . . . You'll be up right away? . . . Fine. . . . Good-by."

"You're not going to have me arrested, Mr. Applegate?" the caretaker cried out in alarm.

"Why not? You're the thief!"

"It might have been better to wait a while," Mr. Hardy interposed. "At least until there was more evidence."

"What more evidence do we want, Mr. Hardy," the owner of Tower Mansion sneered. "If Robinson wants to return the jewels and securities I'll have the charge withdrawn—but that's all."

"I can't return them! I didn't take them!" Mr. Robinson defended himself.

"You'll have plenty of time to think," Mr. Applegate declared. "You'll be in the penitentiary a long time—a long time."

In the hallway the boys listened in growing excitement and dismay. The case had taken an abrupt and tragic turn. Slim looked as though he might collapse under the strain.

"My dad's innocent," the boy muttered over and over again, clenching his fists. "I *know* he is. They can't arrest him. He never stole anything in his life!"

Frank patted his friend on the shoulder. "Brace up, pal," he advised. "It looks discouraging just now, but I'm sure your father will be able to clear himself."

"I— I'll have to tell Mother," stammered Slim. "This will break her heart. And my sisters—"

Frank and Joe followed the boy down the hallway and along a corridor that led to the east wing of the mansion. There, in a neat but sparsely furnished apartment, they found Mrs. Robinson, a gentle, kind-faced woman, who was lame. She was seated in a chair by the window, anxiously waiting. Her two daughters, Paula and Tessie, twelve-year-old twins, were at her side, and all looked up in expectation as the boys came in.

"What news, son?" Mrs. Robinson asked bravely, after she had greeted the Hardys.

"Bad, Mother."

"They're not—they're not—arresting him?" cried Paula, springing forward.

Perry nodded wordlessly.

"But they can't!" Tessie protested. "Dad *couldn't* do anything like that! It's wrong—"

Frank, looking at Mrs. Robinson, saw her suddenly slump over in a faint. He sprang forward and caught the woman in his arms as she was about to fall to the floor.

"Mother!" cried Slim in terror, as Frank laid Mrs. Robinson on a couch, then he said quickly to his sister, "Paula, bring the smelling salts and her special medicine."

Perry explained that at times undue excitement caused an "attack." "I shouldn't have told her about Dad," the boy chided himself.

"She'd have to know it sooner or later," Joe said kindly.

In a moment Paula returned with the bottle of smelling salts and medicine. The inhalant brought her mother back to consciousness, and Paula then gave Mrs. Robinson the medicine. In a few moments the woman completely revived and apologized for having worried everyone.

"I admit it was a dreadful shock to think my husband has been arrested," she said, "but surely something can be done to prove his innocence."

Instantly Frank and Joe assured her they would do everything they could to find the real thief, because they too felt that Mr. Robinson was not guilty.

The next morning, as the brothers were dressing in their room at home, Frank remarked, "There's a great deal about this case that hasn't come to the surface yet. It's just possible that the man who stole Chet Morton's car may have had something to do with the theft."

Joe agreed. "He was a criminal—that much is certain. He stole an automobile and he tried to hold up the ticket office, so why not another robbery?"

"Right, Joe. I just realized that we never inspected Chet's car for any clues to the thief, so let's do it."

The stout boy did not bring his jalopy to school that day, so the Hardys had to submerge their curiosity until classes and baseball practice were over. Then, when Mrs. Morton picked up Chet and Iola, Frank and Joe went home with them.

"I'll look under the seats," Joe offered.

"And I'll search the trunk compartment." Frank walked to the back of the car and raised the cover. He began rooting under rags, papers, and discarded schoolbooks. Presently he gave a cry of victory.

"Here it is! The best evidence in the world!"

Joe and Chet rushed to his side as he held up a man's red wig.

Frank said excitedly, "Maybe there's a clue in this hair piece!"

An examination failed to reveal any, but Frank said he would like to show the wig to his father. He covered it with a handkerchief and put it carefully in an inner pocket. Chet drove the Hardys home.

They assumed that their father was in his study on the second floor, and rushed up there and into the room without ceremony.

"Dad, we've found a clue!" Joe cried. Then he stepped back, embarrassed, as he realized there was someone else in the room.

"Sorry!" said Frank. The boys would have retreated, but Mr. Hardy's visitor turned around and they saw that he was Perry Robinson.

"It's only me," said Slim. "Don't go."

"Hi, Slim!"

"Perry has been trying to shed a little more light on the Tower robbery," explained Mr. Hardy. "But what is this clue you're talking about?"

"It might concern the robbery," replied Frank. "It's about the red-haired man." He took the wig from his pocket and told where he had found it.

Mr. Hardy's interest was kindled at once. "This seems to link up a pretty good chain of evidence. The man who passed you on the shore road wrecked the car he was driving, then stole Chet's, and afterward tried to hold up the ticket office. When he failed there, he tried another and more successful robbery at the Tower."

"Do you really think the wig might help us solve the Tower robbery?" asked Perry, taking hope.

"Possibly."

"I was just telling your father," Slim went on, "that I saw a strange man lurking around the

grounds of the mansion two days before the robbery. I didn't think anything of it at the time, and
in the shock of Dad's arrest I forgot about it."

"Did you get a good look at him? Could you describe him?" Frank asked.

"I'm afraid I can't. It was in the evening. I was
sitting by a window, studying, and happened to
look up. I saw this fellow moving about among the
trees. Later, I heard one of the dogs barking in
another part of the grounds. Shortly afterward, I
saw someone running across the lawn. I thought he
was just a tramp."

"Did he wear a hat or a cap?"

"As near as I can remember, it was a cap. His
clothes were dark."

"And you couldn't see his face?"

"No."

"Well, it's not much to go on," said Mr. Hardy,
"but it might be linked up with Frank and Joe's
idea that the man who stole the jalopy may still
have been hanging around Bayport." The detective thought deeply for a few moments. "I'll bring
all these facts to Mr. Applegate's attention, and
I'm also going to have a talk with the police au-
thorities. I feel they haven't enough evidence to
warrant holding your father, Perry."

"Do you think you can have him released?" the
boy asked eagerly.

"I'm sure of it. In fact, I believe Mr. Applegate

is beginning to realize now that he made a mistake."

"It will be wonderful if we can have Dad back with us again," said Perry. "Of course things won't be the same for him. He'll be under a cloud of suspicion as long as this mystery isn't cleared up. I suppose Mr. Applegate won't employ him or anyone else."

"All the more reason why we should get busy and clear up the affair," Frank said quickly, and Joe added, "Slim, we'll do all we can to help your father."

CHAPTER VIII

An Important Discovery

WHEN the Hardy boys were on their way home from school the next afternoon they noticed that a crowd had collected in the vestibule of the post office and were staring at the bulletin board.

"Wonder what's up now?" said Joe, pushing his way forward through the crowd with the agility of an eel. Frank was not slow in following.

On the board was a large poster. The ink on it was scarcely dry. At the top, in enormous black letters, it read:

$1000 REWARD

Underneath, in slightly smaller type, was the following:

The above reward will be paid for information leading to the arrest of the person or persons who broke into Tower Mansion and stole jewels and securities from a safe in the library.

The reward was being offered by Hurd Applegate.

"Why, that must mean the charge against Mr. Robinson has been dropped!" exclaimed Joe.

"It looks like it. Let's see if we can find Slim."

All about them people were commenting on the size of the reward, and there were many expressions of envy for the person who would be fortunate enough to solve the mystery.

"A thousand dollars!" said Frank, as the brothers made their way out of the post office. "That's a lot of money, Joe."

"I'll say it is."

"And there's no reason why we haven't as good a chance of earning it as anyone else."

"I suppose Dad and the police are barred from the reward, for it's their duty to find the thief if they can. But if we track him down we can get the money. It'll be a good sum to add to our college fund."

"Let's go! Say, there's Slim now."

Perry Robinson was coming down the street toward them. He looked much happier than he had the previous evening, and when he saw the Hardy boys his face lighted up.

"Dad is free," he told them. "Thanks to your father, the charge has been dropped."

"I'm sure glad to hear that!" exclaimed Joe. "I see a reward is being offered."

"Your father convinced Mr. Applegate that it

must have been an outside job. And the work of a professional thief. Chief Collig admitted there wasn't much evidence against Dad, so they let him go. It's a great relief. My mother and sisters were almost crazy with worry."

"No wonder," commented Frank. "What's your father going to do now?"

"I don't know," Slim admitted. "Of course, we've had to move from the Tower Mansion estate. Mr. Applegate said that even though the charge had been dropped, he wasn't altogether convinced in his own mind that Dad hadn't had something to do with the theft. So he dismissed him."

"That's tough luck. But your dad will be able to get another job somewhere," Frank said consolingly.

"I'm not so sure about that. People aren't likely to employ a man who's been suspected of stealing. Dad tried two or three places this afternoon, but he was turned down."

The Hardys were silent. They felt very sorry for the Robinsons and were determined to do what they could to help them.

"We've rented a small house just outside the city," Slim went on. "It's cheap and the neighborhood is kind of bad, but we'll have to get along."

Frank and Joe admired Slim. There was no false pride about him. He faced the facts as they came, and made the best of them. "But if Dad doesn't

get a job, it will mean that I'll have to go to work
full time."

"Why, Slim—you'd have to quit school!" Joe
cried out.

"I can't help that. I wouldn't want to, for you
know I was trying for a scholarship. But—"

The brothers realized how much it would mean
to their chum if he had to leave school. Perry Robinson was an ambitious boy and one of the top ten
in his class. He had always wanted to continue his
studies and go on to a university, and his teachers
had predicted a brilliant career for him as an engineer. Now it seemed that all his ambitions for a
high school diploma and a college education would
have to be given up because of this misfortune.

Frank put an arm around Slim's shoulders.
"Chin up," he said with a warm smile. "Joe and I
are going to plug away at this affair until we get to
the bottom of it!"

"It's mighty good of you fellows," Slim said
gratefully. "I won't forget it in a hurry." He tried
to smile, but it was evident that the boy was deeply
worried. When he walked away it was not with the
light, carefree step which the Hardys associated
with him.

"What's the first move, Frank?" Joe asked.

"We'd better get a full description of those
jewels. Perhaps the thief tried to pawn them. Let's
try all the pawnshops and see what we can find
out."

"Good idea, even if the police have already done it." Frank grinned. Then he sobered. "Do you think Applegate will give us a list?"

"We won't have to ask him. Dad should have that information."

"Let's find out right now."

When the boys returned home, they found their father waiting for them. "I have news for you," he said. "Your theory about the wrecked auto being stolen has been confirmed. Collig phoned just now and told me the true ownership had been traced by the engine number. Car belongs to a man over in Thornton."

"Good. That's one more strike against the thief," Joe declared.

But a moment later the boys met with disappointment when they asked their father for a list of the stolen jewels.

"I'm willing to give you all the information I have," said Fenton Hardy, "but I'm afraid it won't be of much use. Furthermore, I'll bet I can tell just what you're going to do."

"What?"

"Make the rounds of the pawnshops to see if any of the jewels have been turned in."

The Hardy boys looked at each other in amazement. "I might have guessed," said Frank.

Their father smiled. "Not an hour after I was called in on the case I had a full description of all those jewels in every pawnshop in the city. More than that, the description has been sent to jewelry firms and pawnshops in other cities near here, and also the New York police. Here's a duplicate list if you want it, but you'll just be wasting time calling at the shops. All the dealers are on the lookout for the jewels."

Mechanically, Frank took the list. "And I thought it was such a bright idea!"

"It *is* a bright idea. But it has been used before. Most jewel robberies are solved in just this manner—by tracing the thief when he tries to get rid of the gems."

"Well," said Joe gloomily, "I guess *that* plan is all shot to pieces. Come on, Frank. We'll think of something else."

"Out for the reward?" asked Mr. Hardy, chuckling.

"Yes. And we'll get it, too!"

"I hope you do. But you can't ask me to help you any more than I've done. It's my case, too, remember. So from now on, you boys and I are rivals!"

"It's a go!"

"More power to you!" Mr. Hardy smiled and returned to his desk.

He had a sheaf of reports from shops and agencies in various parts of the state, through which he had been trying to trace the stolen jewels and securities, but in every case the report was the same. There had been no lead to the gems or the bonds taken from Tower Mansion.

When the boys left their father's study they went outside and sat on the back-porch steps.

"What shall we do now?" asked Joe.

"I don't know. Dad sure took the wind out of our sails that time, didn't he?"

"I'll say he did. But it was just as well. He saved us a lot of trouble."

"Yes, we might have been going around in circles," Frank conceded.

Joe wagged his head. "It looks as if Dad has the inside track on the case—in the city, anyway."

"What have you got in mind?" Joe asked.

"To concentrate on the country. We started out to find the thief because he stole Chet's car. Let's start all over again from that point."

"Meaning?"

"Mr. Red Wig may have come back to the woods expecting to use Chet's car again, and—"

"Frank, you're a genius! You figure the guy may have left a clue by accident."

"Exactly."

Fired with enthusiasm once more, the brothers called to Mrs. Hardy where they were going, then set off on their motorcycles. After parking them at the picnic site, the brothers once more set off for the isolated spot where the jalopy had been hidden.

Everything looked the same as it had before, but Frank and Joe examined the ground carefully for

Frank and Joe examined the circular marks

new footprints. They found none, but Joe pointed out six-inch circular marks at regular intervals.

"They're just the size of a man's stride," he remarked, "and I didn't notice them before."

"I didn't either," said Frank. "Do you suppose that thief tied pads onto his shoes to keep him from making footprints?"

"Let's see where they lead."

The boys followed the circular marks through the thicket. They had not gone far when their eyes lighted up with excitement.

"Another clue!" Joe yelled. "And this time a swell one!"

CHAPTER IX

Rival Detectives

"MAYBE," Frank said with a grin, "Dad will take us into his camp when he sees these!"

"*Just* a minute," Joe spoke up. "I thought we were rivals now, and you and I have to solve this mystery alone to earn the reward."

Frank held up a man's battered felt hat and an old jacket. "If these belong to that thief, I think we've earned the money already!"

He felt through the pockets of the jacket, but they were empty. "No clue here," he said.

"This hat has a label, though—New York City store," said Joe.

"And the coat, too," Frank added. "Same shop. Well, one thing is sure. If they do belong to the thief, he never meant to leave them. The labels are a dead giveaway."

"He must have been frightened off," Joe concluded. "Maybe when he found that Chet's jalopy was gone, he felt he'd better scram, and forgot the coat and hat."

"What I'd like to know," Frank said, "is whether some hairs from that red wig may be in the hat."

Joe grinned. "Bright boy." He carried the hat to a spot where the sunlight filtered down through the trees and looked intently at the inside, even turning down the band. "Yowee! Success!" he yelled.

Frank gazed at two short strands of red hair. They looked exactly like those in the wig which the boys had found.

Joe sighed. "I guess we'll *have* to tell Dad about this. He has the wig."

"Right."

Frank and Joe hurried home, clutching their precious clues firmly. Mr. Hardy was still in his study when his sons returned. The detective looked up, frankly surprised to see them home so soon. There was the suspicion of a twinkle in his eyes.

"What! More clues!" he exclaimed. "You're really on the job."

"You bet we have more clues!" cried Frank eagerly. He told the boys' story and laid the hat and jacket on a table. "We're turning these over to you."

"But I thought you two were working on this case as my rivals."

"To tell the truth," said Frank, "we don't know what to do with the clue we've found. It leads to New York City."

Mr. Hardy leaned forward in his desk chair as Frank pointed out the labels and the two strands of red hair.

"And besides," Frank went on, "I guess the only way to prove that the thief owns these clothes is by comparing the hairs in the hat with the red wig. And Joe and I don't have the wig."

With a grin the detective went to his files and brought it out. "Chief Collig left this here."

The strands of hair were compared and matched perfectly!

"You boys have certainly made fine progress," Mr. Hardy praised his sons. He smiled. "And since you have, I'll let you in on a little secret. Chief Collig asked me to see what I could figure out of the wig. He says there's no maker's name on it."

"And there isn't?" Joe asked.

His father's eyes twinkled once more. "I guess Collig's assistants weren't very thorough. At any rate, I discovered there's an inner lining and on that is the maker's name. He's in New York City and I was just thinking about flying there to talk to him. Now you boys have given me a double incentive for going."

Frank and Joe beamed with pleasure, then suddenly their faces clouded.

"What's the matter?" Mr. Hardy asked them.

Joe answered. "It looks as if you're going to solve the case all alone."

"Nothing of the sort," the detective replied. "The person who bought the wig may not have given his name. The hat may have been purchased a long time ago, and it isn't likely that the clerk who sold it will remember who bought it. The same with the jacket."

Frank and Joe brightened. "Then the case is far from solved," Frank said.

"All these are good leads, however," Mr. Hardy said. "There is always the chance that the store may not be far from where the suspect lives. Though it's a slim chance, we can't afford to overlook anything. I'll take these articles to the city and see what I can do. It may mean everything and it may mean nothing. Don't be disappointed if I come back empty-handed. And don't be surprised if I come back with some valuable information."

Mr. Hardy tossed the wig, coat, and hat into a bag that was standing open near his desk. The detective was accustomed to being called away suddenly on strange errands, and he was always prepared to leave at a moment's notice.

"Not much use starting now," he said, glancing at his watch. "But I'll go to the city first thing in the morning. In the meantime, you boys keep your eyes and ears open for more clues. The case isn't over yet by any means."

Mr. Hardy picked up some papers on his desk, as a hint that the interview was over, and the boys left the study. They were in a state of high excitement when they went to bed that night and could not get to sleep.

"That thief must be pretty smart," murmured Joe, after they had talked long into the night.

"The smarter crooks are, the harder they fall," Frank replied. "If this fellow has any kind of a record, it won't take long for Dad to run him down. I've heard Dad say that there is no such thing as a clever crook. If he was really clever, he wouldn't be a crook at all."

"Yes, I guess there's something in that, too. But it shows that we're not up against any amateur. This fellow is a slippery customer."

"He'll have to be mighty slippery from now on. Once Dad has a few clues to work on he never lets up till he gets his man."

"And don't forget *us*," said Joe, yawning. With that the boys fell asleep.

When they went down to breakfast the following morning Frank and Joe learned that their father had left for New York on an early-morning plane. Their mother remarked, "I'll be so relieved when he gets back. So often these missions turn out to be dangerous."

She went on to say that her husband had promised to phone her if he wasn't going to be back by suppertime. Suddenly she added with a tantalizing smile, "Your father said he might have a surprise for you if he remains in New York."

Mrs. Hardy refused to divulge another word. The boys went to school, but all through the morning could scarcely keep their minds on studies. They kept wondering how Fenton Hardy was faring on his quest in New York and what the surprise was.

Slim Robinson was at school that day, but after classes he confided to the Hardys that he was leaving for good.

"It's no use," he said. "Dad can't keep me in school any longer and it's up to me to pitch in and help the family. I'm to start work tomorrow at a supermarket."

"And you wanted to go to college!" exclaimed Frank. "It's a shame!"

"Can't be helped," replied Perry with a grimace. "I consider myself lucky to have stayed in school this long. I'll have to give up all those college plans and settle down in the business world. There's one good thing about it—I'll have a chance to learn supermarket work from the ground up. I'm starting in the receiving department." He smiled. "Perhaps in about fifty years I'll be head of the firm!"

"You'll make good at whatever you tackle," Joe assured him. "But I'm sorry you won't be able to go through college as you planned. Don't give up hope yet, Slim. One never knows what may happen. Perhaps the thief who *did* rob Tower Mansion will be found."

Frank and Joe wanted to tell Slim about the clues they had discovered the previous day, but the same thought came into their minds—that it would be unfair to raise any false hopes. So they said good-by and wished him good luck. Perry tried hard to be cheerful, but his smile was very faint as he turned away from them and walked down the street.

"I sure feel sorry for him," said Frank, as he and Joe started for home. "He was such a hard worker in school and counted so much on going to college."

"We've just *got* to clear up the Tower robbery, that's all there is to it!" declared his brother.

As they neared the Hardy home, the boys' steps quickened. Would they find that their father had returned with the information on the identity of the thief? Or was he still in New York? And were they about to share another of his secrets?

CHAPTER X

A Sleuthing Trip

FRANK and Joe's first stop was the Hardy garage. Looking in, they saw that only Mrs. Hardy's car was there. Their father had taken his sedan to the airport and not brought it back.

"Dad's not home!" Joe cried excitedly. "Now we'll hear what the surprise is." Dashing into the kitchen, he called, "Mother!"

"I'm upstairs, dear," Mrs. Hardy called back.

The boys rushed up the front stairway two steps at a time. Their mother met them at the door of their bedroom. Smiling broadly, she pointed to a packed suitcase on Frank's bed. The boys looked puzzled.

Next, from her dress pocket, Mrs. Hardy brought out two plane tickets and some dollar bills. She handed a ticket and half the money to each of her sons, saying, "Your father wants you to meet him in New York to help him on the case."

Frank and Joe were speechless for a moment,

then they grabbed their mother in a bear hug. "This is super!" Joe exclaimed. "What a surprise!"

Frank looked affectionately at his mother. "You sure were busy today—getting our plane tickets and money. I wish you were going too."

Mrs. Hardy laughed. "When I go to New York for a week end I want to have fun with you boys, not trot around to police stations and thieves' hide-outs!" she teased. "I'll go some other time. Well, let's hurry downstairs. There's a snack ready for you. Then I'll drive my detective sons to the airport."

In less than two hours the boys were on the plane to New York City. Upon landing there, they were met by Mr. Hardy. He took them to his hotel, where he had engaged an adjoining room for them. It was not until the doors were closed that he brought up the subject of the mystery.

"The case has taken an interesting turn, and may involve considerable research. That's why I thought you might help me."

"Tell us what has happened so far," Frank requested eagerly.

Mr. Hardy said that immediately upon arriving in the city he had gone to the office of the company which had manufactured the red wig. After sending in his card to the manager he had been admitted readily.

"That's because the name of Fenton Hardy is

known from the Atlantic to the Pacific!" Joe interjected proudly.

The detective gave his son a wink and went on with the story. " 'Some of our customers in trouble, Mr. Hardy?' the manager asked me when I laid the red wig on his desk.

" 'Not yet,' I said. 'But one of them may be if I can trace the purchaser of this wig.'

"The manager picked it up. He inspected it carefully and frowned. 'We sell mainly to an exclusive theatrical trade. I hope none of the actors has done anything wrong.'

" 'Can you tell me who bought this one?' I asked.

" 'We make wigs only to order,' the manager said. He pressed a button at the side of his desk. A boy came and departed with a written message. 'It may be difficult. This wig is not a new one. In fact, I would say it was fashioned about two years ago.'

" 'A long time. But still—' I encouraged him," the detective went on. "In a few minutes a bespectacled elderly man shuffled into the office in response to the manager's summons.

" 'Kauffman, here,' the manager said, 'is our expert. What he doesn't know about wigs isn't worth knowing.' Then, turning to the old man, he handed him the red wig. 'Remember it, Kauffman?'

"The old man looked at it doubtfully. Then he gazed at the ceiling. 'Red wig—red wig—' he muttered.

" 'About two years old, isn't it?' the manager prompted.

" 'Not quite. Year'n a half, I'd say. Looks like a comedy-character type. Wait'll I think. There ain't been so many of our customers playin' that kind of a part inside a year and a half. Let's see. Let's see.' The old man paced up and down the office, muttering names under his breath. Suddenly he stopped, snapping his fingers.

" 'I have it,' he said. 'It must have been Morley who bought that wig. That's who it was! Harold Morley. He's playin' in Shakespearean repertoire with Hamlin's company. Very fussy about his wigs. Has to have 'em just so. I remember he bought this one, because he came in here about a month ago and ordered another like it.'

" 'Why would he do that?' I asked him.

"Kauffman shrugged his shoulders. 'Ain't none of my business. Lots of actors keep a double set of wigs. Morley's playin' down at the Crescent Theater right now. Call him up.'

" 'I'll go and see him,' I told the men. And that's just what we'll do, Frank and Joe, after a bite of supper."

"You don't think this actor is the thief, do you?" Frank asked in amazement. "How could he have gone back and forth to Bayport so quickly? And isn't he playing here in town every night?"

Mr. Hardy admitted that he too was puzzled. He was certain Morley was not the man who had worn the wig on the day the jalopy was stolen, for the Shakespearean company had been playing a three weeks' run in New York. It was improbable, in any case, that the actor was a thief.

The three Hardys arrived at Mr. Morley's dressing room half an hour before curtain time. Mr. Hardy presented his card to a suspicious doorman at the Crescent, but he and his sons were finally admitted backstage and shown down a brilliantly lighted corridor to the dressing room of Harold Morley. It was a snug place, with pictures on the walls, a potted plant in the window overlooking the alleyway, and a rug on the floor.

Seated before a mirror with electric lights at either side was a stout little man, almost totally bald. He was diligently rubbing creamy stage make-up on his face. He did not turn around, but eyed his visitors in the mirror, casually telling them to sit down. Mr. Hardy took the only chair. The boys squatted on the floor.

"Often heard of you, Mr. Hardy," the actor said in a surprisingly deep voice that had a comical effect in contrast to his diminutive appearance. "Glad to meet you. What kind of call is this? Social —or professional?"

"Professional."

Morley continued rubbing the make-up on his jowls. "Out with it," he said briefly.

"Ever see this wig before?" Mr. Hardy asked

him, laying the hair piece on the make-up table.

Morley turned from the mirror, and an expression of delight crossed his plump countenance. "Well, I'll say I've seen it before!" he declared. "Old Kauffman—the best wigmaker in the country —made this for me about a year and a half ago. Where did you get it? I sure didn't think I'd ever see this red wig again."

"Why?"

"Stolen from me. Some low-down sneak got in here and cleaned out my dressing room one night during the performance. Nerviest thing I ever heard of. Came right in here while I was doing my stuff out front, grabbed my watch and money and a diamond ring I had lying by the mirror, took this wig and a couple of others that were around, and beat it. Nobody saw him come or go. Must have got in by that window."

Morley talked in short, rapid sentences, and there was no mistaking his sincerity.

"All the wigs were red," he stated. "I didn't worry so much about the other wigs, because they were for old plays, but this one was being used right along. Kauffman made it specially for me. I had to get him to make another. But say—where did you find it?"

"Oh, my sons located it during some detective work we're on. The crook left this behind. I was trying to trace him by it."

Morley did not inquire further. "That's all the help I can give you," he said. "The police never did learn who cleaned out my dressing room."

"Too bad. Well, I'll probably get him some other way. Give me a list and description of the articles he took from you. Probably I can trace him through that."

"Glad to," said Morley. He reached into a drawer and drew out a sheet of paper which he handed to the detective. "That's the same list I gave the police when I reported the robbery. Number of the watch, and everything. I didn't bother to mention the wigs. Figured they wouldn't be in any condition to wear if I did get them back."

Mr. Hardy folded the list and put it in his pocket. Morley glanced at his watch, lying face up beside the mirror, and gave an exclamation. "Suffering Sebastopol! Curtain in five minutes and I'm not half made up yet. Excuse me, folks, but I've got to get on my horse. In this business 'I'll be ready in a minute' doesn't go."

He seized a stick of grease paint and feverishly resumed the task of altering his appearance to that of the character he was portraying at that evening's performance. Mr. Hardy and his sons left. They made their way out to the street.

"Not much luck there," Frank commented.

"Except through Mr. Morley's stolen jewelry," his father reminded him. "If that's located in a pawnshop, it may lead to the thief. Well, boys,

would you like to go into the theater via the front
entrance and see the show?"

"Yes, Dad," the brothers replied, and Joe added,
"Tomorrow we'll try to find out the name and address of the thief through his coat and hat?"

"Right," the detective said.

The Hardys enjoyed the performance of *The
Merchant of Venice* with Mr. Morley as Launcelot
Gobbo, and laughed hilariously at his comedy and
gestures.

The next morning the detective and his sons
visited the store from which the thief's jacket and
hat had been purchased. They were told that the
styles were three years out of date and there was
no way to tell who had bought them.

"The articles," the head of the men's suit department suggested, "may have been picked up
more recently at a secondhand clothing store."
The Hardys thanked him and left.

"All this trip for nothing." Joe gave a sigh.

His father laid a hand on the boy's shoulder.
"A good detective," he said, "never sighs with dis-
couragement nor becomes impatient. It took years
of persistence to solve some famous cases."

He suggested that their next effort be devoted
to doing some research in the city's police files.
Since Mr. Hardy had formerly been a member of
the New York City detective force, he was permitted to search the records at any time.

Frank and Joe accompanied him to headquarters and the work began. First came a run-down on any known New York criminals who used disguises. Of these men, the Hardys took the reports on the ones who were thin and of medium height.

Next came a check by telephone on the whereabouts of these people. All could be accounted for as working some distance from Bayport at the time of the thefts, with one exception.

"I'll bet he's our man!" Frank exclaimed. "But where is he now?"

CHAPTER XI

Anxious Waiting

THE suspect, the Hardys learned, was out of prison on parole. His name was John Jackley, but he was known as Red Jackley because when caught before going to prison he had been wearing a red wig.

"He lives right here in New York, and maybe he's back home by this time," Joe spoke up. "Let's go see him."

"Just a minute," Mr. Hardy said, holding up his hand. "I don't like to leave Mother alone so long. Besides, in this type of sleuthing three detectives together are too noticeable to a crook. This Jackley may or may not be our man. But if he is, he's probably dangerous. I want you boys to take the evening plane home. I'll phone the house the minute the thief is in custody."

"All right, Dad," his sons chorused, though secretly disappointed that they had to leave.

When they reached home, Frank and Joe learned that their mother had been working on the case from a completely different angle. Hers was the humanitarian side.

"I went to call on the Robinsons to try to bolster their spirits," she said. "I told them about your trip to New York and that seemed to cheer them a lot. Monday I'm going to bake a ham and a cake for you to take to them. Mrs. Robinson isn't well and can do little in the kitchen."

"That's swell of you!" Frank said admiringly. "I'll go."

Joe told them he had a tennis match to play. "I'll do the next errand," he promised.

Monday, during a change of classes, Frank met Callie Shaw in the corridor. "Hi!" she said. "What great problem is on Detective Hardy's mind? You look as if you'd lost your best criminal!"

Frank grimaced. "Maybe I have," he said.

He told Callie that he had phoned home at noon confidently expecting to hear that his father had reported the arrest of the real thief of the Apple-gate money and the exoneration of Mr. Robinson. "But there was no word, Callie, and I'm worried Dad may be in danger."

"I don't blame you," she said. "What do you think has happened?"

"Well, you never can tell when you're dealing with criminals."

"Now, Frank, you're not trying to tell me your

father would let himself get trapped?" Callie said.

"No, I don't think he would, Callie. Maybe Dad hasn't returned because he still hasn't found the man he was looking for."

"Well, I certainly hope that thief is caught," said Callie. "But, Frank, nobody really believes Mr. Robinson did it!"

"Nobody but Hurd Applegate and the men who employ people. Until they find the man who *did* take the stuff, Mr. Robinson is out of a job."

"I'm going over to see the Robinsons soon. Where are they living?"

Frank gave Callie the address. Her eyes widened. "Why, that's in one of the poorest sections of the city! Frank, I had no idea the Robinsons' plight was that bad!"

"It is—and it'll be a lot worse unless Mr. Robinson gets work pretty soon. Slim's earnings aren't enough to take care of the whole family. Say, Callie, how about going over to the Robinsons' with me after school? Mother's sending a ham and a cake."

"I'd love to," Callie agreed. The two parted at the door of the algebra teacher's classroom.

As soon as the last bell had rung, Frank and Callie left the building together. First they stopped at the Shaw house to leave the girl's books.

"I think I'll take some fruit to the Robinsons," Callie said, and quickly filled a bag with oranges, bananas, and grapes.

When the couple reached the Hardy home, Frank asked his mother if any messages had come. "No, not yet," she answered.

Frank said nothing to her about being concerned over his father, as he tucked the ham under one arm and picked up the cakebox. But after he and Callie reached the street, he again confided his concern to Callie.

"It does seem strange you haven't heard anything," she admitted. "But don't forget the old saying, 'No news is good news,' so don't worry."

"I'll take your advice," Frank agreed. "No use wearing a sour look around the Robinsons."

"Or when you're with me, either," Callie said, tossing her head teasingly.

Frank hailed an approaching bus bound for the section of the city in which the Robinsons lived. He and Callie climbed aboard. It was a long ride and the streets became less attractive as they neared the outskirts of Bayport.

"It's a shame, that's what it is!" declared Callie abruptly. "The Robinsons were always accustomed to having everything so nice! And now they have to live here! Oh, I hope your father catches the man who committed that robbery—and soon!"

Her eyes flashed and for a moment she looked so fierce that Frank laughed.

"I suppose you'd like to be the judge and jury at his trial, eh?"

"I'd give him a hundred years in jail!" Callie declared.

When they came to the street where the Robinsons had moved they found that it was an even poorer thoroughfare than they had expected. There were small houses badly in need of paint and repairs. Shabbily dressed children were playing in the roadway.

At the far end of the street stood a small cottage that somehow contrived to look homelike in spite of the surroundings. The picket fence had been repaired and the yard had been cleaned up.

"This is where they live," said Frank.

Callie smiled. "It's the neatest place on the whole street."

Paula and Tessie answered their knock. The twins' faces lighted up with pleasure when they saw who the callers were.

"Frank and Callie!" they exclaimed. "Come in."

The callers were greeted with kindly dignity by Mrs. Robinson. She looked pale and thin but had the same self-possession she had always shown at Tower Mansion.

"We can't stay long," Callie explained. "But Frank and I just thought we'd run out to see how you all are. And we brought something for you."

The fruit, ham, and cake were presented. As the twins ohed and ahed over the food, Mrs. Robinson's eyes filled with tears. "You are dear people," she said. "Frank, tell your mother I can't thank her enough."

Frank grinned as Mrs. Robinson went on, "Callie, we shall enjoy this fruit very much. Many thanks."

Paula said, "It's a wonderful gift. Say, did you know Perry got a better job the second day he was at the supermarket?"

"No. That's swell," Frank replied. "It didn't take the manager long to find out how smart Slim is, eh?"

The twins giggled, but Mrs. Robinson said dolefully, "I wish my husband could find a job. Since no one around here will employ him, he is thinking of going to another city to get work."

"And leave you here?"

"I suppose so. We don't know what to do."

"It's so unfair!" Paula flared up. "My father didn't have a thing to do with that miserable robbery, and yet he has to suffer for it just the same!"

Mrs. Robinson said to Frank hesitantly, "Has Mr. Hardy discovered anything—yet?"

"I don't know," Frank admitted. "We haven't heard from him. He's been in New York following up some clues. But so far there's been no word."

"We hardly dare hope that he'll be able to clear Mr. Robinson," the woman said sorrowfully. "The whole case is so mysterious."

"I've stopped thinking of it," Tessie declared. "If the mystery is cleared up, okay. If it isn't—we won't starve, at any rate, and my father knows *we* believe in him."

"Yes, I suppose it doesn't do much good to keep talking about it," agreed Mrs. Robinson. "We've gone over the whole matter so thoroughly that there is nothing more to say."

So, by tacit consent, the subject was changed and for the rest of their stay Frank and Callie chatted of doings at school. Mrs. Robinson and the girls invited them to remain for supper, but Callie insisted that she must go. As they were leaving, Mrs. Robinson drew Frank to one side.

"Promise me one thing," she said. "Let me know as soon as your father returns—that is, if he has any news."

"I'll do that, Mrs. Robinson," Frank agreed. "I know what this suspense must be like for you and the twins."

"It's terrible. But as long as Fenton Hardy—and his sons—are working on the case, I'm sure it will be straightened out."

Callie and Frank were unusually silent all the way home. They had been profoundly affected by the change that the Tower Mansion mystery had caused in the lives of the Robinsons. Callie lived but a few blocks from the Hardy home, and Frank accompanied her to the door.

"See you tomorrow," he said.

"Yes, Frank. And I hope you'll hear good news from your father."

The boy quickened his steps and ran eagerly into the Hardy house. Joe met him.

"Any phone call?"

Joe shook his head. "Mother's pretty worried that something has happened to Dad."

CHAPTER XII

A Disturbing Absence

ANOTHER whole day went by. When still no word had come from Mr. Hardy, his wife phoned the New York hotel. She was told that the detective had checked out the day before.

Discouraged and nervous about the new mystery of their father's disappearance, Frank and Joe found it almost impossible to concentrate on their studies.

Then, the following morning when Mrs. Hardy came to awaken them, she wore a broad smile. "Your father is home!" she said excitedly. "He's all right but has had a bad time. He's asleep now and will tell you everything after school."

The boys were wild with impatience to learn the outcome of his trip, but they were obliged to curb their curiosity.

"Dad must be mighty tired," Joe remarked, as Mrs. Hardy went downstairs to start breakfast. "I wonder where he came from."

99

"Probably he was up all night. When he's working on a case, he forgets about sleep. Do you think he found out anything?"

"Hope so, Frank. I wish he'd wake up and tell us. I hate to go back to school without knowing."

But Mr. Hardy had not awakened by the time the boys set out for school, although they lingered until they were in danger of being late. As soon as classes were over, they shattered all records in their race home.

Fenton Hardy was in the living room, and as they rushed in panting, he grinned broadly. He looked refreshed after his long sleep and it was evident that his trip had not been entirely without success, for his manner was cheerful.

"Hello, boys! Sorry I worried you and Mother."

"What luck, Dad?" asked Frank.

"Good and bad. Here's the story: I went to the house where Red Jackley was boarding. Although he seemed to be an exemplary parolee, I decided to watch him a while and try to make friends."

"How could you do that?"

"By taking a room in the same house and pretending to be a fellow criminal."

"Wow!" Joe cried. "And then?"

"Jackley himself spoiled everything. He got mixed up in a jewel robbery and cleared out of the city. Luckily, I heard him packing, and I trailed him. The police were watching for him and he couldn't get out of town by plane or bus. He outwitted the police by jumping a freight on the railroad."

"And you still followed?"

"I lost him two or three times, but fortunately I managed to pick up his trail again. He got out of the city and into upper New York State. Then his luck failed him. A railroad detective recognized Jackley and the chase was on. Up to that time I had been content with just keeping behind him. I had still hoped to pose as a fellow fugitive and win his confidence. But when the pursuit started in earnest, I had to join the officers."

"And they caught Jackley?"

"Not without great difficulty. Jackley, by the way, was once a railroad man. Strangely enough, he worked not many miles from here. He managed to steal a railroad handcar and got away from us. But he didn't last long, for the handcar jumped the tracks on a curve and Jackley was badly smashed up."

"Killed?" Frank asked quickly.

"No. But he's in a hospital right now and the doctors say he hasn't much of a chance."

"He's under arrest?"

"Oh, yes. He's being held for the jewel thefts and also for the theft from the actor's dressing room. But he probably won't live to answer either charge."

"Didn't you find out anything that would connect him with the Tower robbery?"

"Not a thing."

The boys were disappointed, and their expressions showed it. If Red Jackley died without confessing, the secret of the Tower robbery would die with him. Mr. Robinson might never be cleared. He might be doomed to spend the rest of his life under a cloud, suspected of being a thief.

"Have you talked to Jackley?" Frank asked.

"I didn't have a chance—he wasn't conscious."

"Then you may never be able to get a confession from him."

Fenton Hardy shrugged. "I *may* be able to. If Jackley regains consciousness and knows he's going to die, he may admit everything. I intend to see him in the hospital and ask him about the Tower robbery."

"Is he far away?"

"Albany. I explained my mission to the doctor in charge and he promised to telephone me as soon as it was possible for Jackley to see anyone."

"You say he used to work near here?" Joe asked.

"He was once employed by the railroad, and he knows all the country around here well. Then he became mixed up in some thefts from freight cars, and after he got out of jail, turned professional criminal. I suppose he came back here because he is so familiar with this area."

"I promised to call Mrs. Robinson," Frank spoke up. "Okay to tell her about Jackley?"

"Yes, it may cheer her up. But ask her not to tell anyone."

Frank dialed the number and relayed part of his father's story. The accused man's wife was overwhelmed and relieved by the news, but promised not to divulge the information. Just as Frank finished the call, the doorbell rang. Frank ushered in the private detective Oscar Smuff.

"Your pa home?" he asked.

"Yes. Come in." Frank led the way into the living room.

Smuff, although he considered himself a topnotch sleuth, stood in awe of Fenton Hardy. He cleared his throat nervously.

"Good afternoon, Oscar," said Mr. Hardy pleasantly. "Won't you sit down?"

Detective Smuff eased himself into an armchair, then glanced inquiringly at the two boys. At once Mr. Hardy said, "Unless your business is *very* private, I'd like to have my sons stay."

"Well, I reckon that'll be all right," Smuff conceded. "I hear you're working on this Applegate case."

"Perhaps I am."

"You've been out of town several days," Smuff remarked cannily, "so I deduced you must be workin' on it."

"Very clever of you, Detective Smuff," Mr. Hardy said, smiling at his visitor.

Smuff squirmed uneasily in his chair. "I'm workin' on this case too—I'd like to get that thousand-dollar reward, but I'd share it with you. I was just wonderin' if you'd found any clues."

Mr. Hardy's smile faded. He said, with annoyance, "If I went away, it is my own business. And if I'm working on the Tower robbery, that also is my business. You'll have to find your own clues, Oscar."

"Well, now, don't get on your high horse, Mr. Hardy," the visitor remonstrated. "I'm just anxious to get this affair cleared up and I thought we might work together. I heard you were with the officers what chased this here notorious criminal Red Jackley."

Mr. Hardy gave a perceptible start. He had no idea that news of the capture of Jackley had reached Bayport, much less that his own participation in the chase had become known. The local police must have received the information and somehow Smuff had heard the news.

"What of it?" Mr. Hardy asked in a casual way.

"Did Jackley have anything to do with the Tower case?"

"How should I know?"

"Wasn't that what you were workin' on?"

"As I've told you, that's my affair."

Detective Smuff looked sad. "I guess you just don't want to co-operate with me, Mr. Hardy. I was thinkin' of goin' over to the hospital where this man Jackley is and questionin' him about the case."

Mr. Hardy's lips narrowed into a straight line. "You can't do that, Oscar. He isn't conscious. The doctor won't let you see him."

"I'm goin' to try. Jackley'll come to some time and I want to be on hand. There's a plane at six o'clock, and I aim to leave my house about five-thirty and catch it." He thumped his chest in admiration. "Detectives don't have to show up for a plane till the last minute, eh, Mr. Hardy? Well, I'll have a talk with Jackley tonight. And I may let you know what he says."

"Have it your own way," said Mr. Hardy. "But if you take my advice you'll not visit the hospital. You'll just spoil everything. Jackley will talk when the times comes."

"So there is somethin' in it!" Smuff said triumphantly. "Well, I'm goin' over there and get a confession!" With that he arose, stumped out of the room, and left the house.

CHAPTER XIII

Teamwork

AFTER Smuff left the house, Mr. Hardy sat back with a gesture of despair. "That man," he said, "handles an investigation so clumsily that Red Jackley will close up like a clam if Smuff manages to question him."

At that moment the telephone rang. The boys listened excitedly as Mr. Hardy answered. "Hello. . . . Oh, yes, doctor. . . . Is that so? . . . Jackley will probably live only until morning? . . . I can see him. . . . Fine. . . . Thank you. Good-by."

The detective put back the receiver and turned to the boys. "I'll take that six-o'clock plane to Albany. But if Smuff goes too, it may ruin everything. The Albany police and I must question Jackley first."

"When's the next commercial flight after six?" Joe asked.

"Seven o'clock."

"Then," said Frank, "Smuff can take that one and question Jackley later. Come on, Joe. Let's see what we can do to help Dad!"

"Don't you boys do anything rash," their father warned.

"We won't."

Frank led the way outdoors and started walking down the street.

"What's on your mind?" Joe asked as they reached the corner.

"We must figure out how to keep Detective Smuff in Bayport until seven o'clock."

"But how?"

"I don't know yet, but we'll find a way. We can't have him bursting into that hospital room and spoiling the chance of Dad's getting a confession. Smuff might ruin things so the case will never be solved."

"You're right."

The brothers walked along the street in silence. They realized that the situation was urgent. But though they racked their brains trying to think of a way to prevent Detective Smuff from catching the six-o'clock plane, it seemed hopeless.

"Let's round up our gang," Joe suggested finally. "Perhaps they'll have some ideas."

The Hardys found their friends on the tennis courts of Bayport High.

"Hi, fellows!" called Chet Morton when he saw

Frank and Joe approaching. "You're too late for a game. Where've you been?"

"We had something important to do," Frank replied. "Say, we need your help."

"What's the matter?" asked Tony Prito.

"Oscar Smuff is trying to win that thousand-dollar reward and get himself on the Bayport police force by interfering in one of Dad's cases," Frank explained. "We can't tell you much more than that. But the main thing is, we want to keep him from catching the six-o'clock plane. We—er—don't want him to go until seven."

"What do you want us to do?" Bill Hooper asked.

"Help us figure out how to keep Smuff in Bayport until seven o'clock."

"Without having Chief Collig lock us up?" Jerry Gilroy put in. "Are you serious about this, Frank?"

"Absolutely. If Smuff gets to a certain place before Dad can, the case will be ruined. And I don't mind telling you that it has something to do with Slim Robinson."

Chet Morton whistled. "Oh, ho! I catch on. The Tower business. If that's it, we'll make sure the six-o'clock plane leaves here without that nutty detective." Chet had a special dislike for Smuff, because the man had once reported him for swimming in the bay after hours.

"So our problem," said Phil solemnly, "is to

keep Smuff here and keep out of trouble ourselves."

"Right."

"Well," Jerry Gilroy said, "let's put our heads
together, fellows, and work out a plan."

A dozen ideas were put forth, each wilder than
the one before. Biff Hooper, with a wide grin, went
so far as to propose kidnaping Smuff, binding him
hand and foot, and setting him adrift in the bay in
an open boat.

"We could rescue him later," he said. The pro-
posal was so ridiculous that the others howled with
laughter.

Phil Cohen suggested setting the detective's
watch back an hour. That plan, as Frank observed,
was a good one except for the minor difficulty of
laying hands on the watch.

"We might send him a warning not to take a
plane before seven o'clock," Tony Prito said, "and
sign it with a skull and crossbones."

"That's a keen idea!" Chet cried enthusiastically. "Let's do it!"

"Wait a minute, fellows," Frank spoke up. "If
Smuff ever found out who wrote it, we'd be up
to our necks in trouble. We could all be arrested!"

"I know!" Joe cried suddenly, snapping his fingers. "Why didn't I think of it before? And it's so
simple, too."

"Well, tell us!" Frank urged.

Joe explained that every once in a while he and Frank went down to Rocco's fruit store to act as clerks while the owner went home to supper. He stayed open evenings until nine.

"Rocco's is only a block from Smuff's house. Smuff knows Frank and I go there, so he wouldn't be surprised to see us in the neighborhood. I suggest that the bunch of us meet casually down near the store and one boy after another stop Smuff to talk. Maybe we can even get him into the shop. You know Smuff loves to eat."

"You can't hate him for that," Chet spoke up. "I'll be glad to invite him in and buy him an apple for his trip."

"A fifteen-minute delay for Smuff is all we need," Frank said.

"I think it's a swell idea," Biff spoke up. "And I'm sure Mr. Rocco will co-operate."

"Who's going to persuade him?" Phil asked.

"That's Frank and Joe's department," Jerry replied.

Rocco was a hard-working man who had come from Italy only a few years ago. He was a simple, genial person and had great admiration for the Hardy boys.

The whole group made their way toward the fruit store, but only the Hardys went inside. The others spread out to watch for Smuff, who was expected to leave his house soon. Each boy went over his part in the plan.

When Frank and Joe walked into the fruit store, they found the dark-eyed Rocco sorting oranges. *"Buona sera,"* he said. "Good evening. How you like my fix the place?"

"Looks swell," Frank answered. "New bins. Better lights." Then he added, "How does your neighbor Smuff like it?"

Rocco threw up his hands in a gesture of disgust. "Oh, that man! He make me mad. He say I charge too much. He tell me I ought to go back to old country."

"Don't pay any attention to him," Joe advised. "Say, Mr. Rocco," he went on, "you look tired. Why don't you go home for an hour or so and let Frank and me take over here?"

"You think I look tired? That worry my wife. Then Rosa say I must close up early." Rocco sighed. "You very kind boys. I do what you say. Come back six-thirty."

As Rocco removed his apron, he said, "I fix trash in yard to burn. You do that?"

"Glad to."

Rocco showed them a wire incinerator in the yard, then left the store. Five minutes later there was a whistle from the street. A signal from Jerry! Frank and Joe went to the front door to watch. Smuff was just backing his car out of the driveway. As prearranged, Phil hurried over and stopped him.

The detective and the boy apparently got into

an argument, but it did not last long enough to satisfy Frank and Joe. The conversation took less than two minutes, then Smuff backed around into the street.

"Hey, Frank," said Joe, "I have an idea. Go light that trash. Make it a roaring fire!"

Without further explanation he dashed into the street, but Frank figured out what was in his brother's mind. He dashed through the store and into the yard. Quickly he lighted the papers in the incinerator in several places. The rubbish blazed lustily.

Joe was intently watching the scene down the street. Smuff was now being "interviewed" by Biff, and Chet came forward to urge Smuff to take some fruit with him on his trip. The detective hesitated, then shook his head and started off in his car.

Only five of the necessary fifteen-minute delay had elapsed! Joe hesitated no longer. Running down the street, he held up one hand for the oncoming car to stop.

"Come quick, Smuff!" he called out. "There's a fire back of Rocco's!"

"Well, you put it out. I'm in a hurry!" the detective told the boy tartly.

"You mean you'd let all of Bayport burn down just because you're in a hurry?" Joe pretended to scoff.

Smuff winced, but still did not move. Joe said,

"Where's the fire?" Smuff cried out

starting back to the store, "Well, Frank and I will have to take care of it alone."

This brought the detective to action. He realized he might be missing a chance to become a hero! In a flash he drove his car down the street and parked in front of the fruit store.

"Where's the fire?" Smuff cried out, nearly bumping into Frank who was dashing from the front door of Rocco's.

"The fire—is—back there—in the yard." Frank pretended to pant. "You go look and see if we ought to turn in an alarm."

Smuff dashed inside the store and hurried to the yard. By this time the Hardys' friends had gathered in Rocco's fruit store. They asked excitedly what was going on.

"Frank! Joe!" yelled Smuff from the rear of the store. "Where's Rocco? Where's a pail? Where's some water?"

CHAPTER XIV

The Confession

"Rocco's not around," Joe replied to Smuff. "There's water in the sink—in the back. Shall I call the fire department?"

"No, I can manage this," Smuff declared. "But where's a pail?"

Frank dashed into the back room and found a pail under the sink. He filled it with water and handed the pail to Smuff, who hurried to the yard. He doused the incinerator flames which hissed and crackled, then died.

"Some people have no sense," Smuff commented. "The idea of anyone starting a fire, then going off and leaving it! I'll bet that was Rocco's work! As for you boys—you had to call me. Didn't have the savvy to put out a simple fire."

"Good thing you were around," Frank observed, suppressing a smile.

"I'll say it was," Smuff agreed. "And Chief Collig is sure goin' to hear about this."

"Oh, please don't tell him about us," Joe spoke up, half closing his eyes so Smuff could not see the twinkle in them.

"I didn't mean that. Oscar Smuff is no squealer. I mean Collig is goin' to hear what *I* did." The detective chuckled. "One more notch in my gun, as the cowboys say."

Suddenly Smuff sobered and looked at his wrist watch. "Oh, no!" he cried out. "Ten minutes to six! I can't make my plane!"

"That's a shame," Frank said consolingly. "But cheer up, Smuff, there's a seven-o'clock plane for Albany. I wish you luck in your interview."

Smuff stormed out of the fruit store and disappeared with his car. The Hardys and their friends burst into roars of laughter which did not stop until a woman customer came into the shop. All the boys but Frank and Joe left.

Rocco returned at six-thirty, pleased that so much fruit had been sold during his absence. "You better salesman than Rocco." He grinned widely.

The Hardys went home, well-satisfied with their day's work. The six-o'clock plane had left without Smuff. Their father could make his trip to the hospital without the annoying detective's interference.

Fenton Hardy did not return home until the

next afternoon. When the boys came from school they found him in high spirits.

"Solved the mystery?" Joe asked eagerly.

"Practically. First of all, Jackley is dead."

"Did he confess?"

"You're not very sympathetic toward the poor fellow, Joe. Yes, he confessed. Fortunately, Oscar Smuff didn't show up while Jackley was talking."

Frank and Joe glanced at each other and their father smiled quietly. "I have an idea," he said, "that you two sleuths know more about this Smuff business than you would care to tell. Well, anyhow, the Albany police and I had a clear field. I saw Jackley before he died and questioned him about the Tower robbery."

"Did he admit everything?"

"Jackley said he came to Bayport with the intention of robbery. He stole a car, smashed it up, and took Chet's. Then he went to rob the ticket office. When he failed in that he decided to hang around town for a few days. He hit upon Tower Mansion as his next effort. Jackley entered the library with gloves on, opened the safe, and took out the jewelry and securities."

"What did he do with the loot?"

"That's what I'm coming to. It was not until Jackley knew he was at the point of death that he did confess to the Tower affair. Then he said, 'Yes, I took the stuff—but I didn't dare try selling any of it right away, so I hid it. You can get all the stuff back easily. It's in the old tower—'

"That was all he said. Jackley lost consciousness then and never regained it."

"When did Smuff get there?" Joe asked eagerly.

"Not until after Jackley had gone into a coma," Mr. Hardy replied. "We both sat by his bed, hoping the man would awaken, but he died within an hour. Just where Jackley hid the loot in the old tower, he was never able to say."

"Does Smuff know what Jackley said?"

"No."

"If the loot's hidden in the old Applegate tower, we'll find it in no time!" Frank exclaimed.

"Tower Mansion has two towers—the old and the new," Joe reminded him.

"We'll search the old tower first."

"The story seems likely enough," Mr. Hardy remarked. "Jackley would gain nothing by lying about it on his deathbed. He probably became panicky after he committed the robbery and hid in the old tower until he was able to get away safely. No doubt he decided to hide the stuff there and take a chance on coming back for it some time after the affair had blown over."

Joe nodded. "That was why Jackley couldn't be traced through the jewels and the bonds. They were never disposed of—they've been lying in the old tower all this time!"

"I tried to get him to tell me in just what part of the tower the loot was hidden," Mr. Hardy continued, "but he died before he could say any more."

"Too bad," said Frank. "But it shouldn't be hard to find the loot, now that we have a general idea where it is. Probably Jackley didn't hide it very carefully. Since the old tower has been unoccupied for a long time, the stuff would be safe there from snoopers."

Joe jumped up from his chair. "I think we ought to get busy and go search the old tower right away. Oh, boy! Maybe we can hand old Mr. Applegate his jewels and bonds this afternoon and clear Mr. Robinson! Let's go!"

"I'll leave it to you boys to make the search," said Mr. Hardy with a smile. "Then you can have the satisfaction of turning over the stolen property to Mr. Applegate. I guess you can get along without me in this case from now on."

"We wouldn't have got very far if it hadn't been for you," Frank declared.

"And I wouldn't have got very far if it hadn't been for you, so we're even." Mr. Hardy's smile broadened. "Well, good luck to you."

As the boys started from the study, Frank said, "Thanks, Dad. I only hope the Applegates don't throw us out when we ask to be allowed to look around inside the old tower."

"Just tell them," his father advised, "that you have a pretty good clue to where the bonds and jewels are hidden and they'll let you search."

Joe grinned. "Frank, we'll have that thousand-dollar reward before the day is over!"

The brothers raced from the house, confident that they were about to solve the Tower Treasure mystery.

CHAPTER XV

The Tower Search

WHEN the Hardy boys reached Tower Mansion at four o'clock the door was opened by Hurd Applegate himself. The tall, stooped gentleman peered at them through his thick-lensed glasses. In one hand he held a sheet of stamps.

"Yes?" he said, seemingly annoyed at being disturbed.

"You remember us, don't you?" Frank asked politely. "We're Mr. Hardy's sons."

"Fenton Hardy, the detective? Oh, yes. Well, what do you want?"

"We'd like to look through the old tower, if you don't mind. We have a clue about the robbery."

"What kind of clue?"

"We have evidence that leads us to believe the jewels and bonds were hidden by the thief in the old tower."

121

"Oh! You have evidence, have you?" The elderly man peered at the boys closely. "It's that rascal Robinson, I'll warrant, who gave it to you. He hid the stuff, and now he's suggesting where you might find it, just to clear himself."

Frank and Joe had not considered the affair in this light, and they gazed at Mr. Applegate in consternation. At last Joe spoke up.

"Mr. Robinson has nothing to do with this," he said. "The real thief was found. He said the loot was hidden in the old tower. If you will just let us take a look around, we'll find it for you."

"Who was the real thief?"

"We'd rather not tell you, sir, until we find the stolen property, then we'll reveal the whole story."

Mr. Applegate took off his glasses and wiped them with his handkerchief. He stared at the boys suspiciously for a few moments. Then he called out:

"Adelia!"

From the dim interior of the hallway a high feminine voice answered.

"What do you want?"

"Come here a minute."

There was a rustle of skirts, and Adelia Applegate appeared. A faded blond woman of thin features, she was dressed in a fashion of fifteen years before, in which every color of the spectrum fought for supremacy.

"What's the matter?" she demanded. "I can't sit down to do a bit of sewing without you interrupting me, Hurd."

"These boys want to look through the old tower."

"What for? Up to some mischief?"

Frank and Joe feared she would not give her consent. Frank said quietly, "We're doing some work for our dad, the detective Fenton Hardy."

"They think they can find the bonds and jewels in the tower," Hurd Applegate explained.

"Oh, they do, do they?" the woman said icily. "And what would the bonds and jewels be doing in the old tower?"

"We have evidence that they were hidden there after the robbery," Frank told her.

Miss Applegate viewed the boys with obvious suspicion. "As if any thief would be silly enough to hide them right in the house he robbed!" she said in a tone of finality.

"We're just trying to help you," Joe put in courteously.

"Go ahead, then," said Miss Applegate with a sigh. "But even if you tear the old tower to pieces, you won't find anything. It's all foolishness."

Frank and Joe followed Hurd Applegate through the gloomy halls and corridors that led toward the old tower. He said he was inclined to share his sister's opinion that the boys' search would be in vain.

"We'll make a try at it, anyway, Mr. Applegate," Frank said.

"Don't ask me to help you. I've got a bad knee. Anyway, I just received some new stamps this afternoon. You interrupted me when I was sorting them. I must get back to my work."

The man reached a corridor that was heavily covered with dust. It apparently had not been in use for a long time and was bare and unfurnished. At the end was a heavy door. It was unlocked, and when Mr. Applegate opened it, the boys saw a square room. Almost in the center of it rose a flight of wooden stairs with a heavily ornamented balustrade. The stairway twisted and turned to the roof, five floors above. Opening from each floor was a room.

"There you are," Mr. Applegate announced. "Search all you want to. But you won't find anything—of that I'm certain."

With this parting remark he turned and hobbled back along the corridor, the sheet of stamps still in his gnarled hand.

The Hardy boys looked at each other. "Not very encouraging, is he?" Joe remarked.

"He doesn't deserve to get his stuff back," Frank declared flatly, then shrugged. "Let's get up into the tower and start the search."

Frank and Joe first examined the dusty stairs carefully for footprints, but none were to be seen.

"That seems queer," Frank remarked. "If Jackley was here recently you'd think his footprints would still show. Judging by this dust, there hasn't been anyone in the tower for at least a year."

"Perhaps the dust collects more quickly than we think," Joe countered. "Or the wind may get in here and blow it around."

An inspection of the first floor of the old tower revealed that there was no place where the loot could have been hidden except under the stairs. But they found nothing there.

The boys ascended to the next floor, and entered the room to the left of the stair well. It was as drab and bare as the one they had just left. Here again the dust lay thick and the murky windows were almost obscured with cobwebs. There was an atmosphere of age and decay about the entire place, as if it had been abandoned for years.

"Nothing here," said Frank after a quick glance around. "On we go."

They made their way up to the next floor. After searching this room and under the stairway, they had to admit defeat.

The floor above was a duplicate of the first and second. It was bare and cheerless, deep in dust. There was not the slightest sign of a hiding place, or any indication that another human being had been in the tower for a long time.

"Doesn't look very promising, Joe. Still, Jackley may have gone right to the top of the tower."

The search continued without success until the

boys reached the roof. Here a trap door which swung inward led to the top of the tower. Frank unlatched it and pulled on the door. It did not budge.

"I'll help you," Joe offered.

Together the brothers yanked on the stubborn trap door of the old tower. Suddenly it gave way completely, causing both boys to lose their balance. Frank fell backward down the stairway.

Joe, with a cry, toppled over the railing into space!

Frank grabbed a spindle of the balustrade and kept himself from sliding farther down the steps. He had seen Joe's plunge and expected the next moment to hear a sickening thud on the floor five stories below.

"Joe!" he murmured as he pulled himself upright. "Oh, Joe!"

To Frank's amazement, he heard no thud and now looked over the balustrade. His brother was not lying unconscious at the bottom of the tower. Instead, he was clinging to two spindles of the stairway on the floor below.

Frank, heaving a tremendous sigh of relief, ran down and helped pull Joe to the safety of the steps. Both boys sat down to catch their breaths and recover from their falls.

Finally Joe said, "Thanks. For a second I sure thought I was going to end my career as a detective right here!"

"I guess you can also thank our gym teacher for the tricks he taught you on the bars," Frank remarked. "You must have grabbed those spindles with flash-camera speed."

Presently the boys turned their eyes upward. An expression halfway between a grin and a worried frown crossed their faces.

"Mr. Applegate," Joe remarked, "isn't going to like hearing we ruined his trap door."

"No. Let's see if we can put it back in place."

The boys climbed the stairway and examined the damage. They found that the hinges had pulled away from rotted wood. A new piece would have to be put in to hold the door in place.

"Before we go downstairs," said Joe, "let's look out on the roof. We thought maybe the loot was hidden there. Remember?"

Frank and Joe climbed outside to a narrow, railinged walk that ran around the four sides of the square tower. There was nothing on it.

"Our only reward for all this work is a good view of Bayport," Frank remarked ruefully.

Below lay the bustling little city, and to the east was Barmet Bay, its waters sparkling in the late afternoon.

"Dad was fooled by Jackley, I guess," Frank said slowly. "There hasn't been anyone in this tower for years."

The boys gazed moodily over the city, then down at the grounds of Tower Mansion. The many roofs of the house itself were far below, and directly across from them rose the heavy bulk of the new tower.

"Do you think Jackley might have meant the *new* tower?" Joe exclaimed suddenly.

"Dad said he specified the old one."

"But he may have been mistaken. Even the new one looks old. Let's ask Mr. Applegate if we may search the new tower, too."

"It's worth trying, anyway. But I'm afraid when we tell him about the trap door, he'll say no."

The brothers went down through the opening. They lifted the door into place, latched it, and then wedged Frank's small pocket notebook into the damaged side. The door held, but Frank and Joe knew that wind or rain would easily dislodge it.

The boys hurried down the steps and through the corridor to the main part of the house.

Adelia Applegate popped her head out of a doorway. "Where's the loot?" she asked.

"We didn't find any," Frank admitted.

The woman sniffed. "I told you so! Such a waste of time!"

"We think now," Joe spoke up, "that the stolen property is probably hidden in the new tower."

"In the new tower!" Miss Applegate cried out. "Absurd! I suppose you'll want to go poking through there now."

"If it wouldn't be too much trouble."

"It *would* be too much trouble, indeed!" she

shrilled. "I shan't have boys rummaging through *my* house on a wild-goose chase like this. You'd better leave at once, and forget all this nonsense."

Her voice had attracted the attention of Hurd Applegate, who came hobbling out of his study.

"Now what's the matter?" he demanded. His sister told him and suddenly his face creased in a triumphant smile. "Aha! So you didn't find anything after all! You thought you'd clear Robinson, but you haven't done it."

"Not yet," Frank answered.

"These boys have the audacity," Miss Applegate broke in, "to want to go looking through the *new* tower."

Hurd Applegate stared at the boys. "Well, they can't do it!" he snapped. "Are you boys trying to make a fool of me?" he asked, shaking a fist at them.

Frank and Joe exchanged glances and nodded at each other. They would have to reveal their reason for thinking the loot was in the new tower.

"Mr. Applegate," Frank began, "the information about where your stolen stuff is hidden came from the man who took the jewels and the bonds. And it wasn't Mr. Robinson."

"What! You mean it was someone else? Has he been caught?"

"He was captured but he's dead now."

"Dead? What happened?" Hurd Applegate asked in excitement.

"His name was Red Jackley and he was a notorious criminal. Dad got on his trail and Jackley tried to escape on a railroad handcar. It smashed up and he was fatally injured," Frank explained.

"Where did you get your information then?" Mr. Applegate asked.

Frank told the whole story, ending with, "We thought Jackley might have made a mistake and that it's the new tower where he hid the loot."

Hurd Applegate rubbed his chin meditatively. It was evident that he was impressed by the boys' story.

"So this fellow Jackley confessed to the robbery, eh?"

"He admitted everything. He had once worked around here and knew the Bayport area well. He had been hanging around the city for several days before the robbery."

"Well," Applegate said slowly, "if he said he hid the stuff in the old tower and it's not there, it must be in the new tower, as you say."

"Will you let us search it?" Joe asked eagerly.

"Yes, and I'll help. I'm just as eager to find the jewels and bonds as you are. Come on, boys!"

Hurd Applegate led the way across the mansion toward a door which opened into the new tower. Now that the man was in a good mood, Frank decided that this was an opportune time to tell him about the trap door. He did so, offering to pay for the repair.

"Oh, that's all right," said Mr. Applegate. "I'll

have it fixed. In fact, Robinson— Oh, I forgot. I'll get a carpenter."

He said no more, but quickened his steps. Frank and Joe grinned. Old Mr. Applegate had not even reprimanded them!

The mansion owner opened the door to the new tower and stepped into a corridor. Frank and Joe, tingling with excitement, followed.

CHAPTER XVI

A Surprise

THE rooms in the new tower had been furnished when it was built. But only on rare occasions when the Applegates had visitors were the rooms occupied, the owner stated.

In the first one Frank, Joe, and Mr. Applegate found nothing, although they looked carefully in closets, bureaus, highboys, and under the large pieces of furniture. They even turned up mattresses and rugs. When they were satisfied that the loot had not been hidden there, they ascended the stairs to the room above. Again their investigation proved fruitless.

Hurd Applegate, being a quick-tempered man, fell back into his old mood. The boys' story had convinced him, but when they had searched the rooms in the tower without success, he showed his disgust.

"It's a hoax!" he snorted. "Adelia was right. I've

been made a fool of! And all because of Robinson!"

"I can't understand it!" Joe burst out. "Jackley said he hid the stuff in the tower."

"If that fellow did hide the jewels and bonds in one of the towers," Applegate surmised, "someone else must have come in and taken them—maybe someone working with him. Or else Robinson found the loot right after the robbery and kept it for himself."

"I'm sure Mr. Robinson wouldn't do that," Joe objected.

"Then where did he get the nine hundred dollars? Explain that. Robinson won't!"

On the way back to the main part of the mansion, Hurd Applegate elaborated on his theory. The fact that the loot had not been found seemed to convince him all over again that Robinson was involved in some way.

"Like as not he was in league with Jackley!" the man stated flatly.

Again Frank and Joe protested that the ex-caretaker did not hobnob with criminals. Nevertheless, the Hardys were puzzled, disappointed, and alarmed. Their search had only resulted in implicating Mr. Robinson more deeply in the mystery.

Back in the hallway of the main house they met Adelia Applegate, who crowed triumphantly when she saw the search party returning empty-handed. "Didn't I tell you?" she cried. "Hurd Applegate, you've let these boys make a fool of you!"

She escorted the Hardys to the front door, while her brother, shaking his head perplexedly, went back to his study.

"We sure messed things up, Frank," Joe declared, as they walked toward their motorcycles. "I feel like a dud rocket."

"Me too."

They hurried home to tell their father the disappointing news. Fenton Hardy was amazed to hear that the stolen valuables had not been located in either tower. "You're sure you went over the place thoroughly?"

"Every inch of it. There wasn't a sign of the loot. From the dust in the old tower, I'd say no one had been there for ages," Frank replied.

"Strange," the detective muttered. "I'm sure Jackley wasn't lying. He had absolutely nothing to gain by deceiving me. 'I hid it in the old tower.' Those were his very words. And what could he mean but the old tower of Tower Mansion? And why should he be so careful to say the *old* tower? Since he was familiar with Bayport, he probably knew that the mansion has two towers, the old and the new."

"Of course, it may be that we *didn't* search thoroughly enough," Joe remarked. "The loot could be hidden under the flooring or behind a movable wall panel. We didn't look there."

"That's the only solution," Mr. Hardy agreed. "I'm still not satisfied that the stolen property isn't there. I'm going to ask Applegate to permit another search of both towers. And now, I think your mother wants you to do an errand downtown."

Mrs. Hardy explained what she wanted and Frank and Joe were soon on their motorcycles again. When the boys reached the business section of Bayport they found that Jackley's confession had already become known. The local radio station had broadcast it in the afternoon news program and people everywhere were discussing it.

Detective Smuff walked along the street looking as if he would bite the head off the first person who mentioned the case to him. When he saw the Hardy boys he glowered.

"Well," he grunted, "I hear you got the stuff back."

"I wish we had," Frank said glumly.

"What!" the detective cried out, brightening at once. "You didn't get it? I thought they said on the radio that this fellow Jackley had told your father where he hid it."

"He did. But how did the news leak out?"

"Jackley's door wasn't closed all the time. One of the other patients who was walking by the room heard the confession and spilled it. So you didn't find the loot after all! Ha-ha! That's a good one! Didn't Jackley say the stuff was hidden in the old tower? What more do you need?"

"Well, it wasn't there!" Joe retorted hotly. "Jackley must have made a mistake!"

"Jackley made a mistake!" Smuff continued cheerfully. "It looks like the joke's on you fellows and your father!" The would-be sleuth went on down the street, chuckling to himself.

When Frank and Joe returned home they found that Mr. Hardy had been in touch with Hurd Applegate and had convinced him that a more detailed search of the towers would be advisable.

"Boys," he said, "we'll go there directly after supper. I think we'd better not wait until tomorrow."

At seven o'clock the detective and his sons presented themselves at the Tower Mansion. Hurd Applegate met them at the door.

"I'm letting you make this search," he said as he led them toward the old tower, "but I'm convinced you won't find anything. I've talked the case over with Chief Collig. He's inclined to think that Robinson is behind it all and I'm sure he is."

"But how about Jackley's confession?" Mr. Hardy asked him.

"The chief says that could be a blind. Jackley did it to protect Robinson. They were working together."

"I know it looks bad for Robinson," Mr. Hardy admitted, "but I want to give the towers another close examination. I heard Jackley make the confession and I don't believe he was lying."

"Maybe. Maybe. But I'm telling you it was a hoax."

"I'll believe that only if I don't find anything inside or outside either tower," Mr. Hardy declared, his mouth set in a grim line.

"Well, come on, let's get started," Hurd Applegate said, unlocking the door leading to the old tower.

Eagerly the four set to work. They started at the top of the old tower and worked downward. Their investigation left no possibility untouched. All the walls were tapped for hollow sounds which might indicate secret hiding places. The floors were examined closely for signs of any recent disturbance to the wood. But the missing jewels and bonds were not located. Finally the group reached the ground floor again.

"Nothing to do but go on to the new tower," Mr. Hardy commented briefly.

"I'll have to rest and eat something before I do any more," Hurd Applegate said wearily. He led the way to the dining room where sandwiches and milk had been set out. "Help yourselves," he invited. He himself took only crackers and milk when they all sat down.

After the brief stop for refreshment, the Hardys and the mansion owner turned their attention to the new tower. Again they searched carefully. Walls and partitions were tapped and floors were sounded. Every bit of furniture was minutely examined. Not an inch of space escaped the scrutiny of the detective and his helpers.

As the search drew to a close and the loot still had not been found, Mr. Hardy remarked, "It certainly looks as if the stolen property was never hidden here by Jackley. And furthermore, there's no evidence that if he did hide it here, anyone came in to take it away."

"You mean," said Frank, "it's proof that Mr. Robinson did *not* come in here?"

"Exactly."

"Maybe not," Mr. Applegate conceded. "But it still doesn't prove he wasn't in cahoots with the thief!"

"I'm not going to give up this search yet," Mr. Hardy said determinedly. "Perhaps the loot was hidden somewhere outside the old tower."

He explained that it would be difficult to examine the grounds properly at night. "With your permission, Mr. Applegate, my sons and I will return at sunrise tomorrow morning and start work again." As the owner reluctantly nodded his assent, Mr. Hardy turned to Frank and Joe and smiled. "We ought to be able to prove our point before schooltime."

The boys, who had had no time to prepare any homework, reminded their father that a note from him to the principal would be a great help. The detective smiled, and as soon as they reached home he wrote one out, then said good night.

Frank and Joe felt as if their eyes had hardly closed when they opened them again to see their father standing between their beds. "Time to get up if you want to be in on the search," he announced.

The boys blinked sleepily, then sprang out of bed. Showers awakened them fully and they dressed quickly. Mrs. Hardy was in the kitchen when they entered it and breakfast was ready. The sun was just rising over a distant hill.

"Everything hot this morning," Mrs. Hardy said. "It's chilly outside."

The menu included hot applesauce, oatmeal, poached eggs on toast, and cocoa. Breakfast was eaten almost in silence to avoid any delay, and within twenty minutes the three Hardy sleuths were on their way.

"I see you put spades in the car, Dad," Frank remarked. "I take it we're going to do some digging."

"Yes, if we don't locate the loot hidden above ground some place."

When the Hardys reached Tower Mansion they instituted their hunt without notifying the Applegates, who, they were sure, were still asleep. Everything in the vicinity of both towers was scrutinized. Boulders were overturned, the space under the summerhouse examined by flashlight, every stone in the masonry tested to see if it could be dislodged. Not a clue turned up.

"I guess we dig," Frank stated finally.

He chose a bed of perennial bushes at the foot of the old tower where there had been recent planting, and pushed one of the spades in deep with his foot. The tool hit an obstruction. Excitedly Frank shoveled away the dirt around the spot. In half a minute he gave a cry of delight.

"A chest! I've found a buried chest!"

CHAPTER XVII

An Unexpected Find

THROWING out the dirt in great spadefuls, Frank uncovered the chest completely. It was about two feet long, six inches wide, and a foot deep.

"The treasure!" Joe cried out, running up.

Mr. Hardy was at his son's heels and looked in amazement at Frank's discovery. The boy lifted the chest out of the hole and instantly began to raise the lid on which there was no lock.

Everyone held his breath. Had the Hardys really uncovered the jewels and securities stolen from the Applegates? Frank flung back the lid.

The three sleuths stared at the contents. They had never been more surprised in their lives. Finally Joe found his voice.

"Nothing but a lot of flower bulbs!"

The first shock of disappointment over, the detective and his sons burst into laughter. The con-

tents of the chest were such a far cry from what
they had expected that now the situation seemed
ridiculous.

"Well, one thing is sure," said Frank. "Red Jackley never buried this chest. I wonder who did?"

"I can answer that," a voice behind them replied, and the Hardys turned to see Hurd Applegate, clad in bathrobe and slippers, walking toward
them.

"Good morning, Mr. Applegate," the boys chorused, and their father added, "You see we're on
the job. For a couple of moments we thought we
had found your stolen property."

Hurd Applegate's face took on a stern look.
"You didn't find my securities," he said, "but
maybe you have found a clue to the thief. Robinson buried that chest full of bulbs. That's what he's
done with Adelia's jewelry and my securities! He's
buried them some place, but I'd be willing to bet
anything it wasn't on the grounds here."

Frank, realizing the man was not in a good humor this morning, tried to steer the conversation
away from the stolen valuables. "Mr. Applegate,"
he said, "why did Mr. Robinson bury these flower
bulbs here?"

The owner of Tower Mansion gave a little snort.
"That man's nutty about unusual flowers. He sent
to Europe for these bulbs. They have to be kept in
a cool, dark place for several months, so he decided
to bury them. He's always doing something queer

like that. Why, do you know what he tried to get me to do? Put up a greenhouse here on the property so he could raise all kinds of rare flowers."

"That sounds like a swell hobby," Joe spoke up.

"Swell nothing!" Mr. Applegate replied. "I guess you don't know how much greenhouses cost. And besides, growing rare flowers takes a lot of time. Robinson had enough to do without fiddling around with making great big daisies out of little wild ones, or turning cowslips into orchids!"

Frank whistled. "If Mr. Robinson can do that, he's a genius!"

"Genius—that's a joke!" said Mr. Applegate. "Well, go on with your digging. I want this mystery cleared up."

It was decided that Mr. Hardy, with his superior powers of observation, would scrutinize the ground near both towers. Wherever it looked as if the ground had been turned over recently, the boys would dig at the spot. The chest of flower bulbs was carefully replaced and the dirt shoveled over it.

"Here's a place where you might dig," Mr. Hardy called presently from the opposite side of the old tower. When the boys arrived with their spades, he said, "I have an idea a dog dug up this spot and probably all you'll find is a beef bone. But we don't want to miss anything."

This time Joe's spade hit the object which had been buried. As his father had prophesied, it proved to be only a bone secreted by some dog.

The three Hardys transferred their work to the new tower. All this time Hurd Applegate had been looking on in silence. From the corners of their eyes, the Hardys could catch an expression of satisfaction on the elderly man's face.

Mr. Hardy glanced at his wrist watch, then said, "Well, boys, I guess this is our last try." He indicated another spot a few feet away. "You fellows must get cleaned up and go to school."

Undaunted by their failures so far, Frank and Joe dug in with a will. In a few moments they had uncovered another small chest.

"Wow, this one is heavy!" Frank said as he lifted it from the hole.

"Then maybe—maybe it's the stolen property!" Joe exclaimed.

Even Mr. Applegate showed keen interest this time and leaned over to raise the lid himself. The box contained several sacks.

"The jewels!" Joe cried out.

"And that flat-shaped sack could contain the securities!" Frank said enthusiastically.

Mr. Applegate picked up one of the circular bags and quickly untied the string wound about the top. His face took on a look of utter disgust. "Seeds!" he fairly shouted.

Mr. Hardy had already picked up the flat sack. He looked almost as disappointed as Mr. Applegate. "Flower catalogs!" he exclaimed. "They seem to be in various foreign languages."

Frank lifted the chest from the hole

"Oh, Robinson was always sending for things from all over the world," the Tower Mansion owner remarked. "I told him to destroy them. He paid too much attention to that stuff when he might have been doing something useful. I suppose he buried the catalogs, so I wouldn't find them."

After a long breath the elderly man went on, "Well, we've reached the end of the line. You Hardys haven't proved a thing, but you've certainly torn up my house and grounds."

The three sleuths had to admit this was true but told him they were still fired by two hopes: to clear Mr. Robinson of the charge against him, and to find the stolen property. As they put their spades back into the Hardy car, Mr. Applegate invited them into the house to wash and have a bite to eat.

"I guess you boys could do with a second breakfast," he added, and the brothers thought, "Maybe at times Mr. Applegate isn't such a bad sort."

They accepted the invitation and enjoyed the meal of waffles and honey. Their father then drove them to Bayport High.

Frank and Joe had no sooner stepped from the car than they heard their names called. Turning, they saw Iola Morton and Callie Shaw coming toward them.

"Hi, boys!"

"Hi, girls!"

"Say, did you hear what happened early this morning?" Callie asked.

"No. School called off for today?" Joe asked eagerly.

"I wish it were." Callie sobered. "It's about Mr. Robinson. He's been arrested again!"

"No!" The Hardys stared at Callie, thunderstruck. "Why?" Frank demanded.

Iola took up the story, saying that she and Chet had heard the bad news on the radio that morning. They had stopped at the Robinsons' home, when their father brought them to school, to find out more about what had happened.

"It seems that Chief Collig has an idea Mr. Robinson was in league with the thief Jackley, that man your father got the confession from. So he arrested him. Poor Mrs. Robinson! She doesn't know what to do."

"And Mr. Robinson had just managed to find another job," Callie said sadly. "Oh, can't you boys do something?"

"We're working on the case as hard as we can," Frank replied, and told the girls about their sleuthing the evening before and early that morning. At that moment the school bell rang and the young people had to separate.

Frank and Joe were deeply concerned by what they had just heard. At lunch they met Jerry, Phil, Tony, and Chet Morton and told them the news.

"This is tough on Slim," Phil remarked.

"Tough on the whole family," Chet declared.

The boys discussed the situation from all angles and racked their brains for some way in which they could help the Robinsons. They concluded that only the actual discovery of the stolen jewels and bonds would clear Mr. Robinson of the suspicion which hung over him.

"That means there's only one thing to do," Frank said. "We *must* find that loot!"

After school he and Joe played baseball for the required period, then went directly home. They had no heart for further sports activities. It was a dull, gloomy day, indicative of rain and this did not raise the boys' spirits.

Frank, who was restless, finally suggested, "Let's take a walk."

"Maybe it'll help clear the cobwebs from our brains," Joe agreed.

They told their mother they would be home by suppertime, then set off. The brothers walked mile after mile, and then, as they turned back, they were drawn as if by magnets to Tower Mansion.

"This place is beginning to haunt me," said Joe, as they walked up the driveway.

Suddenly Frank caught his brother's arm. "I just had an idea. Maybe Jackley in his deathbed confession was confused and meant some other robbery he committed. Besides, at some time in every mystery the most innocent-seeming people become suspect. What proof is there that the Applegates haven't pulled a hoax? For reasons of their own they might say that the things had been stolen from their safe. Don't forget that Dad didn't find any fingerprints on it except Mr. Applegate's."

"Frank, you've got a point there. That man and his sister act so mean sometimes, I wouldn't put it past them to be trying to cheat the insurance company," said Joe.

"Exactly," his brother agreed. "For the moment, let's play it this way. We'll pretend they're suspects and do a little spying about this place."

Instantly the boys left the roadway and disappeared among the shrubbery that lined it. Making their way cautiously, they moved forward toward Tower Mansion. The place was in darkness with the exception of three lighted rooms on the first floor.

"What's your idea, Frank?" his brother whispered. "To learn something that might tell us whether or not the Applegates are implicated in the robbery?"

"Yes. Maybe we'll get a clue if we keep our eyes and ears open."

The boys walked forward in silence. They approached the mansion from the end where the old tower stood. Somewhere, not far from them, they suddenly heard footsteps on the gravel walk. In a flash the brothers dodged behind a tree. The footsteps came closer and the boys waited to see who was approaching. Was it one of the Applegates, or someone else?

Before they could find out, the person's footsteps receded and the boys emerged from their hiding place. Suddenly a glaring light was beamed directly on them.

It came from the top room of the old tower!

CHAPTER XVIII

A Startling Deduction

"Duck!" Frank ordered in a hoarse whisper, quickly dropping to the ground.

Instantly Joe threw himself face down alongside his brother.

"You think the person with the flashlight in the tower saw us?" Frank asked.

"He could have, but maybe not. We sure went down fast."

The strong flashlight was not trained on them again. It was beamed out a window of the tower in another direction, then turned off.

"Well, what say?" Joe asked. "Shall we go on up to the mansion and continue our sleuthing?"

Frank was of the opinion that if they did, they might get into trouble. Even if they had not been recognized, the person in the tower probably had spotted them.

"I'd like to find out who was in the tower," Joe

argued. "It's just possible that the Applegates don't know anything about him."

Frank laughed quietly. "Don't let your imagination run away with you," he advised.

As the boys debated about whether to leave the grounds or to go forward, the matter was suddenly taken out of their hands. From around the corner of the tower rushed a huge police dog, growling and barking. It apparently had scented the brothers and was bounding directly toward them.

Frank and Joe started to run pell-mell, but were unable to keep ahead of the dog. In a few moments he blocked their path menacingly and set up a ferocious barking.

"I guess we're caught," Frank said. "And I hope this old fellow won't take a piece out of my leg."

The two boys tried to make friends with the animal, but he would not let them budge.

"Well, what do we do now?" Joe asked in disgust as the dog continued to growl menacingly.

"Wait to be rescued," Frank replied tersely.

A moment later they saw a bobbing light coming in their direction and presently Mr. Applegate appeared. He looked at the boys in complete astonishment.

"You fellows never give up, do you?" he remarked. "What have you been doing—more digging?"

The brothers did not reply at once. They were embarrassed at having been discovered, but relieved that the man did not suspect what they had really intended to do. The owner of Tower Mansion took their lack of response to mean he was right.

"I'm just not going to have any more of my grounds ruined," he said gruffly. "I've borrowed this watchdog, Rex, and he's going to keep everybody away. If you have any reason for wanting to see me, you'd better phone first, and I'll keep Rex chained."

"Who was up in the tower with a flashlight?" Frank asked the elderly man.

"My sister. She got it into her head that maybe she was smarter than you fellows and could find the stolen stuff in the old tower, but she didn't!" Frank and Joe suppressed grins as he went on. "And then Adelia decided to flash that high-powered flashlight around the grounds, thinking we might have a lot of curious visitors because of the publicity. Apparently she picked you up."

The boys laughed. "Yes, she did," Frank admitted. "Between her and Rex, I guess you needn't worry about any prowlers."

Frank and Joe said good night to Hurd Applegate and started down the driveway. This time the dog did not follow them. He remained at the man's side until the Hardys were out of sight.

As they trudged homeward, Joe remarked, "This seems to be our day for exciting events that fizzle out like wet fireworks."

"Yes. Nothing to show for all our work."

At supper both Mr. and Mrs. Hardy laughed at the boys' story of their encounter with the dog. Then they became serious when Frank asked his father if he thought there was a chance that the Applegates might be guilty of falsely reporting a robbery.

"It's possible, of course," the detective answered. "But the Applegates are so well-to-do I can't see any point in their trying such a thing. I believe it's best for us to stick to the original idea —that someone really did take jewels and securities from the safe, and that the person was Jackley."

As the boys were going to bed that night, Frank remarked to his brother, "Tomorrow is Saturday and we have the whole day free. I vote we set ourselves the goal of solving the mystery before night."

"A big order, but I'm with you," Joe replied with a grin.

They were up early and began to discuss what course of sleuthing they should follow.

"I think we ought to start off on a completely new tack," Joe suggested.

"In which direction?" Frank asked him.

"In the direction of the railroad."

Joe went on to explain that one thing they had not done was find out about Red Jackley's habits when he had worked around Bayport. If they could talk to one or more persons who had known him, they might pick up some new clue which would lead them to the stolen property.

"Good idea, Joe," his brother agreed. "Let's take our lunch and make an all-day trip on our motorcycles."

"Fine."

Mr. Hardy had left the house very early, so his sons did not see him. When his wife heard the boys' plan, she thought it an excellent one and immediately offered to make some sandwiches for them. By the time they were ready to leave she had two small boxes packed with a hearty picnic lunch.

"Good-by and good luck!" Mrs. Hardy called as the brothers rode off.

"Thanks, Mother, for everything!" the young detectives chorused as they started off.

When Frank and Joe reached the Bayport railroad station, they questioned the stationmaster, and learned that he had been with the company only a year and had not known Red Jackley.

"Did he work on a passenger train?" the man asked.

"I don't think so," Frank replied. "I believe he was employed as a maintenance man."

"Then," said the stationmaster, "I'd advise you to go out along the highway to the railroad crossings and interview a couple of old flagmen who are still around. Both of them seem to know everybody and everything connected with the railroad for the past fifty years." He chuckled.

The boys knew of two grade crossings some miles out of town and now headed for them. At the first one they learned that the regular flagman was home ill and his substitute had never heard of Red Jackley. Frank and Joe went on.

At the next crossing they found old Mike Halley, the flagman there, busy at his job. His bright blue eyes searched their faces for a moment, then he amazed them by saying, "You're Frank and Joe Hardy, sons of the famous detective Fenton Hardy."

"You know us?" Frank asked. "I must confess I don't recall having met you before."

"And you ain't," the man responded. "But I make it a rule to memorize every face I see in the newspapers. Never know when there's goin' to be an accident and I might be called on to identify some people."

The boys gulped at this gruesome thought, then Frank asked Halley if he remembered a railroad man named Red Jackley.

"I recollect a man named Jackley, but he wasn't never called Red when I knew him. I reckon he's the same fellow, though. You mean the one that I read went to jail?"

"That's the man!"

"He out of the pen yet?" Mike Halley questioned.

"He died," Joe replied. "Our dad is working on a case that has some connection with Jackley and we're just trying to find out something about him."

"Then what you want to do," said the flagman, "is go down to the Bayport and Coast Line Railroad. That's where Jackley used to work. He was around the station at Cherryville. That ain't so far from here." He pointed in a northerly direction.

"Thanks a million," said Frank. "You've helped us a lot."

The brothers set off on their motorcycles for Cherryville. When they came to the small town, a policeman directed them to the railroad station, which was about a half mile out of town. The station stood in a depression below a new highway, and was reached by a curving road which ran parallel to the tracks for several hundred feet.

The building itself was small, square, and very much in need of paint. A few nearby frame buildings were in a bad state of disrepair. An old wooden water tank, about seventy yards from one side of the station house, sagged precariously. At the same distance on the other side rose another water tank. This one, painted red, was of metal and in much better condition.

Frank and Joe parked their motorcycles and went into the station. A man in his shirt sleeves and wearing a green visor was bustling about behind the ticket window.

"Are you the stationmaster?" Frank called to him.

The man came forward. "I'm Jake—stationmaster, and ticket seller, and baggage slinger, and express handler, and mail carrier, and janitor, and even rice thrower. You name it. I'm your man."

The boys burst into laughter, then Joe said, "If there's anybody here who can tell us what we want to know, I'm sure it's you. But first, what do you mean you're a rice thrower?"

The station agent guffawed. "Well, it don't happen often, but when a bride and groom comes down here to take a train, I just go out, grab some of the rice, and throw it along with everybody else. I reckon if that'll make 'em happy, I want to be part of the proceedin's."

Again the Hardys roared with laughter. Then Frank inquired if the man had known Red Jackley.

"I sure did," Jake replied. "Funny kind of fellow. Work like mad one minute, then loaf on the job the next. One thing about him, he never wanted nobody to give him any orders."

"Did you know that he died recently?" Frank asked.

"No, I didn't," the stationmaster answered. "I'm real sorry to hear that. Jackley wasn't a bad sort when I knew him. Just got to keepin' the wrong kind of company, I guess."

"Can you tell us any particular characteristics he had?" Frank questioned.

Jake scratched his head above his visor. Finally he said, "The thing I remember most about Jackley is that he was a regular monkey. He was nimble as could be, racin' up and down freight-car ladders."

At that moment they heard a train whistle and the man said hurriedly, "Got to leave you now, boys. Come back some other time when I ain't so busy. Got to meet this train."

The Hardys left him and Frank suggested, "Let's eat our lunch and then come back."

They found a little grove of trees beside the railroad tracks and propped their motorcycles against a large tree.

"I'm starved," said Frank, seating himself under the tree and opening his box of lunch.

"Boy, this is good!" Joe exclaimed a moment later as he bit hungrily into a thick roast beef sandwich.

"If Jackley had only stayed with the railroad company," Frank observed as he munched a deviled egg, "it would've been better for everyone."

"He sure caused a lot of trouble before he died," Joe agreed.

"And he's caused a lot more since, the way things have gone. For the Robinsons, especially."

The boys gazed reflectively down the tracks, gleaming in the sun. The rails stretched far into the distance. Only a few hundred feet from the place where they were seated, the Hardys could see both water tanks: the dilapidated, weather-beaten wooden one, with some of the rungs missing from the ladder that led up its side, and the squat, metal tank, perched on spindly legs.

Frank took a bite of his sandwich and chewed it thoughtfully. The sight of the two water towers had given him an idea, but at first it seemed to him too absurd for consideration. He was wondering whether or not he should mention it to his brother.

Then he noticed that Joe, too, was gazing intently down the tracks at the tanks. Joe raised a cooky to his lips absently, attempted a bite, and missed the cooky altogether. Still he continued gazing fixedly in the same direction.

Finally Joe turned and looked at his brother. Both knew that they were thinking the identical thing.

"Two water towers," Frank said in a low but excited tone.

"An old one and a newer one," Joe murmured.

"And Jackley said—"

"He hid the stuff in the old tower."

"He was a railroad man."

"Why not?" Joe shouted, springing to his feet. "Why couldn't it have been this old *water* tower he meant? He used to work around here."

"After all, he didn't say the old tower of Tower Mansion. He just said 'old tower'!"

"Frank, I believe we've stumbled on a terrific clue!" Joe said jubilantly. "It would be the natural thing for Jackley to come to his former haunts after the robbery!"

"Right!" Frank agreed.

"And when he discovered that Chet's jalopy was gone, he probably thought that the police were hot on his trail, so he decided to hide the loot some place he knew—where no one else would suspect. The old water tower! This must be the place!"

CHAPTER XIX

Loot!

LUNCH, motorcycles—everything else was forgotten! With wild yells of excitement, Frank and Joe hurried down the embankment which flanked the right of way.

But as they came to a fence that separated the tracks from the grass and weeds that grew along the side, they stopped short. Someone on the highway above was sounding a car horn. Looking up, they recognized the driver.

Smuff!

"Oh, good night!" Joe cried out.

"The last person we want to see right now," Frank said in disgust.

"We'll get rid of him in a hurry," Joe determined.

The boys turned around and climbed back up the embankment. By this time Oscar Smuff had stepped from his car and was walking down to meet the boys.

"Well, I found you," he said.

"You mean you've been looking for us?" Frank asked in astonishment.

The detective grinned. With an ingratiating air he explained to the boys that he had trailed them for miles. He had seen them leave home on their motorcycles, and almost caught up with them at the Bayport station, only to lose them. But the stationmaster had revealed the Hardys' next destination, and the aspiring sleuth had hastened to talk to the flagman, Mike Halley.

"He told me I'd find you here," Smuff said, self-satisfaction evident in his tone.

"But why do you want us?" Joe demanded.

"I've come to make a proposition," Smuff announced. "I've got a swell clue about Jackley and that loot he hid, but I need somebody to help me in the search. How about it, fellows? If old Smuff lets you in on his secret, will you help him?"

Frank and Joe were astounded at this turn of events. Did the man really know something important? Or was he suddenly becoming clever and trying to trick the Hardys into divulging what they knew? One thing the brothers were sure of: they wanted nothing to do with Oscar Smuff until they had searched the old water tower.

"Thanks for the compliment," Frank said. He

grinned. "Joe and I think we're pretty good ourselves. We're glad you do."

"Then you'll work with me?" Smuff asked, his eyes lighting up in anticipation.

"I didn't say yes and I didn't say no," Frank countered. He glanced at Joe, who was standing in back of the detective. Joe shook his head vigorously. "Tell you what, Smuff," Frank went on. "When Joe and I get back to Bayport, we'll look you up. We came out here to have a picnic lunch and relax."

Smuff's face fell. But he was not giving up so easily. "When I drove up, I saw you running like mad down the bank. Do you call that relaxing?"

"Oh, when you sit around awhile eating, your legs feel kind of cramped," Joe told him. "Anyway, we have to keep in practice for the Bayport High baseball team."

Smuff looked as if he did not know whether or not he was being kidded. But finally he said, "Okay, fellows. If you'll get in touch with me the first of the week, I can promise you a big surprise. You've proved you can't win the thousand-dollar reward alone, so we may as well each get a share of it. I've already admitted I need help to solve this mystery."

He turned and slowly ambled up the embankment to his car. The boys waved good-by to the detective and waited until he was far out of sight and they were sure he would not return. Then Frank and Joe hurried down to the tracks, vaulted the fence, and ran pell-mell toward the old water tower.

"If only we *have* stumbled on the secret!" Frank said enthusiastically.

"It'll clear Mr. Robinson—"

"We will earn the reward by ourselves—"

"Best of all, Dad will be proud of us."

The old water tower reared forlornly alongside the tracks. At close quarters it seemed even more decrepit than from a distance. When the boys glanced at the ladder with its many rungs missing, they wondered if they would be able to ascend to the top on it.

"If Jackley climbed this ladder we can too," said Frank as he stopped, panting, at the bottom. "Let's go!"

He began to scramble up the rotted wood rungs. He had ascended only four of them when there came an alarming *crack!*

"Careful!" Joe cried out from below.

Frank clung to the rung above just as the one beneath him snapped under his weight. He drew himself up and cautiously put his foot on the next rung. This one was firmer and held his weight.

"Hey!" Joe called up. "Don't break all the rungs! I want to come up too!"

Frank continued to climb the ladder as his brother began the ascent. When they came to any place where a rung had broken off, the boys were obliged to haul themselves up by main force. But finally Frank reached the top and waited until Joe was just beneath him.

"There's a trap door up here leading down into the tank," Frank called.

"Well, for Pete's sake, be careful," Joe warned. "We don't want any more accidents with trap doors."

The boys climbed onto the roof of the tower, which swayed under their weight. Both fully realized their peril.

"We can't give up now!" said Frank, and scrambled over the surface of the roof until he reached the trap door. Joe followed. They unlatched and raised the door, then peered down into the recesses of the abandoned water tank. It was about seven feet in depth and twelve in diameter.

Frank lowered himself through the opening, but clung to the rim until he was sure, from feeling around with his feet, that the floor would not break through. "It's okay," he told Joe, who followed his brother inside.

Eagerly the boys peered about the dim interior. The place seemed to be partly filled with rubbish. There was a quantity of old lumber, miscellaneous bits of steel rails, battered tin pails, and crowbars, all piled in helter-skelter fashion. At first glance there was no sign of the Applegates' stolen possessions.

"The jewels and bonds must be here somewhere," Joe declared. "But if Jackley did put the stuff here, he wouldn't have left it right out in the open. It's probably hidden under some of this junk."

Frank pulled out a flashlight and swung it around. In its glow Joe began to hunt frantically, casting aside the old pails and pieces of lumber.

One entire half of the tower was searched without result. Frank turned the flashlight to the far side and noted that a number of boards had been piled up in a rather orderly crisscrossed manner.

"Joe," said Frank, "I'd say these boards hadn't been thrown here accidentally. It sure looks as if somebody had placed them deliberately to hide something underneath."

"You're right."

Like a terrier after a bone, Joe dived toward the pile. Hastily he pulled away the boards.

Revealed in the neat little hiding place lay a bag. It was an ordinary gunny sack, but as Joe dragged it out he felt sure that the search for the Applegate property had come to an end.

"This must be it!" he exulted.

"The Tower treasure!" Frank smothered a whoop of joy.

Joe carried the sack into the light beneath the trap door.

"Hurry up! Open it!" Frank urged.

With trembling fingers Joe began to untie the

cord around the sack. There were many knots, and as Joe worked at them, Frank fidgeted nervously.

"Let me try," he said impatiently.

At last, with both Hardys working on the stubborn knots, the cord was untied and the bag gaped open. Joe plunged one hand into it and withdrew an old-fashioned bracelet of precious stones.

"Jewelry!"

"How about the securities?"

Again Joe groped into the sack. His fingers encountered a bulky packet. When he pulled it out, the boys exclaimed in unison:

"The bonds!"

The bundle of papers, held together by an elastic band, proved to be the securities. The first of the documents was a negotiable bond for one thousand dollars issued by the city of Bayport.

"Mr. Applegate's property!" Frank cried out triumphantly. "Joe, do you realize what this means? We've solved the mystery!"

The brothers looked at each other almost unbelievingly, then each slapped the other on the back. "We did it! We did it!" Joe cried out jubilantly.

Frank grinned. "And without old Smuff," he said.

"Now Mr. Robinson's cleared for sure!" Joe exclaimed. "That's the best part of solving this mystery."

"You're right!"

The boys rejoiced over their discovery for another full minute, then decided to hurry back to Bayport with the precious sack.

"You go down first, Frank," said Joe. "I'll toss the sack to you and then come myself."

He picked up the bag and was about to hoist it to his shoulders when both boys heard a sound on the roof of the tower. They looked up to see an evil-looking, unshaven man peering down at them.

"Halt!" he ordered.

"Who are you?" Frank asked.

"They call me Hobo Johnny," the man replied. "This here is my quarters and anything in it belongs to me. You got no right in my room. You can't take anything away. And t'anks for finding the wad. I never thought to look around."

Joe, taken aback a moment, now said, "You may sleep here, but this is railroad property. You don't own what's in this tower. Now go on down the ladder, so we can leave."

"So you're going to fight, eh?" Hobo Johnny said in an ugly tone. "I'll see about that!"

Without warning the trap door was slammed shut and locked from the outside!

CHAPTER XX

The Escape

"LET us out of here!" Frank shouted at Hobo Johnny.

"You can't get away with this!" Joe yelled.

The man on the water tower roof gave a loud guffaw. "You think I ain't got no brains. Well, I got enough to know when I'm well off. I ain't in no hurry to collect that treasure you found in the tower. A few days from now will be all right for me to sell it."

"A few days from now?" Joe exclaimed, horrified. "By that time we'll be suffocated or die of starvation."

Frank put an arm around his impulsive brother's shoulder. In a low tone he said, "We won't do either, Joe. I don't think it's going to be too hard to get out of here. If not by the trap door, we'll hack our way out through one side of the tank."

Joe calmed down and both boys became silent. This seemed to worry Hobo Johnny, who called down, "What're you guys up to?"

No answer.

"Okay. I'm leaving you now, but I'll be back for that treasure. Don't try any funny stuff or you'll get hurt!"

The man on the roof waited a few moments for an answer. Receiving none, he shuffled across the tower to the ladder.

"I hope he doesn't break all the rungs," said Joe worriedly. "We won't be able to get down."

Again Frank patted his brother on the shoulder. "I noticed an iron pipe running from the top of this tower to the bottom," he said. "If necessary, we can slide down the pipe."

"How long do you think we should wait before trying to break out of here?" Joe asked.

Before replying, Frank pondered the situation. Not knowing anything about Hobo Johnny's habits, he wondered how far away from the tower the man would go. If not far, the boys might find him waiting below and a tough person to handle. Finally, Frank decided that since the tramp had said he would return in an hour, he must be planning to go some distance away, perhaps to get a couple of his hobo friends to come back and help him.

"I'd say that if we leave in fifteen minutes we'll be safe," was Frank's conclusion.

Every second seemed like an hour, but finally when the fifteen minutes were up, the boys lifted a plank and tried to push up the trap door. It would not budge.

"Where do we try next?" Joe questioned.

Frank was examining the seams around the trap door with the flashlight. Presently he pointed out a section where the wood looked completely dried out.

"It shouldn't be too hard to ram a hole here, Joe. Then you can boost me up, so I can reach through and turn the handle on the lock."

Joe picked up a crowbar and jabbed the sharp end between the edge of the trap door and the board next to it. There was a splintering sound. He gave the tool another tremendous push. The seam widened. Now he and Frank together wedged the end of the crowbar up through the opening.

In a few moments they had sprung the two boards far enough apart so that Frank, by standing on Joe's shoulders, could reach his arm through the opening. He found the handle which locked the trap door and turned it. Joe pushed up the door with the plank.

The boys were free!

Frank pulled himself up through the opening and hurried to the edge of the roof. He looked all around below. Hobo Johnny was not in sight; in fact, there was no one to be seen anywhere.

"Clear field ahead!" he announced.

Now the boys began to carry out their original intention of removing the stolen property from the old water tower. Frank went back to the trap door and Joe handed up the sack, then joined his brother on the roof. The older boy went down the ladder quickly and his brother tossed the treasure to him. Joe lost no time in following.

"We'd better get away from here in a hurry!" Frank advised, and both boys sprinted to their motorcycles.

"Let's divide this stuff. It'll be easier to carry," Frank suggested.

He opened the sack and handed Joe the bundle of securities, which the boy jammed into his pocket. Frank stuffed the sack containing the jewelry into his own side pocket. Then they hopped onto their motorcycles, stepped on the starters, and roared down the road toward Bayport. It was not until they were several miles from the old water tower that the Hardys relaxed. Grins spread over their faces.

"I don't know who's going to be the most surprised—Hurd or Adelia Applegate, or Chief Collig or—"

"I have another guess—Dad!" said Frank.

"I guess you're right," Joe agreed. "And the most disappointed person is going to be one Oscar Smuff!"

"What clue do you suppose he wanted us to follow?"

"It's my idea he didn't have any. He just wanted to hook on to us and then claim the glory if we found the treasure, so Collig would give him a job on the force."

"Where do you think we ought to take these valuables?" Joe asked presently.

The boys discussed this as they covered nearly a mile of ground and finally came to the conclusion that since Hurd Applegate had given their father the job of finding the stolen property, the detective should be the one to return it to the owners.

Half an hour later the brothers pulled into the Hardy driveway and soon were overwhelming their parents with the good news.

"It's wonderful! Simply wonderful!" Mrs. Hardy cried out, hugging each of her sons.

Their father's face wore a broad grin. "I'm certainly proud of you," he said, and slapped Frank and Joe on the back. "You boys shall have the honor of making the announcement to the Applegates."

"How about Chief Collig?" Frank asked. "And we'll report Hobo Johnny to him."

"And we'll invite the Robinsons to hear the announcement," Joe added.

The detective said he thought there should be a grand meeting at the Applegates' home of everyone involved with the tower mystery. He suggested that when the boys called up, they try to arrange such a meeting for that very evening.

Frank was selected to make the report to Hurd Applegate; the others could hear the elderly man exclaim in amazement. "I didn't think you'd do it!" he said over and over again.

Shouting for his sister, he relayed the message, then said, "Adelia wants me to tell you she's the most relieved woman in all of Bayport. She never did like any of this business."

The Applegates readily agreed to a meeting at their home early that evening and insisted that Mr. Robinson be there. Mr. Hardy was to see to it that Chief Collig released the man at once.

"This is going to be a lot of fun," Frank declared at supper. "Mother, I think you should come along? Will you?"

"I'd love to," Mrs. Hardy replied. "I'd like to hear what the Applegates and Mr. Robinson and Chief Collig are going to say."

"And Chet should be there too," Joe said. "After all, it was his stolen car that gave us the clue to Red Jackley." Chet was called and gave a whoop of delight. He agreed to meet the Hardy family at the Tower Mansion.

"There's one more person who ought to attend," said Frank with a twinkle in his eye. "Oscar Smuff. I'd like to watch his face, too."

"At least we should tell him that the mystery has been solved," Joe spoke up.

Frank waited until his father had phoned Chief Collig, who promised to release Mr. Robinson at once and bring him out to the Applegates' home. Then Frank called Detective Smuff. He could not resist the temptation to keep Smuff guessing a little longer, and merely invited him to join the conference for a big surprise.

At eight o'clock one car after another arrived at the Tower Mansion. When the Hardy family walked in they found all the Robinsons there. The twins rushed up to Frank and Joe and hugged them. Slim and his father shook the brothers' hands fervently and Mr. Robinson said, "How can I ever thank you?"

There were tears in his wife's eyes and her voice trembled as she added her appreciation for what the Hardy boys had done. "You'll never know what this means to us," she said.

Oscar Smuff was the last to arrive. Instantly he demanded to know what was going on. Frank and Joe had hoped to have a little fun with him, but Tessie and Paula, unable to restrain their enthusiasm, shouted, "Frank and Joe Hardy found the jewelry and the papers! They're real heroes!"

As Frank and Joe reddened in embarrassment, Detective Smuff looked at them disbelievingly. "You!" he almost screamed. "You mean the Hardy boys found the treasure?"

As all the others nodded, Slim spoke up, "This means that my father is completely exonerated."

"But how about that nine hundred dollars?" Smuff demanded suspiciously. "What's the explanation of where your father got that?"

Mr. Robinson straightened up. "I'm sorry," he said, "but I must keep my promise to remain silent about that money."

To everyone's amazement, Adelia Applegate arose and went to stand by the man's side. "*I* will tell you where Robinson got that money," she said dramatically. "At my own suggestion I loaned it to him."

"You!" her brother shouted disbelievingly.

"Yes, this was one time when I didn't ask your advice because I knew you wouldn't agree. I knew Robinson needed the money and I really forced him to borrow it, but made him promise to tell no one where he got it. Then when the robbery took place, I didn't know what to think. I was sick over the whole affair, and I'm very, very glad everything's cleared up."

Miss Applegate's announcement astounded her listeners. Robinson stood up, shook her hand, and said in a shaky voice, "Thank you, Miss Adelia."

Hurd Applegate cleared his throat, then said, "I'd like to make an announcement. Will you all please sit down?"

After everyone had taken seats in the large living room of the mansion, the owner went on, "My sister Adelia and I have been talking things over. This whole robbery business has taught us a great lesson. In the future we're not going to be so standoffish from the residents of Bayport. We're going to dedicate part of our grounds—the part with the pond—as a picnic and swimming spot for the townspeople."

"Super!" exclaimed Chet, and Mrs. Hardy said, "I know everyone will appreciate that."

"I haven't finished," Hurd Applegate went on. "I want to make a public apology to Mr. Robinson. Adelia and I are extremely sorry for all the trouble we've caused him. Robinson, if you will come back and work for us, we promise to treat you like the gentleman you are. We will increase your salary and we have decided to build that greenhouse you want. You'll have free rein to raise all the rare flowers you wish to."

There was a gasp from everyone in the room. All eyes were turned on Mr. Robinson. Slowly he arose from his chair, walked over to Mr. Applegate, and shook his hand.

"No hard feelings," he said. "I'll be happy to have my old position back, and with the new greenhouse, I'm sure I'll win a lot of blue ribbons for you and Miss Adelia."

As he returned to his chair, Mr. Applegate said, "There is just one more item of business—the reward. The thousand-dollar reward goes to Frank and Joe Hardy, who solved the mystery of the Tower treasure."

"A thousand bucks!" exclaimed Detective Smuff.

"Dollars, Mr. Smuff—dollars!" Adelia Applegate corrected him severely. "No slang, please, not in Tower Mansion."

"One thousand iron men," Smuff continued, unheeding. "One thousand round, fat, juicy smackers. For two high school boys! And a real detective like me—"

The thought was too much for him. He dropped his head in his hands and groaned aloud. Frank and Joe did not dare look at each other. They were finding it difficult to restrain their laughter.

"Yes, a thousand dollars," Hurd Applegate went on. "Five hundred to each boy."

He took the two checks from a pocket and handed one each to Frank and Joe, who accepted them with thanks. Mr. Applegate now invited his guests into the dining room for sandwiches, cake, and cold drinks.

As Frank and Joe ate, they were congratulated over and over by the others in the room. They accepted it all with a grin, but secretly, each boy had a little feeling of sadness that the case had ended. They hoped another mystery would soon come their way, and one did at **THE HOUSE ON THE CLIFF.**

"Later, on the way home, Mr. Hardy asked his sons, "What are you fellows going to do with all that money?"

Frank had an instant answer. "Put most of it in the bank."

And Joe added, "Frank and I for some time have wanted to build a crime lab on the second floor of our barn. Now we can do it. All right, Dad?"

The detective smiled and nodded. "An excellent idea!"

THE HOUSE ON THE CLIFF

"Maybe I can give you a tip where to find
your father," said Pretzel Pete

Hardy Boys Mystery Stories

THE HOUSE

ON

THE CLIFF

BY

FRANKLIN W. DIXON

NEW YORK
GROSSET & DUNLAP
A NATIONAL GENERAL COMPANY
Publishers

In this new story, based on the original of
the same title, Mr. Dixon has incorporated
the most up-to-date methods used by police
and private detectives.

CONTENTS

CHAPTER I

Spying by Telescope

"So you boys want to help me on another case?" Fenton Hardy, internationally known detective, smiled at his teen-age sons.

"Dad, you said you're working on a very mysterious case right now," Frank spoke up. "Isn't there some angle of it that Joe and I could tackle?"

Mr. Hardy looked out the window of his second-floor study as if searching for the answer somewhere in the town of Bayport, where the Hardys lived. Finally he turned back and gazed steadfastly at his sons.

"All right. How would you like to look for some smugglers?"

Joe Hardy's eyes opened wide. "You mean it, Dad?"

"Now just a minute." The detective held up his

1

hand. "I didn't say capture them; I just said look for them."

"Even that's a big assignment. Thanks for giving it to us!" Frank replied.

The lean, athletic detective walked to a corner of the study where a long, narrow carrying case stood. Tapping it, he said:

"You boys have learned how to manipulate this telescope pretty well. How would you like to take it out onto that high promontory above the ocean and train it seaward? The place I mean is two miles north of the end of the bay and eight miles from here."

"That would be great!" said seventeen-year-old, blond-haired Joe, his blue eyes flashing in anticipation.

Frank, who was a year older than his brother and less impetuous, asked in a serious tone of voice, "Dad, have you any ideas about the identity of any of the smugglers?"

"Yes, I do," Mr. Hardy answered his tall, dark-haired son. "I strongly suspect that a man named Felix Snattman is operating in this territory. I'll give you the whole story."

The detective went on to say that he had been engaged by an international pharmaceutical company to trace stolen shipments of valuable drugs. Reports of thefts had come from various parts of the United States. Local police had worked on the case, but so far had failed to apprehend any suspects.

"Headquarters of the firm is in India," the detective told the boys. "It was through them that I was finally called in. I'm sure that the thefts are the result of smuggling, very cleverly done. That's the reason I suspect Snattman. He's a noted criminal and has been mixed up in smuggling rackets before. He served a long term in prison, and after being released, dropped out of sight."

"And you think he's working around Bayport?" Joe asked. He whistled. "That doesn't make this town a very healthy place to live in!"

"But we're going to make it so!" Mr. Hardy declared, a ring of severity in his voice.

"Just where is this spot we're to use the telescope?" Frank asked eagerly.

"It's on the Pollitt place. You'll see the name at the entrance. An old man named Felix Pollitt lived there alone for many years. He was found dead in the house about a month ago, and the place has been vacant ever since."

"It sounds as if we could get a terrific range up and down the shore from there and many miles across the water," Frank remarked.

Mr. Hardy glanced at his wrist watch. "It's one-thirty now. You ought to be able to go out there, stay a fair amount of time, and still get home to supper."

"Oh, easily," Joe answered. "Our motorcycles can really burn up the road!"

His father smiled, but cautioned, "This telescope happens to be very valuable. The less jouncing it receives the better."

"I get the point," Joe conceded, then asked, "Dad, do you want us to keep the information about the smugglers to ourselves, or would it be all right to take a couple of the fellows along?"

"Of course I don't want the news broadcast," Mr. Hardy said, "but I know I can trust your special friends. Call them up."

"How about Chet and Biff?" Joe consulted Frank. As his brother nodded, he said, "You pack the telescope on your motorcycle. I'll phone."

Chet Morton was a stout, good-natured boy who loved to eat. Next to that, he enjoyed being with the Hardys and sharing their exciting adventures, although at times, when situations became dangerous, he wished he were somewhere else. Chet also loved to tinker with machinery and spent long hours on his jalopy which he called Queen. He was trying to "soup up" the motor, so that he could have a real "hot rod."

In contrast to Chet, Biff Hooper was tall and lanky. To the amusement—and wonder—of the other boys, he used his legs almost as a spider does, covering tremendous distances on level ground or vaulting fences.

A few minutes later Joe joined his brother in the garage and told him that both Chet and Biff would go along. Chet, he said, had apologized for not being able to offer the Queen for the trip but her engine was "all over the garage." "As usual," Frank said with a grin as the two boys climbed on their motorcycles and set out.

Presently the Hardys stopped at Biff Hooper's home. He ran out the door to meet them and climbed aboard behind Joe. Chet lived on a farm at the outskirts of Bayport, about a fifteen-minute run from the Hooper home. The stout boy had strolled down the lane to the road and was waiting for his friends. He hoisted himself onto Frank's motorcycle.

"I've never seen a powerful telescope in operation," he remarked. "How far away can you see with this thing?"

"It all depends on weather conditions," Frank replied. "On a clear day you can make out human figures at distances of twenty-four miles."

"Wow!" Chet exclaimed. "We ought to be able to find those smugglers easily."

"I wouldn't say so," Biff spoke up. "Smugglers have the same kind of boats as everybody else. How close do you have to be to identify a person?"

"Oh, about two and a half miles," Joe answered.

The motorcycles chugged along the shore

road, with Frank watching his speedometer carefully. "We ought to be coming to the Pollitt place soon," he said finally. "Keep your eyes open, fellows."

The boys rode on in silence, but suddenly they all exclaimed together, "There it is!"

At the entrance to a driveway thickly lined with trees and bushes was a stone pillar, into which the name "Pollitt" had been chiseled. Frank and Joe turned into the driveway. The only part of the house they could see was the top of the roof. Finally, beyond a lawn overgrown with weeds, they came upon the tall, rambling building. It stood like a beacon high above the water. Pounding surf could be heard far below.

"This place sure looks neglected," Biff remarked.

Dank, tall grass grew beneath the towering trees. Weeds and bushes threatened to engulf the whole building.

"Creepy, if you ask me," Chet spoke up. "I don't know why anybody would want to live here."

The house itself was in need of repair. Built of wood, it had several sagging shutters and the paint was flaking badly.

"Poor old Mr. Pollitt was probably too sick to take care of things," Frank commented, as he looked at several weed-choked flower beds.

To the Hardys' disappointment, the sky had

become overcast and they realized that visibility had been cut down considerably. Nevertheless, Frank unstrapped the carrying case and lugged it around to the front of the house.

He unfastened the locks and Joe helped his brother lift out the telescope and attached tripod, pulling up the eye-end section first.

Biff and Chet exclaimed in admiration.

"Boy, that's really neat!" Chet remarked.

He and Biff watched in fascination as Frank and Joe began to set up the telescope. First they unfastened the tape with which the tube and tripod legs were tied together. Joe turned the three legs down and pulled out the extensions to the desired height. Then Frank secured the tripod legs with a chain to keep them from spreading.

"What's next?" Biff asked.

"To get proper balance for the main telescope tube we slide it through this trunnion sleeve toward the eye end, like this." After doing so, Frank tightened the wing nuts on the tripod lightly.

Joe picked up the balance weight from the carrying case and screwed it into the right side of the telescope tube about one third the distance from the eyepiece.

"This'll keep the whole thing from being top heavy," he pointed out.

"And what's this little telescope alongside the big one for?" Chet queried.

"A finder," Frank explained. "Actually, it's a small guide telescope and helps the observer sight his big telescope on the object more easily."

"It's as clear as mud," Chet remarked with a

grin. He squinted through the ends of both the large and the small telescopes. "I can't see a thing," he complained.

Joe laughed. "And you won't until I insert one

of the eyepieces into the adapter of the big telescope and put another eyepiece into the finder."

In a few minutes the Hardys had the fascinating device working. By turning a small knob, Frank slowly swung the telescope from left to right, and each boy took a turn looking out across the water.

"Not a boat in sight!" said Chet, disappointed.

Frank had just taken his second turn squinting through the eyepiece when he called out excitedly, "I see something!"

He now began a running account of the scene he had just picked up. "It's not very clear . . . but I see a boat . . . must be at least six miles out."

"What kind of boat?" Joe put in.

"Looks like a cruiser . . . or a cutter. . . . It's not moving. . . . Want to take a look, Joe?"

Frank's brother changed places with him. "Say, fellows, a man's going over the side on a ladder . . . and, hey! there's a smaller boat down below. . . . He's climbing into it."

"Can you see a name or numbers on the big boat?" Frank asked excitedly.

"No. The boat's turned at a funny angle, so you can't see the lettering. You couldn't even if the weather was clearer."

"Which way is the man in the small boat heading?" Biff asked.

"He seems to be going toward Barmet Bay."

Joe gave up his position to Biff. "Suppose you keep your eye on him for a while, and also the big boat. Maybe it'll turn so you can catch the name or number on the box."

Chet had been silent for several moments. Now he said, "Do you suppose they're the smugglers?"

"Could be," Frank replied. "I think we'd better leave and report this to Dad from the first telephone we—"

He was interrupted by the sudden, terrifying scream of a man!

"Wh-where did that come from?" Chet asked with a frightened look.

"Sounded as if it came from inside," Frank answered.

The boys stared at the house on the cliff. A moment later they heard a loud cry for help. It was followed by another scream.

"Somebody's in there and is in trouble!" Joe exclaimed. "We'd better find out what's going on!"

Leaving the telescope, the four boys ran to the front door and tried the knob. The door was locked.

"Let's scatter and see if we can find another door," Frank suggested.

Frank and Joe took one side of the house, Biff and Chet the other. They met at the rear of the old home and together tried a door there. This, too, was locked.

"There's a broken window around the corner," Biff announced. "Shall we climb in?"

"I guess we'd better," Frank answered.

As the boys reached the window, which seemed to open into a library, they heard the scream again.

"Help! Hurry! Help!" came an agonized cry.

CHAPTER II

Thief at Work

JOE was first to slide through the broken window. "Wait a moment, fellows," he called out, "until I unlock this."

Quickly he turned the catch, raised the window, and the other three boys stepped inside the library. No one was there and they ran into the large center hall.

"Hello!" Frank shouted. "Where are you?"

There was no answer. "Maybe that person who was calling for help has passed out or is unconscious," Joe suggested. "Let's look around."

The boys dashed in various directions, and investigated the living room with its old-fashioned furnishings, the dining room with its heavily carved English oak set, the kitchen, and what had evidently been a maid's bedroom in days gone by. Now it was heaped high with empty boxes and crates. There was no one in any of the rooms and the Hardys and their two friends met again in the hall.

"The man must be upstairs," Frank decided.

He started up the front stairway and the others followed. There were several bedrooms. Suddenly Chet hung back. He wanted to go with his pals but the eeriness of the house made him pause. Biff and the Hardys sped from one to another of the many rooms. Finally they investigated the last of them.

"Nobody here! What do you make of it?" Biff asked, puzzled.

Chet, who had rejoined the group, said worriedly, "M-maybe the place is haunted!"

Joe's eyes were searching for an entrance to the third floor. Seeing none, he opened three doors in the hall, hoping to find a stairway. He saw none.

"There must be an attic in this house," he said. "I wonder how you get to it."

"Maybe there's an entrance from one of the bedrooms," Frank suggested. "Let's see."

The boys separated to investigate. Suddenly Frank called out, "I've found it."

The others ran to where he had discovered a door behind a man's shabby robe hanging inside a closet. This in turn revealed a stairway and the group hurriedly climbed it, Chet bringing up the rear.

The attic room was enormous. Old newspapers and magazines were strewn around among old-fashioned trunks and suitcases, but there was no human being in sight.

"I guess that cry for help didn't come from the house at all," Biff suggested. "What'll we do now? Look outdoors?"

"I guess we'll have to," Frank answered.

He started down the steep stairway. Reaching the foot, he turned the handle of the door which had swung shut. To his concern he was not able to open it.

"What's the matter?" asked Chet from the top of the stairway.

"Looks as if we're locked in," Frank told him.

"Locked in?" Chet wailed. "Oh, no!"

Frank tried pulling and pushing the door. It did not budge.

"That's funny," he said. "I didn't see any lock on the outside."

Suddenly the full import of the situation dawned on the four boys. Someone had deliberately locked them in! The cries for help had been a hoax to lure them into the house!

"You think somebody was playing a joke on us?" Biff asked.

"Pretty rotten kind of joke," Chet sputtered.

Frank and Joe were inclined to think that there was more to it than a joke. Someone had seen a chance to steal a valuable telescope and two late-model motorcycles!

"We've got to get out of here!" Joe said. "Frank, put your shoulder to the door and I'll help."

Fortunately, the door was not particularly sturdy and gave way easily. Frank glanced back a moment as he rushed through and saw two large hooks which he had not noticed before. They had evidently been slipped into the eyes and had been ripped from the framework by the crash on the door.

The other boys followed, running pell-mell through the hallway and clattering down the stairway. They dashed out the front door, leaving it open behind them. To their relief, the telescope still stood at the edge of the cliff, pointing sea-ward.

"Thank goodness!" said Joe. "I'd hate to have had to tell Dad the telescope was gone!"

Frank rushed over to take a quick look through the instrument. It had occurred to him that maybe some confederate of the smugglers had seen them spying. He might even have tricked them into the house during the very time that a smuggling operation would be within range of the telescope!

When Frank reached the edge of the cliff and tried to look through the instrument, he gasped

in dismay. The eyepieces from both the finder and
the telescope tube had been removed!

As he turned to tell the other boys of his discovery, he found that they were not behind him.
But a moment later Joe came running around
the corner of the house calling out:

"The motorcycles are safe! Nobody stole them!"

"Thank goodness for that," said Frank.

Chet and Biff joined them and all flopped down
on the grass to discuss the mysterious happenings
and work out a plan of action.

"If that thief is hiding inside the house, I'm
going to find him," Joe declared finally.

"I'm with you," said Frank, jumping up. "How
about you, Biff, guarding the motorcycles and
Chet taking charge of the telescope? That way,
both the front and back doors will be covered, too,
in case that thief comes out."

"Okay," the Hardys' friends agreed.

As Frank and Joe entered the front hall, Joe remarked, "There's a back stairway. If we don't find
the person on the first floor, I'll take that to the
second. You take the front."

Frank nodded and the search began. Not only
the first, but the second and attic floors were
thoroughly investigated without results.

"There's only one place left," said Frank. "The
cellar."

This area also proved to have no one hiding

in it. "I guess our thief got away," Frank stated.

"And probably on foot," Joe added. "I didn't hear any car, did you?"

"No. Maybe he went down the cliff and made a getaway in a boat," Frank suggested.

In complete disgust the Hardys reported their failure to Biff and Chet. Then they packed up the telescope and strapped it onto Frank's motorcycle.

"We may as well go home," Joe said dolefully. "We'll have a pretty slim report for Dad."

"Slim?" said Biff. "I haven't had so much excitement in six months."

The boys climbed aboard the motorcycles. As the Hardys were about to start the motors, all four of them froze in the seats. From somewhere below the cliff came a demoniacal laugh. Involuntarily the boys shuddered.

"L-let's get out of here!" Chet urged.

Frank and Joe had hopped off the motorcycles, and were racing in the direction from which the eerie laughter was coming.

"It may be another trap!" Chet yelled after them. "Come back!"

But the Hardys went on. Just before they reached the edge of the cliff they were thunderstruck to hear the laughter coming from a completely different area. It was actually in back of them!

"What gives?" Joe asked.

"Search me," his brother answered. "The ghost must have a confederate."

The brothers peered over the edge of the cliff but could see only jagged rocks that led to the booming surf below. Frank and Joe returned to their chums, disappointed that they had learned nothing and had no explanation for the second laugh.

"I'm glad it stopped, anyhow," said Chet. "It gave me goose pimples and made chills run up and down my spine."

Biff looked at his wrist watch. "I really have to be getting home, fellows. Sorry to break up this man hunt. Maybe you can take me to a bus and come back."

The Hardys would not hear of this and said they would leave at once.

They had gone scarcely a mile when the motor on Frank's cycle sputtered and backfired, then died. "A swell time for a breakdown," he said disgustedly as he honked for Joe to stop.

Joe turned around and drove back. "What's the matter?"

"Don't know." Frank dismounted. "It's not the gas. I have plenty of that."

"Tough luck!" Joe said sympathetically. "Well, let's take a look at the motor. Better get out your tools."

As Frank opened the toolbox of his motorcycle, an expression of bewilderment came over his face.

"My tools!" he exclaimed. "They're gone!"

The others gathered around. The toolbox was indeed empty!

"Are you sure you had them when you left Bayport?" Chet asked.

"Of course I did. I never go anywhere without them."

Biff shook his head. "I suppose the guy who took the eyepieces stole your tools too."

Joe dashed to the toolbox on his own motorcycle and gave a cry of dismay.

"Mine are gone, too!"

CHAPTER III

Landslide!

"THAT's a shame, fellows," Chet Morton said. "This is sure your day for bad luck. First the eyepieces from your telescope are taken and now the tools from your motorcycles."

"And all by the same person, I'm sure," Frank remarked grimly.

"Some slick operator, whoever he is," Joe added gloomily.

Chet put his hands into his trouser pockets and with a grin pulled out a pair of pliers, a screw driver, and a wrench.

"I was working on the Queen this morning," he explained. "Good thing I happened to put these in my pocket."

"I'll say," Frank declared gratefully, taking the tools which Chet handed over.

He unfastened the housing of the motor and

began checking every inch of the machinery. Finally he looked up and announced, "I guess I've found the trouble—a loose connection."

Frank adjusted the wires and a moment later the vehicle's motor was roaring normally. The housing was put back on, Chet's tools were returned with thanks, and the four boys set off once more.

"Let's hope nothing more happens before we get home," Biff said with a wry laugh.

"I'll second that," Joe said emphatically.

For five minutes the cyclists rode along in silence, their thoughts partly on the passing scenery, but mostly on the mystery in which they had become involved.

Joe's mind was racing with his throbbing motorcycle. In a few minutes he had far outdistanced his brother. Frank did not dare go any faster because of the telescope strapped onto his handle bars.

Presently Joe reached a spot in the road where it had been cut out of the hillside on the right. There was a sharp curve here. The motorcycle took it neatly, but he and Biff had scarcely reached the straightaway beyond when they heard a thunderous sound back of them.

"What's that?" Joe cried out.

Biff turned to look over his shoulder. "A landslide!" he shouted.

Rocks and dirt, loosened by recent heavy rainstorms, were tumbling down the steep hillside at terrific speed.

"Frank!" Joe cried out in horror. He jammed on his brake and disengaged the engine. As he ran back to warn his brother, Joe saw that he was too late. Biff had rushed up and both could only stare helplessly, their hearts sinking.

Frank and Chet came around the corner at good speed and ran full tilt into the landslide. Its rumbling sound had been drowned out by the pounding surf and their own roaring motor.

The two boys, the motorcycle, and the telescope were bowled over by the falling rocks and earth. As the rain of debris finally stopped, Joe and Biff reached their sides.

"Frank! Chet!" they cried out in unison. "Are you hurt?"

Frank, then Chet, sat up slowly. Aside from looking a bit dazed, they seemed to be all right. "Rock just missed my head," Frank said finally.

"I got a mean wallop on my shoulder," Chet panted gingerly, rubbing the sore spot.

"You fellows were lucky," Biff spoke up, and Joe nodded his intense relief.

"How about the telescope?" Frank asked quickly. "Take a look at it, will you, Joe?"

The battered carrying case, pushed out of the straps which had held it in place on the motorcycle, lay in the road, covered with stone and dirt. Joe opened the heavily lined box and carefully examined the telescope.

"It looks all right to me," he said in a relieved voice. "Of course we won't know for sure until we try other eyepieces in it. But at least nothing looks broken."

By this time Frank and Chet were standing up and Biff remarked, "While you two are getting your breath, Joe and I can take the biggest rocks out of the way. Some motorist may come speeding along here and break his neck or wreck his car unless this place gets cleaned up."

"Oh, I'm okay," Chet insisted. "The rock that hit me felt just like Bender, that big end on the Milton High team. He's hit me many a time the same way."

Frank, too, declared that he felt no ill effects. Together, the boys flung rock after rock into the field between the road and the water and, in pairs, carried the heavier rocks out of the way.

"Guess we're all set now," Frank spoke up. "Biff, I'm afraid you're going to be late getting home." He chuckled. "Who is she?"

Biff reddened a little. "How'd you guess? I have a date tonight with Sally Sanderson. But she's a good sport. She won't mind waiting a little longer."

Again the four boys straddled the motorcycles

and started off. A few minutes later a noise out in the ocean attracted Frank's attention and he peered across the rolling sweep of waters. A powerful speedboat came into view around the base of a small cliff about a quarter mile out. It was followed at a short distance by a similar, but larger craft. Both boats were traveling at high speed.

"Looks like a race!" Joe called out. "Let's watch it!"

The Hardys ran their motorcycles behind a clump of trees and stopped, then walked down to the shore line.

The boats did not appear to be having a friendly speed contest, however. The first boat was zigzagging in a peculiar manner, and the pursuing craft was rapidly overtaking it.

"See! That second boat is trying to stop the other one!" Frank exclaimed.

"It sure is. Wonder what's up," said Joe tensely. "I wish that telescope was working. Can any of you fellows make out the names on the boats?"

"No," the others chorused.

The two men standing in the bow of the pursuing craft were waving their arms frantically. The first boat turned as if about to head toward the shore. Then, apparently, the helmsman changed his mind, for at once the nose of his boat was pointed out into the ocean again.

But the moment of hesitation had given the

pursuers the chance they needed. Swiftly the gap
between the racing craft grew smaller and smaller
until the boats were running side by side. They
were so close together that a collision seemed imminent.

"They'll all be killed if they aren't careful!"
Frank muttered as he watched intently.

The lone man in the foremost craft was bent
over the wheel. In the boat behind, one of the
two men suddenly raised his right arm high. A
moment later he hurled an object through the
air. It landed in back of the engine housing in the
center of the craft. At the same time the larger
boat sped off seaward.

"What was that?" Chet asked. "I—"

Suddenly a sheet of flame leaped high into the
air from the smaller boat. There was a stunning
explosion and a dense cloud of smoke rose in the
air. Bits of wreckage were thrown high and in
the midst of it the boys saw the occupant hurled
into the water.

Swiftly the whole boat caught fire. The flames
raced from bow to stern.

"That man!" shouted Frank. "He's alive!"

The boys could see him struggling in the surf,
trying to swim ashore.

"He'll never make it!" Joe gasped. "He's
all in."

"We've got to save him!" Frank cried out.

CHAPTER IV

The Rescue

THE Hardy boys knew that they had no time to lose. It was evident that the man in the water had been injured by the explosion and could not swim much longer.

"We'll never reach him!" Chet said, as the four boys dashed across the rocks and grass to the shore.

Suddenly Frank cried out, "I see a rowboat up on the beach." His sharp eyes had detected a large rowboat almost completely hidden in a small cove at the bottom of the cliff. "We'd make better time in that!"

A huge rock jutting out of the water cut the cove off from the open part of the beach.

"We'd have to go up to that ridge and then down," Joe objected. "I'll swim out."

"I will too," said Biff.

The two plunged into the water and struck out for the stricken man.

Meanwhile, Frank and Chet sped up the slope, cut across a strip of grass, and began running down the embankment toward the rowboat.

"That man's still afloat," Frank shouted as he looked out over the water.

Joe and Biff were making good time but were a long way from the man, who seemed now to be drifting with the outgoing tide. The explosion victim, fortunately, had managed to seize a piece of wreckage and was hanging onto it.

Slipping and scrambling, Frank and Chet made their way down the slope. Rocks rolled and tumbled ahead of them. But finally they reached the bottom safely and examined the boat. It was battered and old, but evidently still seaworthy. There were two sets of oars.

"Grab hold!" Frank directed Chet.

The boys pulled the boat across the pebbles and into the water. Swiftly they fixed the oars in the locks and took their places. Pulling hard, Frank and Chet rowed toward the distressed swimmer. Presently they overtook Joe and Biff, who clambered aboard. The man had seen the boys and called feebly to them to hurry.

"Faster!" Joe urged. "He looks as if he'll go under any second!"

The motorboat in the background was still

blazing fiercely, flames shooting high in the air. The craft was plainly doomed.

The boys pulled harder and the rowboat leaped across the water. When it was only a few yards away from the man, he suddenly let go his hold on the bit of wreckage and slipped beneath the waves.

"He's drowning!" Chet shouted, as he bent to his oar again.

Joe made a tremendously long, outward dive and disappeared into the water where the man had gone down. Frank and Chet rowed the boat to the spot and leaned over the side to peer down.

Just then, Joe and the stranger broke the surface of the water, with the boy holding an arm under the man's shoulders. His head sagged.

"He's unconscious!" Biff whispered hoarsely, as he helped pull the victim into the boat. The man sprawled helplessly on the bottom, more dead than alive.

"We'd better revive him and get him to the hospital," said Frank.

He applied artificial respiration, forcing a little water from the man's lungs, but the stranger did not regain consciousness.

"I think he collapsed from exhaustion," Joe spoke up.

Frank and Chet took off their jackets and wrapped them around the wet figure.

"How about taking him to that farmhouse over there—along the road?" Chet suggested.

The others agreed. As Frank and Chet rowed toward the farm, the boys discussed the mystery. Who was the victim of the explosion and why had the men in the other motorboat tried to kill him?

The man they had rescued lay face downward in the bottom of the boat. He was a slim, dark-haired man with sharp, clean-cut features, and his clothes were cheap and worn. Biff looked in his pockets for identification but found none.

"Wonder if he's a local man," Joe said. "Never saw him around town."

The other boys declared they never had either.

By this time the boat was close to shore. Joe and Biff leaped out and dragged it part way up on the beach. Then the four boys carried the unconscious man up the rocky shore toward the farmhouse.

At their approach a plump woman came hurrying out of the house. From the orchard nearby a burly man in overalls came forward.

"My goodness! What has happened?" the woman asked, running toward them.

"We just pulled this man out of the water," Frank explained. "We saw your house—"

"Bring him in," boomed the farmer. "Bring him right in."

The woman ran ahead and held the door

open. The boys carried the stranger into the house and laid him on a bed in the comfortably furnished first-floor bedroom. The farmer's wife hastened to the kitchen to prepare a hot drink.

"Rub his ankles and wrists, and get those wet clothes off him," the farmer told the boys. "That will step up his circulation. I'll get him some pajamas."

"How about calling a doctor?" Frank asked.

"No need. He'll be okay," the farmer declared.

The victim was soon under the covers. Frank and Joe continued to massage his wrists and ankles.

At last the stranger stirred feebly. His eyelids fluttered. His lips moved, but no words came. Then his eyes opened and the man stared at those around him, as though in a daze.

"Where am I?" he muttered faintly.

"You're safe," Frank assured him. "You're with friends."

"You saved me?"

"Yes."

"Pretty near—cashed in—didn't I?"

"You nearly drowned, but you're all right now. When you feel like talking, you can tell us the whole story," said Frank. "But, in the meantime, we'll call the police or the Coast Guard and report those men who tried to murder you."

The man in the bed blinked and looked out the

window. Finally he said, "No, no. Don't do that."

The boys were shocked. "Why not?" Joe burst out.

The man was thoughtfully silent for a moment, then said, "Thanks, but I'd rather let matters stand as they are. I'll take care of it as soon as I get my strength back." The rescued man turned to the farmer. "Okay with you if I stay here overnight? I'll pay you, of course."

The farmer put out his hand. "The name's Kane and you're welcome to stay until you feel strong. Nobody can say I ever turned a sick man away. And what's your name?"

The patient hesitated a moment. "Jones. Bill Jones," he said at last.

It was so evidently a false name that the Hardys glanced knowingly at each other. Mr. Kane did not seem to realize that his guest was apparently trying to hide his identity.

Mrs. Kane appeared with hot broth and toast. She suggested that her husband and the boys let the patient rest for a while. When she joined them in the living room she invited the boys to have a snack. Chet readily accepted for all of them.

The snack consisted of sandwiches of home-cured ham with cheese, glasses of fresh milk, and rich lemon pie, frothy with meringue. Chet beamed. "Mrs. Kane, you ought to open a restaurant. I'd be a steady customer. You're the best pie maker I've ever met."

Frank, Joe, and Biff chuckled. How often they had heard their stout, food-loving chum make similar remarks! But in this case they had to agree with him and told Mrs. Kane so.

She smiled. "It's the least I can do for you boys who just saved someone's life."

Her young guests said nothing of their early afternoon's adventure inside the Pollitt house, but Frank casually asked the Kanes if they had known the deceased owner and if anyone were living there now.

"Sure I knew Felix Pollitt," the farmer replied. "Closemouthed old codger, but I did hear him once say somethin' about havin' a no-good nephew. Pollitt said he was his only livin' relative and he supposed he'd have to leave the property to him."

"But who'd want the place?" Mrs. Kane spoke up. "It's falling apart and would cost a mint of money to fix up."

Joe grinned. "Sounds like a haunted house," he remarked pointedly.

"Funny you should say that." Mrs. Kane looked at Joe. "There was a family stopped here the other day. Wanted to buy some eggs. One of the little girls said they'd had a terrible scare. They'd stopped at the old Pollitt place to have a picnic, and were scared out of their wits by moans and groans and queer laughs from the house."

Mr. Kane's face broke into a grin. "The kid's imagination sure was runnin' away with itself."

"I'm not so sure of that," his wife disagreed. "I think some boys were in there playing pranks."

After Frank and Joe and their friends had left the farmhouse, they discussed the strange noises at the Pollitt place from this new angle.

Biff frowned. "If those ghosts are from Bayport High, they'll sure have the laugh on us," he remarked.

"They sure will," Chet agreed. "I'd hate to face them on Monday."

Frank and Joe were not convinced. After they had dropped their chums at the Morton and Hooper homes, they discussed the day's strange and varied adventures all the way to the Hardy house.

"I'm sure that ghost business was meant to be something more than a prank," Frank stated.

"Right," his brother agreed. "I just had an idea, Frank. Maybe nobody was in the house, but he could have rigged up a tape recorder to make those sounds and a remote control to start it. What say we go back sometime and take a look?"

"I'm with you."

By this time the boys had turned into the long driveway of the Hardy home, a spacious, three-story clapboard house on the corner of High and Elm streets. The large two-story garage at the rear of an attractive garden had once been a barn.

Frank and Joe parked their motorcycles, unstrapped the telescope, and carried it to the back porch. As they entered the kitchen, they found their mother, a pretty, sweet-faced woman, with sparkling blue eyes, preparing supper.

"Hello, boys," she greeted them. "Did you have a good day? See any smugglers?"

They kissed her and Frank said, "We have a lot to tell you and Dad."

"He's in the study upstairs. I'll go up with you right away and we can talk while the chicken's roasting and the potatoes baking."

The three hurried up to the room where Mr. Hardy was busy looking in a large metal file in which he kept important records. The detective stopped his work and listened with rapt attention as Frank and Joe gave a detailed account of their adventures.

"We sure fell for that cry for help," Joe explained. "I'm sorry about the stolen eyepieces from the telescope."

"And I hope it wasn't damaged when I had my spill," Frank added. He smiled wanly. "You'll probably want to dismiss us from your detective force."

"Nothing of the kind," his father said. "But

now, let's discuss what you saw through the telescope. You said you spotted a man who climbed
down the ladder of a boat and went off in a smaller
one. Could he have been this same fellow who
calls himself Jones?"

"We couldn't identify him," Joe replied, "but
he might be."

Frank snapped his fingers. "Yes, and he could
be one of the smugglers."

"But who threw that hand grenade at him?"
Joe asked. "Not one of his own gang, surely. And
those guys in the other speedboat—they couldn't
have been Coast Guard men, even in disguise.
They wouldn't use grenades."

"Joe's right on the second point," Mr. Hardy
agreed. "But Jones may still be a smuggler."

"You mean he might have done something to
make his boss mad and the boss sent out a couple
of men to get him?" Joe asked.

The detective nodded. "If this theory is right,
and we can persuade Jones to talk before he either
rejoins the gang or starts trying to take revenge,
then we might get him to turn state's evidence."

The boys were excited. Both jumped from
their chairs and Joe cried out eagerly, "Let's go
talk to him right away! By morning he'll be
gone!"

CHAPTER V

Pretzel Pete

"JUST a minute!" Mrs. Hardy said to her sons. "How about supper?"

"We can eat when we come back from our interview with Jones," Joe answered. "Mother, he may decide to leave the farmhouse any time."

Despairingly Mrs. Hardy returned to her husband. "What do you think, Fenton?"

The detective gave his wife an understanding smile, then turned to Frank and Joe. "Didn't you say Jones was in pretty bad shape?"

"Yes, Dad," Frank replied.

"Then I doubt very much that he'll try to leave the Kanes' home before the time he set—tomorrow morning. I'm sure that it'll be safe for us to eat Mother's good supper and still see our man in time."

Joe subsided, and to make his mother feel better, said with a smile, "Guess I let this mystery go to my brain for a minute. As a matter of fact, I have an empty space inside of me big enough to eat two suppers!"

Mrs. Hardy tweaked an ear of her energetic son, just as she had frequently done ever since he was a small boy. He smiled at her affectionately, then asked what he could do to help with supper.

"Well, suppose you fill the water glasses and get milk for you and Frank," Mrs. Hardy said, as she and Joe went downstairs together.

At the table, as often happened at meals in the Hardy home, the conversation revolved around the mystery. Frank asked his father if he had made any progress on his part in the case concerning the smugglers.

"Very little," the detective replied. "Snattman is a slippery individual. He covers his tracks well. I did find this out, though. The law firm which is handling old Mr. Pollitt's affairs has had no luck in locating the nephew to whom the property was left."

"Mr. Kane said he'd heard Mr. Pollitt call his nephew a no-good," Frank put in.

"That's just the point," Mr. Hardy said. "The lawyers learned from the police that he's a hoodlum and is wanted for burglary."

Frank whistled. "That puts the nephew in a

bad spot, doesn't it? If he shows up to claim the property, he'll be nabbed as a criminal."

"Exactly," Mr. Hardy answered.

"What will become of the property?" Joe queried.

His father said he thought the executors might let the house remain vacant or they might possibly rent it. "They could do this on a month-to-month basis. This would give added income to the estate."

"Which wouldn't do the nephew much good if he were in jail," Mrs. Hardy put in.

"That would depend on how long his sentence was," her husband said. "He may not be a dangerous criminal. He may just have fallen into bad company and unwittingly become an accessory in some holdup or burglary."

"In that case," Frank remarked, "he may realize that he wouldn't have to stay in prison long. He may appear to claim the property, take his punishment, and then lead a normal, law-abiding life out at his uncle's place."

"Well, I sincerely hope so," Mr. Hardy replied. "The trouble is, so often when a young man joins a group of hoodlums or racketeers, he's blackmailed for the rest of his life, even though he tries to go straight." The detective smiled. "The best way to avoid such a situation is never to get into it!"

At this moment the phone rang and Frank went to answer it. "It's for you, Dad!" he called, coming back to the table.'

Mr. Hardy spent nearly fifteen minutes in conversation with the caller. In the meantime, the boys and Mrs. Hardy finished their supper. Then, while Mr. Hardy ate his dessert, he told his family a little about the information he had just received on the phone.

"More drugs have disappeared," he said tersely. "I'm positive now that Snattman is behind all this."

"Were the drugs stolen around here?" Frank asked.

"We don't know," his father answered. "A pharmaceutical house in the Midwest was expecting a shipment of rare drugs from India. When the package arrived, only half the order was there. It was evident that someone had cleverly opened the package, removed part of the shipment, and replaced the wrapping so neatly that neither the customs officials nor the post office was aware that the package had been tampered with."

"How were the drugs sent to this country?" Joe queried.

"They came by ship."

"To which port?"

"New York. But the ship did stop at Bayport."

"How long ago was this?"

"Nearly two months ago. It seems that the pharmaceutical house wasn't ready to use the drugs until now, so hadn't opened the package."

"Then," said Joe, "the drugs could have been removed right on the premises, and have had nothing to do with smugglers."

"You're right," Mr. Hardy agreed. "Each time drugs are reported missing, there's a new angle to the case. Although I'm convinced Snattman is back of it, how to prove this is really a stickler."

Mr. Hardy went on to say that the tip he had received about Snattman being in the Bayport area had been a very reliable one. He smiled. "I'll tell you all a little secret. I have a very good friend down on the waterfront. He picks up many kinds of information for me. His name is Pretzel Pete."

"Pretzel Pete!" Frank and Joe cried out. "What a name!"

"That's his nickname along the waterfront," Mr. Hardy told them. He laughed. "During the past few years I've munched on so many of the pretzels he sells, I think I'm his best customer."

By this time the boys' father had finished his dessert, and he suggested they leave at once for the Kane farmhouse. He brought his black sedan from the garage and the boys hopped in. It did not take long to cover the six miles to the place where Jones was spending the night.

"Why, the house is dark," Frank remarked, puzzled.

"Maybe everyone's asleep," Joe suggested.

"*This* early?" Frank protested.

Mr. Hardy continued on down the lane. There was no sign of anyone around the place. Frank remarked that perhaps the farmer and his wife had gone out for the evening. "But I'm surprised that they would leave Jones alone in his condition," he added.

"I'm quite sure they wouldn't," his father averred. "If they're asleep, I'm afraid we'll have to wake them."

He pulled up in front of the kitchen entrance. Frank was out of the car in an instant, the others followed. He rapped on the door. There was no answer.

"Let's try the front door," Joe suggested. "Maybe that has a knocker on it."

The boys walked around to the ocean side of the house. Although they banged loudly with the brass door knocker, there was still no response.

"The Kanes must have gone out," said Joe.

"But what about Jones? Surely he's here."

"And too weak to come to the door," Frank surmised. "But he *could* call out. I can't understand it."

The brothers returned to the back door and reported to their father. Then, as Joe rapped several more times without response, a sinking feeling came over the brothers.

"I guess Jones recovered fast and has gone," Joe said dejectedly. "We've goofed."

"Try the knob. The door may not be locked," Mr. Hardy ordered. From his tone the boys knew that he shared their fears.

Frank turned the knob and the door swung open. Mr. Hardy felt around for a light switch on the wall.

"We'll go in," he murmured. "If Jones is here we'll talk to him."

By this time the detective had found the switch. As the kitchen became flooded with light, the boys gasped, thunderstruck. On their previous visit they had been impressed by the neatness of the room. Now the place looked as though an earthquake had shaken it.

Pots and pans were scattered about the floor. The table was overturned. A chair lay upside down in a corner. Shattered bits of cups and saucers were strewn on the floor.

"What happened?" Frank exclaimed in bewilderment.

"There's been a fight—or a struggle of some kind," said Mr. Hardy. "Let's see what the rest of the house looks like."

The boys opened the door to the adjoining living room. Frank snapped on the wall switch.

The farmer and his wife were bound and gagged

There a horrifying sight met the Hardys' eyes.

The farmer and his wife, bound and gagged, were tied to chairs in the middle of the room!

Swiftly Frank, Joe, and their father rushed over to Mr. and Mrs. Kane. They had been tied with strong ropes and so well gagged that the couple had been unable to utter a sound. In a minute the Hardys had loosened the bonds and removed the gags.

"Thank goodness!" Mrs. Kane exclaimed with a sigh of relief, stretching her arms.

Her husband, spluttering with rage, rose from his chair and hurled the ropes to one side. "Those scoundrels!" he cried out.

Frank hastily introduced his father, then asked, "What happened?"

For several moments Mr. and Mrs. Kane were too upset to tell their story. But finally the farmer staggered over to the window and pointed down the shore road.

"They went that way!" he roared. "Follow them!"

"Who?"

"Those thugs who tied us up! They took Jones!"

CHAPTER VI

The Strange Message

"How long ago did those kidnapers leave?" Frank asked the Kanes quickly.

"About ten minutes," replied the farmer. "Maybe you can catch them if you hurry!"

"Come on, Dad!" Frank cried. "Let's go after them!"

Mr. Hardy needed no further urging. He and his sons ran out of the house and jumped into the car.

"That's rough stuff," Joe said to his father as they turned onto the shore road, "barging into a house, tying up the owners, and kidnaping a guy!"

"Yes," Mr. Hardy agreed. "It looks as though your friend Jones *is* mixed up in some kind of racket. Those men must have been pretty desperate to risk breaking into an occupied house."

The boys' father was able to follow the tracks of the car from the tread marks in the dusty road. But soon there were signs that another car had turned onto the shore road from a side lane and the trail became confused.

The Hardys passed the lane that led into the Pollitt place and continued on until they came to a hilltop. Here they could get a clear view of the road winding along the coast for several miles. There was no sign of a car.

"We've lost them, I guess," said Frank in disappointment, as Mr. Hardy brought the sedan to a stop.

"They had too much of a head start," Joe remarked. "If only we'd gotten to the farm sooner. Well, we may as well go back."

Mr. Hardy agreed, turned the car around, and once more the Hardys headed for the farm. On the way they discussed the mysterious kidnaping, and speculated on the identity of those responsible.

"I'll bet those men in the other motorboat saw us rescue Jones, or else they heard somehow that he'd been taken to the farmhouse," Joe surmised.

"If they *are* the kidnapers, I wonder what will happen to Jones now," Frank said gravely. "They tried to kill him once."

"Maybe they'll just hold him prisoner," Mr. Hardy stated thoughtfully. "They were probably afraid he'd tell all he knew, and couldn't afford to leave him at the farmhouse."

When they got back to the Kanes', they found the farmer and his wife somewhat recovered from their harrowing experience. Mrs. Kane was busy straightening up the kitchen.

"We couldn't catch them," Frank reported sadly.

"Well, those hoodlums had a high-powered car and they weren't wastin' any time. I could see 'em from the window as they went down the lane," the farmer remarked, frowning angrily at the recollection.

"Please tell us exactly what happened, Mr. Kane," Joe urged.

"Well, Mabel and I were here in the kitchen," the man began. "Mabel was washin' the supper dishes when this fellow came to the door. He was a tall chap with a long, thin face."

"He asked us if we were looking after the man that was almost drowned earlier," the farmer's wife took up the tale. "When we said we were, the fellow told us that Mr. Jones was his brother and he had come to take him away."

"I got suspicious," Mr. Kane broke in. "He didn't look nothin' like Jones. I asked him where he lived."

"At that," Mrs. Kane said, "he walked in the house with another fellow right at his heels.

They grabbed my husband. Henry put up an awful good fight but he was outnumbered. When I tried to help, a third man appeared from nowhere and held me back."

"They dragged us into the livin' room, tied us to those chairs, and put the gags in our mouths," the farmer continued. "Then we heard 'em goin' into Jones's room. Pretty soon they carried him out to a car where a fourth fellow was sittin' at the wheel."

"Did Jones put up a fight when they took him away?" Frank asked.

"He tried to. He hollered for help, but of course I couldn't do anythin' and he was too weak to struggle much."

"This whole affair is very peculiar," Mr. Hardy observed. "Perhaps Jones is mixed up in the smuggling going on around here. But who were those four men, I wonder?"

Mrs. Kane shook her head. "All I know is, we're sure glad you and your sons came out tonight. There's no telling how long we'd have been tied up before somebody found us!"

"We're glad, too, that we got here," Frank replied.

"You folks say your name's Hardy?" said the farmer. "Any relation to Fenton Hardy?"

"Right here." The detective smiled.

"Pleasure to know you!" exclaimed Kane

heartily, putting out his hand. "If anyone can get to the bottom of this business, you can."

"I'll certainly try," the boys' father promised.

The Hardys bade the farmer and his wife good-by. They promised to call again at the Kane farm as soon as they had any further information, and Mr. Kane, in turn, said he would notify them if he found any trace of Jones or his kidnapers.

When they returned home the boys followed their father into his study.

"What do you make of all this, Dad?" Joe asked.

Mr. Hardy sat down at his desk. He closed his eyes and leaned back in his chair a few moments without speaking.

"I have only one theory," he said at last. "The kidnapers probably are Snattman's friends. That means you boys may have uncovered the fact that there is a whole gang of smugglers around here."

The brothers were pleased with their progress. "What do we do next, Dad?" Joe asked eagerly.

"I want to evaluate this case from every angle," their father replied. "I'll think about it and talk to you later." With this the boys had to be content for the rest of the week end.

When the brothers came downstairs Monday morning, Mrs. Hardy was putting their breakfast on the table.

In answer to the boys' inquiries, she replied, "Your father went out early this morning in his car. He didn't say when he would return. But your dad didn't take a bag with him, so he'll probably be back today." Mrs. Hardy was accustomed to her husband's comings and goings at odd hours in connection with his profession and she had learned not to ask questions.

Frank and Joe were disappointed. They had looked forward to resuming a discussion of the case with their father.

"I guess we're left on our own again to try finding out something about those smugglers," Frank remarked, and Joe agreed.

Later, when they reached Bayport High School, the brothers saw Iola Morton standing on the front steps. With pretty, dark-haired Iola was her best friend Callie Shaw. Callie, a blond, vivacious, brown-eyed girl, was Frank's favorite among all the girls in his class.

"How are the ghost hunters this morning?" she asked with a mischievous smile. "Iola told me about your adventures on Saturday."

"Chet was really scared," Iola chimed in. "I think somebody played a good joke on all of you."

"Well, whoever it was had better return the telescope eyepieces and our motorcycle tools," Joe said defiantly.

But as the day wore on and none of their classmates teased them or brought up the subject, the Hardys became convinced that the "ghost" had been serious and not just playing pranks.

"It was no joke," Joe said to Frank on the way home. "If any of the fellows at school had done it, they'd have been kidding us plenty by now."

"Right," Frank agreed. "Joe, do you think the smugglers had anything to do with what happened at the Pollitt place?"

"That's a thought!" exclaimed Joe. "That house on the cliff would be a great hide-out. If the smugglers could make the house appear to be haunted, everyone would stay away."

"I wish Dad would get home, so we could take up this idea with him," Frank said thoughtfully.

But Mr. Hardy did not come home that day. He had often been away for varying lengths of time without sending word, but on this occasion, since he had not taken a bag, the boys felt uneasy.

"Let's not worry Mother about this," Frank said. "But if Dad's not back by Wednesday—at the latest—I think we should do some inquiring. Maybe Pretzel Pete will be able to help us."

Joe agreed. Wednesday was the start of their summer vacation and they could give full time to trying to locate their father.

On Tuesday afternoon the mystery of Mr. Hardy's absence took a strange turn. Frank and Joe came home from school to find their mother seated in the living room, carefully examining a note that she evidently just had received.

"Come here, boys," Mrs. Hardy said in an apprehensive tone. "Look at this and tell me what you think." She handed the note to Frank.

"What is it?" he asked quickly. "Word from Dad?"

"It's supposed to be."

The boys read the note. It was typed on a torn sheet of paper and the signature looked like Fenton Hardy's. It read:

I won't be home for several days. Don't worry. Fenton.

That was all. There was nothing to indicate where the detective was; nothing to show when the note had been written.

"When did you get this, Mother?" asked Frank.

"It came in the afternoon mail. It was addressed to me, and the envelope had a Bayport postmark."

"Why are you worried?" Joe asked. "At least we've heard from Dad."

"But I'm not sure he sent the note."

"What do you mean?"

"Your father and I have an agreement. Whenever he writes me, he puts a secret sign beneath his signature. Fenton was always afraid that someone would forge his name to a letter or note, and perhaps get papers or information that he shouldn't have."

Frank picked up the note again. "There's no sign here. Just Dad's signature."

"It *may* be his signature. If not, it's a very good forgery." Mrs. Hardy was plainly worried.

"If Dad didn't write this note," Joe asked, "who did and why?"

"Your father has many enemies—criminals whom he has been instrumental in sending to prison. If there has been foul play, the note might have been sent to keep us from being suspicious and delay any search."

"Foul play!" exclaimed Frank in alarm. "Then you think something has happened to Dad?"

CHAPTER VII

The Hidden Trail

Joe put an arm around his mother. "Frank and I will start a search for Dad first thing tomorrow," her son said reassuringly.

Next morning, as the boys were dressing, Joe asked, "Where shall we start, Frank?"

"Down at the waterfront. Let's try to find Pretzel Pete and ask him if Dad talked to him on Monday. He may give us a lead."

"Good idea."

The brothers reached the Bayport waterfront early. It was the scene of great activity. A tanker was unloading barrels of oil, and longshoremen were trundling them to waiting trucks.

At another dock a passenger ship was tied up. Porters hurried about, carrying luggage and packages to a line of taxicabs.

Many sailors strolled along the busy street.

Some stepped into restaurants, others into amusement galleries.

"I wonder where Pretzel Pete is," Frank mused. He and Joe had walked four blocks without catching sight of the man.

"Maybe he's not wearing his uniform," Joe surmised. "You know, the one Dad described."

"Let's turn and go back the other way beyond the tanker," Frank suggested.

The boys reversed their direction and made their way through the milling throng for six more blocks.

Suddenly Joe chuckled. "Here comes our man."

Strolling toward them and hawking the product he had for sale came a comical-looking individual. He wore a white cotton suit with a very loose-fitting coat. Around his neck was a vivid red silk handkerchief, embroidered with anchors.

The vendor's trousers had been narrowed at the cuff with bicycle clips to keep them from trailing on the ground, with the result that there was a continuous series of wrinkles from the edge of his coat to his ankles.

The man wore a white hat which came down to his ears. On the wide brown band the name *Pretzel Pete* was embroidered in white letters.

"Boy, that's some gear!" Frank murmured.

Pretzel Pete's garb was bizarre, but he had an

open, honest face. He stopped calling "Pretzels! Hot pretzels! Best in the land!" and smiled at the Hardys. He set down the large metal food warmer he carried. From the top of it rose three short aerials, each ringed with a dozen pretzels.

"You like them hot, or do you prefer them cold?" he asked the brothers.

Joe grinned. "If they're good, I can eat them any way." Then he whispered, "We're Mr. Fenton Hardy's sons. We'd like to talk to you."

At that moment a group of sailors brushed past. Pretzel Pete did not reply until they were out of earshot, then he said to the boys, "Come into this warehouse."

The brothers followed him down the street a short distance and through a doorway into an enormous room which at the moment was practically empty.

"You've brought a message from your pop?" the vendor asked.

Quickly Frank explained to him that their father seemed to be missing. "We thought you might have heard this."

"Yes, I did," Pretzel Pete answered. "But I didn't think nothing about it. I always thought detectives disappeared—sometimes in order to fool people they were after."

"They sometimes do," Joe told him. "But this time seems to be different. Dad said he often came down here to get information from you—because you always give him good tips—and we wondered if you had seen him lately."

"Yes."

"When?"

"Monday morning."

"Dad has been gone ever since."

"Hmm." The man frowned, picked up a pretzel from one of the aerials, and began to munch on it. "Help yourselves, fellows."

Frank and Joe each took one of the pretzels. They had just bitten into the delicious salted rings when Pete continued, "Now you got me worried. Your pop's a fine man and I wouldn't want to see anything happen to him. I'll tell you a place you might look for him."

Pretzel Pete said that he had picked up a bit of information that led him to think an East Indian sailor named Ali Singh might be engaged in some smuggling. The vendor did not know what ship he sailed on, but he understood that the man had come ashore for a secret meeting of some gang.

"This here meeting," Pretzel Pete explained, "was being held out in the country somewhere off the shore road. It was to be in a deserted farmhouse on Hillcrest something or other. I don't remember whether it was 'road' or 'street' or what."

"Was this last Monday?" Frank asked eagerly.

"Oh, no," the vendor answered. "This was about three weeks ago, but when I told your pop he seemed real interested and said he guessed he'd go out there and look around."

Joe broke in, "Dad must have thought the rest of the gang might be living there. Maybe they're holding him a prisoner!"

"Oh, I hope not," Pretzel Pete said worriedly. "But you fellows had better get right out there and take a look."

"We certainly will," Frank told the man.

The brothers thanked Pretzel Pete for the information, then hurried home. Mrs. Hardy was not there, so they did not have a chance to tell her about their plans.

"We'll leave a note," Frank decided and quickly wrote one.

Their hopes high, the brothers set off on their motorcycles on the search for their father. By now they were very familiar with the shore road but did not recall having seen any sign reading Hillcrest.

"Suppose it's not marked," said Joe. "We'll never find it."

Frank gripped his handle bars hard. "If Dad found it, we won't give up until we do."

The motorcycles chugged past side road after side road. The farther away from Bayport the boys went, the farther apart these roads became.

After a while they came to the Kanes' farmhouse and were tempted to stop to see if they might know where Hillcrest was. But just then, a short distance ahead, Joe saw a small car suddenly turn into the shore road. It seemed to have come right out of a clump of bushes and trees.

"Come on, Frank! Let's investigate that place."

The boys pushed ahead, hoping to speak to the driver of the car. But he shot down the road in the opposite direction at terrific speed. When Frank and Joe reached the place from which he had just emerged, they saw that it was a road, though hardly noticeable to anyone passing by.

"I'll take a look and see where it goes," Frank said, shutting off his motorcycle and walking up the grassy, rutted lane. Suddenly he called back, "We're in luck, Joe. I see a homemade sign on a tree. It says Hillcrest Road."

Frank returned to his brother and the boys trundled their machines up among the trees to hide them. Then they set off afoot along the almost impassable woods road.

"There aren't any tire tracks," Joe remarked. "I guess that fellow who drove out of here must have left his car down at the entrance."

Frank nodded, and then in a low tone suggested that they approach the deserted farmhouse very quietly, in case members of the gang were there.

"In fact, I think it might be better if we didn't stay on this road but went through the woods."

Joe agreed and silently the Hardys picked their way along among the trees and through the undergrowth. Five minutes later they came to a clearing in which stood a ramshackle farmhouse. It looked as if it had been abandoned for many years.

The young sleuths stood motionless, observing the run-down building intently. There was not a sound of activity either inside or outside the place. After the boys had waited several minutes, Frank decided to find out whether or not anyone was around. Picking up a large stone, he heaved it with precision aim at the front door. It struck with a resounding thud and dropped to the floor of the sagging porch.

Frank's action brought no response and finally he said to Joe, "I guess nobody's home. Let's look in."

"Right," Joe agreed. "And if Dad's a prisoner there, we'll rescue him!"

The boys walked across the clearing. There was no lock on the door, so they opened it and went inside. The place consisted of only four first-floor rooms. All were empty. A tiny cellar and a loft with a trap door reached by a ladder also proved to have no one in them.

"I don't know whether to be glad or sorry Dad's

not here," said Frank. "It could mean he escaped from the gang if he *was* caught by them and is safely in hiding, but can't send any word to us."

"Or it could mean he's still a captive somewhere else," Joe said. "Let's look around here for clues."

The boys made a systematic search of the place. They found only one item which might prove to be helpful. It was a torn piece of a turkish towel on which the word *Polo* appeared.

"This could have come from some country club where they play polo," Frank figured.

"Or some stable where polo ponies are kept," Joe suggested.

Puzzled, Frank put the scrap in his pocket and the brothers walked down Hillcrest Road. They brought their motorcycles from behind the trees and climbed aboard.

"What do you think we should do next?" Joe asked.

"See Police Chief Collig in Bayport," Frank replied. "I think we should show him this towel. Maybe he can identify it."

Half an hour later they were seated in the chief's office. The tall, burly man took a great interest in the Hardy boys and often worked with Fenton Hardy on his cases. Now Chief Collig gazed at the scrap of toweling for a full minute, then slapped his desk.

"I have it!" he exclaimed. "That's a piece of towel from the *Marco Polo!*"

"What's that?"

"A passenger ship that ties up here once in a while."

Frank and Joe actually jumped in their chairs. Their thoughts went racing to Ali Singh, smugglers, a gang at the deserted farmhouse!

At that moment Chief Collig's phone rang. The Hardys waited politely as he answered, hoping to discuss these new developments with him. But suddenly he put down the instrument, jumped up, and said:

"Emergency, fellows. Have to leave right away!" With that he rushed out of his office.

Frank and Joe arose and disappointedly left headquarters. Returning home, they reported everything to their mother, but upon seeing how forlorn she looked, Frank said hopefully, "That note you received with Dad's name on it *could* have been on the level."

Mrs. Hardy shook her head. "Fenton wouldn't forget the secret sign. I just know he wouldn't."

Word quickly spread through Bayport that the famous Fenton Hardy had disappeared. Early the next morning a thick-set, broad-shouldered young man presented himself at the front door of the Hardy home and said he had something to tell them. Mrs. Hardy invited him to step inside and he stood in the hall, nervously twisting a cap in his hands. As Frank and Joe appeared, the man introduced himself as Sam Bates.

"I'm a truck driver," he told them. "The reason I came around to see you is because I heard you were lookin' for Mr. Hardy. I might be able to help you."

CHAPTER VIII

A Cap on a Peg

"You've seen my father?" Frank asked the truck driver.

"Well, I did see him on Monday," Sam said slowly, "but I don't know where he is now."

"Come in and sit down," Frank urged. "Tell us everything you know."

The four walked to the living room and Mr. Bates sat down uneasily in a large chair.

"Where did you see Mr. Hardy?" Mrs. Hardy asked eagerly.

But Sam Bates was not to be hurried. "I'm a truck driver, see?" he said. "Mostly I drive in Bayport but sometimes I have a run to another town. That's how I come to be out there that mornin'."

"Out where?"

"Along the shore road. I'm sure it was Monday,

because when I came home for supper my wife had been doin' the washin' and she only does that on Monday."

"That was the day Dad left!" Joe exclaimed.

"Well, please go on with the story," Frank prodded Sam Bates. "Where did you see him?"

The truck driver explained that his employer had sent him to a town down the coast to deliver some furniture. "I was about half a mile from the old Pollitt place when I saw a man walkin' along the road. I waved to him, like I always do to people in the country, and then I see it's Mr. Hardy."

"You know my father?" Frank asked.

"Only from his pictures. But I'm sure it was him."

"Dad left here in a sedan," Joe spoke up. "Did you see one around?"

"No, I didn't."

"What was this man wearing?" Mrs. Hardy asked.

"Well, let's see. Dark-brown trousers and a brown-and-black plaid sport jacket. He wasn't wearin' a hat, but I think he had a brown cap in one hand."

Mrs. Hardy's face went white. "Yes, that was my husband." After a moment she added, "Can you tell us anything more?"

"I'm afraid not, ma'am," the trucker said. "You

see, I was in kind of a hurry that mornin', so I didn't notice nothin' else." He arose to leave.

"We certainly thank you for coming to tell us, Mr. Bates," Mrs. Hardy said.

"Yes, you've given us a valuable lead," Frank added. "Now we'll know where to look for Dad."

"I sure hope he shows up," the driver said, walking toward the door. "Let me know if I can help any."

When the man had left, Joe turned to Frank, puzzled. "Do you suppose Dad hid his car and was walking to the Pollitt house? If so, why?"

"Maybe he picked up a clue at that deserted farmhouse on Hillcrest Road," Frank suggested, "and it led to the old Pollitt place. If he left his car somewhere, he must have been planning to investigate the haunted house without being seen."

"Something must have happened to him!" Joe cried out. "Frank, I'll bet he went to Pollitt's and that fake ghost got him. Let's go look for Dad right away!"

But Mrs. Hardy broke in. Her expression was firm. "I don't want you boys to go to that house alone. Maybe you'd just better notify the police and let them make a search."

The brothers looked at each other. Finally Frank, realizing how alarmed she was, said, "Mother, it's possible Dad is there spying on some activities offshore and he's all right but can't leave to phone you. The Pollitt line must have been disconnected. If Joe and I go out there and find him we can bring back a report."

Mrs. Hardy gave a wan smile. "You're very convincing, Frank, when you put it that way. All right. I'll give my permission, but you mustn't go alone."

"Why not, Mother? We can look out for ourselves," Joe insisted.

"Get some of the boys to go with you. There's safety in numbers," his mother said.

The boys agreed to this plan and got busy on the telephone rounding up their pals. Chet Morton and Biff Hooper agreed to go, and they suggested asking Tony Prito and Phil Cohen, two more of the Hardys' friends at Bayport High. Phil owned a motorcycle. He and Tony said they could go along.

Shortly after lunch the group set out. Chet rode with Frank, Biff with Joe, and Tony with Phil. The three motorcycles went out of Bayport, past the Tower Mansion, and along the shore road.

They passed the Kane farmhouse, Hillcrest Road, and at last came in sight of the steep cliff rising from Barmet Bay and crowned by the rambling frame house where Felix Pollitt had lived. All this time they had watched carefully for a sign of Mr. Hardy's car, but found none.

"Your dad hid it well," Chet remarked.

"It's possible someone stole it," Frank told him.

As the boys came closer to the Pollitt property, Phil said to Tony, "Lonely looking place, isn't it?"

"Sure is. Good haunt for a ghost."

When they were still some distance from the lane, Frank, in the lead, brought his motorcycle to a stop and signaled the other two drivers to do likewise.

"What's the matter?" Chet asked.

"We'd better sneak up on the place quietly. If we go any farther and the ghost is there, he'll hear the motorcycles. I vote we leave them here under the trees and go the rest of the way on foot."

The boys hid their machines in a clump of bushes beside the road, and then the six searchers went on toward the lane.

"We'll separate here," Frank decided. "Three of us take one side of the lane and the rest the other side. Keep to the bushes as much as possible, and when we get near the house, lay low for a while and watch the place. When I whistle, you can come out of the bushes and go up to the house."

"That's a good idea," Joe agreed. "Biff, Tony, and I will take the left side of the road."

"Okay."

The boys entered the weeds and undergrowth on either side of the lane. In a few minutes they were lost to view and only an occasional snapping and crackling of branches indicated their presence. The six sleuths crept forward, keeping well in from the lane. After about ten minutes Frank raised his hand as a warning to Chet and Phil. He had caught a glimpse of the house through the dense thicket.

They went on cautiously until they reached the edge of the bushes. From behind the screen of leaves they looked toward the old building. An expression of surprise crossed Frank's face.

"Someone's living here!" he exclaimed in astonishment.

From where the boys stood they hardly recognized the old place. Weeds that had filled the flower beds on their last visit had been completely cleared away. Leaves and twigs had been raked up and the grass cut.

A similar change had been wrought in the house. The hanging shutters had been put in place and the broken library window glass replaced.

"What do you suppose has happened?" Chet whispered.

Frank was puzzled. "Let's wait a minute before we go any farther."

The boys remained at the edge of the bushes, watching the place. A short time later a woman came out of the house carrying a basket of clothes. She walked over to a clothesline stretched between two trees and began to hang up the laundry.

Shortly afterward a man came out, and strode across the yard to a shed where he started filling a basket with logs.

The boys looked at one another in bewilderment. They had expected to find the same sinister and deserted place they had visited previously. Instead, here was a scene of domestic tranquillity.

"There's not much use in our hiding any longer," Frank whispered. "Let's go out and question these people." He gave the prearranged whistle.

The other three boys appeared, and the entire group walked boldly up the lane and across the yard. The man in the woodshed saw them first and straightened up, staring at them with an expression of annoyance. The woman at the clothesline heard their footsteps and turned to face them, her hands on her hips. Her gaunt face wore an unpleasant scowl.

"What do you want?" demanded the man, emerging from the shed.

He was short and thin with close-cropped hair, and he needed a shave. His complexion was swarthy, his eyes narrow under coarse, black brows.

At the same time another man came out of the kitchen and stood on the steps. He was stout and red-haired with a scraggly mustache.

"Yeah, who are you?" he asked.

"We didn't know anyone was living here," Frank explained, edging over to the kitchen door. He wanted to get a look inside the house if possible.

"Well, we're livin' here now," said the red-haired man, "and we don't like snoopers."

"We're not snooping," Frank declared. "We are looking for a man who has disappeared from Bayport."

"Humph!" grunted the woman.

"Why do you think he's around here?" the thin man put in.

"He was last seen in this neighborhood."

"What does he look like?"

"Tall and dark. He was wearing a brown suit and sports jacket and cap."

"There hasn't been anybody around here since we rented this place and moved in," the red-haired man said gruffly.

There seemed to be no prospect of gaining information from the unpleasant trio, so the boys started to leave. But Frank had reached the kitchen door. As he glanced in he gave a start. Hanging on a peg was a brown sports cap!

It looked exactly like the one his father owned, and which he had worn the morning that he had disappeared.

CHAPTER IX

Plan of Attack

"I'M very thirsty," Frank said quickly to the occupants of the Pollitt house. "May I have a drink?"

The red-haired man and the woman looked at each other. They obviously wished to get rid of their visitors as soon as possible. But they could not refuse such a reasonable request.

"Come into the kitchen," said the man grudgingly.

Frank followed him through the door. As he passed the cap he took a good look at it. It *was* his father's, and there were stains on it which looked like blood!

The redheaded man pointed to a sink on the other side of the room. On it stood a plastic cup. "Help yourself," he said gruffly.

Frank went across the room and ran some water from the faucet. As he raised the cup to his lips, his mind was racing. On his way out he glanced again at the peg.

The cap was gone!

Frank gave no sign that he had noticed anything amiss. He walked out into the yard and joined the other five boys.

"I guess we may as well be going," he said nonchalantly.

"You might as well," snapped the woman. "There's no stranger around here, I tell you."

The boys started off down the lane. When they were out of sight of the house, Frank stopped and turned to his companions.

"Do you know what I saw in that kitchen?" he asked tensely.

"What?"

"Dad's cap hanging on a peg!"

"Then he *has* been there!" cried Joe. "They were lying!"

"Yes," Frank continued, "and—and there were bloodstains on the cap!"

"Bloodstains!" Joe exclaimed. "That means he *must* be in trouble. Frank, we've got to go back!"

"We sure do!" his brother agreed. "But I wanted to tell you all about it first."

"What do you think we should do?" Chet asked.

"I'll ask those people in the house about the cap and force a showdown," Frank declared tersely. "We've got to find out where Dad is!"

Resolutely the boys started back to the Pollitt house. When they reached the yard they found the two men and the woman standing by the shed talking earnestly. The woman caught sight of them and spoke warningly to the red-haired man.

"What do you want now?" he demanded, advancing toward the boys.

"We want to know about that sports cap in the kitchen," said Frank firmly.

"What cap? There's no cap in there."

"There isn't now—but there was. It was hanging on a peg when I went in for a drink."

"I don't know anythin' about no cap," persisted the man.

"Perhaps we'd better ask the police to look around," Joe suggested.

The redhead glanced meaningly at the woman. The other man stepped forward. "I know the cap this boy means," he said. "It's mine. What about it?"

"It isn't yours and you know it," Frank declared. "That cap belongs to the man we're looking for."

"I tell you it *is* my cap!" snapped the swarthy man, showing his yellowed teeth in a snarl. "Don't tell me I'm lyin'."

The red-haired man intervened. "You're mistaken, Klein," he said. "I know the cap they mean now. It's the one I found on the road a few days ago."

"Guess you're right, Red," Klein conceded hastily.

"You found it?" asked Frank incredulously.

"Sure, I found it. A brown cap with bloodstains on it."

"That's the one. But why did you hide it when I went into the kitchen?"

"Well, to tell the truth, them bloodstains made me nervous. I didn't know but what there might be some trouble come of it, so I thought I'd better keep that cap out of sight."

"Where did you find it?" Joe asked.

"About a mile from here."

"On the shore road?"

"Yes. It was lyin' right in the middle of the road."

"When was this?"

"A couple of days ago—just after we moved in here."

"Let's see the cap," Chet Morton suggested. "We want to make sure of this."

As Red moved reluctantly toward the kitchen, the woman sniffed. "I don't see why you're makin' all this fuss about an old cap," she said. "Comin' around here disturbin' honest folks."

"We're sorry if we're bothering you," said Joe, "but this is a very serious matter."

Red came out of the house holding the cap. He tossed it to Frank.

The boy turned back the inside flap and there he found what he was looking for—the initials F. H. printed in gold on the leather band.

"It's Dad's cap all right."

"I don't like the look of those bloodstains," said Joe in a low voice. "He must have been badly hurt."

"Are you sure you found this on the road?" Frank asked, still suspicious.

"You don't think I'd lie about it, do you?" Red answered belligerently.

"I can't contradict you, but I'm going to turn this over to the police," Frank told him. "If you know anything more about it, you'd better speak up now."

"He doesn't know anything about it," shrilled the woman angrily. "Go away and don't bother us. Didn't he tell you he found the cap on the road? I told him to burn up the dirty thing. But he wanted to have it cleaned and wear it."

The boys turned away, Frank still holding the cap. "Come on, fellows," he said. "Let's get out of here."

As the boys started down the lane they cast a last glance back at the yard. The woman and the two men were standing just where the young sleuths had left them. The woman was motionless, her hands on her hips. Red was standing with his arms folded, and Klein, the swarthy man, was lean-

"He doesn't know anything about the cap,"
the woman shrilled

ing against a tree. All three were gazing intently and silently after the departing boys.

"I'm sure that those people know more about Dad's cap than they're telling," Frank said grimly, as the boys mounted their motorcycles and rode back toward Bayport.

"What are you planning to do next?" Phil asked as he pulled his machine alongside Frank's.

"I'm going right to Chief Collig and tell him the whole story."

"Okay, we're with you!"

The boys rode directly to police headquarters and left their motorcycles in the parking lot. Chief Collig looked up as his six visitors were ushered into his office.

"Well," he said heartily, "this is quite a delegation! What can I do for you?"

As Frank and Joe took turns, with an occasional graphic illustration from one of the other boys, they told the full story and showed him the blood-stained cap.

Chief Collig looked grave. "I don't like the sound of this at all," he said finally. "We must find your father at once! This cap is a good clue." Then he went on, "Of course you realize that the area where the Pollitt house is located is outside the limits of Bayport, so my men can't go there. But I'll get in touch with Captain Ryder of the State Police at once, so he can assign men to the case."

The boys thanked the chief for his help and left. Chet, Tony, Biff, and Phil went their separate ways while Frank and Joe turned toward home. They decided not to upset their mother about the bloodstained cap, but merely tell her that the State Police would take over the search for her husband.

"I still think there's some connection between Dad's disappearance and the smuggling outfit and the house on the cliff," Frank declared.

"What I've been wondering," said Joe, "is where those two motorboats came from that day Jones was attacked. We didn't see them out in the ocean earlier—at least not both of them."

"That's right. They could have come right out from under the cliff."

"You mean, Frank, there might be a secret harbor in there?"

"Might be. Here's the way it could work. Dad suspects smugglers are operating in this territory from a base that he has been unable to find." Frank spread his arms. "The base is the old Pollitt place! What more do you want?"

"But the house is on top of a *cliff*."

"There could be a secret passage from the house to a hidden harbor at the foot of the cliff."

"Good night, Frank, it sure sounds reasonable!"

"And perhaps that explains why the kidnapers got away with Jones so quickly on Saturday. If

they left the Kane farmhouse just a little while before we did, we should have been able to get within
sight of their car. But we didn't."

"You mean they turned in at the Pollitt place?"

"Why not? Probably Jones is hidden there right
now."

"And maybe Dad too," Joe cried out excitedly.

"That's right. I'm against just sitting and waiting for the state troopers to find him. How about
asking Tony if he will lend us his motorboat, so
we can investigate the foot of that cliff?"

"I get you!" Joe agreed enthusiastically. "And if
we pick up any information we can turn it over to
the State Police and they can raid the Pollitt
place!"

CHAPTER X

A Watery Tunnel

WHEN the brothers arrived home Frank and Joe assured their mother that the State Police would soon find Mr. Hardy. Some of the anxiety left her face as she listened to her sons' reassuring words.

When she went to the kitchen to start preparations for supper, the boys went to phone Tony Prito. After Frank explained their plan to him, he agreed at once to let them use the *Napoli*, provided they took him along.

"I wouldn't miss it for anything," he said. "But I can't go until afternoon. Have to do some work for my dad in the morning. I'll meet you at the boathouse at two o'clock."

"Swell, Tony. I have a job of my own in the morning."

Chet called a few minutes later. As Frank finished telling him about the plan, he whistled.

"You fellows have got your nerve all right. But count me in, will you? I started this thing with you and I'd like to finish it. We've got to find your father!"

After Chet had said good-by, Joe asked his brother, "What's on for the morning?"

"I want to go down to the waterfront and talk to Pretzel Pete again. He might have another clue. Also, I want to find out when the *Marco Polo* is due back here."

Joe nodded. "I get it. You think something may be going on then?"

"Right. And if we can find Dad and lead the Coast Guard to the smugglers before the boat docks—"

"Brother, that's a big order."

By nine o'clock the following morning Frank and Joe were down at the Bayport docks. Pretzel Pete was not in evidence.

"We'd better be cagey about asking when the *Marco Polo's* coming in," Frank cautioned. "The smugglers probably have spies around here and we'd sure be targets."

Acting as if there were no problems on their minds, Frank and Joe strolled along whistling. Once they joined a group of people who were watching a sidewalk merchant. The man was demonstrating little jumping animals. Frank and Joe laughed as they bought a monkey and a kangaroo. "Iola and Callie will get a kick out of these," Joe predicted.

"Say, Frank, here comes Pretzel Pete now!" Joe whispered.

The Hardys went up the street, saying in a loud voice in case anyone was listening, that they were hungry and glad to see Pete.

"Nobody can make pretzels like yours," Joe exclaimed. "Give me a dozen. Two for my mouth and ten for my pockets."

As Pretzel Pete laughed and pulled out a cellophane bag to fill the order, Frank said in a whisper, "Heard anything new?"

"Not a thing, son." Pete could talk without moving his lips. "But I may know something tomorrow."

"How come?"

"The *Marco Polo's* docking real early—five A.M. I heard Ali Singh is one of the crew. I'll try to get a line on him."

"Great! We'll be seeing you."

The boys moved off, and to avoid arousing any suspicion as to why they were in the area, headed for a famous fish market.

"Mother will be surprised to see our morning's catch," Joe said with a grin as he picked out a large bluefish.

The brothers did not discuss the exciting information Pretzel Pete had given them until they were in the safety of their own home. Then Joe burst out, "Frank, if the *Marco Polo* gets offshore during the night, it'll have to lay outside until it's time to dock!"

"And that'll give those smugglers a real break in picking up the stolen drugs!" Frank added. "Maybe we should pass along our suspicions to the Coast Guard."

"Not yet," Joe objected. "All we have to go on is Pretzel Pete's statements about Ali Singh. Maybe we'll learn more this afternoon and then we can report it."

"I guess you're right," Frank concluded. "If those smugglers are holding Dad, and find out that we've tipped off the Coast Guard, they'll certainly harm him."

"You have a point."

When Frank and Joe reached the Prito boathouse at two o'clock, Tony and Chet were already there. Tony was tuning up the motor, which purred evenly.

"No word from your dad yet?" Tony asked. The Hardys shook their heads as they stepped aboard.

The *Napoli* was a rangy, powerful craft with graceful lines and was the pride of Tony's life. The boat moved slowly out into the waters of Barmet Bay and then gathered speed as it headed toward the ocean.

"Rough water," Frank remarked as breaking

swells hit the hull. Salt spray dashed over the bow of the *Napoli* as it plunged on through the whitecaps. Bayport soon became a speck nestled at the curve of the horseshoe-shaped body of water. Reaching the ocean, Tony turned north. The boys could see the white line of the shore road rising and falling along the coast. Soon they passed the Kane farm. Two miles farther on they came within sight of the cliff upon which the Pollitt house stood. It looked stark and forbidding above the rocks, its roof and chimneys silhouetted against the sky.

"Pretty steep cliff," Tony observed. "I can't see how anyone could make his way up and down that slope to get to the house."

"That's probably why nobody has suspected the place of being a smuggling base," Frank replied. "But perhaps when we look around we'll find an answer."

Tony steered the boat closer toward the shore, so that it would not be visible from the Pollitt grounds. Then he slackened speed in order that the sound of the engine would be less noticeable, and the craft made its way toward the bottom of the cliff.

There were currents here that demanded skillful navigation, but Tony brought the *Napoli* through them easily, and at last the boat was chugging along close to the face of the cliff.

The boys eagerly scanned the formidable wall of rock. It was scarred and seamed and the base had been eaten away by the incessant battering of waves. There was no indication of a path.

Suddenly Tony turned the wheel sharply. The *Napoli* swerved swiftly to one side. He gave it power and the craft leaped forward with a roar.

"What's the matter?" Frank asked in alarm.

Tony gazed straight ahead, tense and alert. Another shift of the wheel and the *Napoli* swerved again.

Then Chet and the Hardys saw the danger. There were rocks at the base of the cliff. One of them, black and sharp, like an ugly tooth, jutted out of the water almost at the boat's side. Only Tony's quick eye had saved the *Napoli* from hitting it!

They had blundered into a veritable maze of reefs which extended for several yards ahead. Tony's passengers held their breaths. It seemed impossible that they could run the gantlet of those rocks without tearing out the bottom of the craft.

But luck was with them. The *Napoli* dodged the last dangerous rock, and shot forward into open water.

Tony sank back with a sigh of relief. "Whew, that was close!" he exclaimed. "I didn't see those rocks until we were right on top of them. If we'd ever struck one of them we'd have been goners."

Frank, Joe, and Chet nodded in solemn agreement. Then, suddenly, Frank cried out, "Turn back! I think I saw an opening!"

Tony swung the boat around. The opening which Frank had spotted was a long, narrow tunnel. It led right through the cliff!

"This might be the secret entrance!" Joe exclaimed.

"I think it's large enough for the boat to go through," said Tony. "Want me to try it?"

Frank nodded tensely. "Go ahead."

The *Napoli* slipped through the opening and in a few moments came out into a pond of considerable extent. The boys looked about expectantly. Steep slopes covered with scraggly trees and bushes reached to the water's edge. But there was no path or indication that any human being ever came down to the pond.

Suddenly Frank gave a gasp of surprise and said, "Look to my right, fellows."

Among the thickets at the base of the steepest slope stood a man. He was very tall, his face was weather-beaten, and his lips thin and cruel. He stood quietly, looking at the boys without a shadow of expression on his sinister face.

Upon realizing he had been observed, the man shouted, "Get out of here!"

Tony throttled the engine and Frank called, "We aren't doing any harm."

"I said 'Get out!' This is private property."

The boys hesitated. Instantly the man, as though to back up his commands, reached significantly toward the holster of a revolver.

"Turn that boat around and beat it!" he snapped. "And don't ever come back here! Not if you know what's good for you."

The boys realized that nothing would be gained by argument. Tony slowly brought the boat around.

"Okay," Joe called cheerfully.

The stranger did not reply. He stood gazing fixedly after them, his left hand pointing to the exit, his right tapping the gun holster, as the motorboat made its way out through the tunnel.

"Looks as if he didn't want us around," remarked Tony facetiously, as soon as the *Napoli* was in open water again.

"He sure didn't!" Frank exclaimed. "I expected him to start popping that gun at any moment!"

"He must have an important reason. Who and what do you suppose he is?" Tony asked in bewilderment.

"Fellows," Frank said thoughtfully, "I think that man might have been Snattman!"

CHAPTER XI

Cliff Watchers

"Frank!" Joe exclaimed. "I think you've hit it! That man had no reason to act the way he did unless he's covering up something."

"Something like smuggling, you mean," said Chet. "He must be Snattman or one of his gang."

"And," Frank went on, "the fact that he was in that cove must mean he has some connection with the house on the cliff."

"Snattman, king of the smugglers!" Tony whistled. "You guys really get in some interesting situations!"

"I'll bet that he's one of the fellows who chased Jones that day in the motorboat," Joe cried.

"And tried to kill him," Frank continued the thought.

"Let's get away from here!" Chet urged.

"Why should we go now?" Frank demanded.

"We've stumbled on something important. That hidden pond may be the smugglers' base."

"But if they use the house how do they get to it?" Tony asked. "Those cliffs up from the pond were mighty steep."

"There must be some other way that we couldn't see," Joe said. "What say we hang around here for a while and find out what we can?"

Tony caught the Hardys' enthusiasm and agreed to keep the motorboat in the vicinity of the cliff.

"That fellow may be keeping his eye on us and we don't want him to know that we're watching the place," Frank observed. "Let's run back to the bay and cruise up and down a while, then return."

Chet sighed. "I'm glad none of you argued with that armed man."

"Right," Joe replied. "As it is, he must think we were simply out for a cruise and wandered into that tunnel by mistake."

"Yes," his brother agreed. "If he'd known we're hunting for Dad, he might have acted very differently."

In the late afternoon Tony took the *Napoli* back to the suspected shore spot. Keeping well out from the breaking waves, he cruised along the cliff. The boys kept a sharp eye on the location of the tunnel. As the boat passed it they were just able to distinguish the narrow opening in the rocks.

"I won't be able to go in there after a while," Tony remarked. "The tide's coming in. At high tide I'll bet that tunnel is filled with water."

Suddenly Tony swung his craft so hard to the right that the other boys lost their balance.

"Sorry, fellows," he said. "Saw a log—oh!"

He shut off his engine in a flash and leaned over the gunwale. His companions picked themselves up and asked what had happened.

"Propeller started to foul up with some wire on that log." Tony began to peel off his clothes. "Get me some pliers, will you?"

Frank opened a locker and found a pair. Taking them, Tony dived overboard. A minute later he reappeared and climbed in. "I'm lucky," he said. "Just plain lucky. Two seconds more and all that wire would have been wound around the prop and the log would have knocked it off."

"Good night!" Chet exclaimed. "It would have been a long swim home."

Joe slapped Tony on the back. "Good work, boy. I'd hate to see the *Napoli* out of commission."

Chet and Frank hauled the log aboard, so it would not damage any other craft. "This is a fence post with barbed wire!" Chet said. "Wowee! It's good you spotted that log, Tony."

Tony dressed, then started the engine. He

cruised around for more than an hour, but the boys saw no sign of life about the base of the cliff. They could see the Pollitt house, but to their amazement no lights appeared in it as twilight came.

"How much longer do you think we should stay out here?" Chet asked. "I'm getting hungry."

"I have a few pretzels and a candy bar, but that's not much for four of us," Joe remarked.

"Aha!" crowed Tony. "I have a surprise for you! I stowed away a little food before we took off." With that he pulled a paper bag from the locker and passed each boy a large sandwich, a piece of chocolate cake, and a bottle of lemon soda.

"You deserve a medal," Chet remarked as he bit into a layer of ham and cheese.

"You sure do!" Frank agreed. "I think we should stay right here for a while and watch. It's my guess the smugglers will be on the job tonight. Don't forget that the *Marco Polo* is docking tomorrow morning."

"I get it," said Chet. "If she lays offshore or steams in slowly, it'll give Ali Singh a chance to drop the stolen drugs overboard to Snattman."

"Correct," said Frank.

Tony looked intently at the Hardys. "Is it your idea to keep Snattman from meeting Ali Singh? But what about your father? I thought we came out here to get a line on how to rescue him."

The brothers exchanged glances, then Joe said, "Of course that's our main purpose, but we hope that we can do both."

Twilight deepened into darkness and lights could be seen here and there through the haze. The cliff was only a black smudge and the house above was still unlighted.

Suddenly the boys heard a muffled sound. Tony slowed the *Napoli* and they listened intently.

"Another motorboat," Tony whispered.

The sound seemed to come from near the cliff. Straining their eyes in that direction, the four were at last able to distinguish a faint moving light.

"Can you head over that way, Tony?" Frank asked in a low voice. "And could you take a chance on turning off our lights?"

"Sure. Here goes. The wind's blowing from the land, so our engine won't be heard from the shore."

The boys were tense with excitement as the *Napoli* moved slowly toward the light. As the boat crept nearer the cliff, they could barely distinguish the outline of a motorboat. The craft seemed to be making its way carefully out of the very face of the cliff.

"It must have come from that tunnel!" Joe whispered to Frank.

"Yes."

The *Napoli* went closer, in imminent danger of being discovered or of being washed ashore onto the rocks. Finally the other boat slowed to a crawl. Then came the faint clatter of oars and low voices. The motorboat had evidently met a rowboat.

The next moment, with an abrupt roar, the motorboat turned and raced out to sea at an ever-increasing rate of speed.

"Where can it be going?" said Tony, in amazement. "Out to meet the *Marco Polo?*"

"Probably," Frank replied, "and we'd never catch it. I wonder where the rowboat's going."

The four boys waited in silence for several minutes. Then the rattle of oars came again. This time the sound was closer. The rowboat was coming toward them!

"What'll we do now?" Tony asked.

"Turn off your engine," Frank whispered. Tony complied.

Through the gloom suddenly came snatches of conversation from the rowboat. "—a hundred pounds—" they heard a man say harshly, and then the rest of the sentence was lost. There was a lengthy murmur of voices, then, "I don't know. It's risky—"

The wind died down just then and two voices could be heard distinctly. "Ali Singh's share—" one man was saying.

"That's right. We can't forget him," the gruff voice replied.

"I hope they get away all right."

"What are you worryin' about? Of course they'll get away."

"We've been spotted, you know."

"It's all your imagination. Nobody suspects."

"Those boys at the house—"

"Just dumb kids. If they come nosin' around again, we'll knock 'em on the head."

"I don't like this rough stuff. It's dangerous."

"We've got to do it or we'll end up in the pen. What's the matter with you tonight? You're nervous."

"I'm worried. I've got a hunch we'd better clear out of here."

"Clear out!" replied the other contemptuously. "Are you crazy? Why, this place is as safe as a church." The man laughed sardonically. "Haven't we got all the squealers locked up? And tonight we make the big cleanup and get away."

"Well, maybe you're right," said the first man doubtfully. "But still—"

His voice died away as the boat entered the tunnel.

Joe grabbed Frank's arm. "Did you hear that? All the squealers locked up? I'll bet Dad's one of them and he's a prisoner somewhere around here."

"And this is the hide-out of Snattman and

the other smugglers he was after," Frank added.

"I don't like this," Chet spoke up. "Let's leave here and get the police."

Frank shook his head. "It would take so long we might goof the whole thing. Tell you what. Joe and I will follow that rowboat through the tunnel!"

"How?"

"On foot or swim. I don't think it's deep along the edges."

"You mean Chet and I will wait here?" Tony asked.

"No," Frank answered. "You two beat it back to Bayport and notify the Coast Guard. Tell them we're on the track of smugglers and ask them to send some men here."

"And tell them our suspicions about Ali Singh and the *Marco Polo*," Joe added. "They can radio the captain to keep an eye on him."

"Okay," said Tony. "I'll do that. First I'll put you ashore."

"Don't go too close or you'll hit those rocks and wreck the boat," Frank warned. "Joe and I can swim to shore. Then we'll work around into the tunnel and see what we can find. If we do discover anything, we'll wait at the entrance and show the men from the Coast Guard where to go when they get here."

Tony edged the boat in as close to the dark

shore as he dared without lights. Quickly Frank and Joe took off their slacks, T shirts, sweaters, and sneakers. They rolled them up, and with twine which Tony provided, tied the bundles on top of their heads. Then they slipped over the side into the water. The *Napoli* sped off.

Frank and Joe were only a few yards from the rocks and after a short swim emerged on the mainland.

"Well, here goes!" Joe whispered, heading for the tunnel.

CHAPTER XII

The Secret Passage

CAUTIOUSLY Frank and Joe made their way across the slippery rocks. Suddenly there was a loud splash as Joe lost his footing.

"Are you all right?" Frank whispered, as he came up to where his brother was standing in the shallow water at the edge of the cliff.

"Yes. For a moment I sure thought I'd sprained my ankle," Joe replied tensely, "but it seems to be okay now."

"Give me your hand," Frank whispered and quickly pulled Joe back onto the rocks.

The Hardys had landed at a point some twenty-five yards from the tunnel opening, but the climb over the treacherous rocks was so difficult that the distance seemed much longer. It was very dark in the shadow of the steep cliff. The waves breaking against the rocks had a lonely and foreboding sound.

"Good night!" Joe muttered. "Aren't we ever coming to that tunnel?"

"Take it easy," Frank advised. "It can't be much farther."

"I hope Tony and Chet will hurry back with help," Joe said. "This is a ticklish job."

"If anybody's on guard here, we'll certainly be at a disadvantage," Frank remarked in a barely audible tone. "Watch out!"

By this time they had reached the entrance to the tunnel. After a few cautious steps they discovered that the narrow piece of land between the water and the base of the cliff was covered by a thick growth of bushes.

Frank turned to Joe. "If we try to walk through all that stuff," he whispered, "we're sure to be heard. That is, if those men are in here some place."

Joe grunted in agreement. "What shall we do?"

Tentatively, Frank put one foot into the water from the rock on which he was standing.

"It isn't deep," he said. "I guess we can wade through."

The boys hugged the wall and started off. Fortunately, the water came only to their knees because there was a shelf of rocks all the way along. The brothers' hearts beat wildly. What would they find ahead of them?

The boys had not heard a sound since entering

the tunnel. It appeared that the men in the row-boat had gone on to some secret hiding place.

"I think I'll risk my flashlight," Frank said in a low voice as they reached the pond. "We can't find out anything without it."

He pulled one he always carried from its waterproof case and snapped it on. The yellow beam shone over the pond. There was no sign of the rowboat.

"How do you think those men got out of here?" Joe asked. "Do you suppose there's another open-ing?"

Frank turned the flashlight onto the steep sides surrounding the water. "I don't see any. My guess is that those men hid the boat some place. Let's make a thorough search."

Slowly the brothers began to walk around the edge of the pond, brushing aside the heavy growth and peering among the bushes. They had about given up in despair as they reached the section by the far wall of the tunnel. Then, as Frank beamed the flashlight over the thicket, he exclaimed hoarsely, "Look!"

"A door!" Joe whispered tensely.

The door had been so cleverly concealed that it would not have been seen in full daylight except at close quarters. The glare of the flashlight, how-ever, brought the artificial screen of branches and leaves into sharp relief against the dark cliffside.

"This explains it," Joe said. "The men in the boat went through here. I wonder where it goes."

In order to avoid detection, Frank extinguished his light before trying to open the door. He swung it open inch by inch, half expecting to find lights and people beyond. But there was only darkness. Luckily the door had made no noise. Frank turned on his light again.

Ahead was a watery passageway some ten feet wide and twenty-five feet long, with a ledge running along one side. At the end was a tiny wharf with a rowboat tied to a post.

"This is fantastic!" Joe whispered. "And it must have been here a long time. Do you suppose it's connected with the Pollitt place?"

"If it is, it could mean old Mr. Pollitt was mixed up with the smugglers!" Frank answered. "Hey, do you suppose Snattman is his nephew?"

Excited over this possible new angle to the case, Frank and Joe stepped onto the ledge. They dressed, then quietly inched forward. Reaching the wharf, they looked about them as Frank beamed his flashlight on the walls.

"Hold it!" Joe whispered.

Directly ahead was a crude arch in the rock. Beyond it, the boys could see a steep flight of stone steps. Their hearts pounded with excitement.

"We've found it!" Frank whispered. "This must be the secret passageway!"

"Yes," Joe agreed, "and from the distance we've come I'd figure that we're right underneath the house on the cliff."

"Let's go up."

The light cast strange shadows in the passage through the rocks. Water dripped from the walls. The boys tiptoed forward and stealthily began the ascent.

As they crept up the stairs, Frank flashed the light ahead of them. Shortly they could see that the steps ended at a heavy door. Its framework was set into the wall of rock. Above them was only a rocky ceiling.

When Frank and Joe reached the door, they hesitated. Both were thinking, "If we go through that door and find the gang of smugglers, we'll never get out. But, on the other hand, we *must* find Dad!"

Frank stepped forward, pressed his ear against the door, and listened intently. There was not a sound beyond.

He turned off his light and looked carefully around the sides of the door to see if he could catch a glimmer of any illumination from the other side. There was only darkness.

"I guess there's no one inside," he said to Joe. "Let's see if we can open it."

Frank felt for the latch. The door did not move. "It must be locked," he whispered.

"Try it again. Maybe it's just stuck."

Frank put his hand on the latch, this time also pushing the door with his shoulder. Suddenly, with a noise which echoed from wall to wall, the latch snapped and the door swung open.

Joe stepped forward, but Frank put out a restraining hand. "Wait!" he cautioned. "That noise may bring someone."

Tensely, they stood alert for the slightest sound. But none came. Hopeful that there was no one in the area beyond, Frank switched on the flashlight.

The vivid beam cut the darkness and revealed a gloomy cave hewn out of the rock in the very center of the cliff. The boys wondered if it had been a natural cave. It was filled with boxes, bales, and packages distributed about the floor and piled against the walls.

"Smuggled goods!" Frank and Joe thought.

The fact that the majority of the boxes bore labels of foreign countries seemed to verify their suspicions.

Convinced that the cave was unoccupied, the boys stepped through the doorway and looked about for another door or opening. They saw none. Was this the end of the trail?

"But it couldn't be," the young sleuths thought. "Those men went *some* place."

Bolts of beautiful silk had been tossed on top

of some of the bales. Valuable tapestries were also lying carelessly around. In one corner four boxes were piled on top of one another. Frank accidentally knocked the flashlight against one of these and it gave forth a hollow sound.

"It's empty," he whispered.

An idea struck him that perhaps these boxes had been piled up to conceal some passage leading out of the secret storeroom. He mentioned his suspicion to Joe.

"But how could the men pile the boxes up there after they went out?" his brother questioned.

"This gang is smart enough for anything. Let's move these boxes away and maybe we'll find out."

Frank seized the topmost box. It was very light and he removed it from the pile without difficulty.

"I thought so!" Frank said with satisfaction. The flashlight had revealed the top of a door which had been hidden from view.

The boys lost no time in moving the other three boxes. Then Frank and Joe discovered how it was possible for the boxes to be piled up in such a position, in spite of the fact that the smugglers had left the cave and closed the door behind them.

Attached to the bottom of the door was a thin

wooden platform that projected out over the floor of the cave and on this the boxes had been piled.

"Very clever," Joe remarked. "Whenever any one leaves the cave and closes the door, the boxes swing in with the platform and it looks as though they were piled up on the floor."

"Right. Well, let's see where the door leads," Frank proposed.

He snapped off his light and with utmost caution opened the door. It made no sound. Again there was darkness ahead.

"What a maze!" Frank whispered as he turned on his flash and beamed the light ahead.

Another stone-lined passage with a flight of steps at the end!

Suddenly Frank stiffened and laid a warning hand on his brother's arm. "Voices!" he said in a low tone and snapped off his light.

The boys listened intently. They could hear a man's voice in the distance. Neither could distinguish what he was saying, for he was still too far away, but gradually the tones grew louder. Then, to the brothers' alarm, they heard footsteps. Hastily they retreated into the secret cave.

"Quick! The door!" Frank urged.

They closed it quietly.

"Now the boxes. If those men come in here

they'll notice that the boxes have been moved!" He turned on the light but shielded it with his hand.

Swiftly Joe piled the empty boxes back onto the platform that projected from the bottom of the door. He worked as silently and quickly as possible, but could hear the footsteps drawing closer and closer.

Finally the topmost box was in place.

"Out the other door!" Frank hissed into Joe's ear.

They sped across the floor of the cave toward the door opening onto the stairs they had recently ascended. But hardly had they reached it before they heard a rattle at the latch of the door on the opposite side of the cave.

"We haven't time," Frank whispered. "Hide!"

The beam of the flashlight revealed a number of boxes close to the door. On top of these someone had thrown a heavy bolt of silk, the folds of which hung down to the floor. The brothers scrambled swiftly behind the boxes, pressing themselves close against the wall. They had just enough time to hide and switch out Frank's light before they heard the other door open.

"There's a bunch of drugs in that shipment that came in three weeks ago," they heard a husky voice say. "We'll take it upstairs. Burke says he can get rid of it for us right away. No use leaving it down here. Got to make room for the new shipment."

"Right," the Hardys heard someone else reply. "Anything else to go up?"

"No. I'll switch on the light."

There was a click, and suddenly the cave was flooded with light. It had been wired for electricity.

Frank and Joe crouched in their hiding place, holding their breaths in terror. Would they be discovered?

Footsteps slowly approached the boxes behind which they were concealed!

CHAPTER XIII

A Startling Discovery

FRANK AND JOE tried to crowd themselves into the smallest space possible as the men came nearer to their hiding place. The electric light bulb hanging from the center of the ceiling cast such a strong illumination over the cave that the boys felt certain they would be discovered.

The boxes were placed a small distance apart, and only the fact that folds of silk hung down over the open spaces between the boxes prevented the boys from being seen immediately. However, through a crack in one of the crates, the Hardys could just make out two husky-looking figures.

"Here's some o' that Japanese silk," the boys heard one of the men say. "I'd better take a bolt of that up too. Burke said he could place some more of it."

Instantly the same thought ran through both

the brothers' minds. If the man picked up the silk, they would surely be found!

"Don't be crazy!" the other man objected. "You know you won't get any credit for pushin' a sale. Why break your arm luggin' all that stuff upstairs?"

"Well," the first man explained in a whining tone, "I thought maybe we could get rid of some more of this swag and make ourselves a little extra dough."

"Naw," his companion snarled. "I can tell you ain't been with this gang long. You never get any thanks around here for thinkin'. If Burke don't take the extra stuff, the boss'll make you bring it all the way down again."

"Maybe you're right."

"Sure I'm right! My idea for the rest of us in this gang is to do just what Snattman tells us to and no more."

"You got somethin' there, Bud. Okay. We'll just take up the package of drugs and leave the rest."

To the boys' relief the men turned away and went over to the other side of the room. Frank and Joe did not dare peer out, but they could hear the sound of boxes being shifted.

Then came the words, "All set. I've got the packages. Let's go!"

The switch was snapped and the cave was

plunged into darkness. The Hardys began to breathe normally again. The door to the corridor closed and faintly the boys could detect the men's footsteps as they ascended the stairs at the end of it.

When they had died away completely, Frank switched on the flashlight. "Wow!" he said, giving a tremendous sigh of relief. "That was a close call! I sure thought they had us."

"Me too," Joe agreed. "We wouldn't have had a chance with that pair. Looked like a couple of wrestlers."

"Do we dare follow them?"

"You bet. I'd say we've solved the smuggling mystery, but we've still got to find out if they're holding Dad," Joe said grimly.

"We'll have to watch our step even more carefully. We don't want to walk right into the whole ring of smugglers," Frank reminded him.

"Right. I don't crave anything worse than what we've just gone through," said Joe. "I thought I'd die of suspense while that pair was in here."

They crossed the room, opened the door, and started up the dark passageway. Presently they were confronted by the flight of steps. Part way up there was a landing, then more steps with a door at the top.

"I'll go first," Frank offered. "Stick close behind me. I think I'll keep the flash off."

"That's right," Joe agreed. "Snattman might

have a guard at the top and there's no use advertising our presence."

Step by step, the boys crept upward in the inky blackness. Then they found themselves on a crude landing of planks. Carefully they felt their way along the side of the rock wall until they reached the next flight of steps.

Here the brothers stopped again to listen. Silence.

"So far, so good," Frank whispered. "But somehow I don't like this whole thing. I have a feeling we're walking into a trap."

"We can't quit now," Joe answered. "But I admit I'm scared."

Still groping in the dark, the boys climbed up and up until they were nearly winded.

"Where are we?" Joe panted. "I feel as if I've been climbing stairs for an hour!"

"Me too," Frank agreed. "The cliff doesn't look this high from the outside."

They rested a minute, then continued their journey. Groping around, they finally reached another door. Frank hunted for the door handle. Finding it, he turned the knob ever so slightly to find out if the door was locked.

"I can open it," Frank said in Joe's ear, "but we'd better wait a few minutes."

"Every second is vital if Dad's a prisoner," Joe objected.

Frank was about to accede to his brother's urging when both boys heard footsteps on the other side of the door. A chill ran down their spines.

"Shall we run?" Joe said fearfully.

"It wouldn't do us any good. Listen!"

There came a queer shuffling sound and a sigh from somewhere beyond the door. That was all.

"Someone's in there," Frank breathed. Joe nodded in the darkness.

The boys did not know what to do. The gang might have posted a sentry. If there was only one, the Hardys might be able to jump the man and disarm him. However, they probably could not do it without making some noise and attracting the attention of the rest of the smugglers.

Frank and Joe gritted their teeth. They couldn't give up now!

As they were trying to decide how to proceed, the situation took an unexpected turn. A door slammed in the distance. Then came the murmur of voices and the sound of advancing footsteps.

"This nonsense has gone far enough," a man said angrily. "He'll write that note at once, or I'll know the reason why."

The boys started. The voice was that of the man who had ordered them to leave the pond during the afternoon.

"That's right, chief!" another voice spoke up.

"Make him do as you say and get the heat off us until we've got all the loot moved."

"If he doesn't write it, he'll never get out of here alive," the first man promised coldly.

Instantly Frank and Joe thought of the note their mother had received. Was the man these smugglers were talking about their father? Or was he someone else—maybe Jones, who was to be forced to obey them or perhaps lose his life?

The speakers went a short distance beyond the door behind which Frank and Joe were standing. Then they heard the click of a switch. A faint beam of yellow light shone beneath the door. The brothers figured there was a corridor beyond and three or four men had entered a room opening from it.

"Well, I see you're still here," said the man who had been addressed as chief. "You'll find this an easier place to get into than out of."

A weary voice answered him. The tones were low, so the boys pressed closer to the door. But try as they might, they could not distinguish the words.

"You're a prisoner here and you'll stay here until you die unless you write that note."

Again the weary voice spoke, but the tones were still so indistinct that the boys could not hear the answer.

"You won't write it, eh? We'll see what we can do to persuade you."

"Let him go hungry for a few days. That'll persuade him!" put in one of the other men. This brought a hoarse laugh from his companions.

"You'll be hungry enough if you don't write that letter," the chief agreed. "Are you going to write it?"

"No," the boys barely heard the prisoner answer.

The chief said sourly, "You've got too much on us. We can't afford to let you go now. But if you write that letter, we'll leave you some food, so that you won't starve. You'll break out eventually, but not in time to do us any harm. Well, what do you say? Want some food?"

There was no reply from the prisoner.

"Give his arm a little twist," suggested one of the smugglers.

At this the Hardys' blood boiled with rage. Their first impulse was to fling open the door and rush to the aid of the person who was being tormented. But they realized they were helpless against so many men. Their only hope lay in the arrival of the Coast Guard men, but they might come too late!

"Chief, shall I give this guy the works?" one of the smugglers asked.

"No," the leader answered quickly. "None of

that rough stuff. We'll do it the easy way—starvation. I'm giving him one more chance. He can write that note now or we'll leave him here to starve when we make our getaway."

Still there was no reply.

To Frank's and Joe's ears came a scraping sound as if a chair was being moved forward.

"You won't talk, eh?" The leader's voice grew ugly.

There was a pause of a few seconds, then suddenly he shouted, "Write that note, Hardy, or you'll be sorry—as sure as my name's Snattman!"

CHAPTER XIV

Captured

JOE gave a start. "It *is* Dad!" he whispered hoarsely. "He found the smugglers' hide-out!"

Frank nudged his brother warningly. "Not so loud."

The boys' worst fears were realized—their father was not only a prisoner of the smugglers, but also his life was being threatened!

"Write that note!" Snattman demanded.

"I won't write it," Fenton Hardy replied in a weak but clear voice.

The chief persisted. "You heard what I said. Write it or be left here to starve."

"I'll starve."

"You'll change your mind in a day or two. You think you're hungry now, but wait until we cut off your food entirely. Then you'll see. You'll be ready to sell your soul for a drop of water or a crumb to eat."

"I won't write it."

"Look here, Hardy. We're not asking very much. All we want you to do is write to your wife that you're safe and tell her to call off the police and those kids of yours. They're too nosy."

"Sooner or later someone is going to trace me here," came Mr. Hardy's faint reply. "And when they do, I can tell them enough to send you to prison for the rest of your life."

There was a sudden commotion in the room and two or three of the smugglers began talking at once.

"You're crazy!" shouted Snattman, but there was a hint of uneasiness in his voice. "You don't know anything about me!"

"I know enough to have you sent up for attempted murder. And you're about to try it again."

"You're too smart, Hardy. That's all the more reason why you're not going to get out of here until we've gone. And if you don't co-operate you'll *never* make it. Our next big shipment's coming through tonight, and then we're skipping the country. If you write that letter, you'll live. If you don't, it's curtains for you!"

Frank and Joe were shaken by the dire threats. But they must decide whether to go for help, or stay and risk capture and try to rescue their father.

"You can't scare me, Snattman," the detective

said. "I have a feeling your time is up. You're never going to get that big shipment."

The detective's voice seemed a little stronger, the boys felt.

Snattman laughed. "I thought you were smart, but you're playing a losing game, I warn you. And how about your family? Are you doing them a service by being so stubborn?"

There was silence for a while. Then Fenton Hardy answered slowly:

"My wife and boys would rather know that I died doing my duty than have me come back to them as a protector of smugglers and criminals."

"You have a very high sense of duty," sneered Snattman. "But you'll change your mind. Are you thirsty?"

There was no reply.

"Are you hungry?"

Still no answer.

"You know you are. And it'll be worse. You'll die of thirst and starvation unless you write that note."

"I'll never write it."

"All right. Come on, men. We'll leave him to himself for a while and give him time to think about it."

Frank squeezed Joe's arm in relief and exhilaration. There was still a chance to save their father!

Footsteps echoed as Snattman and the others

left the room and walked through the corridor. Finally the sounds died away and a door slammed.

Joe made a move toward the door, but Frank held him back. "We'd better wait a minute," he cautioned. "They may have left someone on guard."

The boys stood still, listening intently. But there were no further sounds from beyond the door. At length, satisfied that his father had indeed been left alone, Frank felt for the knob.

Noiselessly he opened the door about an inch, then peered into the corridor which was dimly lighted from one overhead bulb. There was no sign of a guard.

Three doors opened from the corridor—two on the opposite side from where the brothers were standing and another at the end.

The passage was floored with planks and had a beamed ceiling like a cellar. Frank and Joe quickly figured where their father was and sped across the planks to the room. They pushed open the door of the almost dark room and peered inside. There was a crude table and several chairs. In one corner stood a small cot. On it lay Fenton Hardy. He was bound hand and foot to the bed and so tightly trussed that he was unable to move more than a few inches in any direction. He was flat on his back, staring up at the ceiling of his prison. On a chair beside the cot was a sheet of paper and a pencil, evidently the materials for the letter Snattman had demanded he write.

"Dad!" Frank and Joe cried softly.

The detective had not heard the door open, but now he looked at his sons in amazement and relief. "You're here!" he whispered. "Thank goodness!"

The boys were shocked at the change in their father's appearance. Normally a rugged-looking man, Fenton Hardy now was thin and pale. His cheeks were sunken and his eyes listless.

"We'll have you out of here in a minute," Frank whispered.

"Hurry!" the detective begged. "Those demons may be back any minute!"

Frank pulled out his pocketknife and began to work at the ropes that bound his father. But the knife was not very sharp and the bonds were thick.

Joe discovered that he did not have his knife with him. "It probably slipped out of my pocket when we undressed on the *Napoli*," he said.

"Mine's gone too," Mr. Hardy told them. "Snattman took everything I had in my pockets, including concentrated emergency rations. Have you anything sweet with you?"

Joe pulled out the candy bar from his pocket and held it, so Mr. Hardy could take a large bite of the quick-energy food. Meanwhile, his eyes roamed over the room in search of something sharp which he might use to help Frank with the ropes. He saw nothing.

Mr. Hardy finished the candy bar, bite by bite. Now Joe started to help Frank by trying to untie the knots. But they were tight and he found it almost impossible to loosen them.

Minutes passed. Frank hacked at the ropes, but the dull blade made little progress. Joe worked at the obstinate knots. Fenton Hardy could give no assistance. All were silent. The only sound was the heavy breathing of the boys and the scraping of the knife against the ropes.

At last Frank was able to saw through one of the bonds and the detective's feet were free. His son pulled the ropes away and began to work on the ones that bound his father's arms. As he reached over with the knife there came a sound that sent a feeling of terror through the Hardys.

It was a heavy footstep beyond the corridor door. Someone was coming back!

Frank worked desperately with the knife, but the ropes still held stubbornly. The dull blade seemed to make almost no impression. But at last a few strands parted. Finally, with Fenton Hardy making a mighty effort and Joe clawing at the rope with his fingers, it snapped.

The detective was free!

But the footfalls of the approaching smuggler came closer.

"Quick!" Frank whispered, as he flung the ropes aside.

"I—I can't hurry!" Mr. Hardy gasped. "I've been tied up so long my feet and legs are numb."

"But we've got to hurry, Dad!" Frank said excitedly. "See if you can stand up."

"I'll—I'll do my best," his father replied, as the boys rubbed his legs vigorously to restore full circulation.

"We must run before those crooks come!" Joe said tensely.

Fenton Hardy got to his feet as hastily as he could. But when he stood up, the detective staggered and would have fallen if Frank had not taken his arm. He was so weak from hunger that a wave of dizziness had come over him. He gave his head a quick shake and the feeling passed.

"All right. Let's go," he said, clinging to both boys for support.

The three hastened out the door of the room and across the corridor to the cave. As they entered it, Mr. Hardy's knees buckled. In desperation his sons picked him up.

"You go on," he whispered. "Leave me here."

"I'm sure all of us can make it," Joe said bravely.

They reached the far door, but the delay had been costly. Just as Frank opened it, clicking off his flashlight, the corridor door was flung open and the ceiling light snapped on.

Frank leaped directly at the smuggler

Frank and Joe had a confused glimpse of the dark man whom they had seen at the pond that afternoon. Snattman! Two rough-looking companions crowded in behind him.

"What's going on here?" Snattman exclaimed, apparently not recognizing the group for a moment.

"It's the Hardys!" one of the other men cried out.

The fleeing trio started down the steps but got no farther than the landing when the smugglers appeared at the stairway and rushed down after them.

"Stop!" cried Snattman, jumping down the last three steps and whipping an automatic from his hip pocket. The place was flooded with light.

As Snattman drew closer, Frank crouched for a spring, then leaped directly at the smuggler. He struck at the man's wrist and the revolver flew out of his grasp. It skidded across the landing and clattered down the steps. Frank closed in on the man. Snattman had been taken completely by surprise. Before he could defend himself, Frank forced him against the wall.

Joe, in the meantime, with a swift uppercut had kayoed one of the other men. And Mr. Hardy, whose strength had partially returned, was battling the third as best he could.

But at this moment the boys saw their father's

adversary dodge to the wall and press a button. In an instant an alarm bell sounded in the corridor. Within seconds a new group of Snattman's gang appeared. As some held drawn revolvers, others overpowered the three Hardys.

In the face of the guns, father and sons were forced to surrender and return to the room where Mr. Hardy had been held captive before.

Within five minutes Fenton Hardy was bound again to the cot, while Frank and Joe, trussed up and unable to move, were tied to two chairs.

CHAPTER XV

Dire Threats

SNATTMAN, once he had recovered from his first consternation and surprise at finding the Hardy boys in the underground room, was in high good humor. He turned to his men.

"Just in time," he gloated, rubbing his hands together in satisfaction. "If we hadn't come here when we did, they'd have all escaped!"

The Hardy boys were silent, sick with despair. They had been sure they were going to succeed in rescuing their father and now the three of them were prisoners of the smuggling gang.

"What are we goin' to do with these guys?" asked one of the men.

The voice sounded familiar to the boys and they looked up. They were not surprised to see that the man was the red-haired one they had met at the

Pollitt place when Frank had discovered his father's cap.

"Do with them?" Snattman mused. "That's a problem. We've got three on our hands now instead of one. Best thing is to leave them all here and lock the door."

"And put gags in their traps," suggested a burly companion.

Red objected. "As long as the Hardys are around here, they're dangerous. They almost got away this time."

"Well, what do you suggest?"

"We ought to do what I wanted to do with the old man in the first place," Red declared doggedly.

"You mean get rid of them?" Snattman asked thoughtfully.

"Sure. All of them!"

"Well—" Snattman gazed at Mr. Hardy with a sinister look.

"I should think you have enough on your conscience already, Snattman!" the detective exclaimed. "I don't expect you to let me go," he added bitterly. "But release my boys. They haven't done anything but try to rescue their father. You'd do the same thing yourself."

"Oh yeah?" Snattman sneered. "Don't bother yourself about my conscience. Nobody—but nobody ever stands in my way.

‌

"As to letting these boys go, what kind of a fool do you take me for?" Snattman shouted. "If you three are such buddies, you ought to enjoy starving together."

The smuggler laughed uproariously at what he considered a very funny remark.

Frank's and Joe's minds were racing with ideas. One thing stood out clearly. Snattman had said the Hardys almost escaped. This meant that no one was guarding the secret entrance!

"If we can only hold out a while," they thought, "the Coast Guard will arrive. There'll be nobody to stop them from coming up here."

Then, suddenly, a shocking possibility occurred to the boys. Suppose the Coast Guard could not find the camouflaged door opening from the pond!

During the conversation four of the smugglers had been whispering among themselves in the corridor. One of them now stepped into the room and faced Snattman.

"I'd like a word with you, chief," he began.

"What is it now?" The smuggler's voice was surly.

"It's about what's to be done with the Hardys, now that we've got 'em," the man said hesitantly. "It's your business what you do to people who make it tough for you when you're on your own. But not in our gang. We're in this for our take out of the smugglin', and we won't stand for too much rough stuff."

"That's right!" one of the other men spoke up.

"Is that so?" Snattman's upper lip curled. "You guys are gettin' awful righteous all of a sudden, aren't you? Look out or I'll dump the lot of you!"

"Oh, no, you won't," replied the first man who had addressed him. "We're partners in this deal and we're goin' to have our full share of what comes in. We ain't riskin' our lives for love, you know."

"We've got another idea about what to do with these three prisoners," a third smuggler spoke up. "I think it's a good one."

"What is it?" Snattman asked impatiently.

"We've been talkin' about Ali Singh."

Frank and Joe started and listened intently.

"What about him?" Snattman prodded his assistant.

"Turn the prisoners over to him. He's got a friend named Foster who's captain of a boat sailin' to the Far East tonight. Put the Hardys on board that ship," the first smuggler urged.

Snattman looked thoughtful. The idea seemed to catch his fancy.

"Not bad," he muttered. "I hadn't thought of Ali Singh. Yes, he'd take care of them. They'd never get back here." He smiled grimly.

"From what he told me about that friend of his,

the captain'd probably dump the Hardys overboard before they got very far out," the man went on smugly. "Seems like he don't feed passengers if he can get rid of 'em!"

"All the better. We wouldn't be responsible."

"Leave them to Ali Singh." Red chuckled evilly. "He'll attend to them."

Snattman walked over to the cot and looked down at Mr. Hardy. "It's too bad your boys had to come barging in here," he said. "Now the three of you will have to take a little ocean voyage." He laughed. "You'll never get to the Coast Guard to tell your story."

The detective was silent. He knew further attempts at persuasion would be useless.

"Well," said Snattman, "haven't you anything to say?"

"Nothing. Do as you wish with me. But let the boys go."

"We'll stick with you, Dad," said Frank quickly.

"Of course!" Joe added.

"You sure will," Snattman declared. "I'm not going to let one of you have the chance of getting back to Bayport with your story."

The ringleader of the smugglers stood in the center of the room for a while, contemplating his captives with a bitter smile. Then he turned suddenly on his heel.

"Well, they're safe enough," he told Red. "We

have that business with Burke to take care of. Come on, men, load Burke's truck. If any policemen come along and find it in the lane we'll be done for."

"How about them?" asked Red, motioning to the Hardys. "Shouldn't they be guarded?"

"They're tied up tight." Snattman gave a short laugh. "But I guess we'd better leave one guard, anyway. Malloy, you stay here and keep watch."

Malloy, a surly, truculent fellow in overalls and a ragged sweater, nodded and sat down on a box near the door. This arrangement seemed to satisfy Snattman. After warning Malloy not to fall asleep on the job and to see to it that the prisoners did not escape, he left the room. He was followed by Red and the other smugglers.

A heavy silence fell over the room after the departure of the men. Malloy crouched gloomily on the box, gazing blankly at the floor. The butt of a revolver projected from his hip pocket.

Frank strained against the ropes that bound him to the chair. But the smugglers had done their task well. He could scarcely budge.

"We'll never get out of this," he told himself ruefully.

Joe was usually optimistic but this time his spirits failed him. "We're in a tough spot," he thought. "It looks as if we'll all be on that ship by morning."

To lighten their spirits the Hardys began to talk, hoping against hope to distract the guard and perhaps overpower him.

"Shut up, you guys!" Malloy growled. "Quit your talking or I'll make it hot for you!" He tapped his revolver suggestively.

After that, a melancholy silence fell among the prisoners. All were downhearted. It looked as if their fate truly were sealed.

CHAPTER XVI

Quick Work

IN DESPAIR the boys glanced over at their father on the cot. To their surprise they saw that he was smiling.

Frank was about to ask him what he had found amusing about their predicament when his father shook his head in warning. He looked over at the guard.

Malloy was not watching the prisoners. He sat staring at the floor. Occasionally his head would fall forward, then he would jerk it back as he struggled to keep awake.

"Snattman sure made a poor selection when he chose Malloy as guard," the boys thought.

Several times the burly man straightened up, stretched his arms, and rubbed his eyes. But when he settled down again, his head began to nod.

In the meantime, the boys noticed their father struggling with his bonds. To their amazement he did not seem to be so tightly bound as they had thought. Both of them tried moving but could not budge an inch.

The boys exchanged glances, both realizing what had happened. "Dad resorted to an old trick!" Frank told himself, and Joe was silently fuming, "Why didn't we think of it?"

Mr. Hardy had profited by his previous experience. When the smugglers had seized the detective and tied him to the cot for the second time, he had used a device frequently employed by magicians and professional "escape artists" who boast that they can release themselves from tightly tied ropes and strait jackets.

The detective had expanded his chest and flexed his muscles. He had also kept his arms as far away from his sides as he could without being noticed. In this way, when he relaxed, the ropes did not bind him as securely as his captors intended.

"Oh, why were Frank and I so dumb!" Joe again chided himself.

Frank bit his lip in utter disgust at not having remembered the trick. "But then"—he eased his conscience—"Dad didn't think of it the first time, either."

Mr. Hardy had discovered that the rope binding his right wrist to the cot had a slight slack in it. He began trying to work the rope loose. This took a long time and the rough strands rubbed his wrist raw. But at last he managed to slide his right hand free.

"Hurray!" Frank almost shouted. He glanced at the guard. Malloy appeared to be sound asleep. "Hope he'll stay that way until we can escape," Frank wished fervently.

He and Joe watched their father in amazement, as they saw him grope for one of the knots. The detective fumbled at it for a while. It was slow work with only his one hand free. But the boys knew from his satisfied expression that the smugglers in their haste apparently had not tied the knots as firmly as they should have.

At this instant the guard suddenly lifted his head, and Mr. Hardy quickly laid his free hand back on the cot. He closed his eyes as if sleeping and his sons followed his example. But opening their lids a slit, they watched the smuggler carefully.

The guard grunted. "They're okay," he mumbled. Once more he tried to stay awake but found it impossible. Little by little his head sagged until his chin rested on his chest. Deep, regular breathing told the prisoners he was asleep.

Mr. Hardy now began work again on the knot of the rope that kept his left arm bound to the cot. In a matter of moments he succeeded in loosening it and the rope fell away from his arm.

After making sure the guard was still asleep, the detective sat up on the cot and struggled to release his feet. This was an easier task. The smugglers had merely passed a rope around the cot to hold the prisoner's feet. A few minutes' attention was all that was necessary for the boys' father to work his way loose.

"Now he'll release us," Joe thought excitedly, "and we can escape from here!"

As Fenton Hardy tiptoed toward his sons, the board floor squeaked loudly. The guard muttered again, as if dreaming, shook his head, then sat up.

"Oh, no!" Frank murmured, fearful of what would happen. He saw his father pick up a white rag someone had dropped.

A look of intense amazement crossed Malloy's face. As he opened his mouth to yell for help, Fenton Hardy leaped across the intervening space and flung himself on the smuggler.

"Keep quiet!" the detective ordered.

Malloy had time only to utter a muffled gasp before the detective clapped a hand over the guard's mouth, jammed the rag in it, and toppled him to the floor. The two rolled over and over in a desperate, silent struggle. The boys, helpless, looked on, their fears mounting. They knew their father had been weakened by his imprisonment and hunger, and the guard was strong and muscular. Nevertheless, the detective had the advantage of a surprise attack. Malloy had had no time to collect his wits.

Frank and Joe watched the battle in an agony of suspense. If only they could join the fight!

Mr. Hardy still had the advantage, for he could breathe better than his opponent. But suddenly Malloy managed to raise himself to his knees. He reached for the revolver at his hip.

"Look out, Dad!" Frank hissed. "He's got his gun!"

Quick as a flash the detective landed a blow on the guard's jaw. Malloy blinked and raised both hands to defend himself as he fell to the ground. Mr. Hardy darted forward and pulled the revolver out of the man's side pocket.

"No funny business!" the detective told him in a low voice.

Without being told, Malloy raised his hands in the air. He sat helplessly on the floor, beaten.

"He's got a knife too, Dad," Joe said quietly. "Watch that."

"Thanks, Joe," his father replied. Then, motioning with the pistol, he said, "All right. Let's have the knife!"

Sullenly the guard removed the knife from its leather sheath at his belt and handed it to Mr. Hardy.

Frank and Joe wanted to shout with joy, but merely grinned at their father.

Still watching Malloy, the detective walked slowly backward until he reached Joe's side. Without taking his eyes from the smuggler, he bent down and with the knife sliced at the ropes that bound his son. Fortunately, the knife was sharp and the ropes soon were cut.

"Boy, that feels good, Dad. Thanks," Joe whispered.

He sprang from the chair, took the knife, and while his father watched Malloy, he cut Frank's bonds.

"Malloy," Mr. Hardy ordered, "come over here!"

He motioned toward the bed and indicated by gestures that the smuggler was to lie down on the cot. Malloy shook his head vigorously, but was prodded over by Joe. The guard lay down on the cot.

The ropes which had held Mr. Hardy had not been cut. Quickly Frank and Joe trussed up Malloy just as their father had been tied, making certain that the knots were tight. As a final precaution they pushed in the gag which was slipping and with a piece of rope made it secure.

The whole procedure had taken scarcely five minutes. The Hardys were free!

"What now?" Frank asked his father out of earshot of Malloy. "Hide some place until the Coast Guard gets here?" Quickly he told about Tony and Chet going to bring the officers to the smugglers' hide-out.

"But they should have been here by now," Joe whispered. "They probably haven't found the secret door. Let's go down and show them."

This plan was agreed upon, but the three Hardys got no farther than the top of the first stairway when they heard rough, arguing voices below them.

"They can't be Coast Guard men," said Mr. Hardy. "We'll listen a few seconds, then we'd better run in the other direction. I know the way out to the grounds."

From below came an ugly, "You double-crosser, you! This loot belongs to the whole gang and don't you forget it!"

"Listen," said the second voice. "I don't have to take orders from you. I thought we was pals. Now you don't want to go through with the deal. Who's to know if we got ten packages or five from that friend o' Ali Singh's?"

"Okay. And the stuff'll be easier to get rid of than those drugs. They're too hot for me. Snattman can burn for kidnapin' if he wants to—I don't."

The voices had now become so loud that the Hardys did not dare wait another moment. "Come on!" the boys' father urged.

He led the way back to the corridor and along it to the door at the end. Suddenly Frank and Joe noticed him falter and were afraid he was going to faint. Joe recalled that his father had had no food except the candy bar. Ramming his hands into his pockets, he brought out another bar and some pieces of pretzel. Quickly he filled both his father's hands with them. Mr. Hardy ate them hungrily as his sons supported him under his arms and assisted him to the door.

As Frank quietly opened it, and they saw a stairway beyond, the detective said, "These steps will bring us up into a shed near the Pollitt house. There's a trap door. That's the way Snattman brought me down. Got your lights? We haven't any time to lose." Mr. Hardy seemed stronger already. "I'll take the lead."

As they ascended, Frank and Joe wondered if they would come out in the shed where they had seen the man named Klein picking up small logs.

When the detective reached the top of the stairs he ordered the lights out and pushed against the trap door. He could not budge it.

"You try," he urged the boys. "And hurry! Those men we heard may discover Malloy."

"And then things will start popping!" Frank murmured.

The boys heaved their shoulders against the trap door. In a moment there came the rumble of rolling logs. The door went up easily.

Frank peered out. No one seemed to be around.

He stepped up into the shed and the others followed.

The three stood in silence. The night was dark. The wind, blowing through the trees, made a moaning sound. Before the Hardys rose the gloomy mass of the house on the cliff. No lights could be seen.

From the direction of the lane came dull, thudding sounds. The boys and their father assumed the smugglers' truck was being loaded with the goods which were to be disposed of by the man named Burke.

Suddenly the Hardys heard voices from the corridor they had just left. Quickly Frank closed the trap door and Joe piled up the logs. Then, silently, the Hardys stole out into the yard.

CHAPTER XVII

Hostages

LITHE as Indians the three Hardys hurried across the lawn and disappeared among the trees. They headed for the road, a good distance away.

"I hope a bus comes along," Frank said to himself. "Then we can get to a phone and report—"

His thought was rudely interrupted as the boys and their father heard a sound that struck terror to their hearts—the clatter of the logs tumbling off the trap door!

An instant later came a hoarse shout. "Chief! Red! The Hardys got away! Watch out for them!"

"He must be one of the men we heard coming up from the shore," Joe decided. "They must have found Malloy trussed up!"

Instantly the place became alive with smugglers flashing their lights. Some of the men ran from the truck toward the road, shouting. Others began to comb the woods. Another man emerged from the trap door. He and his companion dashed to the ocean side of the house.

Two burly smugglers flung open the kitchen door and ran out. One shouted, "They ain't in the house!"

"And they're not down at the shore!" the other yelled. "I just talked to Klein on the phone down there."

"You guys better not let those Hardys get away!" Snattman's voice cut through the night. "It'll be the pen for all of you!"

"Fenton Hardy's got a gun! He took Malloy's!" came a warning voice from the far side of the house. The two men who had gone to the front now returned. "He never misses his mark!"

When the fracas had started, the detective had pulled his sons to the ground, told them to lie flat, face down, and not to move. Now they could hear the pounding steps of the smugglers as they dashed among the trees. The boys' hearts pounded wildly. It did not seem possible they could be missed!

Yet man after man ran within a few yards of the three prone figures and dashed on toward the road. Presently Mr. Hardy raised his head and looked toward the Pollitt mansion.

"Boys," he said tensely, "we'll make a run for

the kitchen door. The men won't expect us to go there."

The three arose. Swiftly and silently they crossed the dark lawn and slipped into the house. Apparently no one had seen them.

"When Snattman doesn't find us outdoors," Joe whispered, "won't he look here to make sure?"

"Yes," Mr. Hardy replied. "But by that time I hope the Coast Guard and State Police will arrive."

"Joe and I found a hidden stairway to the attic," Frank spoke up. "Snattman won't think of looking in it. Let's hide up there."

"You forget the ghost," Joe reminded his brother. "*He* knows we found that stairway."

"Nevertheless, Frank's suggestion is a good one," Mr. Hardy said. "Let's go to the attic. Were any clothes hanging in the closet that might be used to conceal the door?"

"Yes, a man's bathrobe on a rod."

The Hardys did not dare use a light and had to make their way along by feeling walls, and the stair banister, with Frank in the lead and Mr. Hardy between the boys. Reaching the second floor, Frank looked out the rear window of the hall.

"The smugglers are coming back!" he remarked in a low voice. "The lights are heading this way!"

The Hardys doubled their speed, but it was still slow going, for they banged into chairs and a wardrobe as Frank felt his way along the hall toward the bedroom where the hidden staircase was.

Finally the trio reached it. Just as Frank was about to open the door to the attic, a door on the first floor swung open with a resounding bang.

"Scatter and search every room!" Snattman's crisp voice rang out.

"We're trapped!" Joe groaned.

"Maybe not," Frank said hopefully. "I have a hunch Klein was the ghost. It's possible that he's the only one who knows about this stairway and he's down at the shore."

"We'll risk going up," Mr. Hardy decided. "But not a sound." He slid the bathrobe across the rod, so that it would hide the door.

"The stairs creak," Joe informed him.

Mr. Hardy told his sons to push down the treads slowly but firmly with their hands and hold them there until they put one foot between them and then raised up to their full weight.

"And lean forward, so you won't lose your balance," he warned.

Fearful that he could not accomplish this, Frank opened the door carefully and started up in the pitch blackness. But the dread thought of capture made him use extreme caution and he reached the attic without having made a sound.

After closing the door, Joe and his father quickly followed. The three moved noiselessly to a spot out of sight of the stairway behind a large trunk.

They sat down and waited, not daring even to whisper. From downstairs they could hear running footsteps, banging doors, and loud talk.

"Not here!"

"Not here!"

"Not here!"

The search seemed to come to an end, for the second-floor group had gathered right in the room where the secret stairway was.

"This is it! The end! They're going to search up here!" Frank thought woefully.

His father reached over and grasped a hand of each of his sons in a reassuring grip. Someone yanked open the closet door. The Hardys became tense. Would the robe over the entrance to the secret stairway fool him?

"Empty!" the man announced and shut the door. The smugglers went downstairs.

There were fervent handshakes among the detective and his sons. Other than this they did not move a muscle of their bodies, although they inwardly relaxed.

Now new worries assailed the Hardys. It was possible that Snattman and his gang, having been alerted, would move out and disappear before the police or Coast Guard could get to the house on the cliff.

Frank's heart gave a jump. He suddenly realized that his father was hiding to protect his sons. Had he been alone, the intrepid detective would have been downstairs battling to get the better of Snattman and break up the smuggling ring.

"What a swell father he is!" Frank thought. Then another idea came to him. "Maybe being here isn't such a bad plan after all. Dad might have been fatally shot if he'd been anywhere else on the property."

A moment later the Hardys again became aware of voices on the second floor. They recognized one as Snattman's, the other as Klein's.

"Yeah, there's a secret stairway to the attic," Klein announced. "I found it when I was playin' ghost. And them Hardy boys—they found it too. I'll bet my last take on those rare drugs we're gettin' tonight that the dick and his sons are up in that attic!"

The Hardys' spirits sank. They were going to be captured again after all!

They heard the door at the foot of the stairway open. "Go up and look, Klein," ordered Snattman.

"Not me. Fenton Hardy has Malloy's gun."

"I said go up!"

"You can't make me," Klein objected in a whining tone. "I'd be a sure target 'cause I couldn't see him. He'd be hiding and let me have it so quick I'd never know what hit me."

Despite the grave situation, Frank's and Joe's

faces were creased in smiles, but they faded as Snattman said, "I'll go myself. Give me that big light!"

Suddenly a brilliant beam was cast into the attic. It moved upward, accompanied by heavy footsteps.

"Hardy, if you want to live, say so!" Snattman said, an evil ring in his voice.

No answer from the detective.

"We've got you cornered this time!"

Mr. Hardy did not reply.

"Listen, Hardy!" Snattman shouted. "I know you're up there because you moved that bathrobe. I'll give you just one minute to come down out of that attic!"

Still no answer and an interval of silence followed.

Then came Snattman's voice again. "This is your last chance, Hardy!"

Nearly a minute went by without a sign from the two enemy camps. Then Snattman moved up the stairs a few more steps.

"Hardy, I have a proposition to make to you," he said presently. "I know you don't want to die and you want those boys of yours to live too. Well, so do I want to live. So let's call it quits."

The detective maintained his silence and Snattman continued up the steps. "Give you my

"You are my hostages!" the smuggler sneered

word I won't shoot. And I know you never fire first unless you have to."

A moment later he appeared at the top of the stairs, empty-handed except for the light. In a moment he spotted the Hardys with his high-powered flashlight.

"Here's the proposition—your lives in exchange for mine and my gang's."

"How do you mean?" Mr. Hardy asked coldly.

"I mean," the smuggler said, "that you are my hostages."

"Hostages!" Frank and Joe exclaimed together.

"Yes. If my men and I can get our stuff moved away before the police or the Coast Guard might happen in here, then you can leave a little later."

"But if they do come?" Frank asked.

"Then I'll bargain with them," Snattman answered. "And I don't think they'll turn me down. They don't know where you are, but I'll make them understand I mean business. If they take me, you three die!"

Frank and Joe gasped. The famous Fenton Hardy and his sons were to be used as a shield to protect a ruthless gang of criminals!

The boys looked at their father in consternation. To their amazement he looked calm, but his mouth was drawn in a tight line.

"It won't do you any good to shoot me, Hardy," the smuggler said. "Mallory said all the chambers in that gat are empty but one. If the gang hears a shot, they'll be up here in a minute to finish you all off properly."

The Hardys realized that if Snattman's remark about the gun were true, they were indeed at the mercy of this cunning, scheming, conniving smuggler. He now started backing toward the stairway.

"I think I'm a pretty fair guy," he said with the trace of a satisfied smile.

"And one to be hated and feared!" Joe thought in a rage. "We've *got* to outwit this man somehow!" he determined.

But at the moment the possibility of this looked hopeless.

CHAPTER XVIII

Coast Guard Action

WHILE the Hardy boys had been investigating the smugglers' hide-out and had been captured, together with their father, Tony and Chet were trying their best to accomplish the errand which Frank and Joe had given them.

During the early part of their trip back to Bayport to contact the Coast Guard, the *Napoli* had cut through the darkness like a streak. Then suddenly Tony exclaimed, "Oh, oh! My starboard light just went out."

Chet turned to look at the portside. "This light's all right. Must be the bulb in the other one."

"That's what I was afraid of," said Tony. "I'll bet I haven't another bulb."

"You mean, somebody might not see the *Napoli* and ram us?" Chet asked fearfully.

"We'll have to be careful," Tony replied.

"Chet, take the wheel, will you? I'll see if I can find an extra bulb."

Chet changed places with Tony, throttled the motor, and gazed intently ahead. The moon had not yet risen and it was difficult to see very far ahead.

"Find anything?" Chet called out, as Tony finished his round of the lockers and was now rummaging in the last one.

"Not yet." Tony pulled out a canvas bag, a pair of sneakers, and some fishing tackle. As he reached in for the last article in the locker, he gave a whoop of joy. "Here's one bulb—just one—keep your fingers crossed, pal. If this isn't any good, we're in a mess."

"And breaking the law besides," Chet added.

He held his breath as Tony went forward and crawled inside the prow of the *Napoli*. With a flashlight, Tony found the protecting shield for the bulb and unfastened it. After removing the dead bulb, he screwed in the new one. As the light flashed on, Tony breathed a sigh of relief and started to crawl out of the prow.

"Good work!" Chet said. "It's lucky we—"

Chet never finished the sentence. At this instant he saw another speedboat loom up in front of him. Like lightning he swung the wheel around, missing the oncoming craft by inches!

"You fool!" the driver of the other boat

shouted. "Why don't you look where you're going?"

Chet did not reply. He was quivering. Besides, he had stalled the motor, which had been throttled so low it had not been able to take the terrific swerving. "Oh, now I've done it!" the stout boy wailed.

There was no response from Tony for several seconds. He had been thrown violently against the side of the boat and was dazed. But he quickly collected his wits and crawled down beside Chet.

"What happened?" he asked.

Chet told him, then said, "You'd better take over. I'm a rotten pilot."

Tony took the seat behind the wheel, started the motor, and sped off toward Barmet Bay.

"We've sure wasted a lot of time," he remarked. "I wonder how Frank and Joe are making out."

"Hope they found Mr. Hardy," Chet added.

There was no more conversation until the boys turned into the bay. The Coast Guard station for the area was a short distance along the southern shore of the bay and Tony headed the *Napoli* directly for it. He pulled up at the dock, where two patrol boats and a cutter were tied.

The two boys climbed out and hurried up to the white building. As they were about to enter it, Chet and Tony were amazed to find Biff Hooper and Phil Cohen coming out of it. Jerry Gilroy, another Bayport High friend, was with them.

"Well, for Pete's sake!" the three cried out, and Biff added, "Boy, are we glad to see you! Where are Frank and Joe?"

"Still hunting for the smugglers," Chet replied. "What brings you here?"

Biff explained that an hour ago Mrs. Hardy had telephoned him to see if he had heard from Frank and Joe. She confessed to being exceedingly worried about her sons. Mrs. Hardy knew they had gone to look for their father and she was in a panic that they had been captured by the same men who were possibly holding her husband.

"I told her I'd round up a couple of the fellows and go on a hunt," Biff went on. "Jerry thought maybe Frank and Joe had come back to town and were somewhere around. We looked, but we couldn't find them anywhere, so we borrowed Mr. Gilroy's car and came out here to tell the Coast Guard. They're going to send out boats. You'd better come in and talk to Chief Warrant Officer Robinson yourself."

The boys hurried inside. Quickly Chet and Tony told of the Hardys' suspicion that they had found the entrance to the smugglers' hide-out.

"Can you send help out there right away?" Chet asked. "We'll show you where the secret tunnel is."

"This is astounding," said Chief Robinson. "I'll order the *Alice* out. You can start within five minutes."

"I'll phone Mrs. Hardy right away," Jerry offered. "I'm afraid, though, that the news isn't going to make her feel too good."

While Jerry was gone, Chet told the chief warrant officer that the Hardys thought they knew the names of two of the men who were involved in the smuggling racket. Chet revealed the Hardy suspicions about Snattman being one and Ali Singh the other.

"We think Ali is a crewman on the *Marco Polo* that's going to dock early tomorrow morning in Bayport," Chet continued. "Frank and Joe got a tip that makes them think this is the deal: While the ship is offshore, Ali Singh pitches stolen drugs overboard and one of the smugglers picks the package up in a speedboat."

Robinson raised his eyebrows. "Those Hardy boys certainly take after their father," he remarked. "They have the makings of good detectives."

Biff told the Coast Guard officer of the boys' adventure at the haunted house on their first visit to the Pollitt place. "Frank and Joe are sure there is some connection between the house and the smugglers."

"And they are probably right," the chief remarked. "I'll call the State Police at once and tell them the latest developments in this case."

The boys waited while he made the report. Jerry, who had just finished telephoning Mrs. Hardy, said that she seemed even more worried than before but relieved that the Coast Guard was going to take a hand.

The chief warrant officer then told the boys he would get in touch with the captain of the *Marco Polo* at once by ship-to-shore telephone. The connection was made and the boys listened with great interest to the conversation. The captain had a booming voice which they could hear plainly.

"Yes, I have a sailor named Ali Singh," he replied in answer to Chief Robinson's question. "He's a member of the kitchen crew."

After he had been told that Ali Singh was suspected of stealing drug shipments and dropping them overboard to a confederate, he said, "That would be pretty easy for him to do. Singh probably throws them out when he dumps garbage into the water, even though he's not supposed to do it. The drugs could be in an inflated waterproof bag."

"Captain, will you have someone keep an eye on this Ali Singh without his knowing he's being watched?" Chief Robinson requested. "I'll send a patrol boat out from here to watch for any of his gang who may be in a small boat waiting to pick up something he dumps overboard. How far offshore are you?"

"About sixteen miles from your headquarters," was the answer.

"Will you keep in touch with the patrol boat?" Robinson requested. "It's the *Henley*, in charge of Chief Petty Officer Brown."

"I'll do that."

"Ali Singh can be arrested when your ship docks."

As the conversation was concluded, a uniformed coastguardman came in. He was introduced as Chief Petty Officer Bertram in charge of the *Alice*, which would follow Tony and Chet to the smugglers' hide-out.

"I'm ready, sir," he told his chief, after a short briefing. He turned to the boys. "All set?"

Chet and Tony nodded. As they turned to follow Bertram, Biff, Phil, and Jerry looked glum.

Noting the expressions on the three boys, Chief Robinson leaned across his desk and said, "I guess you fellows were hoping to be in on this too. How would you like to go on the *Henley* with Chief Petty Officer Brown and watch the fun?"

The eyes of the three boys lighted up and Phil said, "You mean it?"

"Do you want a formal invitation?" Chief Robinson asked with a laugh.

He rang for Chief Petty Officer Brown, and after introducing the boys, he explained what the mission of the *Henley* was to be.

"I understand, sir," Brown replied. "We'll leave at once."

The three boys followed him down to the dock and went aboard. They met the other Coast Guard men and the fast patrol boat set off. It seemed to the boys as if the sixteen miles were covered in an incredibly short time. The lights of the *Marco Polo* loomed up in the distance.

"She's moving very slowly, isn't she?" Biff asked their skipper.

"Yes, she's making only about four knots."

"So it would be easy for a small boat to come alongside and take something from her?" Phil suggested.

"Yes, it would." Quickly the officer picked up a telescope and trained it on the large craft. "The galley hatches are on the left and the tide is coming in," he reported. "Anything thrown overboard will float toward shore."

He ordered the wheelsman to go past the *Marco Polo,* come down the other side, and approach within three hundred yards, then turn off the engine and lights.

When they reached the designated spot, Petty Officer Brown ordered everyone on board the *Henley* not to talk or to move around. The *Marco*

Polo's decks, as well as the water some distance from the craft, was illuminated by light from some of the stateroom portholes. Biff, Phil, and Jerry crowded close to the chief as he trained his powerful binoculars on the galley hatches, so he could give them a running account of anything that might happen. The officer reported little activity aboard the *Marco Polo* and the boys assumed that the passengers either were asleep or packing their luggage in anticipation of landing the next morning.

Suddenly Petty Officer Brown saw one of the hatches open. A small man, with a swarthy complexion and rather longish coal-black hair, appeared in the circular opening. He looked out, then raised a large pail and dumped its contents into the water. Quickly he closed the hatch.

"Ali Singh!" the three boys thought as Brown reported what he had seen.

They watched excitedly to see what would happen now.

Suddenly Biff grabbed Phil's arm and pointed. Vaguely they could see a long pole with a scooping net fastened to the end of it appear from outside the circle of light and fish among the debris. Petty Officer Brown reported that apparently the person holding the pole had found what he wanted, for he scooped something up and the pole vanished from sight.

The boys strained their ears for the sound of a small boat. It did not come and they were puzzled. They also wondered why Petty Officer Brown seemed to be doing nothing about trying to apprehend the person.

The tense skipper suddenly handed the binoculars to Phil. Without a word the puzzled boy looked through them at the spot where Brown had been gazing. To his amazement he could make out the dim shape of a speedboat with two figures in it. Each held an oar and was rowing the small boat away from the *Marco Polo* as fast as possible.

"We've got the smugglers dead to rights!" Petty Officer Brown whispered to the boys.

"Aren't you going to arrest them?" Phil asked.

"Not yet," the officer told him. "I'm afraid we can't do it without some shooting. I don't want to scare the passengers on the *Marco Polo*. We'll wait a few minutes."

Suddenly the engine of the smugglers' speedboat was started. Tersely, Brown began issuing orders to his men. The motors roared into action.

The chase was on!

CHAPTER XIX

The Chase

In a few minutes the *Henley's* brilliant search-light was turned on. It picked up the speedboat which was racing toward shore at full power. But gradually the Coast Guard boat lessened the distance between them.

Chief Petty Officer Brown picked up a mega-phone and shouted for the fleeing men to stop. They paid no attention.

"We'll have to show them we mean business," the officer told Biff, Phil, and Jerry. "We'll shoot across their bow."

He ordered the boys out of the line of fire, in case the smugglers should attempt to retaliate. They obeyed, and though from their shelter the three could not see the speedboat, they listened intently to what was going on.

The *Henley* plowed ahead and presently the boys heard a shot whistle through the air.

"Stop your engine!" Brown commanded. A second later he added, "Drop those guns!"

The smugglers evidently did both, for Skipper Brown said to the boys, "You fellows can come forward now."

The three scrambled to his side. Biff was just in time to see one of the two captured men half turn and slyly run his hand into the large pocket of his sports jacket. Biff expected him to pull out a gun and was about to warn Brown when the smuggler withdrew his hand and dropped something into the water.

"The rare drugs!" Biff thought.

Instantly he began peeling off his clothes, and when the others asked him what he was doing this for, he merely said, "Got an underwater job to do."

Biff was over the side in a flash and swimming with strong, long strokes to the speedboat. He went beyond it and around to the far side.

In the meantime, Petty Officer Brown had ordered the smugglers to put their hands over their heads. As the *Henley* came alongside, two of the enlisted coastguardmen jumped across and slipped handcuffs on them. Brown instructed one of the enlisted men to take their prisoners back to Coast Guard headquarters in the smugglers' boat.

"You got nothin' on us! You ain't got no right to arrest us!" one of the captured men cried out.

At that moment Biff Hooper's head appeared over the side of the speedboat and a moment later he clambered aboard. He called out, "You've got plenty on these men! Here's the evidence!"

He held up a waterproof bag, tightly sealed. It was transparent and the printing on the contents was easily read. "I happen to know that what's in here is a rare drug," Biff added. "I heard our doctor mention it just a few days ago."

This announcement took the bravado out of the smugglers. The two men insisted they were only engaged to pilot the speedboat and deliver the drugs. But they would not give the name of the person who had hired them, nor the spot to which they were supposed to go.

"We know both the answers already," Petty Officer Brown told the smugglers. Then he said to his wheelsman, "Head for the house on the cliff! They may need a little more help over there."

Biff was hauled aboard, and as he put his clothes back on, the *Henley* shot through the water. He whispered to his pals, "We'll see some more excitement, maybe."

Some time before this, Chet and Tony had reached the area where the secret tunnel was. The patrol boat which had been following them turned on its great searchlight to pick out the exact spot.

"Look!" Chet cried out.

A speedboat with two men in it had just entered

the choppy, rocky waters in front of the tunnel.

"Halt!" Skipper Bertram of the *Alice* ordered.

The man at the wheel obeyed the command and turned off his motor. But instead of surrendering, he shouted to his companion, "Dive, Sneffen!"

Quick as a flash the two smugglers disappeared into the water on the far side of their boat. When they did not reappear, Chet called:

"I'll bet they're swimming underwater to the tunnel. Aren't we going after them?"

"We sure are," Petty Officer Bertram replied. "Tony, can you find the channel which leads to that tunnel?"

"I think so," Tony answered, eying the smugglers' speedboat which now, unattended, had been thrown violently by the waves onto some rocks.

"Then we'll come on board your boat," the chief petty officer stated. He left two of his own men aboard the *Alice* to guard it and to be ready for any other smugglers who might be arriving at the hide-out.

The rest of the crew, including Bertram himself, climbed aboard the *Napoli*, and Tony started through the narrow passage between the rocks leading to the tunnel. One of the enlisted men in the prow of the boat operated a portable searchlight. Everyone kept looking for the swimmers, as they went through the tunnel, but did not see them. When the *Napoli* reached the pond, the man swung his light around the circular shore line.

"There they are!" Chet cried out.

The two smugglers, dripping wet, had just opened the secret door into the cliff. They darted through and the door closed behind them.

Tony pulled his boat to the ledge in front of the door, turned off the engine, and jumped ashore with the others. To their surprise the door was not locked.

"I'll go first," Bertram announced.

"But be careful!" Chet begged. "There may be a man with a gun on the other side!"

The officer ordered everyone to stand back as he pulled the door open. He beamed the searchlight inside. No one was in sight!

"Come on, men!" the skipper said excitedly.

The group quickly went along the route the Hardys had discovered earlier. When they reached the corridor and saw the three doors, Tony suggested that they look inside to see if the Hardys were prisoners. One by one each room was examined but found to be empty.

The searchers hurried on down the corridor and up the stairway which led to the woodshed of the Pollitt place. They pushed the trap door but it did not open. Their light revealed no hidden springs or catches.

"The two smugglers that got away from us may have sounded an alarm," Bertram said. "They probably set something heavy on top of this trap door to delay us."

"Then we'll heave it off!" Chet declared.

He and Tony, with two of the enlisted men, put their shoulders to the trap door and heaved with all their might. At last it raised a little, then fell back into place.

"It isn't nailed shut from the other side at any rate," Bertram said. "Give it another shove!"

The four beneath it tried once more. Now they all could hear something sliding sideways.

"All together now!" Chet said, puffing. "One, two, three!"

The heave that followed did the trick. A heavy object above toppled with a crash, and the trap door opened. As before, Chief Petty Officer Bertram insisted upon being the first one out. There was not a sound from the grounds nor the house and not a light in evidence. He told the others to come up but cautioned:

"This may be an ambush. Watch your step and if anything starts to pop, you two boys go back down through the trap door."

Suddenly there was a sound of cars turning into the lane leading to the Pollitt place. The vehicles' lights were so bright that Bertram said, "I believe it's the police!"

A few moments later the cars reached the rear of the old house and state troopers piled out. Chief

Petty Officer Bertram hurried forward to introduce himself to Captain Ryder of the State Police. The two held a whispered conversation. From what the boys overheard, they figured that the troopers planned to raid the house.

Just as the men seemed to have reached a decision, everyone was amazed to see a man appear at the rear window of the second-floor hall. He held a gun in his right hand, but with his left he gestured for attention.

"My name's Snattman," he announced with a theatrical wave of his hand. "Before you storm this place, I want to talk to you! I know you've been looking for me and my men a long time. But I'm not going to let you take me without some people on your side getting killed first!" He paused dramatically.

"Come to the point, Snattman," Captain Ryder called up to him. He, too, had a gun poised for action should this become necessary.

"I mean," the smuggler cried out, "that I got three hostages in this house—Fenton Hardy and his two sons!"

Chet and Tony jumped. The boys had found their father, only to become captives themselves. And now the three were to be used as hostages!

"What's the rest?" Captain Ryder asked acidly.

"This: If you'll let me and my men go, we'll clear out of here. One will stay behind long

enough to tell you where the Hardys are." Snattman now set his jaw. "But if you come in and try
to take us, it'll be curtains for the Hardys!"

Chet's and Tony's hearts sank. What was going
to be the result of this nightmarish dilemma?

In the meantime Frank, Joe, and their father,
for the past hour, had despaired of escaping before
Snattman might carry out his sinister threat. After
the smuggler left the attic, they had heard ham-
mering and suspected the smugglers were nailing
bars across the door. The Hardys tiptoed to the
foot of the stairway, only to find their fears confirmed.

"If those bars are made of wood," Frank whispered, "maybe we can cut through them with our
knives without too much noise."

"We'll try," his father agreed. "Joe, take that
knife I got from Malloy."

As Detective Hardy sat on the steps, leaning
weakly against the wall, his two sons got to work.
They managed to maneuver the knives through
the crack near the knob. Finding the top of the
heavy crossbars, the boys began to cut and hack
noiselessly. Frank's knife was already dull and it
was not long before Joe's became so. This greatly
hampered their progress.

Half an hour later the boys' arms were aching
so badly that Frank and Joe wondered how they
could continue. But the thought that their lives

were at stake drove them on. They would rest for two or three minutes, then continue their efforts. Finally Joe finished cutting through one bar and started on the second of the three they had found. Ten minutes later Frank managed to cut through his.

"Now we can take turns," he told his brother.

Working this way, with rest periods in between, the boys found the task less arduous.

"We're almost free!" Joe finally said hopefully.

Just then, the Hardys heard cars coming into the driveway. They were sure that the police had arrived because of the illumination flooding the place even to the crack under the attic door.

It was less than a minute later that they heard the cars come to a stop outside and then Snattman's voice bargaining for his own life in exchange for his hostages!

"Let's break this door down and take our chances," Frank whispered hoarsely.

"No!" his father said. "Snattman and his men would certainly shoot us!"

At this instant Frank gave a low cry of glee. His knife had just hacked through the last wooden bar. Turning the knob, he opened the door and the three Hardys stole silently from their prison.

From the bedroom doorway they peered out to where Snattman was still trying to bargain with the police. No one else was around. The boys and their father looked at one another, telegraphing a common thought.

They would rush the king of the smugglers and overpower him!

CHAPTER XX

The Smuggler's Request

As THE three Hardys crept forward, hoping to overpower Snattman before he saw them, they heard a voice outside the house say, "You'll never get away with this, Snattman! You may as well give up without any shooting!"

"I'll never give up!"

"The house is surrounded with troopers and Coast Guard men!"

"What do I care?" Snattman shouted, waving his arms out the window. "I got three hostages here, and I've got one of the Coast Guard."

"He's in the house too?"

Snattman laughed. "Trying to catch me, eh? Well, I'm not going to answer that question."

There was silence outside the house. This seemed to worry the man. He cried out, "It won't do you any good to talk things over! I got you where I want you and—"

Like three stalking panthers Frank, Joe, and their father pounced upon the unwary smuggler. Mr. Hardy knocked the man's gun from his hand. It flew out the window and thudded to the ground below. The boys pinned his arms back and buckled in his knees.

From below came a whoop of joy. "The Hardys have captured Snattman!" The voice was Chet Morton's.

"My men will never let you in here!" the victim screamed. He snarled, twisted, and turned in his captors' grip.

Mr. Hardy, fearful that Snattman would shout to order his men upstairs, clamped a hand over the smuggler's mouth. By this time there was terrific confusion inside and outside the Pollitt place. State troopers and the Coast Guard men had burst into both the front and rear doors.

Others guarded the sides of the house to prevent any escape from the windows. A few shots were fired, but soon the smuggling gang gave up without fighting further. The capture of their leader and the sudden attack had unnerved them.

The Hardys waited upstairs with their prisoner. In a few moments Chet and Tony appeared and behind them, to the utter astonishment of Frank and Joe, were Biff, Phil, and Jerry.

Stories were quickly exchanged and Mr. Hardy praised Frank's and Joe's chums for their efforts.

All this time Snattman glowered maliciously.

In a few moments chief petty officers Bertram and Brown appeared in the second-floor hall with Captain Ryder. Immediately the state trooper fastened handcuffs onto the prisoner. He was about to take him away when Frank spoke up:

"There's someone else involved in this smuggling who hasn't been captured yet."

"You mean the man who got away from here in the truck?" Officer Ryder asked. "We've set up a roadblock for him and expect to capture him any minute."

Frank shook his head. "Ali Singh, the crewman on the *Marco Polo,* has a friend who owns a small cargo ship. Right now, it's lying somewhere offshore. Snattman was thinking of putting my dad, Joe, and me on it and arranging things so that we never got home again."

The king of the smugglers, who had been silent for several minutes, now cried out, "You're crazy! There's not a word of truth in it! There isn't any boat offshore!"

The others ignored the man. As soon as he stopped yelling, Joe took up the story. "I have a hunch you'll find that your Coast Guard man is a prisoner on that cargo ship. The name of the captain is Foster."

"You mean our man Ayres is on that ship?" Petty Officer Brown asked unbelievingly.

"We don't know anyone named Ayres," Frank began. He stopped short and looked at his brother. They nodded significantly at each other, then Frank asked, "Does Ayres go under the name of Jones?"

"He might, if he were cornered. You see, he's sort of a counterspy for the Coast Guard. He pretended to join the smugglers and we haven't heard from him since Saturday."

"I found out about him," Snattman bragged. "That name Jones didn't fool us. I saw him make a sneak trip to your patrol boat."

Frank and Joe decided this was the scene they had seen through the telescope. They told about their rescue of "Jones" after a hand grenade had nearly killed him. They also gave an account of how his kidnapers had come to the Kane farmhouse, bound up the farmer and his wife, and taken "Jones."

Skipper Brown said he would send a patrol boat out to investigate the waters in the area and try to find Captain Foster's ship.

"We'll wait here for you," Captain Ryder stated. "This case seems to be one for both our branches of service. Two kidnapings on land and a theft from the *Marco Polo*, as well as an undeclared vessel offshore."

While he was gone, the Hardys attempted to question Snattman. He refused to admit any guilt in connection with smuggling operations or the shipment of stolen goods from one state to another. Frank decided to talk to him along different lines, hoping that the smuggler would inadvertently confess something he did not intend to.

"I heard you inherited this house from your uncle, Mr. Pollitt," Frank began.

"That's right. What's it to you?"

Frank was unruffled. "I was curious about the tunnel and the stairways and the cave," he said pleasantly. "Did your uncle build them?"

Snattman dropped his sullen attitude. "No, he didn't," the smuggler answered. "My uncle found them all by accident. He started digging through his cellar wall to enlarge the place, and broke right through to that corridor."

"I see," said Frank. "Have you any idea who did build it?"

Snattman said that his uncle had come to the conclusion that the tunnel and pond had been discovered by pirates long, long ago. They apparently had decided it would be an ideal hide-out and had built the steps all the way to the top of the ground.

"Of course the woodshed wasn't there then," Snattman explained. "At least not the one that's here now. The trap door was, though, but there was a tumble-down building over it."

"How about the corridor? Was it the same size when your uncle found it?"

"Yes," the smuggler answered. "My uncle figured that was living quarters for the pirates when they weren't on their ship."

"Pretty fascinating story," Tony Prito spoke up.

Several seconds of silence followed. Snattman's eyes darted from one boy to another. Finally they fastened on Frank Hardy and he said:

"Now that I'm going to prison, the eyepieces to your telescope, and your motorcycle tools, won't do me any good. You'll find them in a drawer in the kitchen."

"Thanks a lot," said Frank.

There was another short silence. Then the smuggler went on, his head down and his eyes almost closed, "Mr. Hardy, I envy you. And I—I never thought I'd be making this kind of a confession. You know almost everything about what I've been doing. I'll tell the whole story later. Since they're going to find that Coast Guard officer, Ayres, on Foster's ship there's no use in my holding out any longer.

"I said I envy you, Mr. Hardy. It's because you brought up two such fine boys and they got swell friends. Me—I wasn't so lucky. My father died when I was little. I was pretty headstrong and my mother couldn't manage me. I began to make the wrong kind of friends and after that—you know how it is.

"My uncle, who owned this place, might have helped me, but he was mean and selfish and never gave us any money. The most he would do was invite my mother and me here once in a while for a short visit. I hated him because he made my mother work very hard around the house all the time we were here. It wasn't any vacation for her.

"One of the times when I was here my uncle showed me the pirates' hide-out and I never forgot it. After I got in with a gang of hoods I kept thinking about this place, and what a swell hideout it would be for smugglers. I was afraid to try it while my uncle was alive. But when I heard he was dead, I thought that was my chance.

"You see, I didn't dare go to claim the property as the rightful heir. But now I'm planning to take it over. Of course it won't do me any good, because I know I'll have to do a long stretch in the pen. But I'm going to ask those executors to use my uncle's money to run this place as a boys' home—I mean a place where boys without proper home training can come to live."

The group listening to Snattman, king of the smugglers, were too overwhelmed by his complete change of heart to say anything for a few seconds. But when the man looked up, as if pleading for his hearers to believe him, Mr. Hardy said, "That's a very fine thing for you to do, Snattman. I'm sure that the boys who benefit from living here will always be grateful to you."

The solemn scene was suddenly interrupted by the return of Chief Petty Officer Brown. He reported that another patrol boat had picked up his message about Captain Foster's ship and within a few minutes had reported sighting it. Then, within a quarter of an hour, word came that Captain Foster had been put under arrest, and that the missing Coast Guard man had been found on the ship, as well as a quantity of merchandise which the captain had expected Snattman to remove.

The prisoners were now taken away from the Pollitt home and the Hardys and their friends found themselves alone.

Chet asked suddenly, "How do we get home?"

Tony grinned. "I guess the *Napoli* will hold all of us."

The group went to the woodshed, opened the trap door, and started down the secret passageway to the pond below. They climbed into the *Napoli* and Tony slipped behind the wheel. The Coast Guard men thoughtfully had left the portable searchlight on the prow and Tony was able to make the trip through the tunnel and the narrow channel out to the ocean without accident.

Suddenly Frank spoke up, "Dad, what happened to your car?"

Mr. Hardy smiled. "It's in Bayport in a garage. I was being followed, so I shook off the shadowers and took the bus." He added ruefully, "But it didn't do me much good. Snattman's men attacked me and took me prisoner on the road."

The famous detective now said, "While I have the chance, I want to thank each of you boys individually for what you did. Without the seven of you, this case might never have been solved and I might not have been found alive."

Modestly Frank and Joe and their friends acknowledged the praise, secretly hoping another mystery would come their way soon. One did and by learning *The Secret of the Old Mill* the Hardy boys encountered a cunning gang of counterfeiters.

Suddenly Joe remarked, "Compliments are flying around here pretty thick, but there's one person we forgot to mention. Without him, Frank and I might never have found Dad."

"Who's that?" Biff asked.

"Pretzel Pete!" Joe replied.

"That's right," said Frank. "All together, fellows! A rousing cheer for Pretzel Pete!"

THE SECRET OF THE OLD MILL

Joe had to act fast to avoid being crushed
beneath the turning wheel!

Hardy Boys Mystery Stories

THE SECRET

OF THE OLD

MILL

BY

FRANKLIN W. DIXON

NEW YORK
GROSSET & DUNLAP
A NATIONAL GENERAL COMPANY
Publishers

In this new story, based on the original of the same title, Mr. Dixon has incorporated the most up-to-date methods used by police and private detectives.

CONTENTS

CONTENTS

CHAPTER I

A Narrow Escape

"WONDER what mystery Dad's working on now?" Joe Hardy asked.

His brother Frank looked eagerly down the platform of the Bayport railroad station. "It must be a very important case, the way Dad dashed off to Detroit. We'll know in a few minutes."

Joe looked at his watch impatiently. "Train's late."

Both boys were wondering, too, about a certain surprise their father had hinted might be ready for them upon his return.

Waiting with Frank and Joe for Mr. Hardy's arrival was their best friend Chet Morton. "Your dad's cases are always exciting—and dangerous," the plump, ruddy-faced boy remarked. "Do you think he'll give you a chance to help out on this one?"

"We sure hope so," Joe replied eagerly.

"Well, if I know you fellows," Chet went on, "you'll get mixed up in the mystery, somehow—and so will I, sooner or later. There goes my peaceful summer vacation!"

Frank and Joe chuckled, knowing that Chet, despite his penchant for taking things easy and avoiding unnecessary risks, would stick by them through any peril.

Dark-haired, eighteen-year-old Frank, and blond impetuous Joe, a year younger, had often assisted their detective father, Fenton Hardy, in solving baffling mysteries. There was nothing the two brothers liked more than tackling a tough case, either with their father, or by themselves.

Chet gave a huge sigh and leaned against a baggage truck as though his weight were too much for him. "I sure could use something to eat," he declared. "I should have brought along some candy or peanuts."

The Hardys exchanged winks. They frequently needled their friend about his appetite, and Joe could not resist doing so now.

"What's the matter, Chet? Didn't you have lunch? Or did you forget to eat?"

The thought of this remote possibility brought a hearty laugh from Frank. Chet threw both boys a glance of mock indignation, then grinned. "Okay, okay. I'm going inside and get some candy from the machine."

As Chet went into the station, the Hardys

looked across to the opposite platform where a northbound train roared in. The powerful diesel ground to a halt, sparks flashing from under the wheels. Passengers began to alight.

"Did you notice that there weren't any passengers waiting to board the train?" Frank remarked.

At that moment a man dashed up the stairs onto the platform toward the rear of the train. As the train started to move, the stranger made a leap for the last car.

"Guess he made it. That fellow's lucky," Joe commented as the train sped away. *"And* crazy!"

"You're telling me!" Chet exclaimed, as he rejoined the brothers. Munching on a chocolate bar, he added, "That same man stopped me in the station and asked me to change a twenty-dollar bill. There was a long line at the ticket window, so he didn't want to wait for change there. He grabbed the money I gave him and rushed out the door as if the police were after him!"

"Boy!" Joe exclaimed. "You must be really loaded with money if you could change a twenty-dollar bill."

Chet blushed and tried to look as modest as he could. "Matter of fact, I do have a good bit with me," he said proudly. "I guess the man saw it when I pulled out my wallet to be sure the money was there."

"What are you going to do with all your cash?"

Frank asked curiously. "Start a mint of your own?"

"Now, don't be funny, Frank Hardy," Chet retorted. "You must have noticed that for a long time I haven't been spending much. I've been saving like mad to buy a special scientific instrument. After your dad arrives, I'm going to pick it up."

"What kind of hobby are you latching onto this time, Chet?" Frank asked, grinning.

From past experience, Frank and Joe knew that their friend's interest in his new hobby would only last until another hobby captured his fancy.

"This is different," Chet insisted. "I'm going to the Scientific Specialties Store and buy a twin-lensed, high-powered microscope—and an illuminator to go with it."

"A microscope!" Joe exclaimed. "What are you going to do with it—hunt for the answers to school exams?"

Frank joined Joe in a loud laugh, but Chet did not seem to think there was anything funny about it.

"Just you two wait," he muttered, kicking a stone that was lying on the platform. "You don't know whether or not I'll decide to be a naturalist or even a zoologist."

"Wow!" said Joe. "I can just see a sign: *Chester Morton, Big-game Naturalist.*"

"Okay," Chet said. "Maybe even you two great detectives will need me to help you with some of your cases."

The conversation ended with Frank's saying, "Here comes Dad's train."

The express from Detroit rolled into the station. The brothers and their friend scanned the passengers alighting. To their disappointment, Mr. Hardy was not among them.

"Aren't there any other Bayport passengers?" Frank asked a conductor.

"No, sir," the trainman called out as he waved the go-ahead signal to the engineer and jumped back onto the car.

As the train pulled out, Joe said, "Dad must have been delayed at the last moment. Let's come back to the station and meet the four-o'clock train."

"That's plenty of time for you fellows to go with me and pick up my microscope," said Chet.

The boys walked to Chet's jalopy, nicknamed Queen, parked in the station lot. The Queen had been painted a brilliant yellow, and "souped up" by Chet during one of the periods when engines were his hobby. It was a familiar and amusing sight around the streets of Bayport.

"She's not fancy, but she gets around pretty quick," Chet often maintained stoutly. "I wouldn't trade her for all the fancy cars in the showrooms."

"The gas gauge reads 'Empty,'" Joe observed, as Chet backed the jalopy from the curb. "How do you figure we'll make it downtown?"

Chet was unconcerned. "Oh, the tank's really half full. I'll have to fix that gauge."

The Hardys exchanged amused glances, knowing that Chet would soon be so absorbed in his

microscope he would forget to tinker with the car.

Suddenly Chet swung the Queen around in the parking lot. The rough gravel caught in the tire treads and rattled against the rear fenders.

"Hey! What's the big rush?" Joe demanded. "We have three whole hours to get back there!"

"Who's in a hurry?" said Chet, adding proudly, "I'm not driving fast. I just wanted to find out if I changed the turning circle of the Queen by adjusting the tie rods."

"Some adjustment!" Joe grimaced. "Think we'll get to town in one piece?"

"Huh!" Chet snorted. "You don't appreciate great mechanical genius when you see it!"

In the business center of Bayport, the boys found traffic heavy. Fortunately, Chet found a parking spot across the street from the Scientific Specialties Store and swung the car neatly into the space.

"See what I mean?" he asked. "Good old Queen. And boy, I can't wait to start working with that microscope!" Chet exclaimed as the three boys got out and walked to the corner.

"All bugs beware." Joe grinned.

"You ought to be a whiz in science class next year," Frank said while they waited for the light to change.

When it flashed green, the trio started across the street. Simultaneously, a young boy on a bicycle began to ride toward them from the opposite side of the street.

The next moment a large sedan, its horn honking loudly, sped through the intersection against the red light and roared directly toward the Hardys and Chet. Instantly Frank gave Joe and Chet a tremendous push and they all leaped back to safety. To their horror, the sedan swerved and the young boy on the bicycle was directly in its path.

"Look out!" the Hardys yelled at him.

CHAPTER II

Trailing a Detective

THE BOY on the bicycle heard the Hardys' warning just in time and swerved away from the onrushing car. He skidded and ran up against the curb.

The momentum carried the boy over the handlebars. He landed in a sitting position on the pavement, looking dazed.

"That driver must be out of his head!" Joe yelled as he, Frank, and Chet dashed over to the boy.

The sedan continued its erratic path, and finally, with brakes squealing and horn blaring, slammed into the curb. It had barely missed a parked car.

By now the Hardys and Chet had reached the boy. He was still seated on the sidewalk, holding his head. "Are you all right?" Frank asked, bending down. The boy was about fourteen years old, very thin and tall for his age.

"I—I think so." A grateful look came into the boy's clear brown eyes. "Thanks for the warning, fellows! Whew! That was close!"

Frank and Joe helped him to his feet. A crowd had gathered, and the Hardys had a hard time keeping the onlookers back. Just then the driver of the sedan made his way through the throng. He was a middle-aged man, and his face was ashen and drawn.

"I'm sorry! I'm sorry! My brakes wouldn't hold. Are you fellows all right?" The driver was frantic with worry. "It happened so fast—I—I just couldn't stop!"

"In that case, you're lucky no one was hurt," Frank said calmly.

The Hardys saw a familiar uniformed figure push through the crowd toward them.

"What's going on?" he demanded. He was Officer Roberts, a member of the local police department and an old friend of the Hardys. The driver of the car started to explain, but by this time he had become so confused, his statements were incoherent.

"What happened, Frank?" Officer Roberts asked.

Frank assured him no one was hurt, and said that apparently the mishap had been entirely accidental, and the only damage was to the boy's bicycle. The front wheel spokes were bent, and some of the paint was scratched off the fender.

The car driver, somewhat calmer now, insisted upon giving the boy five dollars toward repairs.

"I'll phone for a tow truck," Joe offered, and hurried off to make the call while Officer Roberts got the traffic moving again.

After the garage truck had left with the sedan, and the crowd had dispersed, the boy with the bicycle gave a sudden gasp.

"My envelope!" he cried out. "Where is it?"

The Hardys and Chet looked around. Joe was the first to spot a large Manila envelope in the street near the curb. He stepped out and picked it up. "Is this yours?" he asked.

"Yes! I was afraid it was lost!"

As Joe handed over the heavy, sealed envelope, he noticed that it was addressed in bold printing to Mr. Victor Peters, Parker Building, and had *Confidential* marked in the lower left-hand corner.

The boy smiled as he took the envelope and mounted his bicycle. "Thanks a lot for helping me, fellows. My name is Ken Blake."

The Hardys and Chet introduced themselves and asked Ken if he lived in Bayport.

"Not really," Ken answered slowly. "I have a summer job near here."

"Oh! Where are you working?" Chet asked.

Ken paused a moment before replying. "At a place outside of town," he said finally.

Although curious about Ken's apparent evasiveness, Frank changed the subject. He had been observing the bicycle with interest. Its handle-bars were a different shape from most American models. The handgrips were much higher than the center post and the whole effect was that of a deep U.

"That's a nifty bike," he said. "What kind is it?"

Ken looked pleased. "It was made in Belgium. Rides real smooth." Then he added, "I'd better get back on the job now. I have several errands to do. So long, and thanks again."

As Ken rode off, Joe murmured, "Funny he's so secretive about where he lives and works."

Frank agreed. "I wonder why."

Chet scoffed. "There you go again, making a mystery out of it."

Frank and Joe had acquired their keen obser-vation and interest in places and people from their father, one of the most famous investigators in the United States.

Only recently, the boys had solved *The Tower Treasure* mystery. Shortly afterward, they had used all their ingenuity and courage to uncover a dangerous secret in the case of *The House on the Cliff*.

"Come on, you two," Chet urged. "Let's get my microscope before anything else happens."

They had almost reached the Scientific Specialties Store when Joe grabbed his brother's arm and pointed down the street.

"Hey!" he exclaimed. "There's Oscar Smuff. What's *he* up to?"

The other boys looked and saw a short, stout man who was wearing a loud-checkered suit and a soft felt hat. Chet guffawed. "He acts as if he were stalking big game in Africa! Where's the lion?"

"I think"—Frank chuckled—"our friend is trying to shadow someone."

"If he is," Chet said, "how could anybody *not* know Oscar Smuff was following him?"

Oscar Smuff, the Hardys knew, wanted to be a member of the Bayport Police Department. He had read many books on crime detection, but, though he tried hard, he was just not astute enough to do anything right. The boys had encountered him several times while working on their own cases. Usually Smuff's efforts at detection had proved more hindrance than help, and at times actually laughable.

"Let's see what happens," said Joe.

In a second the boys spotted the man Oscar Smuff was tailing—a tall, trim, well-dressed stranger. He carried a suitcase and strode along as though he was going some place with a firm purpose in mind.

The boys could hardly restrain their laughter

as they watched Smuff's amateurish attempts to put into action what he had read about sleuthing.

"He's about as inconspicuous as an elephant!" Chet observed.

Smuff would run a few steps ahead of the stranger, then stop at a store window and pretend to be looking at the merchandise on display. Obviously he was waiting for the man to pass him, but Smuff did not seem to care what kind of window he was looking in. Joe nudged Frank and Chet when Oscar Smuff paused before the painted-over window of a vacant store.

"Wonder what he's supposed to be looking at," Chet remarked.

Smuff hurried on, then suddenly stopped again. He took off his jacket, threw it over his arm, and put on a pair of horn-rimmed glasses.

"Get a load of his tactics now!" Joe laughed. "He's trying to change his appearance."

Frank chuckled. "Oscar's been studying about how to tail, but he needs a lot more practice."

"He probably suspects the man has contraband in his suitcase," Joe guessed, grinning.

The tall stranger suddenly turned and looked back at Smuff. The would-be detective had ducked into a doorway and was peering out like a child playing hide-and-seek. For a moment Smuff and the stranger stared at each other. The man shrugged as though puzzled about what was going on, then continued walking.

Smuff kept up his comical efforts to shadow his quarry, unaware that the boys were following him. Near the end of the block, the man turned into a small variety store and Smuff scurried in after him.

"Come on!" said Joe to Frank and Chet. "This is too good to miss."

The boys followed. Oscar Smuff was standing behind a display of large red balloons. He was so intent on his quarry that he still did not notice the Hardys and Chet.

Frank looked around the store quickly and saw the stranger at the drug counter selecting some toothpaste. The suitcase was on the floor beside him. As they watched, the man picked up the toothpaste and his bag, and went up front to the checkout counter. He took out a bill and gave it to the woman cashier.

Immediately Smuff went into action. He dashed from behind the balloons and across the front of the store. Elbowing several customers out of the way, he grasped the man by the arm and in a loud voice announced, "You're under arrest! Come with me!"

The man looked at Oscar Smuff as though he were crazy. So did the cashier. Other people quickly crowded around.

"What's the matter?" someone called out.

The Hardys and Chet hurried forward, as the man pulled his arm away from Smuff's grasp and demanded angrily, "What's the meaning of this?"

"You know very well what's the meaning of this," Smuff blustered, and grabbed the man's arm again. "Now, miss"—Smuff turned to the cashier—"let me see the bill this man just gave you."

The woman was too surprised to refuse the request and handed the bill to the amateur detective.

Smuff took the money. The Hardys stepped up and peered over his shoulder. The bill was a five-dollar one. Suddenly the expression on Smuff's face changed to confusion and concern.

"Oh—er—a five—" he stuttered.

He dropped his hold on the man's arm and stared down at the floor. "Awfully sorry," he muttered. "It's been—a—mistake."

Both the man and the cashier looked completely bewildered. The next moment Smuff whirled and dashed from the store.

The Hardys and Chet rushed after him. They were overwhelmed with curiosity as to what Smuff thought the man had done. The boys soon overtook the would-be detective.

"What's up?" Joe demanded. "Looking for somebody suspicious?"

Oscar Smuff reddened when he realized the boys had witnessed his entire performance.

"Never mind," he said sharply. "I'll bet even you smart-aleck Hardys have made mistakes. Any-

how, this is different. I'm helping the police on
a very special, very confidential case."

As he made the last statement, Smuff shrugged
off his look of embarrassment and assumed an air
of great importance.

"Well, I can't waste precious time gabbing
with *you* three." Smuff turned and rushed off
down the street.

The boys watched his bustling figure as he
disappeared into the crowd. "I wonder what kind
of case 'Detective' Smuff *is* working on?" Frank
mused.

"I do too," Joe said, as Chet finally led the way
into the Scientific Specialties Store.

Mr. Reed, the shop owner, stood behind the
counter. He was a plump, pleasant man with a
shock of white hair that stood erect on his head.

"Have you come for your microscope, Chet?"
he asked. As he spoke, the man's head bobbed up
and down and his white hair waved back and forth
as though blown by the wind.

"Yes, sir, Mr. Reed," Chet said enthusiastically. "My friends, Frank and Joe, are looking
forward to trying out the microscope just as much
as I am."

Joe smiled a little skeptically, but Frank agreed
with his chum. Chet pulled out his wallet and
emptied it of ten- and twenty-dollar bills. "Here
you are, Mr. Reed. I've been saving for a long
time so I could get the best."

"And the best this is." Mr. Reed smiled. "I'll get the microscope you want from the stockroom." The proprietor picked up the money and disappeared into the back of the store.

While they waited, Chet pointed out the various instruments on display in the showcase. The Hardys were surprised at how much Chet had learned about microscopes and their use.

After waiting five minutes, Chet grew impatient. "Wonder what's keeping Mr. Reed," he said. "I hope he has my 'scope in stock."

At that moment Mr. Reed returned. There was a look of concern on his face.

"Don't tell me you haven't got the model." Chet groaned.

Mr. Reed shook his head. When he spoke, his voice was solemn.

"It's not that, Chet," he said. "I'm afraid that one of the twenty-dollar bills you gave me is a counterfeit!"

CHAPTER III

An Unexpected Return

"*COUNTERFEIT!*" Chet burst out. "*Counterfeit!* It can't be. I just drew the money out of the bank this morning."

The Hardys, nonplused, stared at the twenty-dollar bill Mr. Reed was holding.

"I'm sorry, Chet," Mr. Reed said sympathetically. "But just a few days ago all the storekeepers in town were notified by the police to be on the lookout for fake twenties. Otherwise, I wouldn't have checked it. I can't understand, though, why the bank didn't detect it."

Frank's mind raced. "Wait a minute!" he exclaimed. "Chet, what about the man you made change for at the station?"

"You're right, Frank!" Joe put in. "*He* must have passed Chet the phony twenty!"

"You mean he gave it to me on purpose?" Chet asked indignantly.

"It's possible," Frank said. "Of course it would be pretty hard to prove whether he did it intentionally or not."

"What did the man look like?" Joe questioned Chet. "We got only a glimpse of him running for the train. He was medium height and stocky, but did you notice anything else about him?"

Chet thought for a few seconds. Then he said, "I do remember that the man had a sharp nose. But he was wearing sunglasses and a slouch hat, so I didn't notice much else."

The Hardys tried to fix a picture of the man in their minds. Meanwhile, Chet looked gloomily at the bogus bill.

"What luck!" he complained. "Here I am cheated out of twenty dollars and the microscope."

"I'm sorry, Chet," Mr. Reed said. "I wish there was something I could do about it."

"Don't worry, Chet," said Joe. "You'll get the microscope, anyway." He turned to his brother. "How much money do you have with you?" he asked. "I have five-fifty."

Frank emptied his pockets, but all he had was three dollars in change and bills.

"We'll lend you what we have," Joe offered. "Eight-fifty."

Although Chet protested, the Hardys insisted, and Mr. Reed added, "You can take the microscope along and pay me the balance when you can."

Frank and Joe put their money on the counter, while Mr. Reed went to wrap the instrument.

"Thanks. You're real pals," Chet said gratefully.

When the store owner returned with the package, Chet said, "I'll go right down to Dad's office and borrow the balance. We'll get back here later this afternoon. Thanks very much, Mr. Reed."

The boys were about to leave when Frank had a sudden thought.

"Mr. Reed," he said, "would you let us borrow that counterfeit bill for some close study? We'll be sure to turn it over to Chief Collig."

"Swell idea," Joe said.

The proprietor, who was familiar with the Hardys' reputation as sleuths, readily assented. Frank put the bill in his pocket and the boys left the store.

They hurried back to Chet's car and drove to Mr. Morton's real-estate office several blocks away. The office was on the street level of a small building. They entered and were greeted pleasantly by Mr. Morton's efficient secretary, Miss Benson.

"Hello, boys. Enjoying your summer vacation?"

"Yes, thanks, Miss Benson," Chet said, eying

his father's empty desk. "When will Dad be back?"

"Your father's gone for the day, Chet," she replied. "He decided to go home early."

"That's funny," Chet mused. "Dad usually stays until five at least."

"We have time to drive out to the farm before we meet the train," Joe said. "Let's go."

The Morton farm was on the outskirts of Bayport. When Chet swung the car into the driveway, Joe noticed with pleasure that Iola, Chet's sister, was waving to them from the front porch. Dark-haired Iola, slim and vivacious, was Joe's favorite date.

When they told her about the counterfeit bill, she exclaimed, "What a shame!"

Joe agreed emphatically. "And we'd sure like to get a lead on the man who passed it to Chet."

"Sounds as if you Hardys are in the mood for some sleuthing," Iola said with a twinkle in her eye.

"What's this about sleuthing?" asked attractive Mrs. Morton as she came outside and joined the group.

The boys quickly explained. Then Chet asked his mother, "Is Dad around?"

Mrs. Morton smiled. "He isn't here right now, Chet. He's attending to an important job."

Chet looked disappointed until his sister giggled and said, "Dad's not too far away." Iola winked at her mother and they both began to laugh.

"Your father's important job is at his favorite fishing spot," Mrs. Morton told Chet.

"Fishing!" Chet exclaimed. "He never goes fishing during the week!"

"He did this time," said Mrs. Morton. "I guess the good weather was too much for him to resist."

A few minutes later the boys were in the jalopy and driving down a country road bordered by woods. A half mile farther, Chet stopped and turned off the Queen's engine. The sound of rushing water could be heard.

"This is the spot," Chet announced, and they started off through the woods.

The boys soon came to a clear running stream and spotted Mr. Morton seated contentedly on the bank. He was leaning against a tree, holding his rod lightly between his knees and steadying it with his hands.

Just as the boys called a greeting to him, the line began to jerk and almost immediately the rod bent till the tip was close to the water. Mr. Morton leaped to his feet and shouted, "Just a minute, fellows! I've hooked a lulu!"

Mr. Morton was an expert. He let the fish take just enough line to bury the hook properly, then he very gently braked the reel with his thumb.

So intent was Mr. Morton on his fishing, he

was not aware that his son was now rushing down the slope toward him. Suddenly Chet slipped on a moss-covered rock and fell forward. He lost his grip on the box containing the microscope and it flew toward the water. Joe, behind Chet, leaped forward and grabbed the box.

"Whew!" Chet exclaimed, regaining his balance. "Good work, Joe! Thanks a million!"

The three boys joined Mr. Morton, who was busy landing his catch, a fine, smallmouthed black bass. He held up the fish for them to admire. "Isn't it a beauty, boys?" he said.

"Terrific, Dad," Chet replied, still out of breath from his near tumble. "And I have something to show *you*."

He unwrapped the package and held out the microscope. Mr. Morton put the fish in his creel, then studied the instrument closely.

"It's a topnotch one, son," he declared. "And just the model you wanted."

"Yes, Dad. Only there's a slight problem connected with it."

"Oh—oh." Mr. Morton chuckled good-naturedly. "I should have known from the look on your face. You didn't have enough money, after all. Well, how much do you need?"

"That isn't all there is to it," Chet hastened to inform him, and told about the counterfeit bill.

Mr. Morton's face darkened. "I hope we're not in for a flood of phony bills."

Frank nodded. "Especially since these are very clever imitations."

Chet's father handed over twenty dollars in small bills.

"Thanks, Dad."

"From now on, Chet, be careful about making change for strangers," Mr. Morton cautioned.

"I will," his son promised fervently. "Getting cheated once is enough!"

Chet paid the Hardys the money they had lent him. Then he said to his father, "I sure was surprised when Mother told me you were fishing —in the middle of the week."

Mr. Morton smiled broadly. "I've been working hard the past year on the big sale of land to Elekton Controls," he said. "I thought it was time to take an afternoon off and do some thinking while the fish were nibbling."

"Is that the property in back of the plant they just finished building?" asked Frank.

"That's right." Mr. Morton pointed upstream. "You can just see the top of the main building from here."

"The property you sold has the old Turner mill on it," Joe remarked. "Quite a contrast. A company that makes top-secret control parts for space missiles in a modern building right next to an ancient, abandoned gristmill."

"I suppose they'll tear the old place down," Frank remarked.

"No, Elekton has decided to use it," Mr. Morton went on. "I suggested to them that the old mill would make an attractive gatehouse for the plant's rear entrance. After all, it's a historic place, built by the settlers when this whole area was inhabited by Indians. The company has renovated the old mill a bit, restoring the old living quarters and adding modern facilities."

"Is someone living there?" Joe asked with interest.

"I understand a couple of their employees are," Mr. Morton replied. Then he continued, "They've even repaired the wheel, so it's turning again. Hearing the rushing water and the grinding of the wheel's gear mechanism brought back memories to me."

"About the Indians, Dad?" Chet joked.

"Not quite, son." His father smiled. "But I *can* remember when the mill produced the best flour around here. Your grandmother made many a delicious loaf of bread from wheat ground in the Turner mill."

"That's for me!" Chet said.

Everyone laughed as Mr. Morton reminisced further about having seen the mill in full operation when he was a boy. Suddenly he and the Hardys noticed that Chet had fallen silent. There was a familiar, faraway look in his eyes.

Joe grinned. "Chet, you're turning some new idea over in your mind."

"That's right," Chet said excitedly. "I've been thinking that maybe I could get a summer job at Elekton."

Mr. Morton exchanged amazed glances with the Hardys at the thought of Chet's working during the summer vacation! But, with growing enthusiasm, Chet went on:

"I could earn the twenty dollars I owe you, Dad. Besides, if I am going to be a scientist, I couldn't think of a better place to work."

"Elekton's a fine company," his father said. "I wish you luck, son."

"Thanks, Dad." Chet smiled broadly. "See you later. I have to go now and pay Mr. Reed the money I owe him."

On the drive back to town, Chet told Frank and Joe that he was going to apply for a job at the Elekton plant the next day.

"We'll go along," Joe offered. "I'd like to see the plant and the old mill."

"Swell," said Chet.

When they reached the shopping area in Bayport, Chet drove directly to Mr. Reed's store. The three boys had just alighted from the parked car when Chet excitedly grabbed his friends' arms.

"There he is!" the chubby boy exclaimed. "Right down the street—the man who gave me that phony twenty!"

CHAPTER IV

The Shadowy Visitor

"THERE he goes! Across the street!" Joe said excitedly. "Let's ask him about the counterfeit bill!"

The three boys broke into a run, dodging in and out of the crowd of afternoon shoppers. The Hardys kept their eyes trained on the stocky figure of their quarry.

But their chase was halted at the corner by a red traffic light against them. The street was congested with vehicles and it was impossible for the boys to get across.

"What luck!" Joe growled impatiently.

It seemed to be the longest red light they had ever encountered. When it changed, the threesome streaked across the street—but it was too late. The stocky man was lost to sight. The Hardys raced down the next two blocks, peering in every direction, but to no avail.

Disappointed, Frank and Joe went back to Chet, who had stopped to catch his breath.

"We lost him," Joe reported tersely.

Frank's eyes narrowed. "I have a hunch that man who passed the bogus twenty-dollar bill to Chet knew it was counterfeit. That last-second dash for the train was just a gimmick to make a fast getaway. But his showing up here in Bayport a couple hours after he took the train out of town is mighty peculiar."

Joe and Chet agreed. "He probably got off in Bridgeport," Frank went on. "That's the nearest big town."

As the boys walked back toward the Scientific Specialties Store, they speculated about the source of the supply of bogus money.

"Maybe it's Bridgeport," Frank said. "That could be one of the reasons he took the train there—to get a new supply, or palm off more."

"You mean they might actually make the stuff there?" Chet asked.

Frank shrugged. "Could be," he said. "I hope no more counterfeit bills are passed in Bayport."

"There probably will be," Chet said ruefully, "if this town is full of easy marks like me."

"Let's keep a sharp lookout for that fake-money passer from now on," Joe said, "and other clues to the counterfeit ring."

"Who knows," Chet put in, "it could turn out to be your next case."

As soon as Mr. Reed had been paid, the boys drove to Bayport Police Headquarters. Chet decided to take his microscope into headquarters and show it to Chief Ezra Collig. The keen-eyed, robust officer was an old friend of Fenton Hardy and his sons. Many times the four had cooperated on cases.

"Sit down," the chief said cordially. "I can see that you boys have something special on your minds. Another mystery?"

He leaned forward expectantly in his chair.

"It's possible, Chief," replied Frank as he handed over the counterfeit bill. Quickly the Hardys explained what had happened, then voiced their suspicions of the man who had just eluded them.

"Have there been any other reports of people receiving fake bills?" Joe asked the officer.

Chief Collig nodded. "Chet's not the first to be fooled," he replied. "Since the Secret Service alerted us to watch for these twenty-dollar bills, we've had nearly a dozen complaints. But we've instructed the people involved not to talk about it."

"Why?" Chet asked curiously.

"It's part of our strategy. We hope to trap at least some of the gang by lulling them into a feeling of false security."

The boys learned that Chet's description of

the stocky stranger tallied with what the police had on file.

"He's a slippery one," the chief added. "It sounds to me as if the man wears a different outfit each time he shoves a bill."

"Shoves?" echoed Chet.

"A shover—or passer—is a professional term for people who pass counterfeit money," Chief Collig explained. He rubbed the bogus bill between his fingers. "This is a clever forgery," he said. "Let's see what it looks like under your microscope, Chet."

It took just a minute to rig and focus the microscope. Then, under Chief Collig's directions, the boys scrutinized the faults in the bill.

"Look at the serial number," the chief pointed out. "That's the large, colored group of numbers that appears on the upper right and lower left portions of the bill."

As the boys peered at the number, Chief Collig made some quick calculations on his desk pad. "Divide the serial number by six," he went on, "and in this case, the remainder is two."

When the boys looked puzzled, the chief smiled. "On the upper left portion of the note you'll see a small letter. One that is not followed by a number. That's the check letter and in this case it's B."

The boys listened as Chief Collig further explained, "If the letter B corresponds to the remainder two, after you have done the division, it means the bill is either genuine—or a careful fake. The same way with the remainder, one. The check letter would be A or G; and with the remainder three, the check letter C or I, and so on."

"Wow! Some arithmetic!" Chet remarked.

Frank looked thoughtful. "In this case, the test of the divisional check indicates the bill is genuine."

"Exactly," Chief Collig said. "And the portrait of Jackson is good. The border, sometimes called lathe or scrollwork, is excellent."

"But, Chief," said Joe, puzzled, "everything you've mentioned points toward the bill's being the real thing."

"That's right. However, you'll see through the microscope that the lines in the portrait are slightly grayish and the red and blue fibers running through the bank note have been simulated with colored ink."

In turn, the boys peered through the microscope, observing the points the chief had called to their attention.

Chief Collig snapped off the light in Chet's microscope and pulled the bill out from under the clips that were holding it in place.

He handed the fake bill to Frank and at the same time gave him a genuine one from his wallet. "Now feel the difference in the paper quality," he directed.

Frank did so and could tell immediately that the forged bill was much rougher and thicker than the genuine one.

Just then the chief's telephone rang. He answered it, speaking quickly. When he hung up, Chief Collig said, "I must go out on a call, boys. Thanks for bringing in this bill. If you come across any others like it, or clues that might help the police, let me know. In the meantime, I'll relay your description of the suspect to the Secret Service, and also turn this bill over to them."

Chief Collig arose from his desk, and the boys walked out of the building with him. On the way, Joe said, "I wonder if Oscar Smuff has heard of the counterfeiting racket, and is—er—working on it."

"I wouldn't be surprised." The chief sighed. "That fellow will never give up."

The boys did not mention their encounter with Smuff earlier in the afternoon, but they were fairly certain that Oscar Smuff had trailed the man because he was a stranger in town and had been carrying a suitcase. The aspiring detective undoubtedly had jumped to the conclusion that the suitcase was filled with counterfeit money.

When the chief had gone, Joe glanced at his

watch. "If we're going to meet Dad's train, we'd better get started."

The three boys climbed into the jalopy and drove off. They arrived at the station just as the four-o'clock train was coming to a halt.

A moment later they spotted Mr. Hardy alighting from the rear car. "Dad!" cried Frank and Joe, and dashed to greet him, followed by Chet.

Fenton Hardy, a tall, distinguished-looking man, smiled broadly. "I appreciate this special reception—and a ride home, too," he added, noticing Chet's jalopy in the lot.

"Right this way, sir." Chet grinned.

Joe took his father's suitcase and everyone went to the car. As they rode along, the boys gave Mr. Hardy an account of the afternoon's exciting events.

The detective listened intently. In conclusion, Frank said, "Dad, does your new case have anything to do with the counterfeiting ring?"

Mr. Hardy did not answer for a moment. His mind seemed to be focused on another matter. Finally he said, "No. But I'll be glad to help you boys track down any clues to these counterfeiters. I have a feeling you'll be on the lookout for them!"

"We sure will!" Joe said emphatically.

As they turned into the Hardy driveway, Frank said, "Maybe more leads will show up around here."

Fenton Hardy agreed. "That's a strong possibility."

They were met at the door by Aunt Gertrude, Mr. Hardy's unmarried sister. She was a tall, angular woman, somewhat peppery in manner, but extremely kindhearted. Miss Hardy had arrived recently for one of her frequent long visits with the family. In her forthright manner she was constantly making dire predictions about the dangers of sleuthing, and the terrible fate awaiting anyone who was a detective.

She greeted her brother affectionately as everyone went into the living room. With a sigh she asked, "Will you be home for a while this time, Fenton, before you have to go dashing off on another case?"

Chuckling, Mr. Hardy replied, "I'll probably be around for a while, Gertrude—especially if the boys run into any more counterfeit money."

"What! Laura, did you hear that?" Aunt Gertrude turned to a slim, attractive woman who had just entered the room.

"I did." Mrs. Hardy greeted her husband, then urged the boys to explain.

After hearing of Chet's experience, both women shook their heads in dismay. "Well, the sooner those counterfeiters are caught, the better!" Aunt Gertrude declared firmly.

"That's what we figure, Aunty," Joe spoke up. "We'll see what we can do! Right, Frank?"

"You bet."

Chet added, grinning, "With the Hardy boys on their trail, those counterfeiters won't have a chance!"

"And Laura and I will lose sleep worrying," Aunt Gertrude prophesied.

Frank and Joe exchanged winks, knowing that actually she and Mrs. Hardy were proud of the boys' sleuthing accomplishments, though sometimes fearful of the dangers they encountered.

"What delayed you today, Fenton?" Aunt Gertrude asked her brother. "Another case, I suppose."

Mr. Hardy explained, "There is a special matter I'm investigating, but I'm not at liberty to talk about it yet."

His next remark diverted the boys' attention from the counterfeiters. "Frank and Joe, will you be free tomorrow to see the surprise I have for you both?" he asked. "It'll be ready late in the afternoon."

"We sure will!" his sons exclaimed together. They knew what they hoped the surprise would be, but did not dare count on it.

The brothers tried without success to coax a hint from their family.

"All I can say," Aunt Gertrude remarked, "is that you're mighty lucky boys!" With a deep sigh she added, "But this surprise certainly won't help my peace of mind!"

"Oh, Aunty!" said Joe. "You don't really worry about us, do you?"

"Oh, no!" she exploded. "Only on weekdays, Saturdays, and Sundays!"

Before Chet left for home, he reminded Frank and Joe of his intention to apply to Elekton Controls Limited for a job.

Overhearing him, Mr. Hardy was immediately interested. "So you want to enter the scientific field, Chet?" he said. "Good for you and lots of luck!"

The detective told the boys that the company, in addition to manufacturing controls, was engaged in secret experiments with advanced electronic controls.

"Not too long ago," he concluded, "I met some of Elekton's officers."

It flashed through Chet's mind that he might ask the detective to make an appointment for him, but he decided not to. He wanted to get the job without an assist from anyone. Frank and Joe suggested that Chet come for them early the next afternoon.

"I have an idea!" Chet exclaimed. "Let's go earlier and take along a picnic lunch. We'll be right near Willow River. After I apply for a job, we can eat by the water. Then you fellows can help me collect bark and stone specimens."

"Microscope study, eh?" Frank grinned. "Okay. It's a deal."

At supper Aunt Gertrude commented wryly, "There'll be two moons in the sky when Chet Morton settles down to a job!"

The others laughed, then the conversation reverted once more to counterfeiting. Mr. Hardy backed up Chief Collig's statement that the bogus twenty-dollar bills being circulated were clever imitations. "I heard that the Secret Service is finding it a hard case to crack," he added.

Frank and Joe were wondering about their father's other case. They realized it must be extremely confidential, and refrained from questioning him.

In the middle of the night, Joe was suddenly awakened by a clattering sound. He leaped out of bed and rushed across the room to the front window. It was a dark, moonless night, and for a moment Joe could see nothing.

But suddenly he detected a movement near the front door, then saw a shadowy figure running down the walk to the street.

"Hey!" Joe called out. "Who are you? What do you want?"

At the end of the walk, the mysterious figure leaped onto a bicycle. It swerved, nearly throwing the rider, but he regained his balance and sped off into the darkness.

"What's going on?" Joe cried out.

CHAPTER V

The Bicycle Clue

Joe ran downstairs to the front door, flung it open, and dashed outside. He reached the end of the walk and peered in the direction the mysterious cyclist had taken. The person was not in sight.

Puzzled, Joe walked back slowly to the house. Had the stranger come there by mistake? "If not, what did he want?" Joe wondered.

The rest of the Hardy family had been awakened by Joe's cries to the stranger. By this time, they were clustered at the doorway and all the lights in the house were on.

"What's the matter, Joe?" Aunt Gertrude demanded. "Who were you calling to at this unearthly hour?"

Joe was about to reply when he noticed a large white envelope protruding from the mailbox. He pulled it out, and saw that his father's name was typed on the front. "This is for you, Dad."

Joe handed the envelope to Mr. Hardy. "That fellow on the bike must have left it."

Joe was besieged with questions, and he explained what had happened.

"It's a funny way to deliver a message," Frank commented.

"Very suspicious, if you ask me!" Aunt Gertrude snapped.

Suddenly they all noticed that Mr. Hardy was frowning at the contents of the envelope—a plain piece of white paper.

"What does it say, Fenton?" Mrs. Hardy asked anxiously.

He read the typed message: " 'Drop case or else danger for you and family.' "

There was silence for a moment, then Aunt Gertrude exclaimed, "I knew it! We can't get a decent night's sleep with three detectives in the family! I just *know* there's real trouble brewing!"

Although she spoke tartly, the others realized Miss Hardy was concerned, as always, for her brother's safety.

"Now, don't worry, Gertrude," Fenton Hardy said reassuringly. "The boys and I will be on guard against any danger. This note probably is the work of a harmless crank."

Aunt Gertrude tossed her head as though she did not believe this for a moment.

"Let's all look around for clues to the person on the bike," Frank suggested.

Flashlights were procured, and the entire family searched the grounds thoroughly on both sides of the stoop and the walk. As Frank and his aunt neared the end of the front walk, Miss Hardy cried out, "There's something—next to that bush."

Frank picked up the object. "A bicycle pedal!" he exclaimed. "Aunty, this is a terrific clue! I think we have *four* detectives in the family!"

His aunt forced a rather embarrassed smile.

"The pedal must've fallen off the bike Joe saw," Frank said. "That's why it swerved."

Back in the house, the family gathered in the kitchen. They were too excited to go back to bed immediately, and the boys were eager to question their father. They all had cookies and lemonade.

"What case did the warning refer to?" Joe asked Mr. Hardy.

"I can't be sure," the detective replied slowly.

Again the boys wondered about Mr. Hardy's secret case, and longed to know what it involved. "Maybe the threat is connected with that one," Frank thought. Before the boys went to sleep, they decided to track down the pedal clue early the next morning.

Right after breakfast, Chet telephoned. He told Frank, who took the call, that his sister Iola and her friend Callie Shaw had offered to pack lunch if they could go along on the picnic.

"Swell," Frank said enthusiastically. Callie was his favorite date. "In the meantime, how'd you like to do some sleuthing with us?"

"Sure! What's up?"

Frank quickly told Chet about the excitement of the previous night. "Meet us here as soon as you can."

When Frank and Joe informed Mr. Hardy of their plan to trace the pedal, he nodded approval. "I must go out of town for a short while," he said. "But first, I'd like to examine the warning note in the lab."

The boys went with him to their fully equipped laboratory over the garage. Mr. Hardy dusted the note carefully, but when he blew the powder away, there was no sign of a fingerprint.

Holding the note up to the light, Mr. Hardy said, "There's no watermark. Of course, this is not a full sheet of paper."

"Dead end, so far." Joe frowned. "If we could only locate the typewriter this message was written on—"

Shortly after Mr. Hardy had driven off in his sedan, Chet arrived. "Where to, fellows?" he asked as they set off in the Queen.

"Center of town," Joe replied.

On the way, the brothers briefed Chet on their plan, which was to make inquiries at all the bicycle supply stores. In the first four they visited,

Frank showed the pedal and asked if there had been any requests for a replacement that morning. All the answers were negative. Finally, at the largest supply store in Bayport, they obtained some helpful information.

"This particular pedal comes from a bike made in Belgium," the proprietor said. "There isn't a store in town that carries parts for it."

The boys were disappointed. As Frank put the pedal back in his pocket he asked the proprietor where parts for the Belgian bicycle could be purchased.

"It might be worth your while to check over in Bridgeport," the man said. "I think you'll find Traylor's handles them."

"It's an odd coincidence," Frank remarked, when the boys were back in the car. "We've come across two Belgian bikes in two days."

When they reached the Traylor store in Bridgeport, the young detectives learned they had just missed a customer who had purchased a pedal for a Belgian bike.

"Who was he?" Frank inquired.

"I don't know."

"What did he look like?" Joe asked.

The proprietor's brow wrinkled. "Sorry. I was too busy to pay much attention, so I can't tell you much. As far as I can remember, he was a tall boy, maybe about fourteen."

The three friends knew this vague description

was almost useless. There probably were hundreds of boys living in the surrounding area who fitted that description.

As the boys reached the street, Joe said determinedly, "We're not giving up!"

"Hey!" Chet reminded his friends. "It's almost time to pick up the girls."

Within an hour the five young people were turning off the highway onto a side road paralleling Elekton's east fence. A little farther on Chet made a right turn and followed the dirt road that led to the rear entrance of the plant.

"Any luck sleuthing?" Pretty, brown-eyed Callie Shaw asked the Hardys.

"What makes you think we were sleuthing?"

"Oh, I can tell!" Callie said, her eyes twinkling. "You two always have that detective gleam in your eyes when you're mixed up in a mystery!"

"They certainly have!" Iola agreed, laughing.

When they reached a grove bordering Willow River, which was to their left, Chet pulled over. "I'll park here."

The girls had decided they would like to see the changes which had been made in the old mill. As the group approached Elekton's gatehouse, they were amazed at the transformation.

No longer did the mill look shabby and neglected. The three-story structure had been completely repainted and the weeds and overgrowth of years cleared away. The grounds and shrubbery of the whole area were neatly trimmed.

"Look!" said Frank. "There's the mill wheel!"

As the Hardys and their friends watched the huge wheel turning, they felt for a moment that they were living in olden days. Water which poured from a pond over a high stone dam on the south side and through an elevated millrace caused the wheel to revolve.

"Oh!" Callie exclaimed admiringly as she spotted a little bridge over the stream from the falls. "It looks just like a painting!"

About three hundred yards from the north side of the mill was the closed rear gate to Elekton's ultramodern plant.

"Some contrast between the old and the new!" Joe remarked as they left the dirt road and walked up the front path to the gatehouse.

Suddenly the door opened and a dark-haired, muscular man in uniform came out to meet them. "What can I do for you?" he asked. "I'm the gate guard here."

"I'd like to apply for a summer job at Elekton," Chet told him.

"Have you an appointment?"

"No," replied Chet. "I guess I should have phoned first."

The guard agreed. "You would've saved yourself time and trouble," he said. "I'm sure there aren't any openings, especially for temporary help."

"Well, couldn't I go in and leave an application with the personnel manager?" Chet asked.

The guard shrugged. "Tell you what—I'll phone the personnel office instead," he offered, and went back into the mill.

While they waited, the five looked around. At the south side of the mill grounds, a slender, graying man who wore overalls was clipping the low hedges.

"Look, Callie," said Iola, pointing toward a spot near the hedges. "Isn't that quaint? An old flour barrel with ivy growing out of it!"

"Charming." Callie smiled.

The girls and boys started over toward the mill for a closer inspection. At that same moment the guard came to the door. "Just as I told you," he called out to Chet. "No openings! Sorry!"

"Too bad, Chet," Joe said sympathetically. "Well, at least you can keep on relaxing."

Despite his disappointment, Chet grinned. "Right now I'm starved. "Let's go down to the river and have our picnic."

He thanked the guard, and the young people started to walk away. Suddenly Frank stopped and looked back at the mill. Propped against the south wall was a bicycle. Quickly he ran over to examine it. "This looks like a Belgian model," Frank thought. "Sure is," he told himself. "The same type Ken Blake has."

On impulse Frank pulled the pedal from his

pocket and compared it to those on the bike. They matched exactly. Frank noticed that one of the pedals looked much less worn than the other. "As if it had been replaced recently," he reflected, wondering excitedly if someone had used this bicycle to deliver the warning note.

"And could this bike be Ken's?" the young detective asked himself.

He inspected the front-wheel spokes. None was twisted, but several had slight dents. "They could've been straightened out easily," Frank reasoned, "and the paint scratches on the fender touched up."

He felt his heart beat faster as he waved his companions to join him. When Frank pointed out the clues to his brother, Joe agreed immediately.

"It could be the bicycle which was used to deliver the message—"

Joe was interrupted by a strange voice behind them. "Pardon me, but why are you so interested in that bike?"

Frank quickly slipped the pedal into his pocket as the group swung around to face the speaker. He was the man who had been clipping the hedges.

"Because just yesterday we met a boy, Ken Blake, who was riding a bike of the same model. We don't often see this Belgian make around."

For a moment the man looked surprised, then smiled. "Of course! Ken works here—does odd jobs for us around the mill. You must be the boys he met yesterday when he was delivering some copy to the printer."

"Yes," Frank replied. "When we asked Ken about his job he was very secretive."

"Well," the maintenance man said, "he has to be! This plant is doing top-secret work. All of us have been impressed with the necessity of not talking about Elekton at all."

"Is Ken around?" Joe asked nonchalantly. "We'd like to say hello."

"I'm afraid not," was the reply. "We sent him by bus this afternoon to do an errand. He won't be back until later." The man excused himself and resumed his clipping.

"We'd better eat." Iola giggled. "My poor brother is suffering."

"I sure am!" Chet rolled his eyes. Laughing, the picnickers started away.

Joe, who was in the rear, happened to glance up at the front of the mill. He was startled to catch a glimpse of a face at one of the second-story windows. He stopped in his tracks.

"Ken Blake!" Joe said to himself.

As the young sleuth stared, mystified, the face disappeared from the window.

CHAPTER VI

A Mysterious Tunnel

PUZZLED, Joe continued looking up at the window of the old mill.

"What's the matter?" Iola asked him. "Did you see a ghost?"

In a low whisper Joe explained about the face which had disappeared. "I'm sure it was Ken Blake I saw at that window!"

The others followed his gaze. "No one's there now," Iola said. "Of course the glass in all the windows is old and wavy. The sunlight on them could cause an illusion."

Chet agreed. "How could Ken be here if he was sent on an errand?"

Joe stood for a minute, deep in thought. "I can't figure it out, but I'm sure that it was no illusion. Come on, Frank. Let's go check."

While the others walked down the hill, the

Hardys strode up to the maintenance man, who was still trimming hedges.

"Are you sure Ken went into town?" Joe asked. "Just now I thought I saw him looking out a second-floor window."

"You couldn't have. You must have been dreaming." The man gave a jovial laugh.

Joe was still not convinced. Impulsively he asked, "Does Ken ever run any errands for you at night?"

"No," the man answered readily. "He leaves his bike here and walks home when we close at five-thirty."

"Does anyone else have access to the bike after that?" Frank queried.

"It's kept in an open storage area under the rear of the mill and could be taken from there easily."

Although obviously curious, the man did not ask the Hardys the reason for their questions. He looked at his watch.

"Excuse me, boys, I'm late for lunch." He turned and hurried into the mill.

As the brothers hastened to catch up with Chet and the girls, Frank said, "Another thing which makes me wonder if that bicycle is connected with the warning is the description of the boy who bought the pedal. *He* could be Ken Blake."

"I agree," Joe said. "I'd sure like to question Ken."

"We'll come back another time," Frank proposed.

The group picked up the picnic hamper from the Queen and strolled down a narrow path through the woods leading to Willow River.

"Here's a good spot." Callie pointed to a shaded level area along the bank. "We haven't been in this section before."

Soon everyone was enjoying the delicious lunch the girls had prepared: chicken sandwiches, potato salad, chocolate cake, and lemonade. While they were eating, the girls were the targets of good-natured kidding.

"Boy!" Joe exclaimed as he finished his piece of cake. "This is almost as good as my mother and Aunt Gertrude make."

"*That's* a compliment!" Chet said emphatically.

Callie's eyes twinkled. "I know it is. Joe's mother and aunt are the best cooks ever!"

Iola sniffed. "I don't know about this compliment stuff. There's something on your mind, Joe Hardy!"

Joe grinned. "How are you on apple pie and cream puffs and—?"

"Oh, stop it!" Iola commanded. "Otherwise, you won't get a second piece of cake!"

"I give up." Joe handed over his paper plate.

After lunch everyone but Chet was ready to relax in the sun. Normally he was the first one to suggest a period of rest, even a nap, but now his new project was uppermost in his mind.

"Let's start to collect the specimens for my microscope," he urged his friends.

The Hardys groaned good-naturedly at Chet's enthusiasm, but readily agreed.

"We'll need some exercise to work off that meal." Frank grinned.

The girls packed the food wrappings in the hamper. Then, single file, the group walked downstream, paying careful attention to the rocks and vegetation. Chet picked up several rocks and leaves, but discarded them as being too common.

"Are you looking for something from the Stone Age?" Joe quipped. "Maybe a prehistoric fossil?"

"Wouldn't you be surprised if I found one?" Chet retorted.

They followed a bend in the river and came to a small cove with a rocky, shelving beach. Here the willow trees did not grow so thickly. The shoreline curved gently around to the right before it came to a halt in a sandy strip along the riverbank.

"What a nice spot," said Callie. "We'll have to come here again and wear our swim suits."

"Look!" cried Iola. "What's that?"

She pointed to a dark opening beneath a rocky ledge which bordered the beach.

"A cave!" exclaimed Joe and Frank together.

Intrigued, the five hurried along the beach for

"Hey! This looks like a tunnel!"

a closer look. Eagerly the Hardys and Chet peered inside the entrance. The interior was damp, and the cave's walls were covered with green growth.

"This'll be a perfect spot to look for specimens," Chet said. "Let's go in!"

The boys entered the cave. The girls, however, decided to stay outside.

"Too spooky—and crowded!" Callie declared. "Iola and I will sun ourselves while you boys explore."

The Hardys and Chet could just about stand up in the low-ceilinged cave. Frank turned on his pocket flashlight and pointed to an unusual yellow-green fungus on the right side of the cave. "Here's a good sample of lichens, Chet."

Soon the boys were busy scraping various lichens off the rocks. Gradually they moved deeper into the cave. Frank halted in front of a pile of rocks at the rear.

"There ought to be some interesting specimens behind these stones," he said. "They look loose enough to move."

Together, the three boys rolled some of the rocks to one side. To their great surprise, the stones had concealed another dark hole.

"Hey! This looks like a tunnel!"

Excitedly Joe poked his flashlight into the opening. In its beam they could see that the hole appeared to extend into the side of the bank.

"Let's see where the tunnel goes!" Joe urged.

"Okay," Frank agreed eagerly. "We'll have to move more of these rocks before we can climb through. I wonder who put them here and why."

Rapidly the boys pushed rocks aside until the narrow tunnel entrance was completely exposed. Joe crawled in first, then Frank.

Chet tried to squeeze his bulky form through the space but quickly backed out. "It's too tight for me," he groaned. "I'll stay here and collect more specimens. Anyhow, I'll bet some animal made the tunnel and it doesn't lead anywhere."

"I'm sure no animal did this," Joe called back, aiming his flashlight at the earthen walls of the tunnel. "Look how hard-packed the sides are—as if dug out by a shovel."

Frank was of the same opinion. He pointed to rough-hewn wooden stakes placed at intervals along the sides and across the ceiling. "I wonder who put those supports here—and when."

The Hardys crawled ahead carefully. There was just room in the passageway for a normal-sized person to get through.

Presently Joe called back to his brother, "Look ahead! I can see a sharp bend to the right. Let's keep going."

Frank was about to reply when the brothers were startled by a girl's scream from outside.

"That's Callie!" Frank exclaimed. "Something's wrong!"

CHAPTER VII

Sleuthing by Microscope

FRANK and Joe scrambled through the tunnel and out of the cave. They found Chet and the girls staring at an arrow embedded in the sandy beach.

"It—it almost hit us," Iola quavered. Callie, who was white-faced with fear, nodded.

Joe was furious. "Whoever shot it shouldn't be allowed to use such a dangerous weapon!" he burst out. "That's a hunting arrow—it could have caused serious injury."

Chet gulped. "M-maybe the Indians haven't left here, after all," he said, trying to hide his nervousness.

Joe turned to dash off into the woods to search for the bowman.

"Wait!" Frank called. He had pulled the arrow from the sand. "This was done deliberately," he announced grimly, holding the arrow up for all of them to see. Attached to the shaft just below the

56

feathers was a tiny piece of paper. It had been fastened on with adhesive tape.

Frank unrolled the paper and read the printed message aloud: " 'Danger. Hardys beware.' "

Chet and the girls shuddered and looked around fearfully, as though they expected to see the bowman behind them.

"You boys *are* involved in a new mystery!" Callie exclaimed. "Your own or your father's?"

Frank and Joe exchanged glances. It certainly seemed as though they were involved, but they had no way of knowing *which* case. Did it involve the counterfeit money? Or was it the case their father could not divulge?

"A warning did come to Dad," Frank admitted. "This one obviously was meant for Joe and me. Whoever shot the arrow trailed us here."

Joe frowned. "I wonder if the same person sent both warnings."

"I still think Ken Blake could give us a clue," Frank said. "But we must remember that anybody could have taken the bike from the storage place under the mill."

Frank pocketed the latest warning, then the five searched quickly for any lead to the bowman. They found none. When the group returned to the beach, Joe looked at the sky. "We're in for a storm—and not one of us has a raincoat."

The bright summer sun had disappeared behind towering banks of cumulus clouds. There were rumbles of heavy thunder, followed by vivid flashes of lightning. The air had become humid and oppressive.

"Let's get out of here!" Chet urged. "This isn't a picnic any more!"

The young people hastened through the woods and up the road to Chet's jalopy. As they drove off, rain began coming down in torrents. The sky grew blacker.

Callie shivered. "It seems so sinister—after that awful arrow."

Chet dropped his sister off at the Morton farm and at the same time picked up his new microscope. He begged to try out the instrument on both warning notes and the Hardys smilingly agreed, although they had an up-to-date model of their own.

By the time they had said good-by to Callie at her house, and Chet had driven the Queen into the Hardys' driveway, the storm had ended. The sun shone brightly again.

Immediately the three boys went to the laboratory over the garage. Here Frank carefully dusted the arrow and the second warning note for prints. He blew the powder away, and Joe and Chet looked over his shoulder as he peered through the magnifying glass.

"Nothing. Same as the warning to Dad. The person no doubt wore gloves."

"Now to compare this paper to the first note," Joe said.

"Right," his brother agreed. "You have the combination to the cabinet in Dad's study. Chet and I will rig up his microscope while you get the note from the file."

Frank and Chet focused and adjusted the microscope, making sure it was level on the table. They plugged in the illuminator and checked to see that it did not provide too dazzling a reflection. When Joe returned, Chet took the two pieces of paper and fitted them side by side under the clips on the base.

"Okay. Want to take a look, fellows?"

Frank, then Joe, studied both papers. "The quality and texture are definitely the same," Frank observed.

Next, he lifted the second note from under the clips and slowly moved the paper back and forth under the lenses.

"A watermark!" he exclaimed, stepping back so the others could look at the small, faint imprint.

"Sure is!" said Joe. "A five-pointed star. This could be a valuable clue! We can try to track down exactly where this paper came from."

"And also the arrow," said Chet. "I'll make the rounds of sport stores in town."

"Swell, Chet. Thanks," Frank said.

After their friend had left, the Hardys consulted the classified directory for paper manufacturers.

They made several calls without any luck. Finally they learned that the Quality Paper Company in Bridgeport manufactured paper bearing the five-pointed star watermark. The brothers wanted to go at once to get more information, but realized this errand would have to wait.

"Dad will be home soon," Frank reminded his brother. "We don't want to miss our surprise!"

"Right. And I'd like to tell him about the warning on the arrow."

When Chet returned from a round of the sports shops, he was glum. "I wasn't much help," he said. "The arrow isn't new, and all the stores I checked told me it was a standard model that could be purchased at any sports shop in the country."

"Never mind, Chet," said Frank. "At least giving your microscope a trial run helped us to spot the watermark on the second warning note. We've located a company that manufactures paper with the star watermark."

Chet's face brightened. "Let me know if you find out anything else," he said, packing up his microscope. "I guess I'll take off—and do some nature study for a change."

After he had driven off, Frank and Joe walked to the house. Their minds once more turned to the surprise Mr. Hardy had for them.

"Wouldn't it be terrific if—" Joe said to Frank excitedly. "Do you think it *is?*"

"I'm just hoping." Frank grinned.

Just then a newsboy delivered the evening newspaper. The brothers entered the house and went into the living room. Frank scanned the front page and pointed out an item about new trouble in an Indiana electronics plant.

"That's where an explosion took place a couple of months ago," Joe remarked. "Sabotage, the investigators decided."

"And before that," Frank added, "the same thing happened at a rocket research lab in California. Another unsolved case."

"Seems almost like a chain reaction," Frank remarked.

Any mystery appealed to the boys, but they did not have much chance to discuss this one. The telephone rang. Aunt Gertrude, after taking the call, burst into the living room. From the look on her face Frank and Joe could tell she was indignant, and at the same time, frightened.

"What's the matter, Aunty?" Joe asked.

"More threats—that's all!" she cried out. "This time by telephone. A man's voice—he sounded sinister—horrible!"

Mrs. Hardy came into the living room at that moment. "What did he say, Gertrude?" she asked.

Aunt Gertrude took a deep breath in an effort to calm down. " *'Hardy and his sons are playing with fire,*' the man said. '*They'll get burned if they don't lay off this case.*' " Miss Hardy sniffed. "I don't know what case he meant. What kind of danger *are* you boys mixed up in now?"

Frank and Joe smiled wryly. "Aunt Gertrude," Frank replied, "we really don't know. But please try not to worry," he begged her and his mother. "You know that Dad and the two of us will be careful."

When Mr. Hardy came home a little later, his family told him about the threatening telephone call. The boys, however, did not mention the arrow warning in the presence of their mother and Aunt Gertrude. They knew it would only add to their concern.

Mr. Hardy was as puzzled as his sons. "It's a funny thing," he said. "At this point it's impossible to tell which 'case' the person is referring to. If I knew, it might shed light on either one."

The detective grinned and changed the subject. "Right now, I want you all to come for a drive and have a look at the boys' surprise."

"Swell!" Frank and Joe exclaimed in unison.

While Aunt Gertrude and Mrs. Hardy were getting ready, Frank and Joe went out to the car with their father. Quickly the boys related their afternoon's experience, concluding with the arrow incident.

The detective looked grim. "Whoever is responsible for these warnings is certainly keeping close tabs on us."

Mr. Hardy and his sons speculated for a few minutes on the fact that the pedal found in front of the house apparently had belonged to Ken's bike.

"I think Joe and I should go back tonight to the place where we had the picnic," Frank told his father. "In the darkness we'll have a better chance to sleuth without being seen. And there might be some clue we missed this afternoon."

"I suppose you're right," agreed his father. "But be cautious."

As Aunt Gertrude and Mrs. Hardy came out of the house, conversation about the mystery ceased. Everyone climbed into the sedan and Mr. Hardy drove off. Frank and Joe, seated alongside him, were in a state of rising suspense. Was the surprise the one thing they wanted most of all?

CHAPTER VIII

The Strange Mill Wheel

A FEW minutes later Mr. Hardy was driving along the Bayport waterfront.

"Is the surprise here, Dad?" Joe asked excitedly.

"That's right."

Mr. Hardy drove to a boathouse at the far end of the dock area and parked. He then invited the others to follow him. He walked to the door of a boathouse and unfastened the padlock.

Frank and Joe held their breaths as Mr. Hardy swung back the door. For a moment they stared inside, speechless with delight. Finally Joe burst out, "Exactly what we had hoped for, Dad!" and put an arm affectionately around his father.

"What a beauty!" Frank exclaimed and wrung Mr. Hardy's hand.

Rocking between the piles lay a sleek, completely equipped motorboat. It nudged gently against clean white fenders as the waves from the bay worked their way under the boathouse door.

The boys' mother exclaimed in delight, and even Aunt Gertrude was duly impressed by the handsome craft.

"This is the same model we saw at the boat show," Joe said admiringly. "I never thought we'd own one."

"She even has the name we picked out," Frank observed excitedly. "The *Sleuth!*"

Shiny brass letters were fitted on the bow of the boat, with the port of registry, Bayport, underneath them.

Mr. Hardy and his wife beamed as their sons walked up and down, praising every detail of the graceful new craft. It could seat six people comfortably. The polished fore and aft decks carried gleaming anchor fittings, and the rubbing strakes were painted white. The *Sleuth* seemed to be waiting to be taken for a run!

"May we try her out now, Dad?" Joe asked.

"Of course. She's fueled up."

Aunt Gertrude shook her head. "The *Sleuth's* an attractive boat, all right. But don't you two start doing any crazy stunts in it," she cautioned her nephews. "And be back for supper."

When the adults had left, Frank and Joe climbed aboard and soon had the *Sleuth* gliding into the bay. The boys had no difficulty operating the motorboat. They had gained experience running their friend Tony Prito's boat, the *Napoli*, which had similar controls.

Taking turns at the wheel, the brothers ran the boat up and down the bay. "Terrific!" Joe shouted.

Frank grinned. "Am I glad we stuck to our agreement with Dad, and saved up to help buy this!"

For some time the boys had been putting money toward a boat of their own into a special bank account. Mr. Hardy had promised that when the account reached a certain sum, he would make up the necessary balance.

Now, as the *Sleuth* knifed through the water, Frank and Joe admired the way the stern sat down in the water when the boat gathered speed. Joe was impressed with the turning circle and the fact that no matter how sharp the twist, none of the spume sprayed into the cockpit.

"Wait until Tony and Chet see this!" Joe exclaimed, when they were pulling back toward the boathouse.

"Speaking of Tony—there he is," Frank said. Their dark-haired classmate was standing on the dock, shouting and waving to them.

Joe, who was at the wheel, brought the *Sleuth* neatly alongside. He turned off the engine as Tony rushed up.

"Don't tell me this dreamboat is yours?" he demanded in amazement.

"Nothing but," Joe said proudly.

Tony and the brothers inspected the boat carefully, comparing her various features with the *Napoli*. They lifted the battens from the *Sleuth's* cowling and admired the powerful motor underneath.

"She's neat all right," said Tony. "But I'll still promise you a stiff race in the *Napoli!*"

"We'll take you up on it after the *Sleuth's* broken in," Joe returned, laughing.

Tony became serious. "Say, fellows, something happened today in connection with my dad's business that I want to tell you about. Your mother said you were down here," he explained.

"What's up?" Frank asked.

Tony's father was a building contractor and also had a construction supply yard where Tony worked during the summer. "Today I went to the bank, just before it closed, to deposit the cash and checks we took in this week," he said. "The teller discovered that one of the bills was a counterfeit!"

"A twenty-dollar bill?" Frank guessed.

"Yes. How'd you know?"

The Hardys related Chet's experience. Tony's dark brows drew together. "I'd like to get my hands on the guy making the stuff!" he said angrily.

"So would we!" Joe stated.

The Hardys learned that the head teller had told Tony he would make a report to the Bayport police and turn the bill over to the Secret Service. "Did he explain how he could tell that the bill was a fake?" Frank asked.

"Yes," replied Tony, and from his description, the Hardys were sure that the bill had come from the same batch as the one passed to Chet.

"Think back, Tony," Frank urged. "Have you any idea who gave it to you—or your father?"

Tony looked doubtful. "Three days' trade— pretty hard to remember. Of course, we know most of the customers. I did ask Mike, our yard-man, who helps with sales. He mentioned one purchaser he didn't know."

Frank, eager for any possible lead, carefully questioned Tony. The Hardys learned that three days before, just at closing time, a faded green panel truck had driven into the Prito supply yard. "Mike remembers there were no markings on the truck—as if the name might have been painted out."

"Who was in it?" Joe prompted.

"A young boy—about fourteen—was with the driver. Mike says they bought about fifty dollars' worth of old bricks and lumber. The boy paid him in assorted bills. One was a twenty. Our other cash customers had given smaller bills."

"What did the driver look like?" Frank probed.

"Mike said he didn't notice—the fellow stayed behind the wheel. There was a last-minute rush at the yard, so the boy and Mike piled the stuff into the back of the truck. Then the driver gave the boy money to pay the bill."

Frank and Joe wondered the same thing: Had the man driving the truck passed the bogus bill deliberately? If so, was he the one who had fooled Chet? "It seems funny he'd go to so much trouble to dump one phony twenty-dollar bill," Joe said.

Frank agreed and added, "Besides, what would a person in league with counterfeiters want with a pile of old bricks and lumber?"

He turned to Tony. "Did Mike notice anything in particular about the boy?"

"He was tall and thin. Mike thinks he was wearing a striped shirt."

Frank and Joe exchanged glances. "Could be Ken Blake!" Joe declared. Briefly, the Hardys explained their first encounter with the boy.

"He might have been helping pick up the load for Elekton," Frank reasoned. "But why would a modern plant want secondhand building material? And why wouldn't they have the purchase billed to them?"

"What's more," his brother put in, "why didn't the driver get out and help with the loading? Unless, perhaps, he wanted to stay out of sight as much as possible."

"Too bad Mike didn't notice the truck's license number," Tony said. "Naturally he had no reason to at the time."

"Was there anything unusual about the truck besides the fact it wasn't marked?" Frank asked his chum.

Tony thought for a moment. "Mike did say there was a bike in the back. He had to move it out of the way."

"Ken rides one," Joe remarked.

"Well, Dad will be glad if you two pick up any clues to these counterfeiters," Tony said. "He's hopping mad at being cheated, and Mike feels sore about it."

"We'll keep our eyes open for that green truck," Frank assured him. "The whole business sounds suspicious—though the bill could have been passed accidentally."

"Let's question Ken Blake," Joe proposed.

He and his brother housed the *Sleuth,* and the three boys started homeward. On the way they continued to speculate on the counterfeiting racket.

"Let me know if I can help you detectives," Tony said as he turned into his street.

"Will do."

That evening, when it grew dark, Frank and Joe told their mother and aunt that they were going out to do some investigating. Before they left, the boys had a chance to speak to their father in private about Tony's report of the counterfeit bill and green truck and their own hunches.

Mr. Hardy agreed that the purchase of lumber and bricks seemed odd, but he felt that until more positive evidence could be obtained, it was best not to approach Elekton officials on the matter.

"I guess you're right, Dad," said Frank. "We might be way off base."

The detective wished them luck on their sleuthing mission. The boys decided to make the trip in the *Sleuth*. They rode their motorcycles down to the boathouse, parked them, then climbed aboard the new boat. Joe took the wheel and soon the sleek craft was cutting across the bay toward the mouth of Willow River.

When they entered it, Joe throttled down and carefully navigated the stream. Meanwhile, Frank shone his flashlight on the wooded banks.

"There's the cave—ahead!" he whispered.

Joe ran the boat astern a few yards and Frank dropped anchor. The brothers waded ashore, carrying their shoes and socks.

When they reached the mouth of the cave, Joe said, "Let's investigate this place first."

They went into the cave and moved forward to the tunnel. One glance told them that the tunnel had become impassable—it was filled with water.

"Must have been the cloudburst," said Frank, as they emerged from the cave. "We'll have to wait until the ground dries out. At least we can take a look through the woods and the area around the mill for clues to the bowman."

Shielding the lenses of their flashlights, so that the light beams would not be easily detected by anyone lurking in the vicinity, the boys began a thorough search of the wooded section. As they worked their way noiselessly uphill among the trees, the only sound was the eerie rattling the wind made in the leaves and branches.

Frank and Joe shone their lights beneath shrubs and rocks, and even crawled under some fallen trees. They found nothing suspicious. They were approaching the edge of the woods and could see the outline of the mill beyond. The old wheel creaked and rumbled.

Suddenly Frank whispered hoarsely, "Look! Here's something!"

Joe joined his brother, and together they examined the leather object Frank had picked up.

"An archer's finger guard," he said.

"It may be a valuable clue to the arrow warning," Joe said, as Frank pocketed the guard. "Let's go up to the mill," he proposed. "Maybe the men there have seen something suspicious."

As the boys crossed the clearing toward the gatehouse, they saw that it was in darkness.

"Probably everyone has gone to bed," Frank remarked.

For a moment the brothers stood wondering

what to do next. "Something's missing," Joe said in a puzzled voice. "I have it! The mill wheel has stopped turning."

"Maybe it was switched off for the night," Frank observed.

The boys were eager to question the occupants, but decided not to awaken them.

"Let's walk around the mill," said Frank, "and look through the woods on the other side."

The boys had just passed the north corner of the building when, with a creaking groan, the wheel started to turn again.

"There must be something wrong with the mechanism," Frank deduced. "The wheel hasn't been used for so many years that adapting it to work the generator may have put a strain on it."

"We'd better let the men know it's acting up," Joe said.

The boys retraced their steps to the mill door. As they reached it, the wheel stopped turning.

Frank and Joe stood staring off to their left where the mass of the motionless wheel was outlined against the night sky.

"Spooky, isn't it?" Joe commented.

Frank nodded, and knocked on the door. There was no response. After a short wait, he knocked again—louder this time. The sound echoed in the deep silence of the night. Still no one answered.

The Hardys waited a while longer. Finally they turned away. "Must be sound sleepers," Joe commented. "Well, maybe they'll discover what's wrong tomorrow."

Frank and Joe were about to resume their search for clues when they heard a loud crashing noise from the woods which bordered Willow River.

The boys dashed ahead to investigate. Entering the woods, they made their way stealthily forward, flashlights turned off. Silently they drew near the river.

After a few minutes they stopped, and listened intently. The sound was not repeated.

"Must have been an animal," Joe whispered.

Just then they heard a rustling sound behind them and turned to look. The next instant each received a terrific blow on the back of the head. Both boys blacked out.

CHAPTER IX

Tracing a Slugger

WHEN Frank regained consciousness, his first thought was of his brother. He turned his throbbing head and saw that Joe was lying next to him.

"Joe!" he exclaimed anxiously.

To his relief, Joe stirred and mumbled, "W-what happened?"

"Someone conked us on the head—"

Frank broke off as he became aware of a gentle rocking motion. He sat up. Was he still dizzy or were they moving? When his mind and vision cleared, he knew they were certainly moving.

"Hey!" he said. "We're on the *Sleuth!*"

Astonished, Joe raised himself and looked around. They were indeed aboard their boat— lying on the foredeck and slowly drifting down Willow River toward the bay. The anchor lay beside them.

"A fog's rolling in," Frank said uneasily, observing white swirls of mist ahead. "Let's start 'er up before visibility gets worse."

The boys wriggled into the cockpit and Joe pressed the starter. It would not catch. While Joe stayed at the controls, Frank climbed to the foredeck and lifted the cowling from the engine. He quickly checked to see if the distributor wires were in place. They were. There did not seem to be anything visibly wrong with the engine, but when he lifted the top off the carburetor, he found it empty.

A quick check of the gas tank revealed the cause of the trouble. The tank had been drained.

"Fine mess we're in," he mumbled. "What was the idea?"

"The man who hit us on the head can answer that one," Joe said bitterly. "He sure did a complete job—even took both the oars!"

"We'll have to tow her," Frank said tersely, "to make more speed and guide her."

While Joe stripped to his shorts, Frank quickly led a painter through one of the foredeck fairleads.

"Take this painter," Frank said, handing Joe the rope. "Make it fast around your shoulder and swim straight ahead. I'll unhinge one of the battens and use it as a paddle and try to keep her straight. In a few minutes I'll change places with you."

The Hardys knew that keeping a dead weight

like the *Sleuth* moving in a straight line would be a tough job. However, with Joe swimming ahead and Frank wielding the batten, they managed to make fairly steady progress.

It was slow, backbreaking work, and before they reached the bay, the boys had changed places three times. Their heads were pounding more than ever from the physical strain. Also, the fog had grown so dense that it was impossible to see very far ahead.

Frank, who was taking his turn in the water, did not know how much longer he could go on.

Suddenly Joe shouted from the boat, "There's a light! Help! Help! Ahoy! Over here!" he directed at the top of his lungs.

Gradually the light approached them. Frank clambered back into the *Sleuth* as a Harbor Police boat, making its scheduled rounds, pulled alongside.

"You're just in time!" Frank gasped to the sergeant in charge. "We're exhausted."

"I can see that. You run out of gas?" the police officer asked.

"Worse than that. Foul play," Frank replied.

"Tough luck," the sergeant said. "You can tell your story when we get to town."

The officer gave orders to his crew, and a towline was put on the *Sleuth*. The boys were given blankets to throw around themselves.

When the two crafts reached the Harbor Police

pier, the boys went inside and gave a full account of what had happened to them and asked that the report be relayed to Chief Collig.

"We'll give you some gas," said the sergeant who had rescued the boys. "Then do you think you can make it home alone?"

"Yes, thank you."

A half hour later the boys, tired and disappointed, cycled home. Their mother and aunt gasped with dismay at the sight of the weary boys in the water-sodden clothing. Joe and Frank, however, made light of the evening's experience.

"We ran out of gas," Joe explained, "and had to swim back with the *Sleuth*."

Aunt Gertrude sniffed skeptically. "Humph! It must have been some long ride to use up all that fuel!" She hustled off to make hot chocolate.

Mrs. Hardy told the boys that their father had left the house an hour before and would be away overnight working on his case. Again Frank and Joe wondered about it. And did the attack tonight have any connection with either case?

After a hot bath and a good night's sleep, Frank and Joe were eager to continue their search for clues to the bowman, the counterfeiters, and the writer of the first warning note to Mr. Hardy.

Breakfast over, Frank and Joe went to the lab and dusted the archer's finger guard. To the brothers' delight they lifted one clear print.

"We'll take this to Chief Collig on our way to

the paper company in Bridgeport," Frank decided.

Just before they left, Chet telephoned. "Guess what!" he said to Frank, who answered. "I have an appointment at Elekton to see about a job!"

"How'd you do it?" Frank asked, amazed. "You sure work fast."

Chet laughed. "I decided to telephone on my own," he explained. "The man in the personnel office told me there might be something available on a part-time basis. How about that?"

"Swell," Frank said. "The vacancy must have come up since yesterday."

"Funny thing," Chet added. "The personnel manager asked me if I'd applied before. I said No, though the guard had phoned about me yesterday. The manager said he didn't remember this, but that somebody else in the office might have taken the call."

Chet became more and more excited as he talked about the prospect of getting a job in the Elekton laboratory. "I'm going to make a lot of money and—"

"Don't get your hopes up too high," Frank cautioned his friend. "Elekton is such a top-secret outfit they might not hire anyone on a part-time basis for lab work. But you might get something else."

"We'll see," Chet replied optimistically.

"Joe and I have something special to show you," Frank told him. "After you have your interview, meet us at the north end of the Bayport waterfront."

Chet begged to know why, but Frank kept the news about the *Sleuth* a secret. "You'll see soon enough," he said.

"Okay, then. So long!"

The Hardys hopped on their motorcycles and rode to police headquarters. They talked to Chief Collig in detail about the attack on them, and left the bowman's fingerprint for him to trace.

"Good work, boys," he said. "I'll let you know what I find out."

Frank and Joe had decided not to mention to him the green truck and its possible connection with the counterfeiters until they had more proof.

The boys mounted their motorcycles and rode to Bridgeport. They easily located the Quality Paper Company, and inquired there for Mr. Evans, the sales manager, with whom they had talked the day before.

When Frank and Joe entered his office and identified themselves, Mr. Evans looked at the brothers curiously. But he was most cooperative in answering their questions.

"No," Mr. Evans said, "we don't sell our star watermark paper to retail stores in this vicinity. All our purchasers are large industrial companies. Here is a list." He handed a printed sheet across the desk to Frank.

The boys were disappointed not to have obtained any individual's name. Nevertheless, Frank and Joe read the list carefully. Several names, including Elekton Controls Limited, were familiar to them. The warning note could have come from any one of thousands of employees of any of the firms.

"I guess there's no clue here to the man we want to locate," Frank said to Mr. Evans.

The boys thanked him. As they started to leave, he called them back.

"Are you boys, by any chance, related to Mr. Fenton Hardy?" he asked.

Joe, puzzled, nodded. "He's our father. Why?"

"Quite a coincidence," Mr. Evans said. "Mr. Hardy was here a little while ago."

"He was!" Frank exclaimed in surprise. The brothers exchanged glances, wondering what mission their father had been on.

"Maybe I shouldn't have mentioned Mr. Hardy's visit," Mr. Evans said.

"That's all right," Joe assured him. "If Dad had wanted the visit kept secret, he would have told you."

When the boys were outside again, Frank said, "I hope Dad will be home. I'd like to find out what brought him here."

Frank and Joe rode directly home and were glad to see Mr. Hardy's sedan in the driveway. The boys rushed into the house.

They found the detective in his study, talking on the telephone. The boys paused next to the partly open door.

". . . the same eight-and-one pattern, I believe," their father was saying. . . . "Yes—I'll be there. . . . Good-by."

Frank knocked and the boys entered the room. Mr. Hardy greeted them warmly. He was startled when Joe told him, "We know where you've been this morning, Dad."

"Were you two shadowing me?" the detective joked.

"Not exactly." Frank grinned, and explained why they had visited the Quality Paper Company.

"Good idea," said the detective. "Did you learn anything?"

"No," Joe replied glumly, then asked suddenly, "Dad, did you go to Quality Paper in connection with the warning note on the arrow?"

Mr. Hardy admitted that he had gone there to investigate the watermark. "I believe I did find a clue to confirm a suspicion of mine. But I'm not sure yet where it will lead."

The boys sensed that their father's trip had been linked to his secret case. "If it was to help us on the counterfeiting mystery, he'd say so," Frank thought. "And he hasn't mentioned Elekton, so I guess he doesn't suspect any of that company's employees."

Mr. Hardy changed the subject. He looked at his sons quizzically. "What's this I hear from Aunt Gertrude about you boys coming home last night half dead?"

The boys explained, omitting none of the details. "We didn't want to alarm Mother and Aunt Gertrude," Frank said, "so we didn't tell them about the attack."

Mr. Hardy looked grim and warned his sons gravely to be extra cautious.

"There's one bright spot," he added. "The print you found on that finger guard. It could be a big break."

During lunch the detective was unusually pre-occupied. The boys tried to draw him out by questions and deductions about the counter-feiting case. He would say very little, however, and seemed to be concentrating on a knotty problem.

A little later the boys rode their motorcycles straight to the boathouse and parked at the street end of the jetty. "Chet ought to show up soon," Joe remarked.

As the brothers walked toward the boathouse Frank commented on his father's preoccupation during luncheon.

"I have a hunch Dad's assignment is even tougher than usual," he confided. "I wish we could help him on it."

Frank seemed to be only half listening and nodded absently.

"What's the matter with you?" Joe laughed. "I'm talking to myself!"

Suddenly Frank stopped. He grasped his brother's arm firmly.

"Joe!" he said. "We may have found a clue in Bridgeport this morning, and didn't realize it!"

CHAPTER X

The Sign of the Arrow

"What clue do you mean, Frank?" Joe demanded eagerly.

"Elekton's name was on that list Mr. Evans showed us this morning."

"Yes, I know. But Dad didn't seem excited over that."

"Well, I am," Frank said. "Put two and two together. Every time we've been near the Elekton area, something has happened. First, the warning on the arrow, then the attack last night."

"Of course!" Joe said. "I get you! Someone who has access to the company's paper supply could have sent the warnings, and knocked us out. But who? An employee of Elekton?"

"That's the mystery," said Frank. "Is the person trying to get at Dad through us? And which of the cases is this mysterious person connected with —the counterfeit case or Dad's secret one?"

"Then there's the bike," Joe recalled. "Someone from the company easily could have taken it from the storage area under the mill at night when the guard and maintenance man were inside the gatehouse."

"Joe," said Frank slowly, "we're theorizing on the case having a connection with Elekton. Do you think Dad is, too, even though he didn't tell us? The Elekton name may have been the clue *he* found at Quality Paper!"

Joe snapped his fingers. "My guess is that Dad is doing some detective work for Elekton! That would explain why he can't say anything. Elekton *is* doing top-secret space missile work."

"It's possible," Frank speculated, "that Elekton retained Dad because of the chain of sabotage acts in plants handling similar jobs for the government."

"Sounds logical," Joe agreed. "I guess Dad's main assignment would be to ward off sabotage at Elekton. No wonder he is so anxious to find out who sent the warnings."

Just then Chet arrived in the Queen and leaped out.

"I have a job!" he announced to Frank and Joe. Then he looked a bit sheepish. "It's—er—in the cafeteria, serving behind the food counter. The cafeteria is run on a concession basis, and the people working there aren't as carefully screened as the plant employees."

Joe grinned. "It's not very scientific, but think of the food! You'll be able to eat anything you want."

Chet sighed, and did not respond with one of his usual humorous comebacks. A worried expression spread over his face. He shifted from one foot to the other.

"What's on your mind?" Joe prodded. "Not nervous about the job, are you?"

Chet shook his head. He dug into his pocket and pulled out a piece of white paper. "I *am* nervous about this—another warning note! It was on the seat of my car when I came out after the job interview." He handed the note to Frank.

Unfolding it, Frank read aloud, " *'You and your pals watch out!'* " There was no signature on the boldly printed note, but at the bottom was the crude drawing of an arrow.

Chet gulped. "Must be that arrow shooter. He's keeping tabs on all of us!" he said.

Frank and Joe studied the note intently for a minute, then Frank asked Chet, "Where did you park?"

"Near the front entrance. The guard at the mill told me to go in that way to reach the personnel office." Chet smiled faintly. "Boy, was *he* surprised when I told him I had an appointment."

The Hardys were more convinced than ever that their unknown enemy must somehow be linked with the Elekton company. "We'll compare this note with the others," Frank said. "But first, Chet, we'll show you something to cheer you up."

The brothers led their friend into the boathouse. "Feast your eyes!" Joe grinned. "This is our surprise."

Chet gasped when he saw the *Sleuth*. "Wow! She's really yours?"

"You bet! How about a ride?"

Eagerly Chet accepted. As the Hardys refueled from the boathouse tank, they told Chet about the adventure they had had the previous night.

"You suspect there's a connection between somebody at Elekton and the counterfeiting?" Chet guessed.

"That's right," Frank replied.

He then told Chet about the Pritos having received a counterfeit bill. "We think," said Joe, "the boy in the panel truck who gave Mike the counterfeit twenty *might* have been Ken Blake."

"Ken Blake again," Chet commented. "Funny how he keeps turning up."

The Hardys agreed. As Frank steered the *Sleuth* into the bay, Joe suggested, "Let's run up Willow River to the mill. That'll give you a good chance to see how the boat rides, Chet, and also we can stop to question the guard and maintenance man, and Ken Blake. They might have seen some suspicious people in the area."

"I should've known this would turn into a

"Something's wrong!" Joe shouted.
"I can't slow her down."

sleuthing trip." Chet sighed. "Oh, well, I'm with you if we can learn anything about the counterfeiters."

When Frank had the *Sleuth* well away from shore and out of the path of other craft on the bay, he pushed the throttle for more speed and steered the boat toward the mouth of the river.

The *Sleuth* responded like a thoroughbred. The stern sat back in the water and in a second it was planing wide open across the bay.

"How do you like this?" Frank called from the cockpit.

"Terrific!" Chet yelled back enthusiastically.

Frank now swung the wheel back and forth to show his friend how stable the boat was. Then he said, "Joe, take the wheel and show Chet your stuff!"

The brothers changed places and Joe made a wide circle to port, with the *Sleuth* heeling beautifully. Then he headed for the river's narrow mouth.

"Better slow down!" Frank warned him.

Obediently Joe began to ease the throttle. The *Sleuth* did not respond! And there was no lessening of the roar of the engine.

Quickly Joe turned the throttle all the way back. Still there was no decrease in speed.

"Something's wrong!" he shouted. "I can't slow her down!"

CHAPTER XI

Sinister Tactics

"WHAT do you mean you can't slow down?" Chet yelled. "Turn off the engine!"

"Joe can't," Frank said grimly. "He has the throttle to *off* position and we're still traveling at full speed."

There was no choice for Joe but to swing the *Sleuth* into another wide, sweeping turn. It would have been foolhardy to enter the river at such speed, and Joe knew that under the circumstances he needed lots of room to maneuver. The motorboat zoomed back into the middle of the bay. It seemed to the boys that suddenly there was far more traffic on the bay than there had been before.

"Look out!" Chet yelled. Joe just missed a high-speed runabout.

He turned and twisted to avoid the small pleasure boats. The young pilot was more worried about endangering these people than he was about colliding with the larger vessels, which were commercial craft.

"Keep her as straight as you can!" Frank shouted to Joe. "I'll take a look at the engine and see what I can do with it."

Frank stood up and leaned forward to open the cowling in front of the dashboard, as the boat leaped across the waves in the bay.

"Watch out!" Chet yelled, as Frank almost lost his balance.

Joe had made a sharp turn to avoid cutting in front of a rowboat containing a man and several children. Joe realized that the wash of the speeding *Sleuth* might upset it.

"If those people are thrown overboard," he thought, "we'll have to rescue them. But how?" Fortunately, the boat did not overturn.

Frank quickly lifted the cowling from the engine and stepped into the pit. He knew he could open the fuel intake and siphon off the gas into the bay, but this would take too long.

"I'll have to stop the boat—right now!" he decided.

Frank reached down beside the roaring engine and pulled three wires away from the distributor. Instantly the engine died, and Frank stood up just as Joe made another sharp turn to miss hitting a small outboard motorboat that had wandered across their path.

"Good night!" Chet cried out. "That was a close one!"

Even with the *Sleuth*'s reduction in speed, the other boat rocked violently back and forth as it was caught in the wash. Frank grasped the gunwale, ready to leap over the side and rescue the man if his boat overturned.

But the smaller craft had been pulled around to face the wash. Though it bounced almost out of the water, the boat quickly resumed an even keel.

The lone man in it kept coming toward the *Sleuth*. As he drew alongside, he began to wave his arms and shout at the boys.

"What's the matter with you young fools?" he yelled. "You shouldn't be allowed to operate a boat until you learn how to run one."

"We couldn't—" Joe started to say when the man interrupted.

"You should have more respect for other people's safety!"

Frank finally managed to explain. "It was an accident. The throttle was jammed open. I had to pull the wires out of the distributor to stop her."

By this time the outboard was close enough for its pilot to look over the *Sleuth*'s side and into the engine housing where Frank was pointing at the distributor.

The man quickly calmed down. "Sorry, boys," he said. "There are so many fools running around in high-powered boats these days, without knowing anything about the rules of navigation, I just got good and mad at your performance."

"I don't blame you, sir," said Joe. Then he asked, "Do you think you could tow us into the municipal dock so that we can have repairs made?"

"Glad to," said the man.

At the dock, the Hardys and Chet watched while the serviceman checked the *Sleuth* to find out the cause of the trouble. Presently he looked up at the boys with an odd expression.

"What's the trouble?" Frank asked. "Serious?"

The mechanic's reply startled them. "This is a new motorboat and no doubt was in tiptop shape. But somebody tampered with the throttle!"

"What!" Joe demanded. "Let's see!"

The serviceman pointed out where a cotter pin had been removed from the throttle group. And the tension spring which opened and closed the valve had been replaced with a bar to hold the throttle wide open, once it was pushed there.

The Hardys and Chet exchanged glances which meant: "The unknown enemy again?"

The boys, however, did not mention their suspicions to the mechanic. Frank merely requested him to make the necessary repairs on the *Sleuth*. Then the trio walked back to the Hardys' boathouse.

Several fishermen were standing at a nearby

wharf. Frank and Joe asked them if they had seen anyone near the boathouse.

"No," each one said.

The three boys inspected the boathouse. Frank scrutinized the hasp on the door. "The *Sleuth* must have been tampered with while it was inside. Unless it was done last night while we were unconscious."

There was no sign of the lock having been forced open, but near the edge of the loose hasp there were faint scratches.

"Look!" Joe pointed. "Somebody tore the whole hasp off the door and then carefully put it back on."

Frank looked grim. "I'm sure this was done by the same person who attacked us last night, and sent us the warnings."

"You're right," said Joe. "This is what Dad would call sinister tactics."

Again both brothers wondered with which case their enemy was connected. There seemed to be no answer to this tantalizing question which kept coming up again and again.

Chet drove the Queen back to the Hardys', and the brothers rode their motorcycles. When they reached the house they went at once to the lab with the note Chet had found in his car.

They dusted it for fingerprints but were disappointed again. There was not one trace of a print. The boys found, however, that the paper was the same as that used for the previous warnings.

"Well," said Joe, "I vote we go on out to the mill."

The boys went in the Queen. Chet had just brought his car to a stop on the dirt road when Joe called out, "There's Ken Blake trimming the grass over by the millrace. Now's our chance to talk to him."

The three jumped out. Ken looked up, stared for a second, then threw his clippers to the ground. To the boys' surprise, he turned and ran away from them, along the stream.

"Wait!" Frank yelled.

Ken looked over his shoulder, but kept on running. Suddenly he tripped and stumbled. For a moment the boy teetered on the bank of the rushing stream. The next instant he lost his balance and fell headlong into the water!

At once the Hardys and Chet dashed to the water's edge. Horrified, they saw that the force of the water was carrying the boy, obviously a poor swimmer, straight toward the plunging falls!

CHAPTER XII

An Interrupted Chase

FRANK, quick as lightning, dashed to the mill-stream and plunged in after Ken Blake. The boy was being pulled relentlessly toward the water-fall. In another moment he would be swept over the brink of the dam!

With strong strokes, Frank swam toward the struggling boy. Reaching out desperately, he managed to grasp Ken's shirt.

Joe jumped in to assist Frank. The two boys were buffeted by the rushing water but between them they managed to drag Ken back from the falls.

"Easy," Frank cautioned the frightened youth. "Relax. We'll have you out in a jiffy."

Despite the weight of their clothes, the Hardys, both proficient at lifesaving techniques, soon worked Ken close to the bank. Chet leaned over and helped haul him out of the water. Then Frank and Joe climbed out.

To their relief, Ken, though white-faced and panting from exhaustion, seemed to be all right. The Hardys flopped to the ground to catch their breath.

"That was a whale of a rescue!" Chet praised them.

"You bet!" Ken gasped weakly. "Thanks, fellows! You've saved my life!"

"In a way it was our fault," Joe replied ruefully. "You wouldn't have fallen in if we hadn't come here. But why *did* you run away when you saw us?"

Ken hesitated before answering. "Mr. Markel —the guard at the gatehouse—said you wanted to talk to me. He warned me about talking to outsiders, because of the strict security at Elekton."

Joe nodded. "We understand, Ken. But," he added, "we have something important to ask you, and I don't think you will be going against company rules if you answer. Did anybody use your bike the night before last to deliver a message to our house?"

"Your house?" Ken sounded surprised. "No. At least, not that I know of."

Joe went on, "Did you buy a pedal in Bridgeport to replace the one missing from your bike?"

Ken again looked surprised. "Yes. It was gone yesterday morning when I came to work. I suspected someone must have used my bike and lost the pedal. When I couldn't find it around here, Mr. Markel sent me to Bridgeport to buy a new one."

It was on the tip of Frank's tongue to ask the boy if he had seen any person in the area of the mill carrying a bow and arrow. But suddenly Mr. Markel and the maintenance man came dashing from the mill.

"What's going on here?" the guard demanded, staring at the Hardys and Ken, who were still dripping wet.

Briefly, Frank told the men what had happened. They thanked the brothers warmly for the rescue, and the maintenance man hustled Ken into the mill for dry clothes. He did not invite the Hardys inside.

Frank and Joe turned to Mr. Markel, intending to question him. But before they could, a horn sounded and a shabby green panel truck approached the plant gate.

The guard hurried over to admit the truck and it entered without stopping. Suddenly Joe grabbed Frank's arm. "Hey! That truck's unmarked—it looks like the one Tony described."

The brothers peered after the vehicle, but by this time it was far into the grounds, and had turned out of sight behind one of the buildings.

"I wonder," Joe said excitedly, "if the driver is the man who gave the Pritos the counterfeit bill!"

The boys had noticed only that the driver wore a cap pulled low and sat slouched over the wheel.

"If this truck's the same one, it may be connected with Elekton," Frank said tersely.

Both Hardys, though uncomfortably wet, decided to stay and see what they could find out. They hailed Mr. Markel as he walked back from the Elekton gate.

"Does that truck belong to Elekton?" Frank asked him.

"No, it doesn't," the guard answered.

"Do you know who does own it?" asked Joe.

Mr. Markel shook his head regretfully. "Sorry, boys. I'm afraid I'm not allowed to give out such information. Excuse me, I have work to do." He turned and went back into the gatehouse.

"Come on, fellows," Chet urged. "You'd better not hang around in those wet clothes."

The Hardys, however, were determined to stay long enough to question Ken Blake further, if possible.

"He'll probably be coming outside soon," said Joe. "Frank and I can dry out on the beach by the cave. It won't take long in this hot sun."

Chet sighed. "Okay. And I know what I'm supposed to do—wait here and watch for Ken."

Frank chuckled. "You're a mind reader."

Chet took his post at the edge of the woods, and the Hardys hurried down to the river's edge.

They spread their slacks and shirts on the sun-warmed rocks. In a short while the clothing was dry enough to put on.

"Say, maybe we'll have time to investigate that tunnel before Chet calls us," Joe suggested eagerly.

He and Frank started for the cave, but a second later Chet came running through the woods toward them.

"Ken came out, but he's gone on an errand," he reported, and explained that the boy had rushed from the mill dressed in oversize dungarees and a red shirt. "He was riding off on his bike when I caught up to him. I told Ken you wanted to see him, but he said he had to make a fast trip downtown and deliver an envelope to the Parker Building."

"We'll catch him there," Frank decided.

The three boys ran up the wooded slope and jumped into the Queen. They kept on the main road to Bayport, hoping to overtake Ken, but they did not pass him.

"He must have taken another route," Joe said.

At the Parker Building there were no parking spaces available, so Chet stopped his jalopy long enough to drop off Frank and Joe.

"I'll keep circling the block until you come out," Chet called as he drove away.

There was no sign of Ken's bicycle outside the building. The Hardys rushed into the lobby and immediately were met by a five-o'clock crowd of office workers streaming from the elevators. Frank and Joe made their way through the throng, but saw no sign of Ken.

Joe had an idea. "Maybe he was making the delivery to Mr. Peters, the name I saw on the Manila envelope I picked up the other day. Let's see if Ken's still in his office."

The boys ran their eyes down the building directory, but Mr. Peters was not listed. The brothers questioned the elevator starter, who replied that so far as he knew, no one by the name of Peters had an office in the building.

Joe asked the starter, "Did you notice a boy wearing dungarees and a bright-red shirt in the lobby a few minutes ago?"

"Sure," was the prompt reply. "Just before the five-o'clock rush started. I saw the boy come in and give an envelope to a man waiting in the corner over there. The man took the envelope and they both left right away."

"I guess he must be Mr. Peters," Frank said.

"Could be," the starter agreed. "I didn't recognize him."

As the Hardys hurried outside, Joe said, "Well, we got crossed up on that one. Let's get back to the mill. Ken will have to drop off the bike."

The brothers waited at the curb for Chet. In a few minutes the Queen pulled up. "All aboard!" Chet sang out. "Any luck?"

"No."

When Frank told Chet they were returning to the mill, their good-natured friend nodded. "It's fortunate I bought these sandwiches," he said, indicating a paper bag on the seat beside him. "I had a feeling we'd be late to supper."

Joe snapped his fingers. "That reminds me. I'll stop and phone our families so they won't wait supper for us."

After Joe had made the calls and they were on their way again, he told Frank and Chet that Mr. Hardy had left a message saying he would not be home until after ten o'clock.

As the Queen went down the side road past the Elekton buildings, Frank thought, "If Dad *is* working for Elekton, he might be somewhere in the plant right this minute."

The same possibility was running through Joe's mind. "Wonder if Dad is expecting a break in his secret case."

As Chet neared the turn into the mill road, a green truck zoomed out directly in front of the Queen. Chet jammed on his brake, narrowly avoiding a collision. The truck swung around the jalopy at full speed and roared off toward the highway.

"The green truck we saw before!" Joe exclaimed. "This time I got the license number, but couldn't see the driver's face."

"Let's follow him!" Frank urged.

Chet started back in pursuit. "That guy ought

to be arrested for reckless driving!" he declared indignantly.

The Hardys peered ahead as they turned right onto the main road, trying to keep the truck in sight. Suddenly the boys heard a tremendous *bo-o-om* and felt the car shake.

"An explosion!" Joe cried out, turning his head. "Look!"

Against the sky a brilliant flash and billows of smoke came from the direction of Elekton. Another explosion followed.

"The plant's blowing up!" Joe gasped.

CHAPTER XIII

Sudden Suspicion

THE roar of the explosion and the sight of smoke and flames stunned the three boys for a moment. Chet stepped on the brake so fast that his passengers hit the dashboard.

"Take it easy!" urged Frank, although he was as excited as Chet.

All thoughts of chasing the mysterious green truck were erased from the Hardys' minds.

"Let's get as close as possible," Frank said tersely, as Chet headed the car back toward the plant. "I'd like to know what—"

Frank broke off as a series of explosions occurred. The brothers sat forward tensely.

As the Queen drew near the main entrance, the boys could see that the flames and smoke were pouring from a single building at the northeast corner.

"It's one of the labs, I think," said Frank.

Quickly Chet pulled over and parked, and the boys hopped out of the jalopy. The series of explosive sounds had died away, but the damage appeared to be extensive. Most of the windows in the steel-and-concrete building had been blown out by the force of the blast.

Smoke and flames were pouring out of the blackened spaces where the windows had been. As the boys ran toward the front, the roof of the west wing caved in. The rush of oxygen provided fuel for a new surge of flames that reached toward the sky.

"Lucky this happened after closing time," Chet murmured, staring wide-eyed at the fire. "There might have been a lot of injuries."

"I hope no one was inside." Joe exchanged worried glances with his brother. Both shared the same concern. It was for their father.

"I wish we could find out whether or not Dad's at Elekton," Frank whispered to Joe.

At this point, the boys heard the scream of sirens. Soon fire trucks and police cars from Bayport pulled up at the front gate. The Hardys saw Chief Collig in the first police car. They rushed up to him and he asked how they happened to be there.

"Sleuthing," Frank answered simply. Without going into detail, he added, "Joe and I aren't sure, but we have a hunch Dad may have been—

or still is—here at Elekton. All right if we go into the grounds and look around?" he asked eagerly. "And take Chet?"

The officer agreed.

By this time the guard had opened the wide gate, and the fire apparatus rushed in. Some of the police officers followed, while others took positions along the road and directed traffic so it would not block the path of emergency vehicles.

As the boys rode inside with the chief, Joe asked him, "Any idea what caused the explosion?"

"Not yet. Hard to tell until the firemen can get inside the building."

When they reached the burning structure, Chief Collig began directing police operations, and checking with the firemen. As soon as they seemed to have the flames under control, the firemen entered the laboratory building to look for any possible victims of the explosions.

The Hardys and Chet, meanwhile, had searched the outdoors area for Mr. Hardy, but did not see the detective.

"Maybe we were wrong about Dad's coming here," Joe said to his brother, more hopeful than before. "Dad probably wouldn't have been in the lab."

The brothers went back to Chief Collig, who told them he had not seen Fenton Hardy. Just then the fire chief came up to the group.

"I'll bet this fire was no accident," he reported

grimly to Collig. "The same thing happened in Indiana about two months ago—and that was sabotage!"

Frank and Joe stared at each other. "Sabotage!" Joe whispered.

A startling thought flashed into Frank's mind, and, drawing his brother aside, he exclaimed, "Remember what we overheard Dad say on the phone? 'The same eight-and-one pattern. I'll be there.' "

"And two months equal about eight weeks," Joe added excitedly. "That might have been the saboteurs' time schedule Dad was referring to! So maybe the explosion at Elekton was set for today!"

Frank's apprehension about his father returned full force. "Joe," he said tensely, "Dad might have been inside the lab building trying to stop the saboteurs!"

Deeply disturbed, the Hardys pleaded with Chief Collig for permission to enter the building and search for their father.

"I can tell you're worried, boys," the officer said sympathetically. "But it's still too risky for me to let you go inside. It'll be some time before we're sure there's no danger of further explosions."

"I know," Frank agreed. "But what if Dad *is* in there and badly hurt?"

The police chief did his best to reassure the brothers. "Your father would never forgive me if I let you risk your lives," he added. "I suggest that you go on home and cheer up your mother in case she has the same fears you do. I promise if I see your dad I'll call you, or ask him to."

The boys realized that their old friend was right, and slowly walked away. Frank and Joe looked back once at the blackened building, outlined against the twilight sky. Wisps of smoke still curled from the torn-out windows. It was a gloomy, silent trio that drove to the Hardy home in the Queen.

Frank and Joe decided not to tell their mother or aunt of their fear, or to give any hint of their suspicions. When the boys entered the living room, both women gave sighs of relief. They had heard the explosions and the subsequent news flashes about it.

Aunt Gertrude looked at the boys sharply. "By the way, where have you three been all this time? I was afraid that you might have been near Elekton's."

Frank, Joe, and Chet admitted that they had been. "You know we couldn't miss a chance to find out what the excitement was about," Joe said teasingly, then added with an assurance he was far from feeling, "Don't worry. The fire was pretty much under control when we left."

To change the subject, Frank said cheerfully, "I sure am hungry. Let's dig into those sandwiches you bought, Chet!"

"Good idea!" Joe agreed.

"Are you sure you don't want me to fix you something hot to eat?" Mrs. Hardy asked.

"Thanks, Mother, but we'll have enough." Frank smiled.

Chet called his family to let them know where he was, then the three boys sat down in the kitchen and halfheartedly munched the sandwiches. Aunt Gertrude bustled in and served them generous portions of deep-dish apple pie.

"This is more super than usual," Chet declared, trying hard to be cheerful.

The boys finished their pie, but without appetite. When they refused second helpings, however, Aunt Gertrude demanded suspiciously, "Are you ill—or what?"

"Oh, no, Aunty," Joe replied hastily. "Just—er—too much detecting."

"I can believe that!" Miss Hardy said tartly.

The evening dragged on, tension mounting every minute. The boys tried to read or talk, but their concern for the detective's safety made it impossible to concentrate on anything else.

Eleven o'clock! Where *was* their father? Frank and Joe wondered.

"Aren't you boys going to bed soon?" Mrs. Hardy asked, as she and Aunt Gertrude started upstairs.

"Pretty soon," Frank answered.

The three boys sat glumly around the living

room for a few minutes until the women were
out of earshot.

"Fellows," said Chet, "I caught on that you're
sure your dad is working on an important case for
Elekton, and it's a top-secret one—that's why you
couldn't say anything about it."

"You're right," Frank told him.

Chet went on to mention that his father had
heard of various problems at Elekton—produc-
tion stoppages caused by power breaks, and, before the buildings were completed, there were reports of tools and equipment being missing.

"This ties in with our hunch about the secrecy
of Dad's case," Frank said. "The company must
have suspected that major sabotage was being
planned, and retained Dad to try and stop it."

Talking over their speculations helped to re-
lieve some of the tension the boys felt and made
the time pass a little faster as they waited for news
of Fenton Hardy.

"I wonder how the saboteurs got into the
plant?" Joe said, thinking aloud. "Both the gates
are locked and well guarded. It seems almost impossible for anyone to have sneaked in the necessary amount of explosives—without inside help."

A sudden thought flashed into Frank's mind.
He leaped to his feet. "The green truck!" he exclaimed. "It was unmarked, remember? It could
have been carrying dynamite—camouflaged under ordinary supplies!"

"That could be, Frank!" Joe jumped up. "If so, no wonder it was in such a rush! I'll phone the chief right now and give him the truck's license number."

Frank went with Joe to the hall telephone. As they approached the phone, it rang. The bell, shattering the tense atmosphere, seemed louder than usual.

"It must be Dad!" exclaimed the brothers together, and Chet hurried into the hall.

Frank eagerly lifted the receiver. "Hello!" he said expectantly.

The next moment Frank looked dejected. He replaced the receiver and said glumly, "Wrong number."

The Hardys exchanged bleak looks. What *had* happened to their father?

CHAPTER XIV

Prisoners!

THE HARDYS' disappointment in discovering that the telephone call was not from their father was intense. Nevertheless, Joe picked up the receiver and dialed police headquarters to report the truck's license number.

"Line's busy," he said.

Joe tried several more times without success. Suddenly he burst out, "I can't stand it another minute to think of Dad perhaps lying out there hurt. Let's go back to Elekton and see if we can learn something."

"All right," Frank agreed, also eager for action, and the three rushed to the front door.

Just as they opened it, the boys saw the headlights of a car turning into the driveway.

"It's Dad!" Joe barely refrained from shouting so as not to awaken Mrs. Hardy and Aunt Gertrude.

The detective's sedan headed for the garage at the back of the house. Heaving sighs of thankful relief, the boys quietly hurried through the house into the kitchen to meet him.

"Are we glad to see you, Dad!" Frank exclaimed as he came into the house.

His father looked pale and disheveled. There was a large purple bruise on his left temple. He slumped wearily into a chair.

"I guess I'm lucky to be here." Mr. Hardy managed a rueful smile. "Well, I owe you boys an explanation, and now is the time."

"Dad," Joe spoke up, "you *are* working on the sabotage case for Elekton, aren't you?"

"And you were in the lab building during the explosions?" Frank put in.

"You're both right," the detective replied. "Of course I know I can depend on all of you to keep the matter strictly confidential. The case is far from solved."

Mr. Hardy was relieved that Frank and Joe had kept their fears for his safety from his wife and sister. He now revealed to the boys that for the past several hours he had been closeted with Elekton's officials. Suspecting that the saboteurs had inside help, the detective had screened the records of all employees. He and the officials had found nothing suspicious.

"I'll submit a full report to the FBI tomorrow morning, and continue a search on my own."

When Joe asked if the eight-and-one pattern referred to the saboteurs' schedule, his father nodded. "In the other plants, the sabotage took place eight weeks plus one day apart.

"In each of those plants," the detective went on, "the damage occurred right after closing time. Figuring the schedule would be exactly right for an attempt on Elekton in a couple of days, I started a systematic check of the various buildings. I planned to check daily, until the saboteurs had been caught here or elsewhere. At my request, one company security guard was assigned to assist me. I felt that the fewer people who knew what I was doing, the better. That's how I ruined the saboteurs' plan in Detroit.

"Nothing suspicious occurred here until today when I took up a post in the section of the building where the experimental work is being conducted. After all the employees had left, and the dim night-lights were on, I went toward the east lab wing to investigate."

Mr. Hardy paused, took a deep breath, and continued, "Just as I reached the lab, I happened to glance back into the hall. Things started to happen—fast."

"What did you see, Dad?" asked Joe, and all the boys leaned forward expectantly.

The detective went on, "Hurrying down the

hall from the west lab were two men in work clothes, one carrying a leather bag. I knew there weren't supposed to be any workmen in the building. I stepped out to question them, but the pair broke into a run and dashed past me down the stairs."

"Did you see what either of them looked like?" Frank asked.

"I did catch a glimpse of one before they broke away. He had heavy features and thick eyebrows. But just as I was about to take off after them, I smelled something burning in the east lab and went to investigate. The first thing I saw was a long fuse sputtering toward a box of dynamite, set against the wall.

"I didn't know if it was the kind of fuse that would burn internally or not, so I took my penknife and cut it close to the dynamite. Professional saboteurs don't usually rely on just one explosive, so I started for the west wing to check the lab there."

Mr. Hardy leaned back in his chair and rubbed the bruise on his temple. In a low voice he said, "But I didn't make it. I was running toward the hall when there was a roar and a burst of flame. The explosion lifted me off my feet and threw me against the wall. Though I was stunned, I managed to get back to the east wing. I reached for the phone, then blacked out.

"I must have been unconscious for some time because when the firemen found me and helped me out of the building, the fire had been put out."

"You're all right now?" asked Frank.

"Yes. It was a temporary blackout from shock. What bothers me is that I had the saboteurs' pattern figured out—only they must have become panicky, and moved up their nefarious scheme two days."

Joe looked grim. "I wish we'd been there to help you capture those rats!"

Chet asked Mr. Hardy if he would like a fruit drink. "I'll make some lemonade," he offered.

"Sounds good." Mr. Hardy smiled.

As they sipped the lemonade, Frank and Joe questioned their father about his theories.

"I'm still convinced," said Mr. Hardy, "that one of those men works in the plant. How else would he have known when the watchman makes his rounds and how to disconnect the electronic alarms? But I *can't* figure how the outside accomplice got in—those gates are carefully guarded."

At this point, Frank told his father about the green truck. "We suspected at first it might be connected with the counterfeiters. Now we have a hunch the saboteurs may have used it."

Fenton Hardy seemed greatly encouraged by this possible lead. Joe gave him the license number, which Mr. Hardy said he would report to Chief Collig at once.

When Mr. Hardy returned from the telephone, he told the boys the chief would check the license number with the Motor Vehicle Bureau in the morning and by then he also would have some information about the print on the archer's finger guard.

The next morning after breakfast Frank said he wanted to take another look at the warning notes.

"Why?" Joe asked curiously as they went to the file.

Frank held up the "arrow" warning, and the one received by Chet. "I've been thinking about the printing on these two—seems familiar. I have it!" he burst out.

"Have what?" Joe asked.

"This printing"—Frank pointed to the papers —"is the same as the printing on Ken's envelope addressed to Victor Peters. I'm positive."

Excitedly the brothers speculated on the possible meaning of this clue. "I'd sure like to find out," said Joe, "who addresses the envelopes Ken delivers, and if they're always sent to Mr. Peters in the Parker Building. And why—if he doesn't have an office there. And who *is* Victor Peters?"

"If the person who addresses the envelopes and the sender of the warnings are the same," Frank declared, "it looks as though he's sending something to a confederate, under pretense of having work done for Elekton. I wonder what that something could be?"

"At any rate," Joe added, "this could be a link either to the counterfeiters or to the saboteurs. Which one?"

The boys decided to go out to the mill again, in hopes of quizzing Ken Blake. Just then their father came downstairs. Frank and Joe were glad to see that he looked rested and cheerful.

Mr. Hardy phoned Chief Collig. When the detective hung up, he told his sons that the license number belonged to stolen plates and the fingerprint to a confidence man nicknamed The Arrow.

"He's called this because for several years he worked at exclusive summer resorts, teaching archery to wealthy vacationers, then fleecing as many of them as he could. After each swindle, The Arrow disappeared. Unfortunately, there's no picture of him on file. All the police have is a general description of him."

Frank and Joe learned that the swindler had a pleasant speaking voice, was of medium height, with dark hair and brown eyes.

"Not much to go on," Joe remarked glumly.

"No, but if he *is* working for Elekton, he must be pretty shrewd to have passed their screening."

Mr. Hardy agreed, and phoned Elekton, requesting the personnel department to check if anybody answering The Arrow's description was employed there.

The brothers then informed their father about the similar lettering on the warnings and Ken's Manila envelope.

"A valuable clue," he remarked. "I wish I could go with you to question Ken." The detective explained that right now he had to make his report of the explosion to the nearby FBI office.

When he had left, Frank and Joe rode off to the mill on their motorcycles.

At the gatehouse the guard had unexpected news. "Ken Blake isn't working here any more," Mr. Markel said. "We had to discharge him."

"Why?" asked Joe in surprise.

The guard replied that most of the necessary jobs had been done around the mill grounds. "Mr. Docker—my coworker—and I felt we could handle everything from now on," he explained.

"I see," said Frank. "Can you tell us where Ken is staying?"

Markel said he was not sure, but he thought Ken might have been boarding in an old farmhouse about a mile up the highway.

When the brothers reached the highway, they stopped. "Which way do we go? Mr. Markel didn't tell us," Joe said in chagrin.

"Instead of going back to find out, let's ask at that gas station across the way," Frank suggested. "Someone there may know."

"An old farmhouse?" the attendant repeated in answer to Frank's query. "There's one about a mile from here going toward Bayport. That might be the place your friend is staying. What does he look like?"

Frank described Ken carefully. The attendant nodded. "Yep. I've seen him ride by here on his bike. A couple of times when I was going past the farm I noticed him turn in the dirt road to it."

"Thanks a lot!" The Hardys cycled off quickly.

Soon they were heading up the narrow, dusty lane, which led to a ramshackle, weather-beaten house. The brothers parked their motorcycles among the high weeds in front of it and dismounted.

"This place seems deserted!" Joe muttered.

Frank agreed and looked around, perplexed. "Odd that Ken would be boarding in such a rundown house."

Frank and Joe walked onto the creaky porch and knocked at the sagging door. There was no answer. They knocked again and called. Still no response.

"Some peculiar boardinghouse!" Joe said. "I wouldn't want a room here!"

Frank frowned. "This must be the wrong place. Look—it's all locked up and there's hardly any furniture."

"I'll bet nobody lives in this house!" Joe burst out.

"But the attendant said he has seen Ken riding in here," Frank declared. "Why?"

"Let's have a look," Joe urged.

Mystified, Frank and Joe circled the house. Since they were now certain it had been abandoned, they glanced in various windows. When Joe came to the kitchen he grabbed Frank's arm excitedly.

"Somebody *is* staying here! Could it be Ken?"

Through the dusty glass the boys could see on a rickety table several open cans of food, a carton of milk, and a bowl.

"Must be a tramp," Frank guessed. "I'm sure Ken wouldn't live here."

In turning away, the young detectives noticed a small stone structure about ten yards behind the house. It was the size of a one-car garage. Instead of windows, it had slits high in the walls.

"It probably was used to store farm equipment," Frank said. "We might as well check."

They unbolted the old-fashioned, stout, wooden double doors. These swung outward, and the boys were surprised that the doors opened so silently. "As if they'd been oiled," Frank said.

"No wonder!" Joe cried out. "Look!"

Inside was a shabby green panel truck! "The same one we saw yesterday!" Joe exclaimed. "What's it doing here?"

The boys noticed immediately that the vehicle

"We're prisoners!" Frank exclaimed

had no license plates. "They probably were taken off," Frank surmised, "and disposed of."

Frank checked the glove compartment while Joe looked on the seat and under the cushion for any clue to the driver or owner of the vehicle. Suddenly he called out, "Hey! What's going on?"

Joe jumped from the truck and saw with astonishment that the garage doors were swinging shut. Together, the boys rushed forward but not in time. They heard the outside bolt being rammed into place.

"We're prisoners!" Frank exclaimed.

Again and again the Hardys threw their weight against the doors. This proved futile. Panting, Frank and Joe looked for a means of escape.

"Those slits in the wall are too high and too narrow, anyway," Frank said, chiding himself for not having been on guard.

Finally he reached into the glove compartment and drew out an empty cigarette package he had noticed before. He pulled off the foil. Joe understood immediately what his brother had in mind. Frank lifted the truck's hood and jammed the foil between the starting wires near the fuse box. "Worth a try," he said. "Ignition key's gone. If we can start the engine—we'll smash our way out!"

Joe took his place at the wheel and Frank climbed in beside him. To their delight, Joe gunned the engine into life.

"Here goes!" he muttered grimly. "Brace your-self!"

"Ready!"

Joe eased the truck as far back as he could, then accelerated swiftly forward. The truck's wheels spun on the dirt floor and then with a roar it headed for the heavy doors.

CHAPTER XV

Lead to a Counterfeiter

C-R-A-S-H! The green truck smashed through the heavy garage doors. The Hardys felt a terrific jolt and heard the wood splinter and rip as they shot forward into the farmyard.

"Wow!" Joe gasped as he braked to a halt. "We're free—but not saying in what shape!"

Frank gave a wry laugh. "Probably better than the front of this truck!"

The boys hopped to the ground and looked around the overgrown yard. No one was in sight. The whole area seemed just as deserted as it had been when they arrived.

"Let's check the house," Joe urged. "Someone *could* be hiding in there."

The brothers ran to the run-down dwelling. They found all the doors and windows locked. Again they peered through the dirty panes, but did not see anyone.

"I figure that whoever locked us in the garage would decide that getting away from here in a hurry was his safest bet."

"He must have gone on foot," Joe remarked. "I didn't hear an engine start up."

The Hardys decided to separate, each searching the highway for a mile in opposite directions.

"We'll meet back at the service station we stopped at," Frank called as the boys kicked their motors into life and took off toward the highway.

Fifteen minutes later they parked near the station. Neither boy had spotted any suspicious pedestrians.

"Did you see anybody come down this road in a hurry during the past twenty minutes?" Joe asked the attendant.

"I didn't notice, fellows," came the answer. "I've been busy working under a car. Find your friend?"

"No. That farmhouse is apparently deserted except for signs of a tramp living there," Joe told him.

The Hardys quickly asked the attendant if he knew of any boardinghouse nearby. After a moment's thought, he replied:

"I believe a Mrs. Smith, who lives a little ways beyond the old place, takes boarders."

"We'll try there. Thanks again," Frank said as he and Joe went back to their motorcycles.

Before Frank threw his weight back on the starter, he said, "Well, let's hope Ken Blake can give us a lead."

"If we ever find him," Joe responded.

They located Mrs. Smith's boardinghouse with no trouble. She was a pleasant, middle-aged woman and quickly confirmed that Ken was staying there for the summer. She was an old friend of his parents. Mrs. Smith invited the Hardys to sit down in the living room.

"Ken's upstairs now," she said. "I'll call him."

When Ken came down, the Hardys noticed that he looked dejected. Frank felt certain it was because of losing his job and asked him what had happened.

"I don't know," Ken replied. "Mr. Markel just told me I wouldn't be needed any longer. I hope I'll be able to find another job this summer," he added. "My folks sent me here for a vacation. But I was going to surprise them—" His voice trailed off sadly.

"Ken," Frank said kindly, "you may be able to help us in a very important way. Now that you're not working at the Elekton gatehouse, we hope you can answer some questions—to help solve a mystery."

Frank explained that he and Joe often worked on mysteries and assisted their detective father.

Ken's face brightened. "I'll do my best, fellows," he assured them eagerly.

"Last week," Joe began, "a shabby green panel truck went to Pritos' Supply Yard and picked up old bricks and lumber. Our friend Tony Prito said there was a boy in the truck who helped the yardman with the loading. Were you the boy?"

"Yes," Ken replied readily.

"Who was the driver?" Frank asked him.

"Mr. Docker, the maintenance man at the mill. He said he'd hurt his arm and asked me to help load the stuff." Ken looked puzzled. "Is that part of the mystery?"

"We think it could be," Frank said. "Now, Ken —we've learned since then that one of the bills you gave the yardman is a counterfeit twenty."

Ken's eyes opened wide in astonishment. "A— a counterfeit!" he echoed. "Honest, I didn't know it was, Frank and Joe!"

"Oh, we're sure you didn't," Joe assured him. "Have you any idea who gave Docker the cash?"

Ken told the Hardys he did not know. Then Frank asked:

"What were the old bricks and lumber used for, Ken?"

"Mr. Docker told me they were for repair work around the plant. After we got back to the mill, Mr. Markel and I stored the load in the basement."

"Is it still there?" asked Frank.

"I guess so," Ken answered. "Up to the time I left, it hadn't been taken out."

The Hardys determined to question Markel and Docker at the first opportunity. Then Frank changed the subject and asked about the day of the picnic when Joe thought he had seen Ken at the window.

"I remember," the younger boy said. "I *did* see you all outside. I never knew you were looking for me."

"When we told Mr. Docker," Frank went on, "he said Joe must have been mistaken."

Ken remarked slowly, "He probably was worrying about the plant's security policy. He and Mr. Markel were always reminding me not to talk to anybody."

"During the time you were working at the Elekton gatehouse, did you see any strange or suspicious person near either the plant or the mill grounds?" Frank asked.

"No," said Ken in surprise. Curiosity overcoming him, he burst out, "You mean there's some crook loose around here?"

Frank and Joe nodded vigorously. "We're afraid so," Frank told him. "But who, or what he's up to, is what we're trying to find out. When we do, we'll explain everything."

Joe then asked Ken if he had seen anyone in the area of the mill with a bow and arrow.

"A bow and arrow?" Ken repeated. "No, I never did. I sure would've remembered that!"

Frank nodded and switched to another line of

questioning. "When you delivered envelopes, Ken, did you always take them to Mr. Victor Peters?"

"Yes," Ken answered.

The Hardys learned further that Ken's delivery trips always had been to Bayport—sometimes to the Parker Building, and sometimes to other office buildings in the business section.

"Did Mr. Peters meet you in the lobby every time?" Frank queried.

"That's right."

"What was in the envelopes?" was Joe's next question.

"Mr. Markel said they were bulletins and forms to be printed for Elekton."

"Were the envelopes always marked confidential?" Joe asked.

"Yes."

"Probably everything is that Elekton sends out," Frank said.

"Sounds like a complicated delivery arrangement to me," Joe declared.

Ken admitted that he had not thought much about it at the time, except that he had assumed Mr. Peters relayed the material to the printing company.

Frank and Joe glanced at each other. Both remembered Frank's surmise that the bulky Manila envelopes had not contained bona fide Elekton papers at all!

"What does Mr. Peters look like?" asked Joe, a note of intense excitement in his voice.

"Average height and stocky, with a sharp nose. Sometimes he'd be wearing sunglasses."

"Stocky and a sharp nose," Frank repeated. "Sunglasses." Meaningfully he asked Joe, "Whom does that description fit?"

Joe jumped to his feet. "The man who gave Chet the counterfeit twenty at the railroad station!"

The Hardys had no doubt now that the mysterious Victor Peters must be a passer for the counterfeit ring!

CHAPTER XVI

A Night Assignment

GREATLY excited at this valuable clue to the counterfeiters, Frank asked, "Ken, who gave Mr. Markel the envelopes for Victor Peters?"

"I'm sorry, fellows, I don't know."

The Hardys speculated on where Peters was living. Was it somewhere near Bayport?

Joe's eyes narrowed. "Ken," he said, "this morning we found out that sometimes you'd ride up that dirt road to the deserted farmhouse. Was it for any particular reason?"

"Yes," Ken replied. "Mr. Markel told me a poor old man was staying in the house, and a couple of times a week I was sent there to leave a box of food on the front porch."

"Did you ever see the 'poor old man'?" Frank asked. "Or the green panel truck?"

The Hardys were not surprised when the answer to both questions was No. They suspected the "poor old man" was Peters hiding out there and that he had made sure the truck was out of sight whenever Ken was expected.

The brothers were silent, each puzzling over the significance of what they had just learned. If the truck was used by the counterfeiters, how did this tie in with its being used for the sabotage at Elekton?

"Was The Arrow in league with the saboteurs? Did he also have something to do with the envelopes sent to Victor Peters?" Joe asked himself.

Frank wondered, "Is The Arrow—or a confederate of his working at Elekton—the person responsible for the warnings, the attack on us, and the tampering with the *Sleuth?*"

"Ken," Frank said aloud, "I think you'd better come and stay with us for a while, until we break this case. Maybe you can help us."

He did not want to mention it to Ken, but the possibility had occurred to him that the boy might be in danger if the counterfeiters suspected that he had given the Hardys any information about Victor Peters.

Ken was delighted with the idea, and Mrs. Smith, who knew of Fenton Hardy and his sons, gave permission for her young charge to go.

As a precaution, Frank requested the kindly woman to tell any stranger asking for Ken Blake that he was "visiting friends."

"I'll do that," she agreed.

Ken rode the back seat of Joe's motorcycle on the trip to High Street. He was warmly welcomed by Mrs. Hardy and Aunt Gertrude.

"I hope you enjoy your stay here," said Mrs. Hardy, who knew that Frank and Joe had a good reason for inviting Ken. But neither woman asked questions in his presence.

"Your father probably will be out all day," Mrs. Hardy told her sons. "He'll phone later."

While lunch was being prepared, Frank called police headquarters to give Chief Collig a report on what had happened at the deserted farmhouse.

"I'll notify the FBI," the chief said. "I'm sure they'll want to send men out there to examine that truck and take fingerprints. Elekton," the chief added, "had no record of any employee answering The Arrow's description."

"We're working on a couple of theories," Frank confided. "But nothing definite so far."

After lunch the Hardys decided their next move was to try to find out more about the contents of the envelopes Ken had delivered to Peters.

"We could ask Elekton officials straight out," Joe suggested.

His brother did not agree. "Without tangible evidence to back us up, we'd have to give too many reasons for wanting to know."

Finally Frank hit on an idea. He telephoned Elekton, asked for the accounting department,

and inquired where the company had its printing done. The accounting clerk apparently
thought he was a salesman, and gave him the information.

Frank hung up. "What did they say?" Joe asked
impatiently.

"All Elekton's printing is done on the premises!"

"That proves it!" Joe burst out. "The setup
with Ken delivering envelopes to Peters isn't a
legitimate one, and has nothing to do with Elekton business."

Meanwhile Ken, greatly mystified, had been
listening intently. Now he spoke up. "Jeepers,
Frank and Joe, have I been doing something
wrong?"

In their excitement the Hardys had almost forgotten their guest. Frank turned to him apolo-
getically. "Not you, Ken. We're trying to figure
out who has."

Just then the Hardys heard the familiar chug
of the Queen pulling up outside. The brothers
went out to the porch with Ken. Chet leaped
from his jalopy and bounded up to them. His
chubby face was split with a wide grin.

"Get a load of this!" He showed them a badge
with his picture on it. "I'll have to wear it when
I start work. Everybody has to wear one before he
can get into the plant," he added. "Even the
president of Elekton!"

Suddenly Chet became aware of Ken Blake. "Hello!" the plump boy greeted him in surprise. Ken smiled, and the Hardys told their friend of the morning's adventure.

"Boy!" Chet exclaimed. "Things are starting to pop! So you found that green truck!"

At these words a strange look crossed Frank's face.

"Chet," he said excitedly, "did you say *everybody* must show identification to enter Elekton's grounds?"

"Yes—everybody," Chet answered positively.

"What are you getting at, Frank?" his brother asked quickly.

"Before yesterday's explosion, when we saw the gate guard admit the green truck, the driver didn't stop—didn't show any identification at all!"

"That's true!" Joe exclaimed. "Mr. Markel doesn't seem to be the careless type, though."

"I know," Frank went on. "If the green truck was sneaking in explosives—what better way than to let the driver zip right through."

Joe stared at his brother. "You mean Markel deliberately let the truck go by? That he's in league with the saboteurs, or the counterfeiters, or both?"

As the others listened in astonishment, Frank replied, "I have more than a hunch he is—and Docker, too. It would explain a lot."

Joe nodded in growing comprehension. "It sure would!"

"How?" demanded Chet.

Joe took up the line of deduction. "Markel himself told Ken the envelopes were for the printer. Why did Docker say Ken wasn't at the mill the day I saw him? And what was the real reason for his being discharged?"

"I'm getting it," Chet interjected. "Those men were trying to keep you from questioning Ken. Why?"

"Perhaps because of what Ken could tell us, if we happened to ask him about the envelopes he delivered," Joe replied. Then he asked Ken if Markel and Docker knew that Joe had picked up the envelope the day of the near accident.

"I didn't say anything about that," Ken replied. The boy's face wore a perplexed, worried look. "You mean Mr. Docker and Mr. Markel might be—crooks! They didn't act that way."

"I agree," Frank said. "And we still have no proof. We'll see if we can find some—one way or another."

The Hardys reflected on the other mysterious happenings. "The green truck," Frank said, "could belong to the gatehouse men, since it seems to be used for whatever their scheme is, and *they* are hiding it at the deserted farmhouse."

"Also," Joe put in, "if Victor Peters is the 'old man,' he's probably an accomplice."

"And," Frank continued, "don't forget that the bike Ken used was available to both Docker and Markel to deliver the warning note. The arrow shooting occurred near the mill; the attack on us in the woods that night was near the mill. The warning note found in Chet's car was put there after Markel told him to go to the front gate. The guard probably lied to Chet the first day we went to the mill—he never did phone the personnel department."

"Another thing," Joe pointed out. "Both men are more free to come and go than someone working in the plant."

There was silence while the Hardys concentrated on what their next move should be.

"No doubt about it," Frank said finally. "Everything seems to point toward the mill as the place to find the answers."

"And the only way to be sure," Joe added, "is to go and find out ourselves. How about tonight?"

Frank and Chet agreed, and the boys decided to wait until it was fairly dark. "I'll call Tony and see if he can go with us," Frank said. "We'll need his help."

Tony was eager to accompany the trio. "Sounds as if you're hitting pay dirt in the mystery," he remarked when Frank had brought him up to date.

"We hope so."

Later, Joe outlined a plan whereby they might

ascertain if Peters *was* an accomplice of Docker and Markel, and at the same time make it possible for them to get into the mill.

"Swell idea," Frank said approvingly. "Better brush up on your voice-disguising technique!"

Joe grinned. "I'll practice."

Just before supper Mr. Hardy phoned to say he would not be home until later that night.

"Making progress, Dad?" asked Frank, who had taken the call.

"Could be, son," the detective replied. "That's why I'll be delayed. Tell your mother and Gertrude not to worry."

"Okay. And, Dad—Joe and I will be doing some sleuthing tonight to try out a few new ideas *we* have."

"Fine. But watch your step!"

About eight-thirty that evening Chet and Tony pulled up to the Hardy home in the Queen.

Ken Blake went with the brothers to the door. "See you later, Ken," Frank said, and Joe added, "I know you'd like to come along, but we don't want you taking any unnecessary risks."

The younger boy looked wistful. "I wish I could do something to help you fellows."

"There *is* a way you can help," Frank told him.

At that moment Mrs. Hardy and Aunt Gertrude came into the hall. Quickly Frank drew Ken aside and whispered something to him.

CHAPTER XVII

Secret Signal

WITH rising excitement, Frank, Joe, Chet, and Tony drove off through the dusk toward the old mill.

Chet came to a stop about one hundred yards from the beginning of the dirt road leading to the gatehouse. He and Tony jumped out. They waved to the Hardys, then disappeared into the woods.

Joe took the wheel of the jalopy. "Now, part two of our plan. I hope it works."

The brothers quickly rode to the service station where they had been that morning. Joe parked and hurried to the outdoor telephone booth nearby. From his pocket he took a slip of paper on which Ken had jotted down the night telephone number of the Elekton gatehouse.

Joe dialed the number, then covered the

mouthpiece with his handkerchief to muffle his voice.

A familiar voice answered, "Gatehouse. Markel speaking."

Joe said tersely, "Peters speaking. Something has gone wrong. Both of you meet me outside the Parker Building. Make it snappy!" Then he hung up.

When Joe returned to the Queen, Frank had turned it around and they were ready to go. They sped back toward the mill and in about ten minutes had the jalopy parked out of sight in the shadows of the trees where the dirt road joined the paved one.

The brothers, keeping out of sight among the trees, ran to join Chet and Tony who were waiting behind a large oak near the edge of the gatehouse grounds.

"It worked!" Tony reported excitedly. "About fifteen minutes ago the lights in the mill went out, and Markel and Docker left in a hurry."

"On foot?" Joe asked.

"Yes."

"Good. If they have to take a bus or cab to town, it'll give us more time," Frank said.

Tony and Chet were given instructions about keeping watch outside while the Hardys inspected the mill. The brothers explained where the Queen was parked, in case trouble should arise and their friends had to go for help.

Frank and Joe approached the mill cautiously. It was dark now, but they did not use flashlights. Though confident that the gatehouse was deserted, they did not wish to take any chances. As they neared the building the Hardys could see that the shutters were tightly closed. Over the sound of the wind in the trees came the rumble of the turning mill wheel.

The Hardys headed for the door. They had just mounted the steps when the rumbling sound of the wheel ceased.

In the silence both boys looked around, perplexed. "I thought it had been fixed," Joe whispered. "Seemed okay the other day."

"Yes. But last time we were here at night the wheel stopped when we were about this distance away from it," Frank observed.

Thoughtfully the boys stepped back from the mill entrance to a point where they could see the wheel. They stood peering at it through the darkness. Suddenly, with a dull rumble, it started to turn again!

Mystified, the Hardys advanced toward the gatehouse and stopped at the entrance. In a short while the wheel stopped.

"Hm!" Joe murmured. "Just like one of those electric-eye doors."

"Exactly!" Frank exclaimed, snapping his fingers. "I'll bet the wheel's *not* broken—it's been rigged up as a warning signal to be used at night!

When someone approaches the mill, the path of the invisible beam is broken and the wheel stops. The lack of noise is enough for anyone inside to notice, and also, the lights would go out because the generator is powered by the wheel."

The Hardys went on a quick search for the origin of the light beam. Frank was first to discover that it was camouflaged in the flour-barrel ivy planter. Beneath a thin covering of earth, and barely concealed, were the heavy batteries, wired in parallel, which produced the current necessary to operate the light source for the electric eye.

The stopping and starting of the wheel was further explained when Frank found, screened by a bushy shrub, a small post with a tiny glass mirror fastened on its side.

"That's the complete secret of the signal!" he exclaimed. "This is one of the mirrors a photo-electric cell system would use. With several of these hidden mirrors, they've made a light-ring around the mill so an intruder from any side would break the beam. The barrel that contains the battery power also contains the eye that completes the circuit."

"I'll bet Markel and Docker rigged this up," Joe said excitedly. "Which means there must be something in the mill they want very badly to keep secret! We must find a way inside!"

The Hardys did not pull the wires off the battery connection, since they might have need of the warning system. Quietly and quickly the brothers made a circuit of the mill, trying doors and first-floor windows, in hopes of finding one unlocked. But none was.

"We can't break in," Joe muttered.

Both boys were aware that time was precious—the men might return shortly. The young sleuths made another circle of the mill. This time they paused to stare at the huge wheel, which was turning once more.

"Look!" Joe whispered tensely, pointing to an open window-shaped space above the wheel.

"It's our only chance to get inside," Frank stated. "We'll try climbing up."

The Hardys realized it would not be easy to reach the opening. Had there been a walkway on top of the wheel, as there was in many mills, climbing it would have been relatively simple. The brothers came to a quick decision: to maneuver one of the paddles on the wheel until it was directly below the ledge of the open space, then stop the motion. During the short interval which took place between the stop and start of the wheel, they hoped to climb by way of the paddles to the top and gain entrance to the mill.

Joe ran back through the beam, breaking it, while Frank clambered over a pile of rocks across the water to the wheel. It rumbled to a stop, one paddle aligned with the open space above. By the time Joe returned, Frank had started to climb up, pulling himself from paddle to paddle by means of the metal side struts. Joe followed close behind.

The boys knew they were taking a chance in their ascent up the wet, slippery, mossy wheel. They were sure there must be a timing-delay switch somewhere in the electric-eye circuit. Could they beat it, or would they be tossed off into the dark rushing water?

"I believe I can get to the top paddle and reach the opening before the timer starts the wheel turning again. But can Joe?" Frank thought. "Hurry!" he cried out to his brother.

Doggedly the two continued upward. Suddenly Joe's hand slipped on a slimy patch of moss. He almost lost his grip, but managed to cling desperately to the edge of the paddle above his head, both feet dangling in mid-air.

"Frank!" he hissed through clenched teeth.

His brother threw his weight to the right. Holding tight with his left hand to a strut, he reached down and grasped Joe's wrist. With an aerialist's grip, Joe locked his fingers on Frank's wrist, and let go with his other hand.

Frank swung him out away from the wheel. As Joe swung himself back, he managed to regain his footing and get a firm hold on the paddle supports.

"Whew!" said Joe. "Thanks!"

The boys resumed the climb, spurred by the thought that the sluice gate would reopen any second and start the wheel revolving.

Frank finally reached the top paddle. Stretching his arms upward, he barely reached the sill of the opening. The old wood was rough and splintering, but felt strong enough to hold his weight.

"Here goes!" he thought, and sprang away from the paddle.

At the same moment, with a creaking rumble, the wheel started to move!

CHAPTER XVIII

The Hidden Room

WHILE Frank clung grimly to the sill, Joe, below him, knew he must act fast to avoid missing the chance to get off, and perhaps being crushed beneath the turning wheel. He leaped upward with all his might.

Joe's fingers barely grasped the ledge, but he managed to hang onto the rough surface beside his brother. Then together they pulled themselves up and over the sill through the open space.

In another moment they were standing inside the second floor of the building. Rickety boards creaked under their weight. Still not wishing to risk the use of flashlights, the Hardys peered around in the darkness.

"I think we're in the original grinding room," Frank whispered as he discerned the outlines of two huge stone cylinders in the middle of the room.

"You're right," said Joe. "There's the old grain hopper." He pointed to a chute leading down to the grinding stones.

Though many years had passed since the mill had been used to produce flour, the harsh, dry odor of grain still lingered in the air. In two of the corners were cots and a set of crude shelves for clothes. Suddenly the boys' hearts jumped. A loud clattering noise came from directly below. Then, through a wide crack in the floor, shone a yellow shaft of light!

"Someone else must be here!" Joe whispered.

The Hardys stood motionless, hardly daring to breathe, waiting for another sound. Who *was* in the suddenly lighted room?

The suspense was unbearable. Finally the brothers tiptoed over and peered through the wide crack. Straightening up, Frank observed, "Can't see anyone. We'd better go investigate."

Fearful of stumbling in the inky darkness, the boys now turned on their flashlights, but shielded them with their hands. Cautiously they found their way to a door. It opened into a short passageway which led down a narrow flight of steps.

Soon Frank and Joe were in another small hall. Ahead was a partially opened door, with light streaming from it.

Every nerve taut, the young sleuths advanced. Frank edged up to the door and looked in.

"Well?" Joe hissed. To his utter astonishment Frank gave a low chuckle, and motioned him forward.

"For Pete's sake!" Joe grinned.

Inside, perched on a chipped grindstone, was a huge, white cat. Its tail twitched indignantly. An overturned lamp lay on a table.

The Hardys laughed in relief. "Our noise-maker and lamplighter!" Frank said as the boys entered the room. "The cat must have knocked over the lamp and clicked the switch."

Although the room contained the gear mechanism and the shaft connected to the mill wheel, it was being used as a living area by the present tenants. There were two overstuffed chairs, a table, and a chest of drawers. On the floor, as if dropped in haste, lay a scattered newspaper.

"Let's search the rest of the mill before Markel and Docker get back," Joe suggested. "Nothing suspicious here."

The Hardys started with the top story of the old building. There they found what was once the grain storage room. Now it was filled with odds and ends of discarded furniture.

"I'm sure nothing's hidden here," Frank said.

The other floors yielded no clues to what Docker and Markel's secret might be.

Frank was inclined to be discouraged. "Maybe our big hunch is all wet," he muttered.

Joe refused to give up. "Let's investigate the cellar. Come on!"

The brothers went into the kitchen toward the basement stairway. Suddenly Joe gave a stifled yell. Something had brushed across his trouser legs. Frank swung his light around. The beam caught two round golden eyes staring up at them.

"The white cat!" Joe said sheepishly.

Chuckling, the Hardys continued down into the damp, cool cellar. It was long and narrow, with only two small windows.

Three walls were of natural stone and mortar. The fourth wall was lined with wooden shelves. Frank and Joe played their flashlights into every corner.

"Hm." There was a note of disappointment in Joe's voice. "Wheelbarrow, shovels, picks—just ordinary equipment."

Frank nodded. "Seems to be all, but where are the old bricks and lumber that Ken said were stored here?"

"I'm sure the stuff was never intended for Elekton," Joe declared. "More likely the mill. But where? In a floor? We haven't seen any signs."

Thoughtfully the boys walked over to inspect the shelves, which held an assortment of implements. Frank reached out to pick up a hammer.

To his amazement, he could not lift it. A further quick examination revealed that all the tools were glued to the shelves.

"Joe!" he exclaimed. "There's a special reason for this—and I think it's camouflage!"

"You mean these shelves are movable, and the tools are fastened so they won't fall off?"

"Yes. Also, I have a feeling this whole section is made of the old lumber from Pritos' yard."

"And the bricks?" Joe asked, puzzled.

His brother's answer was terse. "Remember, this mill was used by settlers. In those days many places had hidden rooms in case of Indian attacks—"

"I get you!" Joe broke in. "Those bricks are in a secret room! The best place to build one in this mill would have been the cellar."

"Right," agreed Frank. "And the only thing unusual here is this shelf setup. I'll bet it's actually the entrance to the secret room."

"All we have to do is find the opening mechanism," Joe declared.

Using their flashlights, the boys went over every inch of the shelves. These were nailed to a backing of boards. The Hardys pulled and pushed, but nothing happened. Finally, on the bottom shelf near the wall, Frank discovered a knot in the wood. In desperation, he pressed his thumb hard against the knot.

There was the hum of a motor, and, as smoothly

"The door to the secret room!" Frank exulted

as though it were moving on greased rails, the middle section of shelves swung inward.

"The door to the secret room!" Frank exulted.

Quickly the boys slipped inside the room and shone their flashlights around. The first thing they noticed was the flooring—recently laid bricks. Frank snapped on a light switch beside the entrance.

The boys blinked in the sudden glare of two high-watt bulbs suspended from the low ceiling. The next instant both spotted a small, hand-printing press.

"The counterfeiters' workshop!" they cried out.

On a wooden table at the rear of the room were a camera, etching tools, zinc plates, and a large pan with little compartments containing various colors of ink. At the edge of the table was a portable typewriter.

Frank picked up a piece of paper, rolled it into the machine, and typed a few lines. Pulling it out, he showed the paper to Joe.

"The machine used to type the warning note Dad got!" Joe exclaimed excitedly. "The counterfeiters must have thought he was on their trail."

"And look here!" exclaimed Frank, his voice tense. A small pile of twenty-dollar bills lay among the equipment. "They're fakes," he added, scrutinizing the bills. "They're the same as Chet's and Tony's."

Joe made another startling discovery. In one corner stood a bow, with the string loosened and carefully wound around the handgrip. A quiver of three hunting arrows leaned against the wall nearby.

Excitedly Joe pulled one out. "The same type that was fired at the girls," he observed. "This must belong to The Arrow!"

"Docker matches his description," Frank pointed out. "He easily could have colored his hair gray."

The Hardys were thrilled at the irrefutable evidence all around them. "Now we know why Markel and Docker rigged the mill wheel—to give a warning signal when they're working in this room!"

"Also, we have a good idea what was being sent to Peters in the envelopes—phony twenty-dollar bills!"

"Let's get Dad and Chief Collig here!" Joe urged, stuffing several of the counterfeits into a pocket.

As the boys turned to leave, the lights in the secret room went out. Frank and Joe froze. They realized the mill wheel had stopped turning.

"The signal!" Joe said grimly. "Someone is coming!"

CHAPTER XIX

Underground Chase

THE HARDYS knew this was the signal for them to get out of the secret room—and fast! As they hurried into the cellar, the lights came on again. With hearts beating faster, they started for the stairway. But before the boys reached it, they heard the mill door being unlocked, then heavy footsteps pounded overhead.

"Docker!" a man's voice called. "Markel! Where are you!"

The Hardys listened tensely, hoping for a chance to escape unseen. When they heard the man cross the ground floor and go upstairs, Joe whispered, "Let's make a break for it!"

The boys dashed to the steps. They could see a crack of light beneath the closed door to the kitchen. Suddenly the light vanished, and the rumble of the mill wheel ceased.

The Hardys stopped in their tracks. "Somebody else is coming!" Frank muttered. "Probably Docker and Markel. We're trapped!"

Again the brothers heard the mill door open. Two men were talking loudly and angrily. Then came the sound of footsteps clattering down the stairs to the first floor.

"Peters!" The boys recognized Docker's voice. "Where in blazes were you?"

Frank and Joe nudged each other. Victor Peters *was* in league with the gatehouse men!

"What do you mean? I told you I'd meet you here at eleven," snarled Peters.

"You must be nuts!" retorted Markel. "You called here an hour ago and said there was trouble and to meet *you* at the Parker Building."

Peters' tone grew menacing. "Something's fishy. I didn't phone. You know I'd use the two-way radio. What's the matter with you guys, anyway?"

"Listen!" Markel snapped. "*Somebody* called here and said he was you. The voice did sound sort of fuzzy, but I didn't have a chance to ask questions—he hung up on me. I thought maybe your radio had conked out."

The Hardys, crouched on the cellar stairs, could feel the increasing tension in the room above. Docker growled, "Something funny *is* going on. Whoever phoned must be on to us, or suspect enough to want to get in here and snoop around."

"The Feds! We'll have to scram!" said Markel, with more than a trace of fear in his voice. "Come on! Let's get moving!"

"Not so fast, Markel!" Docker barked. "We're not ditching the stuff we've made. We'll have a look around first—starting with the cellar."

The men strode into the kitchen. Below, Frank grabbed Joe. "No choice now. Into the secret room!"

Quickly the brothers ran back into the workshop. Frank pulled the door behind him and slid the heavy bolt into place.

Tensely the brothers pressed against the door as the three men came downstairs into the basement. Frank and Joe could hear them moving around, searching for signs of an intruder.

"I'd better check the rest of the mill," Docker said brusquely. "You two get the plates and the greenbacks. Go out through the tunnel, and I'll meet you at the other end. We'll wait there for Blum to pay us off, then vamoose."

"We're in a fix, all right," Joe said under his breath. "What tunnel are they talking about?"

"And who's Blum?" Frank wondered.

The boys heard the hum of the motor that opened the secret door. But the bolt held it shut.

"The mechanism won't work!" Markel rasped.

"Maybe it's just stuck," said Peters.

The men began pounding on the wood.

"What's going on?" Docker demanded as he returned.

"We can't budge this tricky door you dreamed up," Peters complained.

"There's nothing wrong with the door, you blockheads!" Docker shouted. "Somebody's in the room! Break down the door!"

In half a minute his order was followed by several sharp blows.

"Oh, great!" Joe groaned. "They're using axes!"

"We won't have long to figure a way out," Frank said wryly.

"Way out!" Joe scoffed. "There isn't any!"

Frank's mind raced. "Hey! They said something about leaving through a tunnel! It must be in here."

Frantically the Hardys searched for another exit from the secret room. They crawled on the floor, and pried up one brick after another looking for a ring that might open a trap door.

"Nothing!" Joe said desperately.

All the while the men in the cellar kept battering away at the door. "Good thing that old lumber is such hard wood," Frank thought. "But they'll break through any minute."

"Look!" Joe pointed. "Under the bench!"

Frank noticed a shovel lying beneath the worktable. The boys pushed it aside, and saw that the wall behind the table was partially covered with loose dirt. On a hunch Frank grabbed the shovel and dug into the dirt.

"This dirt might have been put here to hide the entrance to the tunnel!" he gasped.

"It better be!" His brother clawed frantically at the dirt.

At the same moment there was a loud splintering noise. The Hardys looked around. A large crack had appeared in the bolted door.

One of the men outside yelled, "A couple more blows and we'll be in."

Frank dug furiously. Suddenly his shovel opened up a small hole in the crumbly dirt. Joe scooped away with his hands. Finally there was a space big enough for the boys to squeeze through. Without hesitation, Frank wriggled in, then Joe.

From behind them came a tremendous crash and the sound of ripping wood. Markel's voice shouted, "Into the tunnel! After 'em!"

The Hardys heard no more as they pushed ahead on hands and knees into the damp darkness of an earthen passageway.

Joe was about to call out to his brother when he became aware that someone was crawling behind him. "No room here for a knockdown fight," he thought, wondering if the pursuer were armed.

The young detective scrambled on as fast as he could in the narrow, twisting tunnel. He managed to catch up to Frank, and with a push warned him to go at top speed.

"Somebody's after us!" Joe hissed. "If only we can outdistance him!"

The underground route was a tortuous, harrowing one. The Hardys frequently scraped knees and shoulders against sharp stones in the tunnel floor and walls. They had held onto their flashlights, but did not dare turn them on.

"This passageway is endless!" Frank thought. The close, clammy atmosphere made it increasingly difficult for him and his brother to breathe.

Joe thought uneasily, "What if we hit a blind alley and are stuck in here?"

The boys longed to stop and catch their breath, but they could hear the sounds of pursuit growing nearer, and forced themselves onward faster than ever.

Frank wondered if Chet and Tony had seen the men enter the mill and had gone for help.

"We'll need it," he thought grimly.

Suddenly the brothers came to another turn and the ground began to slope sharply upward.

"Maybe we're getting close to the end," Frank conjectured hopefully.

Spurred by possible freedom, he put on a burst of speed. Joe did the same. A moment later Frank stopped unexpectedly and Joe bumped into him.

"What's the matter?" he barely whispered.

"Dead end," reported his brother.

Squeezing up beside Frank, Joe reached out and touched a pile of stones blocking their path. The boys now could hear the heavy breathing of their pursuer.

"Let's move these stones," Frank urged.

Both Hardys worked with desperate haste to pull the barrier down. They heaved thankful sighs when a draft of fresh air struck their faces.

"The exit!" Joe whispered in relief.

The brothers wriggled through the opening they had made and found themselves in a rock-walled space.

"It's the cave by the river, Joe!" Frank cried out. "Someone put back the rocks we removed!"

The boys clicked on their flashlights and started toward the entrance of the cave.

"We beat 'em to it!" Joe exclaimed.

"That's what you think!" came a harsh voice from the entrance.

The glare from two flashlights almost blinded the Hardys. Docker and Markel, with drawn revolvers, had stepped into the cave.

CHAPTER XX

Solid Evidence

For a second the two armed men stared in disbelief at Frank and Joe. "The Hardy boys!" Docker snarled. "So you're the snoopers we've trapped!"

There was a scuffling in the tunnel behind the boys. A stocky man, huffing and puffing, emerged from the tunnel. The Hardys recognized him instantly: the counterfeit passer, Victor Peters.

The newcomer gaped at the Hardys. "What are *they* doing here?"

"A good question!" Markel snapped at his accomplice. "You told us on the two-way radio you'd locked 'em up with the truck."

Peters whined, "I *did*. They must've broken out."

"Obviously." Docker gave him a withering look.

Frank and Joe realized that Peters had not returned to the old farmhouse.

Docker whirled on them. "How *did* you escape?"

The boys looked at him coldly. "That's for you to find out," Joe retorted.

"It's a good thing Markel and I decided to head 'em off at the cave," Docker added angrily. "Otherwise, they would have escaped again."

The Hardys could see that the men were nervous and edgy. "I'm not the only one who made a mistake," Peters growled. "I told you a couple of days ago to get rid of that kid Ken when these pests started asking about him, and then found the tunnel. We could have thrown 'em off the scent!"

While the men argued, the Hardys kept on the alert for a chance to break away. Markel's eye caught the movement, and he leveled his revolver. "Don't be smart!" he ordered. "You're covered."

Peters continued the tirade against his confederates. "Docker, you should've finished these Hardys off when you put 'em in the boat that night! And you"—Peters turned on Markel—"*you* could have planted a dynamite charge in their boat instead of just monkeying with the throttle."

The Hardys, meanwhile, were thankful for the precious minutes gained by the men's dissension.

"Tony and Chet might come back in time with help," Joe thought.

Simultaneously, Frank hoped that Ken Blake had carried out his whispered instructions.

Docker glanced nervously at his watch. "Blum ought to be here," he fumed.

"Who's Blum?" Frank asked suddenly. "One of your counterfeiting pals?"

Docker, Markel, and Peters laughed scornfully. "No," said Markel. "We're the only ones in our exclusive society. Paul Blum doesn't know anything about our—er—mill operation, but it was through him we got the jobs at the gatehouse. The whole deal really paid off double."

Docker interrupted him with a warning. "Don't blab so much!"

Markel sneered. "Why not? What I say won't do these smart alecks any good."

Joe looked at the guard calmly. "Who paid you to let the green panel truck into Elekton?"

All three men started visibly. "How'd you know that?" Markel demanded.

"Just had a hunch," Joe replied.

The former guard regained his composure. "We'll get our money for that little job tonight."

Frank and Joe felt elated. Paul Blum, whom these men expected, must be the sabotage ringleader! "So that's what Markel meant by the deal paying off double," Frank thought. "He and Docker working the counterfeit racket on their own—and being in cahoots with the saboteurs."

Frank addressed Markel in an icy tone. "You call blowing up a building a 'little job'?"

The counterfeiters' reactions astonished the Hardys. *"What!"* bellowed Markel, as Docker and Peters went ashen.

Joe snorted. "You expect us to believe you didn't *know* explosives were in that truck?"

Victor Peters was beside himself with rage. *"Fools!"* he shrilled at Docker and Markel. "You let yourselves be used by saboteurs? This whole state will be crawling with police and federal agents."

The gatehouse men, though shaken, kept their revolvers trained on the Hardys. "Never mind," Docker muttered. "Soon as Blum shows up we'll get out of here and lie low for a while."

Frank and Joe learned also that Docker and Markel actually were brothers, but the two refused to give their real names.

"You, Docker, are known as The Arrow, aren't you?" Frank accused him.

"Yeah. Next time I'll use *you* boys for targets!" the man retorted threateningly.

The Hardys kept egging the men on to further admissions. Docker and Markel had been approached several months before by Blum who tipped them off to good-paying jobs at the Elekton gatehouse. Docker had cleverly forged references and identification for Markel and himself.

As soon as he and Markel had obtained the jobs, Blum had instructed them to buy the truck secondhand in another state, and told them only that Markel was to lend Blum the truck on a certain day when notified, let him through the gate, then out again soon after closing time. The guard would be handsomely paid to do this.

When Markel and Docker had become settled in the mill, the two had discovered the secret room and tunnel, which once had been a settlers' escape route. The men had wasted no time in setting it up for their counterfeiting racket, and often used the nondescript green truck to sneak in the required equipment.

"Who rigged up the electric-eye signal?" Frank queried.

"My work," Docker replied proudly.

As the boys had surmised, Peters, an old acquaintance of theirs, was "the old man" at the deserted farmhouse. When the boys had left the mill that morning Docker had radioed Peters, telling him if the Hardys showed up at the farm, he was to trap them.

"No doubt you planned to finish us off when you came back," Joe said.

Peters nodded.

Frank said to Docker, "I must admit, those

twenties are pretty good forgeries. The police think so, too."

The counterfeiter smiled in contempt. "Your fat friend sure was fooled."

He explained that his skill at engraving, which he had learned years ago, had enabled him to make the plates from which the bills were printed.

"Which one of you rode Ken's bike and left the typed warning for our father?" Frank asked.

"I did," Markel replied promptly.

"Why? He wasn't involved with the counterfeiting case."

We thought he was when we overheard a company bigwig say Fenton Hardy was 'taking the case.' "

"Yeah," Docker said. "I wasn't kidding when I sent the warnings—on paper and by phone."

He had acquired some sheets of bond paper from Elekton on a pretext; also the Manila envelopes used to deliver the bogus money to Peters. Docker admitted he had "unloaded" the counterfeit twenty at Pritos' yard by mistake.

Peters broke in abruptly. "We'd better get rid of these kids right now!"

The three men held a whispered conference, but Docker and Markel did not take their eyes from the Hardys. Suddenly the boys' keen ears detected the put-put of an approaching motorboat.

One thought flashed across their minds—Chet and Tony were bringing help. But in a few minutes their hopes were dashed! A heavy-set, dark-haired man peered into the mouth of the cave.

"Blum!" Markel said.

"Who are these kids?" Blum asked, squinting at Frank and Joe.

"Their name is Hardy—" Docker began, but Blum cut him short.

"Hardy!" he said sharply. "Listen—I just gave Fenton Hardy the slip at the Bayport dock. He was on a police launch."

"We've got to move fast!" Markel urged. "Docker and I caught these sons of his snooping. Pay us what you promised and we'll scram."

Blum looked disgusted. "Stupid amateurs! You let kids make it so hot you have to get out of town?" The heavy-set man pulled out his wallet. "Here's your cut for letting me into the plant," he continued scornfully. "I'm glad to get rid of such bunglers."

"It's not just these kids that made it hot for us!" Docker stormed. "If we'd known you were going to blow up that lab, we never would've gotten mixed up with you."

The Hardys noticed that Paul Blum appeared startled at Docker's words.

Frank spoke up boldly. "Sure. We all know you're back of the sabotage. Who pays *you* for doing it? And who's *your* inside man at Elekton?"

Blum glared, then in a sinister tone replied, "You'll never live to sing to the cops, so I'll tell you. Several countries that want to stop United States progress in missiles are paying me. My friend in the plant is a fellow named Jordan."

The saboteur revealed that his accomplice had first carried out smaller acts of sabotage, the ones which Chet had heard about from his father. It had been Blum himself who had driven the truck into the grounds and placed the dynamite in the laboratory. "Jordan and I gave your father the slip, then, too!"

"You guys can stand here and talk!" snapped Peters. "I'm going. You'd better take care of these Hardys." He backed out of the cave and raced off.

The counterfeiters discussed heatedly whether "to get rid" of Frank and Joe immediately, or take "these kids" and dispose of them later.

"That's your worry!" Blum said. "*I'm* taking off!"

"Oh, no, you're not. You can't leave us in the lurch." Markel waved his gun meaningfully.

At that instant there was a crashing noise outside the cave. The three men swung around.

This was all the Hardys needed. They hurled themselves at their captors, forcing them backward onto the rocky beach. From the woods they heard Chet yell, "Here we come, fellows!"

Frank had tackled Blum, and Joe was wrestling with Docker on the beach.

Tony Prito yelled, "Got you!" as he took a flying leap at Markel and brought him to the ground.

The older men, though strong, were no match for the agile Hardys and the furious onslaught of Chet and Tony. Finally the struggle ended.

The saboteur and counterfeiters were disarmed and lined up before the cave, their arms pinioned behind them by Joe, Chet, and Tony. Frank took charge of the revolvers.

"Good work, you two!" he said to his friends.

Chet, out of breath, grinned proudly. "I'm glad Tony and I stuck around when we saw these guys high-tailing it through the woods."

Now Frank turned to the prisoners. "Okay. March!" he ordered.

But before anyone could move, footsteps were heard approaching through the woods. A moment later Chief Collig and another officer appeared. With them, in handcuffs, was Victor Peters.

"Chief! Are we glad to see you!" Joe exclaimed.

The chief stared in amazement at the boys and their captives. "I got your message from Ken Blake," he told Frank. "Looks as if you have your hands full!"

"Oh, we have!" Joe grinned, then, puzzled, he asked his brother, "What message?"

"Just before I left the house I told Ken to call

Chief Collig if we weren't back by eleven, and tell him where we had gone."

While Blum and the counterfeiters stood in sullen silence, the four boys learned that Ken had called the chief just minutes after Fenton Hardy had left in the police launch in pursuit of Paul Blum.

"When we reached the mill we met this crook running out of the woods." Chief Collig gestured toward the handcuffed Peters. "I recognized him from Chet's description. When we found phony money on him, he told me where you were, hoping to get off with a lighter sentence."

"You rat!" Docker's face contorted with rage.

At that moment the group became aware of a police launch churning toward them, the beam from its searchlight sweeping the water. In the excitement, no one had heard the sound of its engine.

"Dad!" cried the Hardys, spotting the detective's erect figure standing in the bow. Soon the launch was beached, and Mr. Hardy, with several officers, leaped ashore.

"Well," Mr. Hardy said sternly when he saw Blum, "you won't be escaping again."

The captured lawbreakers were handcuffed and put aboard the launch. Mr. Hardy looked at his sons and their friends proudly. "You've done a yeoman's job—on both cases, yours and mine," he said.

After the police cruiser had departed, Frank and Joe led their father and the others into the mill cellar and showed them the secret room.

"This is all the evidence you need against the counterfeiters, Chief," said Mr. Hardy. "I can see there are plenty of fingerprints on this equipment. We know some will match the one on the finger guard. Besides your evidence, boys, Ken's testimony should be more than enough to convict them."

"What about Jordan, Blum's confederate at Elekton?" Frank asked.

Mr. Hardy smiled. "He was my big prize and I'm glad to say he is in jail!" The detective explained that further sleuthing had led to Jordan —and through him, Paul Blum. Mr. Hardy's first break had come when he learned that one Elekton employee had seen Jordan going toward the laboratory building at closing time on the day of the explosion.

A police guard was assigned to watch the counterfeiters' workshop and its contents. Then the four boys, Mr. Hardy, and the chief left the mill. Outside, they paused and looked back at the turning wheel.

Frank laughed. "Its signaling days are over."

"Sure hope so," Chet declared firmly. "No more mysteries for a while, please!"

Tony chuckled. "With Frank and Joe around, I wouldn't count on it."

His words proved to be true. Sooner than even the Hardy boys expected, they were called upon to solve the mystery of **THE MISSING CHUMS.**

Now Joe turned to their plump friend. "Good thing you bought that microscope, Chet. We started to look for nature specimens and dug up the old mill's secret!"